1st PLACE TIE IN THE

PACIFIC NORTHWEST WRITERS'

LITERARY CONTEST

"From adults to 13-year-olds, Wildfire's a fast read...how can you go wrong with a town called Potshot, a wolf, fires...I hated to come to the end...the story is superb."

--Comments from PNWA *judges*

"Jessie Jayne Smith brings the town of Potshot, Nevada to vivid life as a timeless setting. Adept at depicting complex family drama, romance and our connection with nature all rolled into one strong story, Smith has created a book as hot as, well, wildfire."

--Anjali Banerjee, Author of the Book Sense *Notable Book,* Imaginary Men

Wildfire

Dear Heidi,
From one intrepid
woman to another.
Jessie Jayne Smith

BY
JESSIE JAYNE SMITH

CMP Publishing Group, LLC
Okanogan, WA

Cover art created by Janine Marie Donoho with assistance from the Publisher.

All inquiries should be addressed to:

CMPPG, LLC
27657 Highway 97
Okanogan, WA 98840

Wildfire may be ordered from CMPPG, LLC at the above address and at **cmppg.com**

Wildfire is also available at **Amazon.com**.

Contact Publisher for distributor information.

email: **cmppg@cmppg.org**
website: **cmppg.com**

ISBN: 0-9801554-0-1

This one is for my dad, Jesse Bushyhead Smith—a native Oklahoman and one-legged Korean War vet whose generous heart ultimately failed him.

Chapter One

The fire's banshee wail filled Althea MacTavish's ears. Heat singed her hair and the burnt feather stench triggered a cough. Thea took that as a warning and rested for a moment. With one hand braced against a knee, her other clutched the blackened shovel handle. Panting breaths scalded her throat as a searing gust billowed over her. Ashes and sparks swirled, obscuring the blazing structure before her. One-handed, Thea retrieved the nearly dry towel now draping her shoulders and swaddled her neck and crown. After a lifetime spent in wildfire country, she knew better than to cover her mouth; superheated steam in the lungs trumped scorched hair. Through her gardening gloves, tender spots warned of blisters. Renewed purpose focused Thea on smoldering grasses nearer the flaming building.

"Dig in, MacTavish!" She scolded herself as anger fueled her. "*How—dare—you—spoil—all—our—work!*" Thea yelled at the flames as she pounded the shovel blade against flickering embers in time to her words. Acrid smoke burned her eyes as residue scattered.

Strong hands gripped her shoulders from behind. "Thea! Enough! The smoke-eaters are here. You've done all you can."

She shrugged him off and snarled, "Back off, Dwaine!"

The deputy's arms closed around her. "For crying out loud, MacTavish, your clothes are smoking! Don't argue."

He manhandled her to a rocky outcropping. The buckles

1

on his turnout coat dug into her back. Fresh air acted like cold water in her face and she blinked. *How long ago had the sun gone down?*

"All right, all right! Let me go."

He set her on a granite outcropping, none too gently. Her knees collapsed and she crumpled onto the rock.

"Whoa! You okay, Thea?"

She stared at the fire. Twenty yards away, the framework of Potshot's new spa glowed and shimmered in a flaming maw. The roof trusses crashed down, scattering sparks and firefighters. A roiling smoke beast engulfed them. She wiped her eyes and teetered to her feet.

Was she all right? Hardly. "What do *you* think?"

He shrugged. "Looks like a total loss to me." In true Dwaine Hollis form, he missed her point completely. "'Scuse me, Thea. Looks like Hulon's in a bind." She barely glanced at him as he headed toward the blaze.

Thea's eyes stung, but she couldn't tell if it was from smoke or her own reek. Even from here, the fire's heat parched her face. Hunched into herself, she watched the holocaust devour eight months of bone-jarring labor, two years of planning, and thousands of volunteer hours. Never mind the shoestring funds gone up in smoke. Ash eddies danced around the remaining structure as firefighters shot pitiful streams of water from their hoses.

"Might as well spit on it," she muttered.

Thea's tired regard settled on the gaggle of townsfolk there for the pyrotechnics. Her son broke away from a group near the water tanker and pelted toward her. Thank goodness Alex had actually listened to her and run to Potshot. He must have caught a ride back with one of   the volunteers.

With any luck, he hadn't witnessed her making a spectacle of herself. Alex's recent investment in the teenage code of parental shame hurt. Lately, almost everything she did

2

embarrassed him. He would never forgive her for matching her puny efforts against the fire. Who did she think she was anyway? She grinned without much humor and her fire-dried lips cracked. Looking back at the blaze, Thea dismissed the irritating concepts guiding his thirteen-year-old brain.

A grimy hand tugged her bare wrist, disrupting the death grip she had on her ribs. "Mom? Why're you crying?"

She glanced at her son. The top of his head reached her shoulders—he really had grown this last month. "I'm not crying, Alex. It's this dratted smoke. Aren't your eyes burning?"

"Nope." Riveted on the inferno, his wide eyes reflected flame.

"Crying doesn't accomplish anything anyway. What we need is a recovery plan." Thea draped an arm around his shoulders. For once, he didn't shrug her off. Complete devastation could draw people together. Or more likely, his fascination with the fire made him oblivious.

Edging closer to the two MacTavishes, other Potshot residents clustered in rapt groups. Watching money burn could be therapeutic, she supposed. In this case, stock options turned to ash. Potshot, Nevada would not be plush for some time.

"Look, Mom, there's Sheriff Benton. Uh-oh. I think he's heading up here."

In the surreal glow of parking lot lights filtered through smoke, Thea watched as Sy leaned down to kiss his wheelchair-bound wife before coming uphill toward Alex and her.

"Hey, there's Sherm. And Keith! See ya." Alex hurtled away before asking permission. So much for his being grounded. Thea suspected the sheriff lumbering toward them had as much to do with Alex making himself scarce as wanting to see his best friends.

"Althea." The bulky man nodded before joining her on the

3

outcrop.

"Sy." She trained her gaze on the volunteer firefighters, who wrestled an inferno.

"Hell of a setback. Looks like a complete loss."

"So I've been told. Not to worry, though. We'll have our insurance money for materials. I'm more concerned about the time crunch. With only three months left…"

"If we still aim to open by July 1ˢᵗ. Saw the ads in those swank leisure magazines at Jessie's hair salon. Spa looked real good on paper, Thea."

"It did, didn't it?"

He shook his head. "Don't see how we're going to get this mess whipped into any kind of shape, though. Not before July and especially with volunteer labor. Since Bud Senior fell off that ladder, the upgrade on his hotel's behind, too."

"Nearly everyone's lent a hand." She flexed her fingers. *Definitely blistered.*

"Mighty fortunate you called in the fire when you did. This could have been a whole lot worse."

Thea squeezed her eyes shut against a brief flash of Ricochet Mountain in flame.

Sy cleared his throat. "You said Alex discovered the fire?"

Queasiness hit Thea's gut. "Yes. I let him come up here to soak in the springs after weeding. He came tearing down the mountain less than half an hour after he left, hollering about the fire."

"Only thirty minutes? You're sure?"

Thea faced the sheriff, whose weathered face flickered uncertainly in the firelight. "Sy, I know what you're getting at, but Alex had nothing to do with this."

"Now, Thea…"

"I know, I know. First the miner's ghost, then the incident with the old sheepherder's shack…"

"And the abominable snowman."

She took a shallow breath, bitter with smoke. "You know it takes me a good twenty minutes to jog here from my place. Walking takes longer. With my car on the blitz, hoofing it was my only option. So after grabbing a wet towel, gloves, and a shovel, it took me nearly twenty minutes to get here and I was fueled by adrenaline. Even if Alex ran all the way, he couldn't make a round trip in less than half an hour. No way could he have set this fire, Sy."

Sy adjusted his cowboy hat. "You know I have to check all the particulars. Hell, Thea, that's why you all voted me into office. My findings of fact will protect Alex as much as anyone else here."

Her shoulders relaxed fractionally. "I know. And I suppose that since I called it in, you needed to start with me."

"That's right." Another smoky surge made them step back a few paces.

"Sorry, Sy. With all the mischief Alex has been causing, I guess I'm feeling a little defensive right now. Has your wife found any sources for restocking Boondoggle Pond?"

"As a matter of fact, April *did* work out a deal with the Department of Fish and Wildlife. They'll be here by week's end with a truckload of fingerling trout."

"Thank goodness!" Thea closed her eyes and recalled the faded rainbow hues of dead trout floating on the town's lagoon. She opened her eyes to flame. "What could those boys have been thinking—tossing firecrackers into the lagoon like that."

Sy grunted. "I don't believe any thought at all crossed their hormone-rattled brains. Never have seen three boys more upset. They turned green as Granny Smith apples. There's not a cruel bone in any of them and they sure as shootin' didn't expect their prank to kill those fish. Still, remorse isn't enough for the infraction. I know for a fact, Sherman and Keith aren't taking much joy in their lives right now."

5

Thea cracked a grim smile. "Neither is Alex. I've consigned him to a fate worse than death. He's grounded and weeding my beds. Now, instead of Sherm and Keith, he's spending spring break with me."

Sy's snort covered a chuckle. "Can't say I envy you, Thea."

"What do you think the chances are of Marine recruiters in Reno sending a van for Alex?"

"Slim to none. Shanghaiing isn't how they work, more's the pity. 'Sides, they're not allowed to recruit thirteen-year-old hooligans."

Thea's peripheral vision caught Meg Connor a moment before the diminutive librarian slipped an arm around her ribs.

"Merciful God, Thea! What a mess! Thank goodness the people from Oklahoma were here to help fight the fire. No telling whether we could have contained it otherwise."

"Oklahoma?"

Sy said, "Those university folks here on that grant. You know, the ones who're doing the study on fire safety?"

"I'd forgotten. And they rolled into town today? Now there's irony for you."

Meg chimed in. "The plot sickens. The town commissioners told them the hotel would be ready. With Bud's injury, we have only two rooms suitable for lodgers."

"The rest are somewhere between hell and damnation," added Sy. He dropped his voice a register. "I know things've been tight for you over the last months. Thought maybe you could rent out your basement. The head guy seems like a stand-up fellow; a safety engineer and all."

A safety engineer, huh? Much as Thea despised stereotypes, a vision of pocket protectors and bifocals, the entire spectrum of buttoned-up and tucked-in, reeled through her mind.

"He's willing to pay the same as he would've for the hotel.

6

You don't have to cook or anything." Sy had eaten enough of Thea's cooking to know her limitations.

"While I haven't met the man, it sounds like a splendid opportunity," added Meg.

Thea shook her head. "No way!"

"Althea MacTavish, this is not the time to let false pride stand in your way—" the librarian began.

"Whoa! Am I being double-teamed here or what?"

"Yes," they harmonized.

She crossed her arms over her chest. "You know I'm working out of my home. I can't afford distractions right now. This set of paintings has to be done by June when my sabbatical ends. Now with rebuilding the spa—"

Sy waved away her reservations. "We all respect your work habits, Thea. I've already read this guy the riot act. He says he won't be any trouble. The room's only his base camp. His *team*—that's what he calls them—they're planning on being out nearly every day. Pitching tents on the mountain when they have to. All Dr. Hayes needs is a bed, a shower, and a room to set-up his computer stuff."

Thea studied the man-shapes stationed between fire and pedestrians. "Can you at least point the guy out to me?"

"Aw, now Thea, you know firemen all look alike in soot and turnouts." Sy squinted into the fire, much reduced over what it had been.

Not much fuel left. Despair rolled in, thick as fog in Eden Valley.

"There! See the tallest one?"

"That's our trusty Hulon Peabody," Meg stated.

"No, the guy with the shovel—closest to the flames. I think that's Dr. Hayes."

Thea studied the man. Backlit by fire in the twilight, she could see nothing more than a silhouette. At least he looked more competent with a shovel than she had been.

7

"Whew! You're not making this easy on me. Unfortunately, you're right about my finances. My savings are disappearing nearly as fast as Alex when I ask him to clean his room."

She swept a hand through her singed hair. "Oh, fuchsia! All right. Bring the good doctor over tomorrow afternoon, Sy. I'll have to move my supplies from the room, but that won't take long. I'll wait until he agrees to stay—and I have veto power."

"Good enough."

Meg squeezed her arm. "Come along, Thea, you're dead on your feet. Let me drive you home. It's time to let the experts do what they do best and clean up this mess."

"No, Meg. There's too much to do. I'd rather help Sissy get the buffet ready. Isn't she here?" Thea asked.

Meg answered. "Of course not. She's at the club. There's money to be made, after all,"

Thea shook her head. Sissy Peabody, town pharmacist and mother to Alex's best friend Sherman, would be setting up the local eatery and gambling joint to feed the firefighters. While her husband and partner Hulon figuratively managed Peabody's Bar and Grill, Sissy made the business profitable. Earnings were bound to go up when you fed the volunteer fire department. The town council always compensated her afterward from the city coffers, nearly empty now after underwriting the new spa.

She suspected Sissy claimed these post-blaze gatherings as donations on her income tax, too. Still, the smoke-eaters needed to eat and Hulon's club provided. When a quick reconnaissance around the hot springs failed to unearth Alex, Sherman, or Keith Bodeen, Thea spread the word. "Have my son meet me in town at the Bar and Grill."

She rode the winding road into Potshot with Meg. From three blocks away, Hulon's neon sign captured the eye. Having experienced the fire, Thea decided the revamped sign looked somewhat less garish than it had yesterday, when Hulon installed it.

Sissy met them at the buffet tables. She gasped, "Thea?"

"No, Siss, Harrison Ford." Thea gave her best lopsided grin.

"Oh, bosh! I don't know why you all tease me so."

Meg and Thea exchanged a look. Sissy wrote elaborate fan mail to the actor and, frankly, Thea couldn't blame her. She might write to Mr. Ford herself if she was married to Hulon.

"I mean, Thea, you're a mess! What did you do? Put out that fire by yourself? You're covered with soot head-to-toe. And your hair—" With a gingerly nudge, Sissy aimed her toward the back. "Go hose yourself down. Use plenty of soap, mind you. You, too, Meg. You're not as bad as Thea, but you both reek."

After one unfortunate look in the bathroom mirror, Thea concentrated on changing the color of her skin from streaked black and gray to golden olive tones. Afterward she confronted her reflection. Her dark hair formed a botched nimbus around her head. Thea leaned over the sink and finger-combed it. Charred strands fell into the basin. She straightened.

Meg hugged her. "I'll be over tomorrow with my razor. We can trim back the frazzled ends."

"You think?"

"Just don't tell Jessie I cut your hair."

"Like I can afford her prices right now."

"She'd do it for free. Like you, she's an artist. Unfortunately, she's booked solid for the next two weeks. I tried to get in for a trim yesterday."

The two returned to the dining area. By then, more wives, daughters, sisters, and mothers had arrived. The noise level rivaled the fire scene, but with less order.

Sissy rolled her eyes. "Megan! Please will you organize

these ladies? I have a crisis in the kitchen."

Thea smiled. No one created order from chaos like Meg did. Even Sissy bowed to her greater abilities. Thea stationed herself behind a buffet table originally setup for tonight. Tying an apron over her cropped sweatshirt and jeans, now laced with charred holes, she slumped by the Joe Special, a savory concoction of eggs, spinach and ground beef steaming beneath the cover. Her location allowed her to observe her friends and neighbors. A contingent from Eden Valley worked alongside town residents, all differences aside.

Contentment spread through her tired body. Community. That's what Potshot, Nevada meant to Thea.

Basking in her sense of belonging, it took awhile for her to intercept the looks. Odd moments of quiet overtook the room, too. At first, she blamed it on Meg's efficiency in coordinating her neighbors' efforts. Then she caught snatches of 'Alex' this and 'Alexander' that. Add to the murmurs the fact that no one attempted to include her in obvious discussion about her son and Thea's defenses rose. Comfort evaporated as righteous anger buoyed her. She marched around her table with the vigor of any mother protecting her young, as indeed she was. Thea headed for the closest group, where April Benton presided over place settings from her wheelchair.

The older woman said, "Nonsense, Una. We're lucky Alex went to the spa when he did. No telling the damage we'd be facing otherwise. The whole of Ricochet Mountain could have gone up."

As Thea drew nearer, Jessie Moran caught her eye. "Oh, my goodness, Thea! What did you do to your face? You're sunburned!" She spoke louder than necessary,

The gathering grew suspiciously quiet. Thea tamped down her ire and entered the fray. "I must have stood too close to the fire, Jessie." Looking at Una Bodeen, she said, "Did I hear Alex's name taken in vain?"

Uneasy quiet rippled to nearby clusters and further until only one person could be heard. Sissy Peabody's voice carried across the room. "—expect from a fatherless boy. A wonder he didn't burn the entire town down around our ears."

Thea turned slowly. Siss had the grace to look embarrassed, but pitched her chin at a stubborn angle. Others shifted on their feet, faces hot with blushes. A few just looked confused. Only four moved closer and met her regard with clear gazes: Meg, Letty, April, and Jessie. *So, that's how it stands.*

Thea said, "If you'd taken the time to get the facts, Sissy Peabody, you'd have learned that Alex didn't have time to set any fires. None of you saw his face when he bolted into our house. I did. He's as innocent as you of starting that fire."

Thea held her hands wide. "Besides, why treat this like an arson? We won't know what happened until the insurance people study the site. It could have been anything.

"Why just last year that folded electric blanket smoldered at the Donaldson's hotel. If Bud Senior hadn't found it in time, Letty and him would have lost their place. And what about the faulty wiring in your own house, Siss? When Hulon decided to save a few bucks and do it himself? As I remember it, you had a couple of close calls before hiring an electrician from Reno."

Meg added, "You'll note we didn't let your Hulon help with the electrical wiring at the spa, Sissy."

A few titters accompanied her pronouncement.

Siss huffed. "Well, there weren't any electric blankets at the spa, Thea. And as you said, Hulon didn't do the wiring. No lightning today, either."

"But accidental fires do start all the time," Jessie inserted.

"Why are you so eager to believe not only that someone started the spa fire, but that my son was involved? He's gotten into mischief, yes, but he's never set out to do damage."

Before Sissy could mount another attack, Mayor Letty said, "Well now ladies, I'd say we've had enough idle talk for one evening. The crews should be coming down shortly. I suspect they'll have to monitor the place all night, checking for hot spots and such. We have plenty of work to do yet. Not to mention figuring out a way to get our spa done in time for our grand opening."

The talk grew animated with potential solutions and obstacles. Thea tried not to listen to the doomsayers, of which there were many, and faded back to her station at the buffet. Meg followed. The first rush of smoke-eaters pushed through the door, carrying with them the combined stench of smoke and sweat. Alex and Sherman, topped with oversized helmets, milled at their center.

Fatigue hit in a wave and Thea swayed beneath its assault. Fifteen years older than Thea at forty-seven, Meg steadied her. "You're exhausted, Althea. We have plenty of help here. Why don't you collect Alex and head home?"

Thea lifted her chin. "And let Sissy spread her poison?"

"You have good friends here. We'll quell any slander."

"I know you will. Maybe I'll go after serving the first group. I don't want it to look like I'm turning tail."

Meg chuckled. "As though anyone could think such a thing."

"Thanks, Meg. But I'll stay, at least until Alex gets a plate. I'd never be able to pry him loose otherwise. Maybe I'll get a look at my new tenant, too."

So Thea stood her watch, dishing up a mountain of chow to the returned warriors. She nodded and smiled as they told of their exploits. Like fish stories, their tales grew with each recounting. Thea had no doubt that by buffet's end, each fireperson would have single-handedly saved Potshot and the Sierra Nevada Mountain range. As Alex finished his third plate, she signaled to the sheriff's wife, who rolled her chair over to take her place.

"Thanks, April." Thea kissed the older woman on her cheek.

The crew from Oklahoma still hadn't made their entrance. *Tomorrow will have to be soon enough.* Pulling loose her apron ties, where she'd wrapped them twice around her waist, Thea removed the smock. All the while she zigzagged through the crowd toward the table where her son sat with his friends.

"—weirdest looking guy. Really old and skinny. He was trying to put the fire out with his shirt. He had like really gross *scars* all over his back. He yelled at me to get help, so I ran all the way home."

"Jeez, Alex, do you think *he* started the fire?" Sherman leaned forward.

"Hell, no. Why would he be trying to put it out if he did it?"

Thea placed her hands over her son's shoulders. "Alex, it's time to go."

"Aw, Mom—"

"Come on, honey. I'm bushed."

He tilted his head back and must have seen 'irrevocable' on her face. Alex gave a disgusted snort before shoving his chair from the table.

Stiff with tiredness and more pressing matters, Thea hustled him outside into a cool March night that revived her. She steered her son along the sidewalk until he evaded her touch.

"We're walking home?"

"You don't see the car, do you?"

"Jeez, just asking. You don't have to be so cranky."

"Sorry, but you know I took the path to the hot springs. The car's at home." *And barely running.*

"Oh, yeah."

Thea frowned and gathered her thoughts. "Did you tell

Sheriff Benton about the man you saw at the hot springs?"

"Didn't have a chance."

They passed *Guinevere's Locks*, Jessie's beauty salon. The mural Thea had painted for the grand opening looked fine by streetlight. For a long moment, she yearned toward Perceval, the hero of the fresco. Thea bet he had never dealt with ambivalence or needed to cajole a teenager. A life of garden-variety quests and requited love sounded good about now. She traced the back of her fingers along the painted wall to its end. The darkened bakery next door smelled of cinnamon and sweet breads. Her belly grumbled.

Alex edged away. "Jeez, Mom."

"I'm just hungry. I haven't eaten since lunch." In the glow of the next street lamp, Thea clutched her son's thin shoulder and turned him to face her. "Tomorrow, you need to tell Sheriff Benton everything you saw."

"Ouch! That hurts!" Alex tried to shrug off her tense hold.

She released her grip. "Sorry, honey, but this is very important. You need to remember everything as it happened, and write it down when we get home. Okay?"

He shrugged and eyed her askance. "Sure."

Walking again, she took a deep breath. The knot within her loosened. "You didn't recognize this guy?"

"*Duh.*"

"Come on, Alex."

"No! Never seen him before."

"Well, he's a witness now. Sy will need his account of the fire to get the facts straight." She picked up their pace, even skipped a few beats.

"Mom! Someone'll see you."

"So." She grinned at his mortified expression. On impulse, she sang, "Come on, Alex! Race you home!"

He left her in his dust within a block. At the town hall, he slowed, then trotted backward until she caught up.

14

"For a jogger, you sure can't run." He settled into her methodic pace.

"Tortoise and hare. I can go miles further than most sprinters."

"Yeah, yeah." Still, he stayed by her side. They reached home twenty minutes later, then he sprinted up the drive to tag the door.

"First!"

She hugged him. *Please let Sy find the other witness.* "You're the best, honey."

Chapter Two

"Meg? You're sure no one believes Alex started the fire?" Thea asked. She twisted on the three-legged stool. Through an open window, she heard the song of wind-teased chimes.

"Once Sy explained the circumstances, the naysayers had no ammunition. Now, don't fidget!"

Thea tucked her chin and stilled her tapping foot. Her friend snipped more frizzed hair from her head. The pieces looked like magnetic filings as they wafted in the afternoon breeze. Crisped tresses drifted onto Thea's painting smock.

Using peripheral vision, Thea tried for a better view of her latest painting. She must have cocked her head, since her friend hissed like a bee-stung goose.

"You're going to look like Hulon's mangy dog if you keep moving while I cut."

A finger-long strand settled on her lap. "If you wanted me to sit still, you shouldn't have put me next to my easel."

The librarian heaved a long-suffering sigh. "All right, Althea. Let's turn you toward your artwork. Then you can look to your heart's content."

Thea repositioned her stool.

"Now, are you where you want to be?"

"Yes. But it's just as I thought." She caught her bottom lip in her teeth.

Snip, snip, scritch. "What?"

"My hero's refusing to cooperate. I mean he develops a new blemish with each brush stroke. Today he looks spiteful.

He has an arrogant lift to his lips, too." She squinted her eyes. A slight tug came from the crown of her head.

"Nonsense."

"Oh, yes he does."

"Well, perhaps a bit of a sneer." Her friend paused and Thea contorted herself to read Meg's expression. The librarian's regard fastened on the lower half of the painting. "He's really quite heroic in his other—proportions."

A blush heated Thea's chest and moved upward. "It was a long night. I was feeling lonely."

"*Lonely* isn't the word I'd have used."

"He'll be wearing a loincloth by tomorrow."

"A pity."

Thea sighed. "Well, I still don't know what to do about his face. You're right, he *is* heroic—from his neck down. Mr. Fantasy comes to life. Let's face it, Meg. I don't have any business painting a suite of legendary heroes." Inadequacy sucked the joy from her and she leaned her elbows onto her knees.

"What nonsense is this?"

"I *mean*, look at the dearth of heroes in my life."

Meg sidestepped the chair and draped an arm over Thea's shoulders. "Drivel. What about Sy and Dwaine? They're valiant—in a rather prosaic way. Hulon and Bud also have much to recommend them. What about wonderful Mr. Sakamura, who's a war hero no less?"

Thea leapt to her feet, snatching up a brush and palette. A touch of paint here and there, then smudging her champion's ear, she stepped back and said, "*Voila!* Sy's bulbous nose. And here, Dwaine's cauliflower silhouette. Whoever said heroes have to be good-looking?"

Meg crossed her arms and cocked her head. "You're not addressing the problem, Thea. All the men you know are *friends*. What you *need* is a heroic love interest."

"That's even more complicated." Her impetus toward fun slipped sideways and Thea's smile faltered. She dropped her brush into a cleaning jar and balanced her palette nearby.

Their gazes caught, reminding Thea of how long they had been friends—and that Meg had started as her college advisor and mentor. Then this university librarian had chosen to move with a pregnant Thea back to Potshot, where Meg campaigned for a branch library, which she now ran with joyous verve. Meg claimed all along that she missed the Irish hamlet where she'd grown up and that Potshot filled her need for community.

Thea drew a deep breath. "I'm serious, Meg. What can I possibly know about heroic love?"

"If you're referring to Salinger, I'll agree. He certainly acted more like villain than hero. I still think we should have taken out a contract on him. He's scum of the earth."

Thea noted the grim set to Meg's jaw. "Like you would know anyone who kills for pay. Besides, Salinger did give me Alex."

Her friend's mouth softened. "True. He gets full credit as sperm donor. But that leaves only your stepfather as a role model. Lord knows he didn't revise your opinion of men."

"He raised a child who wasn't his own. What could you expect?"

"Honor and compassion," snapped Meg. She stepped forward and surveyed Thea's new 'do. "Now, fluff your hair, dear."

Thea complied. No strand felt longer than her little finger. Gone was her chic bob. She raised her chin. "Well?"

"I think it suits you." Meg's russet brown eyes twinkled.

Thea retrieved the hand mirror from beneath her vacated seat. "Hmm. Not bad actually and sort of gamine. Very Demi Moore in *GHOST*."

Meg glanced out the window. "The afternoon's slipped

away. I have my senior citizens coming today."

"That's the one reading group that doesn't need supervision."

"I know, but I do like to brew tea for them, bless their hearts. Which reminds me of two other subjects I intended to broach."

"Oh, boy. When you get that look—"

Meg held up her index finger. "First, Sy wanted me to warn you that Hulon will be burning sagebrush from his lot today. If you smell smoke, you're not to worry. The volunteer fire department's standing by."

"What get-rich-quick scheme is it this time?"

"Evidently Hulon's decided to grow a rare garlic as a money crop. I believe even Sy invested in this one."

Thea shook her head. "Those two."

Meg huffed. "At least it isn't a mother ship landing site."

"Only because Sissy refused to let him visit Roswell last summer." Thea slipped off her smock, carefully folding it around loose hairs.

"Just as well. We're still trying to stabilize the slope from the slide he started last year with his earthworm farm."

"Alex says it's a good place to find worms for fishing, though." Thea walked Meg toward the front door. Barefoot she noticed it was time to swab the parquet floor again.

At the door, Meg faced her. "The other topic I wanted to broach ties into our spa project."

Thea leaned into the macramé hanging on her entry wall. "I haven't heard from the insurance company yet. They promised to get back to me this afternoon. It's getting late."

Meg patted her arm. "Don't started fretting now. And as you might have suspected, Sy asked me to lodge a member of this grant team. However, I've been mulling over another idea."

Thea grimaced. "I hope it's creative. Our contractor's long

gone. Even with money from insurance, we'll only be able to get raw materials. What we're going to do for labor…"

"That's just what I've been thinking about. Do you remember Jake Seeker, who originally bid on the contract?"

"Of course! He *was* the only other one."

"Well, I left a message for him last night. He called me this morning. I explained the circumstances and Jake said he would forego wages for stock options."

Thea's mouth dropped open. "You're kidding? What's the catch?"

"Full room and board. I'd like to have him stay in my extra room." The irascible set of Meg's chin warned her.

Thea met the obstinate brown of her friend's gaze.

"Meg, when we considered his original offer we expected him to stay with one of the men in town. Dwaine's place would be ideal. I don't think I'd be comfortable with him staying at your house." She tried unsuccessfully to revamp her first impression of the carpenter.

Meg's look rebuked. "It's my choice, not yours. Besides, aren't you planning to house this safety engineer? Sy *did* identify him as *male*."

"But a buttoned-down, tucked-in kind of guy. Jake is… well, he's…"

Her friend's foot began tapping. "I know he's had problems orienting himself since the War."

Thea smiled at Meg's reference to Vietnam. She pictured her friend as she must have been in her radical activism period: directed, fiery, and joyous all at once. Not much had changed.

The librarian continued. "I don't have a problem with his former affiliations. Jake's as much a victim as anyone."

Again, Thea tried. "I liked him, too, but, Meg, he's been *more* than out of it. When I couldn't get any references, he told me he's lived on the streets for years. Who knows how much his experiences still affect him? I'm not sure how stable his behavior is. I got the impression that he suffers from flashbacks. What if he decides you're the enemy?" More personal demons made her shudder.

"We *did* consider hiring him."

"Yes, when he was the only one who applied."

"I believe his post-war episodes are behind him. Remember, I met him, too. I found him wonderfully literate and charming. Why he's practically a Renaissance man. Do you know he's read Chaucer in old English? And James Joyce's *ULYSSES*?"

"But Meg—"

"This isn't at all like you, my dear. Why are you being so uncharitable toward Jake Seeker?"

Thea gnawed her lip before saying, "It isn't Jake Seeker. Not really."

"Well?"

Thea opened the door and walked onto the porch and Meg followed. "We still have the labor problem. We're not going to get the volunteer hours we need."

Meg smiled. "That's the beauty of it! Jake mentioned potential work forces from Reno and Carson City."

"People who don't need to be paid? What planet are they from?"

"Actually, Jake proposed setting up a tent city. Between Peabody's club and Bodeen's bakery, we can feed them. I think the city's coffers can manage that…"

"Whoa! Who are these people?"

"An *itinerant work force* is how Jake described them."

"Meg, you're not telling me all—"

"I have to run, Thea. Just think! We can meet our date for the grand opening after all." Off she bustled.

Thea closed her gaping mouth. Then she called, "I'll corner you tomorrow during our book club meeting, Megan

Connor. You won't slide out of answering me so easily then."

Inside her car now, Meg offered a merry wave good-bye. Thea watched the sedan disappear around the blind corner in her driveway. An illusive warbler flashed from a nearby tree, flying up Ricochet Mountain. Its yellow breast flashed like a warning as it headed for cover.

"I wonder what Alex's up to?" She backtracked through the house, noticing signs of disarray. Months of working either on the spa or her paintings showed. Pillowcases needed washing, couch and chairs plumping, floors and rugs cleaning. Dust lined all surfaces. Wind set off the chimes lining her back porch and drew her through the sliding door off the kitchen. From the veranda, the spicy bouquet of scarlet gilia, blue dicks, orange monkey flower, and butter-and-egg toadflax leading to Jack Rabbit Creek filled her nose.

Thea gave her smock a vigorous shake over the rail. Singed hairs floated away on the breeze. *Even mice and birds, which favored hair for nest materials, would reject these burnt offerings.* Hanging the old shirt on a hook, she breathed deeply. Subtle scents of lavender and basil quieted her unease. Then she heard Alex's lilting voice from the creek bed.

"Alex? Alexander MacTavish! Who're you talking to?"

An intense rustling of foliage traversed the creek bed along the abrupt slope up the mountain. Thea followed the sound with her gaze, but saw nothing.

His reluctance obvious in his sluggishness, Alex slogged up the bank and into view. He slouched at the rim, his golden hair mussed and blue eyes the telling shade of his father's. Right now those eyes filled with censure.

"Jeez, Mom! Why'd you have to yell? You scared him off."

"Scared who off? Whoever he is, if he's afraid of your mother's voice I don't want him here anyway." As Alex spun away from her, she said, "Not yet, mister. Come here. *Pronto.*"

As he ambled toward her, she cleared her mind of both undue concern and fuzzy anger. Yet relief made her lips twitch. He didn't always do what she asked of him. *What's he up to this time?*

Once he climbed the stairs, she said, "Want some iced tea, sport? To loosen your tongue?"

His hostile shrug made her wish she hadn't offered. A new twinge of hurt flayed the emotional callus acquired during the last year. This constant jockeying for advantage with her son exhausted her if she let it. She strode to her favorite willow chair, noting as she did that the cushion fabric needed replacing.

Who am I kidding? Hulon's mother ship had landed and its alien life forms now colonized the pillow. Maybe Alex had become a repository for extraterrestrials, too.

She relegated such trivial concerns to later, once she returned to her advertising career. Or after she sold another painting. For now, she plunked onto the weathered cloth, sweeping a hand toward the rocker facing her.

"Please sit, Alex."

He complied, perching warily on the edge. She loosened her fingers from their death grip on the armrests and rotated her shoulders. "Now, spill your guts, mister. Who was that?"

Fuchsia, I hate this tough love approach. A longing for gentler days brought a lump to her throat. She swallowed it. The art of hiding frailty thrived with practice.

He met her gaze with one just as steady. His sweeping gold-tipped lashes and creamy complexion didn't fool Thea for one minute; Alex was definitely no cherub. "*That* was a wolf."

She leaned toward him. "Hah! Come on, Alex! There aren't any wolves around here. Coyotes, yes. Stray dogs, yes. Wolves, no. And whatever it was, we need to let Sheriff Benton know. It's early in the year for rabies, but…"

His jaw tightened. "I don't know why you even ask. You never believe me anyway."

"Oh, come on. Give me the chance. I'd like nothing more than to take every word you say as fact. But let's look at your track record. Last year, it was the abominable snowman; the year before, the ghost of an old miner; now this latest episode with the trout pond..."

He bounded to his feet with all the energy of a natural disaster. His hands fisted and he pounded them against his thighs. "It was a wolf! It was a big, hungry wolf! Maybe a werewolf. And I'm going to start feeding him. But first, I'm going to take a soak." He whirled from her, vaulted the three steps and then headed down the path toward the hot springs.

Since the upper springs weren't really affected by yesterday's fire, Thea swallowed the words to call him back. They had moved past any chance at rational discussion. In fact, she didn't think they had even come close to coherent. She rolled her head onto the headrest and called,   "Stay away from that dog, Alex!"

He didn't acknowledge her words, but moved into a lope.

"And I should go soak, too. My head if nothing else. What was I thinking of anyway? Nothing like a little conflict to reinforce the Great Wall of Discord."

With a groan, she pushed herself to her feet. Thea started back into the house, intent on throwing together a late lunch, but changed her mind. Instead, she slipped into an old pair of sneakers, without laces of course, since Alex still exploited shoestrings to make parachutes for his action figures along with other bizarre uses. Thea straightened with a sigh, then backtracked along the path Alex followed from the creek.

Thea noticed anew that her son's feet were the same size as hers. This explained why her favorite jogging shoes smelled like a decaying animal. She had bought him new sneakers only two months ago. It must be time for another pair. Yet

24

another case of more debt than income.

At the streambed, she located Alex's footprints. A trail of colored stones curved along the border between clear water and fine-grained sand, evidence of her son's morning activity. Pyrite flakes glittered in the shallows as her gaze followed the direction of the earlier commotion. She hopped across the creek, careful to stay on the stepping-stones, then traced the deer run along the tributary for about fifteen feet.

Squatting to study the mud, she detected the cloven hoof prints of deer along with the unique claw and pad combination of raccoons. Late afternoon sun warmed the back of her neck and lulled her, bringing to mind the soothing days of summer ahead. Scents of crushed mint and silty mud filled her nose. Brushing aside sharp-edged grasses to study the muck more closely, the hairs along her nape and arms lifted. She stared at a paw print six inches across with pinkie length claws described from each pad.

Thea rocked onto her heels. "Holy fuchsia! That's one big dog."

Worse yet, she knew of no domestic dogs that used this trail as part of their circuit. While many Potshot residents kept pets, most treated their critters like family and kept them close to home. She understood their concern; her spaniel Dognabbit had died of old age last year. If she'd let him run free, he would have made some coyote family a nutritious snack.

She wobbled to her feet, looking long and hard along the creek for more disturbed vegetation. The sun no longer warmed her. Thea would not pretend to call herself a tracker, but she did know that whatever the animal was, stray dog or monster coyote, it must have been bigger across than the deer who normally traveled the path. It would not have made such a ruckus in the foliage otherwise. Still, neither dog nor coyote would attack a human the size and temperament of her son. Alex knew how to handle himself.

Rubbing dread-chilled arms, she returned to the house. When Sy stopped by with her tenant, she would let the sheriff know of her suspicions. Sy could enlist Deputy Dwaine's vaunted tracking skills. They'd get to the bottom of this.

Her mind fully occupied, she went through the motions of putting together something for lunch. A glance at the clock changed her mind. She would forego the midday meal and get dinner started. To brown a package of Dwaine's venison burger for spaghetti sauce took only a few minutes.

After chopping onions, she poured a dollop of olive oil in the heated pan. The phone rang. Her grip on the receiver failed, smacking it hard against her barely hardened blisters, souvenirs of the fire. "Ouch! Yes?"

Thea listened intently as the formal voice of the insur-ance agent detailed his findings. "Arson? You're sure?"

Then, "You're not going to reimburse us until *when*?"

After that, nothing he said mattered. She hung up, taking special care to place the handset in its cradle. Thea drifted onto the porch. Staring at the lofty tree whose base supported Alex's fort, she murmured, "What's wrong with me? I love spring. The sap's flowing in the silver birch. Jack Rabbit Creek's practically leaping from its bed and two kestrel falcons have moved into a woodpecker hole in the lightning struck tree."

Thea circled her ribs with her arms. "So why do I feel sapless? Parched. I'm all out of ideas. And what in *fuchsia* are we going to do about the spa now?"

A huge *whoosh!* erupted from inside. She raced into her kitchen. Flames on her stove leaped as high as the fan overhead. Black smoke roiled from the pan she had left on the hot burner. The chimes at her front door sang out.

"Oh, fuchsia," she protested. Thea grabbed her dishtowel while visions of beating the flames into submission pranced through her head.

She barely saw Sy from the corner of her eye. A stranger wrenched the pan's lid off the counter. He clattered it into place over the flame. Then the man grabbed her potholders and pulled the pan from the burner. With a loud click of finality, he flipped the burner control to 'off'. Salt granules from an overturned shaker bounced across the stovetop and onto her bare feet.

"Wow! That was incredible," she said as she faced the man. She raised her gaze a good six inches to make eye contact.

Umber brown eyes with pupils shrunken to pinpricks met her regard. The directness of his gaze called to mind a hawk at hunt, although this man dwarfed even the largest eagle. Every alarm in her head screamed 'danger' as she fought to break eye contact.

"Just what were you planning to do with that tea towel, Ma'am? Fan the flames higher? I don't hear any smoke alarm either." His tone, as heavy with Southern charm as Spanish moss, flooded her face with shame. He gingerly rubbed his right forearm.

"Fuchsia, you've burned yourself!" In one movement, she captured his arm between her hands, intent on towing him toward the sink. The scarlet ridge of flesh between her fingers transfixed her. It looked like an old injury, but he must have reinjured it. "Cold water—that should minimize the damage."

The man refused to budge. Thea stopped trying to drag him and really looked at him. His face had gone pale beneath tanned skin and white indentations bracketed his ashen mouth. He swayed on his feet.

"Holy fuchsia! You're not all right at all. Sy? Get that chair behind you, will you?"

As the sheriff slid the seat toward the listing giant, Thea urged him into it. It creaked as he folded onto the cushion. She prayed the chair would hold up under his solid mass.

At the same moment, she became aware of how his forearm felt beneath her touch; how smooth and warm the skin surrounding the burn; how well put together he was. Her breath wove into a knot below her diaphragm. As the man's physical beauty overcame concern, she practically flung his arm away from her.

Sy's voice broke her study. "Thea, this here's Dr. Bramden Youngwolf Hayes. Bram, this is Althea MacTavish, Potshot's resident artist. Maybe your landlady, too."

Chapter Three

Once the woman's kitchen quit spinning, Bram rolled his sleeve down to cover his scar. The action offered him a brief respite from the adrenaline rage filling him. More than that, he needed time to recover after MacTavish zapped him with those mossy soft eyes. *How in blazes could this woman be so ignorant about safety?* Fire killed—a fact he knew firsthand. Momentary bleakness escalated again into angry frustration.

"You okay, Dr. Youngwolf?" The sheriff leaned toward him, evidently looking for signs of equilibrium.

"It's 'Hayes' and I'm fine. Fires sometimes affect me this way."

"I've never met a fire guy who faints when confronted with fire. Of course, I only know volunteer firemen." The woman's husky voice rolled over him.

"I'm a fire safety engineer. And I did *not* faint." He hoisted himself from the chair.

Aiming an assessing look at her, he then turned his attention to the blackened wall and stove. "My actions *did* save your kitchen, if not your supper. No permanent damage. Nothing a scrub brush and some whitewash won't fix."

When he again regarded the woman, she stepped toward the counter and braced herself there. "*You* need to reacquaint yourself with basic fire safety, Miz MacTavish."

Her eyes reddened with tears. *Oh, no. Not a crier.*

This time she stopped short of touching him. Cynicism curled his lips. Even though her skin tone looked more golden than lily-white, the lady must have just registered his Indian heritage and taken offense.

"But what about your arm?" she quavered.

"It's an old scar. What in tarnation?" He focused on her hands. Bram touched her in spite of himself. The coolness of her fingers beneath her inflamed flesh baffled him. While he wallowed in confusion, she laughed. *Laughed!*

"Oh, that's just paint. It's leftover from my morning session. An evil wizard's cloak, if you can imagine. Plus a few blisters from yesterday's fire." He raised his gaze to meet dancing lights in hers. She tugged her hands free and dabbed them against denim shorts.

"I thought you were burned." His tone rang with accusation.

"I, for one, am not sorry to disappoint you."

"You're a testy little thing."

The woman shot a glint toward the sheriff. "Neither *little* nor a *thing*. Sy, could I speak to you? Privately, please. If you'll excuse us, Dr. Youngwolf?"

She didn't wait for him to correct her misconception before seizing the sheriff's arm. The woman hauled the much bigger man from the room. As they exited, the muscles in Bram's neck and shoulders tightened. He knew what came next. It wouldn't be the first time a woman turned him away because of his Cherokee blood. More recently, white women flocked to him as though he had a hotline to a higher power—shamanic connection incurred by blood, if you will. Neither response left room for a guy to be human. Worse yet, Bram suspected that if Miz MacTavish used tears on the sheriff, the man would crumble like old cheese.

Bram retrieved the tea towel from the floor. Embossed watermelon slices covered the fabric, recalling him to balmy evenings on Grandfather's back porch. The dust-laden air had smelled of summer. No drifting ash, no burned flesh...

The strain in his forearms brought his mind back to the present. He had coiled the dishcloth into a taut cable. When he released one end, it whipped like a whirligig before returning to a semblance of its former shape. He spread the fabric on the counter, where he pressed out the wrinkles with his hands.

Methodically, he rolled up his sleeves again. The damage was done here; it did little good to close the gate after the shoats had bolted. *Let them look. In fact, let them make a study of what wildfire did to flesh.* Twenty-four years ago on a warm summer night, fire had branded him as one of its own. Maybe the sight of his maimed flesh would open this snug community to the lessons he could teach.

Bram went to the sink and flipped the cold water on, then doused his face, neck, and arms. *Damn that felt good.* No longer overpowered by the stink of smoke, he finished drying his face. Strong essence of onion assaulted him as he lowered the towel. With a glance, he took in a cutting board covered with quartered bulbs. *Not tears, then, onions.* Somehow, that failed to comfort. Bram knew how to handle tears; quiet determination was another story. He went to the sliding glass door.

From an enclosed porch, a carpet of wildflowers the color of cardinals' wings directed his scrutiny to a bank twenty yards away. The path probably led to surface water judging from the cottonwoods. What looked like a kid's fort squatted midway between house and creek. Like a huge fungus, the fort encircled the trunk of a birch tree.

The sheriff and woman returned and Bram braced himself before facing them.

"Well, Dr. Hayes. Seems Thea here was expecting a boarder a bit more weathered. Say, someone closer to my age."

Bram looked right into the woman's eyes. Big mistake. *She had real pretty eyes for a bigot.* "So you think maturity relates

31

directly to age, Miz MacTavish? I'm thirty-five and head of this grant team. That makes me neither the oldest nor the youngest of my crew. Just the one in charge."

He stalked her, stopping a foot away. Every once in a while, he wielded Rez upbringing like a shield. She planted her feet. *Little hypocrite, her hair's as black as mine.*

"The University of Oklahoma felt confident putting trust in me. Why don't you?" Belatedly he realized her towel dangled from his fingers. He passed it to her.

She fumbled the handoff. A flush of color stained her cheeks. Good, Bram decided, let her stew in her intolerance. Her gaze dropped from his, then flashed toward the sheriff. When the sheriff grinned and shrugged, her regard returned to Bram.

The woman straightened, bringing the top of her head to his collarbone. "Look, Dr. Youngwolf—er—Hayes, I'm a single mom with a teenaged son. I can't have just any man living with me. You're not exactly what I expected, you know."

Was she for real? He cocked his head, listening for truth beneath the words.

"I mean I'm sure you're a very responsible person, but you're hardly a buttoned-up, tucked-in kind of guy. You don't even have a pocket-protector! And you're definitely no grandfather figure. As it turns out, you're only two years older than me. So you see? You can't stay here." She nodded as though justified.

He pushed a hand through his hair and stepped away from her. Maybe ethnicity had nothing to do with this after all. Cousin Challie always told him how thin-skinned he was. "Therefore, you're concerned about what? Your reputation?"

He leaned into the counter. The odor of onions assailed him, threatening to bring tears to his eyes, too. "Look, Miz MacTavish, we work long hours. I won't be here enough to damage anything. Certainly not your social status. Besides, you owe me." He gestured toward the stove.

"Now wait just a minute," she sputtered.

"It seems that having me around here, even infrequently, would be to your advantage. I certainly know more about fire prevention. Besides, the sheriff thought you'd appreciate the income."

"Don't you have any women in your—ah—group? I'm sure that would work out much better."

Bram decided this wasn't going the direction he wanted. He turned his attention to the sheriff. "Look. Potshot agreed to host my team four months ago. I have all the documents in order, signed by your mayor and blessed by your council members. Can your town afford the problems that breaking this contract would cause? I'm prepared to be reasonable. This is quibbling."

He looked at MacTavish again. "Yes, I have a woman on my team. She prefers to stay in one of the available rooms at your hotel. However, *I* need a room and *yours* is the one I want."

"You haven't even seen it!"

"No, I haven't. Now's as good a time as any." He gestured with his hands in what he hoped translated into 'after you, ma'am'.

The sheriff cleared his voice. "Well, Thea, now that you have this situation in control—"

"Sy!"

She looked apprehensive. Forcing her to abide with his wishes started a pang of discomfort in Bram. He felt like a bully.

The sheriff said, "I'd best be getting back to town. Thanks for Alex's write-up about what happened yesterday. Meg dropped it off before we came up here. I'll put it in the file." The big man lumbered to the front door, his much-creased cowboy hat in hand.

"The Wife got another shipment in this morning. God knows my April's hell on wheels, but I like to help when I can. Sometimes that wheelchair can slow even her down."

Bram and MacTavish trailed the sheriff. She looked in need of a reprieve. *Shoats and razorbacks, did the woman actually see him as a threat?*

The peace officer paused with the door open and faced Bram. "Now I know you'll be the perfect gentleman, Dr. Hayes. Or you *will* answer to me." The older man's gaze grew decidedly chilly.

Miz MacTavish shut the door behind the receding back of Potshot's sheriff. She leaned her forehead into the frame before facing him. For a brief moment, he almost offered reassurance. Her lifted chin warned him off. She was one fractious filly.

"I thought I'd have veto power."

A tinge of shame grazed Bram. "There's no reason for concern. Even if I were a lecherous sort, you're really not my type." Against his wishes, a smile crept onto his face.

Her eyes, mouth, and chin tensed. In fact, her jaw took on a decidedly mutinous cast. "How very reassuring. And how wonderful for you to categorize people so neatly." Frost sharpened her eyes. "Follow me, please."

He trailed her stiff back through the entranceway, noticing for the first time the scuffling sounds of her bare feet on hardwood floors. She wore ragged cutoffs and an equally disreputable tee shirt. The original color proved indeterminate, as age-faded and splotched with paint as the shorts were. While her hair mirrored his in shade, he noticed that far from the heavy coarseness of his, hers caught air and lifted as she marched through the house. Long earrings of ceramic beads and oddly shaped metals clinked from multi-pierced ears. He identified a floral scent, too. Since he preferred his women

34

blonde, tall, and voluptuous, this little gypsy presented little obstacle to his composure.

She glanced at him. Except for her eyes, he amended, which now held all the warmth of arctic ice. Her look played havoc with his poise.

"You're an artist?"

"Yep." Had the word been a blade, he'd have been shorter from the knees down.

Self-preservation warned him to ride her wave of silence. Instead, he asked, "What kind of a living can a person make in art?"

She shot him a glare over one shoulder. "Not much of one. Actually, I'm on sabbatical from my paying job through July. Normally I live the opulent life of a graphics designer in advertising." When he made no response, she added, "That was supposed to be *funny*. The opulent part anyway."

Bram scowled. "With a growing boy and all, I'd think fiscal responsibility…"

She stopped so quickly he nearly rammed her. Delicate muscles clenched in her jaw, calling attention to her lush mouth, chapped lips, and firm chin when she faced him. Skin on one cheek had begun to peel; an obvious side effect of getting too close to the spa fire. "My finances, stable or otherwise, are none of your business. Our contract is through Potshot."

"Fine by me."

"Furthermore, Sy ran a background check on you or you wouldn't be here. Even so, it's my intent that you'll have little or no association with either my son or me, Dr. Hayes. That's why I'm putting you in the basement."

She whirled around, nearly sprinting in her haste. *Looks like she can't wait to consign me to subterranean levels.* Bram nearly laughed aloud. He hadn't had so much fun since Challie's pigs razed Grandfather's corn patch. He took his time following her, giving him the chance to peruse his new surroundings.

From the twig furniture in the living room to the carelessly tossed rugs and pillows along much of the floor space, the woman's house reflected her, bright and disarrayed. Her housekeeping skills left much to be desired, too. There must have been a run of demented dust bunnies taking cover inside when winter hit.

Then there was her deficiency in the kitchen. That pan had overheated for quite awhile before reaching flashpoint. Add that fact to no discernible smoke alarms, and Bram decided MacTavish was in dire need of his expertise.

Too many of the people where he had grown up lived in such havoc. Perhaps not the same mayhem this woman encouraged, but close enough. Those friends he kept track of still squatted on the Rez in places he would no longer consider living. He worked hard to escape the Rez—and its inherent chaos. *Give me my upscale condo in Norman, Oklahoma any day.*

So why had it suddenly seemed so important that he stay here? He blamed it on his intolerance for nitpicking. She really had no legitimate excuse for rebuffing him. Despite her contrariness, she and the boy could use the added income.

His new landlady paused to switch on a light, then he followed her down narrow stairs toward what had looked like a daylight basement when he drove up. Not a word had passed her chapped lips since she turned her back on him. Silence from a woman was almost startling; his cousins chattered like magpies. Bram's last woman friend had barely paused for breath. *She's probably sulking at not getting her way*, he concluded.

With little effort, he continued his catalog of her negative points. Even her car, beside which he had parked his Land Rover, looked like it belonged on the Rez. Still, he smiled

36

at the bumper sticker: "THIS IS NOT AN ABANDONED VEHICLE".

When she stopped at the bottom of the stairs, he braced a hand against the wall to keep from colliding with her. She stepped aside and switched on an overhead light. It illuminated a room paneled in pale walnut. Recessed lighting shone from the finished ceiling. The space possessed more order than anything he had seen thus far. Raw pine shelves packed with painting supplies lined one wall. Opposite that crouched a queen-sized bed smothered under a comforter and pillows in the same hectic colors as the rest of the house. At one end, a helter-skelter mass of frames and stretched canvases wedged between mattress and wall. Mismatched bureau, armoire, and desk with a chair completed the rest of the furnishings. On a brick hearth in the niche closest to the desk hunkered a wood stove. The southern exposure of the sliding glass doors along with a couple of narrow windows allowed plenty of light into the room. Through the glass door, he viewed his rig parked next to her disreputable Honda.

"Well?" she asked in a clipped manner.

"This looks fine."

"We have one bathroom. You passed it in the hall. You'll find towels and sheets under the sink there. Now, if that's all, I have dinner to prepare. I'll move my frames out tomorrow— *after* you leave." She turned her cool gaze on him.

"Fine. I'll just unload. Oh, and do you have a connection box down here? I need a separate phone line for my laptop. Unless you have wireless?"

She gave him a look of pity, then kneeled by the desk and pointed. Leaning into the small space, he noticed more colossal dust bunnies, which had yet to migrate back to the great outdoors. Then Bram smelled the distinct fragrance of honeysuckle. It recalled his mother's garden. When Miz MacTavish straightened, the scent faded.

He turned as she headed for the steps. "I may have my team over tonight. This will be our base of operation. I doubt you'll even notice we're here. I'll tell them to come through this door." With a nod, she continued up the   stairs, taking her oddly vital presence and sunny fragrance with her.

Hours later, Bram jogged up the basement stairs two at a time. Clutched in one hand, he brandished a list of questions for Miz MacTavish. He strode by the bathroom, where he had excavated sun-dried sheets earlier, then down the hall toward the living room and kitchen. The clatter of silverware against china keyed him to where he might find her. Aromas of marinara and garlic drew him. He rounded the corner between front room and dining area before coming to a halt. The tableau before him struck him as unusual, to say the least.

Bram's experiences at dinner tables revolved around a riot of talk. Yet here he found the MacTavish woman sitting mute across from a skinny kid, most likely her son. He briefly noticed the dazzling blue cloth covering the table along with scarlet, blue and yellow flowers in an asymmetrical vase. What really caught his attention was the saturated quiet. The room teemed with unspoken words. Miz MacTavish's face looked strained even to him, a virtual stranger. The boy appeared morose, or at least he did until Bram wandered into view. Then the kid slanted a glance at him. Keen intelligence sparkled from eyes the clearest blue Bram had experienced since summer skies in Oklahoma.

"May I help you?" Althea MacTavish rose from the table. Her eyes changed from resigned to bleak between heartbeats.

He indicated the slip of paper. "No, I—ah—didn't intend to interrupt your supper. I just had a few questions. I'll come back after you're done."

"Too late. You might as well have a seat."

38

Now Bram sensed her relief at his interruption, but stifled any comment.

"I made enough spaghetti to freeze some." She moved nonchalantly toward a cabinet near the stove.

His stomach snarled, a badger too long without food. It *had* been over six hours. "Actually, I could eat a charred buffalo, but the sheriff told me meals weren't included in my lease agreement. In fact, I was hoping to get our deal in writing so I'd know where I stand."

Miz MacTavish trapped her lower lip with her teeth. "In writing? I suppose I could do that. For now, why don't you join us? We'll make this one a freebie." She turned to the stove, which revealed a good deal less fire damage now, and dished food from a blackened pot.

"I made the sauce with venison burger. There's garlic bread on the table. I can only offer you milk, herb tea, or instant coffee."

The boy leaned toward Bram and warned, "Don't ask for milk; it's *powdered.* Tastes like crap."

Bram said, "Water would be fine. Let me wash up first."

He escaped down the hall and into the bathroom, all the while kicking himself for being drawn into what was obviously an awkward family situation. The last thing he wanted was any involvement deeper than monthly rent and bathroom privileges. He told his reflection, "It's only supper."

When he returned to the table, Bram settled himself into the remaining chair between the woman and her son. The boy looked him over, then stuck out his right hand. "I'm Alex. Better known in Potshot as 'Althea's bane'."

His mother choked on her last bite, while Bram took the proffered hand. "Bramden Youngwolf Hayes. I'll be boarding here until the hotel's ready."

The boy gave him an adult nod before releasing his hand. Bram planted a napkin on his lap, then picked up his fork. At least the pasta *smelled* good enough to eat.

The boy asked, "So you're the guy who saved my mom from the inferno? I might as well warn you, her cooking's just as deadly."

"Come on, Alex. My cooking isn't that bad."

The boy looked Bram straight in the eye, so he set his fork down, spaghetti untouched. Clearing his throat, Bram said, "I suppose in retrospect it wasn't a bad fire."

With a snort of disbelief, the kid said, "Oh, come on. We scrubbed the stove for *hours*. Now I have to help paint the wall tomorrow. So Mom really screwed up, huh?"

Miz MacTavish's fork hit her plate with a heavy clatter as she raised an eyebrow and said, "I thought you were hungry, Alex. A little respect, please."

"Sorry, Mom," the boy mumbled.

Bram said, "Hot oil ignites. It's not a thing to be taken lightly."

"Jeez, from the soot all over the hood, the flames must have been huge. I'll bet…"

"Alex, enough. Please let *Doctor* Hayes eat before he keels over from hunger."

"A doctor? No shit."

"Alex! Watch your language."

Bram chewed and swallowed a single mouthful by applying pure concentration to his food. "I got my PhD in environmental engineering. It doesn't have much to do with sick people other than causal effects. My actual title's 'fire safety engineer'."

The boy mulled that over. Bram managed another bite before the kid asked, "What does that mean, 'environmental engineering'?"

"In this case, it means I can assess an area for fire hazards. Then I make recommendations to minimize damage." He sounded stilted, but his answer didn't faze the kid.

40

"Wow." The boy had one of those angelic faces that concealed satanic tendencies. Except for the kid's big almond-shaped eyes and firm little chin, he sure didn't look much like his mother. "So I guess it's a good thing you're here, with Mom's thing for stove fires and all. Guess Sheriff Benton must have told you about…"

"Alex, that's enough. I've only had one other stove fire." His new landlady turned toward Bram.

"What about the one in the hibachi? Couldn't tell the burgers from the briquettes," quipped the Devil's advocate. He looked at Bram.

With a shake of her head and a slight smile, his landlord said, "Dr. Hayes, my son's obsessed by natural disasters. Some would say he *is* a natural disaster."

"Mom, can I tell Dr. Hayes about the firestorm on the other side of Ricochet Mountain last year?"

The woman conceded with a smile, bringing to mind sunlight on water. Bram's attitude about her veered south. He shook it off. So she could smile; big deal. Unlike Bram's stomach, the MacTavish woman evidently thrived on the kid's nonstop discourse.

The boy swung his clear gaze back to Bram. "We thought for sure it was going to come over the peak and crisp us. I stood outside and ran the garden hose on the roof all night. Mom and a bunch of other people dug a big ditch on the slope."

A thrill of fear clenched Bram's gut. He put his fork down. "I read about that. You had a plume."

The boy leaned forward. "We did? What's that?"

"A plume can happen as a growing fire sucks harder at the oxygen around it. Since cooler air pushes up hot air, a convection column develops. Some plumes rise high enough into the atmosphere that they make their own weather systems."

"Cool," said Alex.

Bram nodded. "Plumes generate enormous heat. Hot enough to melt steel. This area has a high potential for having more wildfires of that type, especially in the next few years. That's why I brought my team here. According to our data, you're overdue." He moved his gaze to the woman as she hurriedly reached for her glass.

"Coo-o-ol," the boy said again. His mother had trouble swallowing her last mouthful and gulped water.

"We have some applications that should increase this area's durability. There *are* preparations you can make, even some relatively minor topographical ones. Our grant targets preventative measures." He took a breath, ready to launch into the findings of his research, when Miz MacTavish broke his concentration.

"Dr. Hayes! How's your dinner? Please, have some garlic bread." He registered her helpless look.

Alex leapfrogged in with, "Don't feel bad, Dr. Hayes. Ever since Sherm and me torched the old sheepherders' shack, Mom goes postal when anybody talks about fires."

That stopped Bram cold. A tiny fissure appeared along the lid of the Pandora's box he carried within. He tamped it down ruthlessly. His look caused Alex to flash from bravado to wariness.

The boy squirmed in his chair. Words tumbled from his mouth. "You know, we really didn't mean to do it. It's just that Sherm—that's Sherman Peabody whose dad had the absolute *best* earthworm farm last year—he got this way cool magnifying glass from the drugstore where his mom works. So we went up to the shack and burned holes in leaves and things." Alex licked his lips, passing a quick glint toward his silent mother.

"You know, the closer you bring the glass to the leaf, the faster it burns. Only the holes get smaller and smaller..." The kid's voice dwindled.

On autopilot, Bram said, "Basic physics. Magnifying glasses concentrate light energy."

"Yep. That's what it did. But I guess when we left, we didn't stamp out all the sparks. Later that night, the whole side of the mountain lit up when the shack burned down. Boy, did we catch hell." His head drooped as he used a crust of bread to probe the sauce streaks on his plate.

"I think that's enough conversation for now, Alex."

Bram had nearly forgotten about the boy's mother, who continued with, "Since you worked so hard on helping me clean around the stove, I'll do dishes."

"Cooo-ool. Can I watch…"

She held up a hand to forestall him. "You're still on restriction. No T.V." When his face fell in disappointment, she added, "Meg brought you a new 'Pick Your Adventure' book from the library. It's on my dresser."

With a thousand-watt smile, the kid hopped up, plate in hand. He put his dish and silverware in the sink with a clatter that made Bram visualize shards of china. Then the boy headed out one side of the kitchen, only to pop into the other entrance a heartbeat later.

"Thanks, Mom. Nice meeting you, Dr. Hayes." Off he pelted.

Bram envisioned the wreckage left in his wake; destruction the equivalent of a small twister in a confined space no doubt. A door slammed hard enough to shake the windows. As he turned toward the table and his cold plate of spaghetti, Bram's landlady whisked it away from him. His stomach protested.

"I'll just put this in the microwave for you. Alex willing, you can finish in peace."

Since he saw the logic behind her statement, he said nothing until she plopped the reheated plate in front of him. He thanked her. She returned to the stove. For a few moments, he concentrated on his meal. It was pretty good considering what he had seen of her competence at the range. As he pondered sopping up the tangy sauce with his bread, the room's silence trickled through his self-absorption.

He glanced up to find the woman poised over the sink. A dishrag dangled forgotten from her fingers. She had finally gotten the paint stains off her fingers. Without the camouflage, he saw how narrow, even graceful, her hands were. The compact lines of her body looked coiled. Thick as pitch from a loblolly pine, raw emotions oozed from her. Bram figured that if he so much as exhaled, she would fly apart. He had the urge to rattle his plate and scrape his chair along the floor. Instead, he sat quietly and let his unlikely landlady finish whatever journey she was making.

As she emerged from her fugue, she turned toward the table. The sight of him made her jump and put a hand over her chest. "I thought you'd gone." She stalked forward, reaching for his plate as he lifted it toward her.

"I was letting my meal settle. Didn't mean to startle you."

She shrugged. "Guess I have a lot on my mind."

He decided now was as good a time as any to make his escape. Instead, he opened his mouth and said, "How about if I give you a hand with the dishes?"

She rewarded him with a suspicious look. "Why?"

"Hey, you fed me."

"Suit yourself. I'll wash; you can rinse."

That's what they did, until he said, "One of the things I hoped to negotiate was some kitchen time."

She kept washing. Only now did he realize that all the dinner plates matched. That surprised him, although their riotous fruit design did not. Finally, she said, "I really value my solitude. I'm not sure I like the thought of you wandering through my house any time of the day."

The muscles in his neck tightened. "I *am* house trained. I

44

clean up after myself and buy my own groceries. Plus I'll pay you something extra for the privilege."

She slanted a curious look at him from the corner of her eyes. The thick curtain of black lashes nearly hid her assessment. Her look seemed to find him wanting. "You think you can buy just about anything, don't you?"

"Look, I'll work out a time schedule. It'll either be early or late in the day." He grabbed the dishtowel off the refrigerator handle and used the action to regain control of his temper. Bram scrubbed a plate hard enough to rub the flowers off.

She took the dish from him and put it in the drainer. "I let my dishes air dry."

As MacTavish drained the water from the sink, she said, "All right. Draw up your schedule. If it doesn't suit me, I'll let you know and that'll be the end of it. Deal?" She pinned him with her lucid gaze.

He nodded. Just then, the chimes at the front of the house set up a horrible clatter.

"Now who would that be?" She took the towel from him and dried her hands.

He detoured to the table for his list before following. "Could be my crew. I asked them to come through the basement entrance, but…"

The din erupted again as his landlady opened the door. *How did the woman stand the racket?*

Bram didn't recognize the person framed there. Tall and clad in what looked like a custom-made silk suit, the man hesitated. The porch light burnished his blond hair to gold.

"Derek?"

"Thea! How are you, my dear?" With a move Bram could only admire, the man slid into the entranceway. He caught Miz MacTavish by the wrist with one hand before she could slam the door in his face. The man's maneuver brought Bram onto the balls of his feet. The tension between the two bordered on tangible.

"What are you doing here?" Her voice vibrated.

This should have been the cue for Bram to make his exit. Now that he analyzed this situation, it looked too personal. Still, he felt a strong urge to spoil the guy's plans, even ruin the city slicker's manicure. Bram stayed.

Blue eyes the same shade as Alex's caught him in their high beams and the man mouthed, "Temper, temper, my sweet."

Fashion Plate kept Miz MacTavish from shoving the door at him. She finally dropped her arms to her sides in obvious disgust. All the while, Mr. Elite picked Bram apart with venomous regard. Bram responded like a junkyard dog, hackles raised and a growl forming deep in his chest. No woman deserved this scum in her life, not even the annoying Miz MacTavish.

The man's suave voice sharpened, "Who the hell is he?"

Chapter Four

"He doesn't concern you, Salinger. And who are you to barge into my home and ask me anything?" Thea crossed her arms over her chest, where her heart slammed hard enough to bruise. As she studied the predator before her, she knew she would do whatever needed to be done to protect her son. Her peripheral vision picked up Hayes' movement. She swung to face him.

"I'm not going anywhere, Miz MacTavish," he said.

"Big mistake on your part, buddy," Derek intoned.

She ignored Derek Salinger. Instead, she said to Hayes. "It's 'Thea'. Just Thea, Dr. Hayes, and thank you. I really need a witness to what I have to say to this viper," she added to counter the disquiet she saw in his dark eyes. Whatever she had to do for Alex . . .

Hayes nodded, settling onto his heels. That was all, but unexpected warmth rushed through her. "Thank you." She whipped around to the man who had gouged a swathe of ruin in her life fourteen years ago.

"You, get out!" When the blond man balked she paced closer to him. "Get out. I won't have Alex involved in this."

"A little late now, sweetheart," but Derek stepped through the doorway and into the night.

Thea sensed Hayes at her back as she cut off Derek's reentry into her home. Her unlikely supporter showed the good sense to shut the door behind them. Out of the tailspin into which Derek's arrival had thrust her, having a man called

Youngwolf at her back gave her a peculiar sense of security.

Thea scrutinized Derek Salinger as he filled her view with his carnal beauty, murky soul and all. Fallen angel that he was, he seemed to draw strength from her study. What could he possibly want from her now? Unless he intended to demand his legal rights…

"Thea, you've got me all wrong. Look, I even brought us a ceremonial bottle of champagne." He extended the offering.

Her mouth dry as desert sand, she shoved aside the bottle. Her hands shook so badly she clenched her fingers into a fist and clamped both arms to her sides. "You're fourteen years too late. Keep your poison to yourself. Now, Salinger, you have two minutes to state your business before I ask Dr. Hayes to call the sheriff."

Derek's calculating look hit her dead center. Her stomach turned to iced jelly. A smile transformed him into Beauty incarnate. "Two minutes? Well, that's not going to be nearly long enough. Maybe I'll just let you stew in your own bitter juices for a time instead. Yes, I think I'll do just that, my dear." He started toward his car, a sleek coupe bleached white by the full moon.

Salinger paused to set the paper-wrapped bottle on the lowest step. With careless leisure, he adjusted his cuffs under a suit that probably cost more than she made in two months as a graphics designer. Her rage crested. She welcomed the heat. Suspicion that she was doing exactly what he expected vaporized under the onslaught. She refused to be his victim—again.

Before he reached his car, he paused. "Oh. How foolish of me. I forgot to give you my card. In case you want to reach me before this week's town meeting. I'm staying at Lake Tahoe. You don't need to know exactly where. My service will have instructions to put you through immediately, old *friends* that we are."

He prowled to within four feet of her and made a show of opening a gleaming case and extracting a card. Salinger flicked it onto the bottom step. The card bumped against the bottle, then drifted to its base. "Wouldn't want to get too close you know. Haven't had my rabies vaccine." He shot her the venomous grin Thea once found so seductive, but now associated with bone deep despair.

She swallowed hard. "Get off my land. Get out of my town. Leave Alex and me alone." Anger pitched her voice harsh and low.

"Anything for a—lady." He tipped a nonexistent hat toward her, then pivoted on his well-heeled Loafers.

Thea refused to accept his intent to leave until the oversized motor in his auto roared to life. Within seconds of ignition, all that remained of Derek was his business card and the champagne, both glowing a malignant white in the moonlight. The rooster tail of dust raised by the wheels of Salinger's car took on the aspect of a fall of sorcerer's powder, as though Derek had disappeared into thin air. The surging roar from his vehicle's engine belied her fancy even as it grew more distant.

She raced to where Salinger's tires had gouged a furrow into her driveway. Digging her toes into the yielding earth, she gathered rocks into one hand, muttering the entire time. "You scum! Coming to *my* town and onto *my* mountain. Threatening me in *my* house."

Using short wind-ups with inaccurate releases, she pelted stones in the general direction of his retreat. After firing three handfuls of missiles, her throwing arm ached enough that she decided to quit. Besides, she had torn open a blister or two.

Her teeth chattered as she returned to her house. She closed the distance between herself and Salinger's business card, gingerly lifting it. It took more will power than she believed she had not to rip the thing into shreds. She stuffed it into a pocket of her cutoffs, then hefted the bottle. Feeling every one of her thirty-three years, she climbed the stairs to face her boarder. He looked solid as a lodgepole pine. Thea sought her tenant's gaze with hers. Backdropped by weak porch light, she could not decipher his expression.

"Nice guy," he drawled.

His obvious skepticism startled a dismal croak from her. That would have been all right, but it didn't stop there. She proceeded to a choking laugh until it sounded more like a wrenching sob. Thea swallowed hard. Uncomfortable silence thickened the space between them.

"I'm not going to cry, if that's what you're waiting for."

"It had crossed my mind."

"Only onions make me cry." Burrowing one handed into the front pocket of her shorts, she dug out a wadded tissue. Turning away from him, she blew her nose.

"Dust," she explained when she faced him again. His cedar scent wafted to her. The man's vitality hit her harder than at any other time during this long day.

"Dr. Hayes, you must feel like you've been dropped into a loony bin."

"Into an alternate reality, anyway," he replied.

"And to think I believed you lacked a sense of humor. That was humor, wasn't it?" She reached for the door.

"A piss-poor attempt, obviously."

They stood in the entry hall and Thea scrutinized him. She owed him a level of honesty, especially after what he witnessed. Thea saw no reason for any illusions. "How about if I make some tea? Or instant coffee. You choose."

His guarded look slipped into place, reminding her of what had been missing. "My crew could be here at anytime."

"So take your tea downstairs when they show up. No biggie." When she turned to check on Alex, he followed. "You can meet me in the kitchen." This she tossed over her shoulder.

For some reason, Dr. Hayes refused to behave and, instead of meeting her in there, he tracked her. He must have thought it his duty to keep her in sight; no telling what a crazy woman might do. At the door to her son's room, she pressed the bottle into Hayes' hands. When he hesitated to accept, she said, "Consider it a hospitality gift, since I didn't put any gourmet chocolates on your pillow."

She ignored his coolness. Rapping softly first, she opened the door. Amid the confusion of last year's bird nests, posters of alternative rock idols, books and futuristic action figures, she found Alex on his bed. Relief eased the tightness in her chest when she saw him asleep, the headset of his much-despised portable disc player in place—he'd been lobbying for an iPod. An open book draped his narrow chest. Raw tenderness made her ache. She glanced back and laid a finger over her lips, probably unnecessarily, since an oddly vulnerable expression covered her houseguest's face.

Thea tiptoed through debris generated by a week out of school. She pried the earphones from Alex's head, then closed his book after slipping a scrap of paper inside to mark his place. Since he was already barefoot, she decided to let him sleep in his jeans and shirt, both so soft from repeated washings that they wore like pajamas anyway. She fetched a light comforter, more suited to summer, from the top of his closet and covered him. Stroking his silky hair, she kissed his downy cheek.

"I'll keep you safe, my little love, I promise," she whispered. Good thing Alex couldn't hear. He would be mortified.

Thea backtracked from his room, turning off the light before closing the door. Her boarder, who leaned against the doorframe throughout the nightly ritual, said nothing, but traced her steps into the kitchen. Her eyes gritty and skin tight, she went to the sink where she doused her face in cold water. The chill water cooled the blossom of shame.

As she dabbed her face dry with the damp dishtowel, she faced the window over her sink and said, "I hope you'll believe me when I say that this is not business-as-usual in the MacTavish household. It speaks well of you that you haven't run from the house shrieking, bags in hand. I'm not usually such a maniac." She turned toward him.

Her gaze dipped from his steady look to a splotchy remnant of his tussle with her kitchen fire on his chambray blue shirt. The gaping fabric at his throat and upper chest, where a button had come undone, revealed sun-touched skin. Solid looking flesh peeked from the recesses. In his own way, Hayes was every bit as good-looking as Salinger. Blood rushed to her face. She hung the towel to dry. "It looks like you'll need laundry privileges."

Setting the champagne on the counter, he worked a slip of paper from his shirt pocket. Even from here, she could see the ink had run. His comical expression brought laughter bubbling from her. "Looks like my stint as dish rinser left its mark. Laundry *was* on my list of questions. Guess you'll have to take my word for it."

"I will. Now about that tea."

Brewing the drink offered a brief respite. For Thea, small talk equated with wearing shoes, an uncomfortable formality at best. She took time to reflect on Derek's sudden appearance and what it meant. His crack about the town meeting bothered her. As she puzzled it out, more questions than answers formed.

She and her new tenant sat for a time in repose, sipping an apple spice brew. Night sounds moved into the kitchen from outside: an owl's forlorn call, the leathery rustle of bat wings, the scurry of prey through the undergrowth, and the constant background of creek song. Hayes was one of few people Thea knew who seemed comfortable in this quiet she savored. He wrapped stillness around him like a cloak.

Finally, she said, "Derek Salinger is Alex's biological father." She almost said 'sperm donor'. Never mind how the truth of that encounter might shock even this composed man.

Hayes' penetrating gaze held hers. Drops of residual water trapped in the kitchen faucet splattered onto stainless steel. He took a breath, released it. "I don't really want to know about your private life, Thea. Like you, I prefer limited contact."

His words abraded the scar within her. "It wasn't an invitation, Dr. Hayes. Just a barebones explanation for the insanity you just witnessed."

Gulping his tea, he clunked the cup onto the table. "Understand where I'm coming from. I'm here to do a six-month study for a project best done over five years. I need a tight focus." He studied the depths of his mug before again meeting her regard.

Thea ached with each word of dismissal, although she refused to dwell on why that would be. After all, she had just met this guy. *Ambivalence sucks.* With that thought, her initial sense of peril returned. His kindness must have been nothing more that an attempt at damage control.

She raised her chin. "A tight focus, huh? Well, that suits me, too. Please forgive me for not anticipating Derek's little visit. After thirteen years of silence, I couldn't have foreseen his arrival. Now, if we're finished here, I've some things to do." Face stiff and body rigid, she stood.

His eyes widened with her words. What did he expect? That she might beg for his help? Fall blubbering onto his brawny chest?

She decided then and there that her first instincts were correct and not the delusions of a woman too long alone. Much like Derek, Dr. Bramden Youngwolf Hayes was much too good-looking and self-absorbed for her piece of mind.

So what if he had supported her when she needed it? His had been a convenient presence, nothing more. If the sensual creature within her, so long dormant, bounded to life at his woodsy male scent, well, she expected to deal with *her*, too. Thea would *not* break her vow to herself and seek false solace from any source, no matter how muscular a chest he sported. No matter how well his jeans fit his hips. No matter how interesting the fade patterns on those jeans. She promised.

Cross her fingers and hope to die.

She checked the time, then her personal calendar before going to the phone and dialing Meg's number. Conscious of the tenant at her table, she planted her feet more firmly and straightened her shoulders.

When her best friend picked up, she said, "Meg, I need to make a run to Reno. Would you mind coming to the house and staying with Alex while I'm gone?"

"Why, of course, Thea. Are you sure you don't want me to come with you? I'll bet Jessica wouldn't mind staying at the house."

Thea paused briefly, understanding Meg's shorthand for 'If you need me, I'm here'. "No, I just have to drop by Mother's. I meant to go earlier, but life intruded."

"All right, I'll be there shortly. Maybe we can have a good heart-to-heart when you get back." Meg rang off.

Thea turned to her boarder. "Just turn off the lights when you leave." She headed for the shower.

True to his word, Dr. Hayes left the house as Thea awakened to amber light coming through her windows. A twinge of unease, compounded by the presence of a man in her house, hastened her from slumber. At least Alex still slept. The melee of the previous night, followed by a requisite visit to her mother's place, must have manifested in a catharsis.

She woke refreshed and ready to face anew the fact that sometimes, emotional recovery equated with hand-to-hand combat with demons.

Which could explain why in one hand, Thea now held the first demon she intended to exorcise today. A crumpled brown bag encased the champagne left by Salinger. Left on the counter by her boarder, Thea accepted it as yet another degree of separation between her and Hayes.

"Bramden Youngwolf Hayes' no-man's land. Or no-woman's either."

She slipped the bottle into a discarded cereal box. In her other hand, Thea hefted a hammer. She carried both to the garbage can at one side of her house. Once she popped the lid and plunked it onto the ground, an almost unholy glee overtook her. She balanced the twice-wrapped bottle on the upturned lid and raised her hammer. For a brief moment, sensory images made her hesitate. It had been well over a decade since she had a glass of really good champagne.

"Damn you to hell, Salinger."

She swung her hammer down, fueled by new rage and old injury. The head hit the center with a satisfying explosion of glass and released pressure. The saturated paper bag didn't survive the first strike, but the chipboard did and kept splinters from showering her. Thea ignored the sweet smell of addiction and hit the bottle again—and again—until only pulpy shards in a pool of champagne remained. Then she dropped her hammer and flipped the lid back onto the garbage. The tinkle of glass hurtling against aluminum sounded like a good day's work.

She swept the cement footing around the can. As she gathered glass fragments into a dustpan, Thea wished she could dispose of Derek as easily. The reek of fermented grapes saturated the air, intensifying the itch in her nose and palate. Thea concentrated on the early morning bouquet of pine and sage instead. Maybe this evening, she would walk up to the hot springs and take a long soak.

"I definitely need to unwind."

She stood and meandered the driveway, viewing a sapphire mantle of lupines in bloom. Her late night call to Sy had turned up no clue as to Derek's intent, although the sheriff promised keep his ear to the ground. With a deep breath, Thea released her anxiety over what she could not control. As she walked back toward the house, puffs of soil kicked up with each step of her sandaled feet. She enjoyed a shiver of coolness. The buzz of newly emergent insects soothed as their presence underscored the richness of her life here in Potshot. Fuchsia, but she loved early spring on her mountain.

A loud report followed by two more, obviously from an automatic rifle, broke the peace. The gunshots echoed along the creek. Thea shaded her eyes from morning sun and tried to make out the source, a futile effort given the distance. She knew the origin anyway.

Eden Valley. Only one mile southwest as the crow flies, it was a good five-mile hike from here, but only two from Potshot. She would bet anything that the shot had been fired in the valley. A compound of survivalists lived there. Whenever they launched into their militia-style drills, rifle reports could be heard for miles. There had been only three shots this time, but it didn't sound like the kind of gun used for bird hunting.

"Great! Guns in the hands of fanatics. What next?" she muttered, rubbing goose bumps along her arms. She paced quickly back to the house and, after a cold breakfast, herded a recalcitrant Alex into the car.

"I don't see why you have to drive me to the library," he groused.

"You had other plans?"

He shrugged. "You're always watching me. Like I've done something wrong when I haven't."

56

Thea fixed her regard back on the road and tried to still the blood creeping into her face. To no avail. "Too bad, Alex. You're grounded and should be counting your lucky stars that I'm letting you go to the library today."

"Like Miz Connors won't tell you everything that goes on there."

She grinned and pulled into the parking lot. "That's the idea, sport."

When she got out of the car with him, he crossed his arms and glared. "Aw, Mom, you're not walking me in, too?"

"Actually, I need to see Meg about something else. However, if you want an escort. . ."

"No way," and he pelted up the stairs and through the front door.

Thea took a slower pace, avoiding the children gathered at the largest table and wandering through the stacks toward the back office. She found Meg sipping coffee.

"A cup of courage before facing the hellions?"

"Nonsense, Althea. You know I love their youthful exuberance. The chance to shape bright minds always fires my imagination."

"And every parent in town lives for your Thursday 'Reading Room'. It's saved more parent-child relationships than you know."

Meg eyed her over the rim of her mug. Lowering the cup to her desk, she said, "I know you're not here to discuss Alex."

Thea's breath left in a gust. "Well, you're right about that. Or mostly. Derek Salinger showed up on my doorstep last night."

Meg's hand covered her heart. "Heavens above! What does that nasty piece of work want now?"

Thea slouched into a folding chair. "I wish I knew. That's why I'm here. Sy's promised to follow up on any leads. I thought you might. . .but of course, if you knew anything, so would I. Derek said he would be at the town meeting next week."

"Did he now?"

Thea ran a hand through her hair. "He left a bottle of extremely expensive champagne and his business card." At Meg's look, she added, "I smashed the bottle to smithereens this morning."

"No doubt visualizing Derek's smug face the entire time."

"Some other part of his anatomy, if you must know."

Raucous laughter from the main library distracted them. Thea stood. "You'd better get in there before the horde destroys your library. I just wish I knew more about Derek's intent. He's planning something and knowing him, I'm sure I won't like it."

"I agree and I'll certainly check with Letty. If he asks to be placed on the agenda, I'll let you know."

"Thanks, Meg."

"And Althea? You keep your chin up, my dear. If you need anything, anything at all, call me."

After a fierce hug, her friend headed toward another explosion of mirth in the bowels of her library. Thea slipped out the back.

A few minutes later, she stepped into the sheriff's office. Dwaine lolled in his chair, slamming his feet onto the floor when the door opened. "Thea! What brings you here? Not your kid again—"

"Nope. Alex is at the library under Meg's eagle eye."

"Well, that's a comfort. So what can I do you for?"

"I heard three shots this morning from Eden Valley. I was hoping you or Sy might investigate."

"Aw, Thea, it's bird season."

"You don't shoot birds with an automatic, Dwaine."

"I know that. And you know those militant fellas're always

getting a few shots off on the sly."

Thus reminding her of the deputy's own abiding love of guns. She fixed him with her Stern Mom look and said, "Still, it's a congested area and kids are on spring break. Either the kids are shooting or they're in danger of being shot. Are you going to follow-up on this or should I?"

"Put it that way. Hell, woman, you'd face down Billy the Kid himself. 'Sides, wouldn't do to have kids messing around with their daddy's guns. I'll make the rounds once Sy gets back. He's on the mountain, checking out those college folks."

Thea smiled, softening toward the deputy, normally a generous man. "Thanks, Dwaine. I cooked up some of your venison burger last night for my spaghetti sauce. It made even my cooking palatable."

He grinned sheepishly. "Hope that means you're considering making another batch of lasagna."

"Could be. I'll make extra if I do," she said, lasagna being her one claim to fame in the kitchen arena.

She headed out the door, yearning for home, but edgy and watching for any sign of Salinger along the way. She saw neither him nor his car. By the time she got home, Thea settled into her painting routine.

Later, in the slanted light of late afternoon, she faced Jake Seeker over a cup of coffee in the cafe portion of Bodeen's bakery. Florid and plump as their yeast buns, the Bodeen team bustled around their pride and joy. The Mister stayed as far away as possible from the counter, while the Missus waited on customers. Just now, Una scurried over to their table with a large platter of raspberry scones and two smaller plates for individual servings.

Jake raised a bushy eyebrow, while Thea smiled and thanked the proprietress, who before dashing off to greet another customer said, "There's been a coyote coming too close to town again. Might have gotten one of Letty's cats last night." Then, off she went.

For a second, Thea flashed to Alex's wolf story, which she quickly discounted. Letty was always misplacing her cats. This one would probably show up after an extended prowl, thinner but no wiser for the escapade.

Thea noticed Jake's wistful scan of the sweet cakes. "You might as well dig in. It does no good to protest Una's generosity. She'll be offended if we don't eat every crumb. Besides, she hopes to use her part of the spa income to pay for her trip to Graceland next year."

"A worthy cause indeed," the older man said, then bit into a blue ribbon scone.

Thea slid a look out the window and down Main Street to the library. Meg should be closing for the day. Thea expected to see her friend at any moment. Once she got here, Thea would tell her that no one else had agreed to board this man. Having to put the grant team up had taken Thea's options away; her primary choices for housing space had been taken by the new people. Even neatly dressed in clean flannel shirt and jeans as he was, Jake's appearance probably hindered his cause.

Looking at this man again, she tried to see him as others did, without the strange affinity she had felt for him right from the start. She supposed that his craggy face, ravaged as it was by both time and scars, could repel. His hollowed body had been ground down by years of hard living. How his spirit remained in tact, Thea could only guess.

Unfortunately, his honesty about his past at last year's town meeting had not served him well either. Not many people wanted to let a shell-shocked and fragmented personality into their homes, even if he had gotten that way saving the lives of other Americans in battle. But Thea found true gentleness in the tarnished depths of his eyes; that and a likeness that should have frightened her, but did not. No one in her right mind wanted to see herself reflected in human wreckage. It was just too scary.

On that thought, Alex whirled into the cafe. Thea almost expected the glass to blow out of the windows with his approach. Daypack flapping over one shoulder, he ran to their table.

"Hiya, Mom. Mr. Seeker," he added, his gaze fixed on the pastry. Thea put one on her plate, then scooted it toward her son. He straddled the wire-backed chair and started in with a muffled, "Thanks."

Meg entered the cafe more sedately, probably pulled along in the wake of Alex's tsunami. The petite brunette turned wide eyes toward them from the door and smiled. Even after a day of having Alex close at hand, Meg's grooming remained impeccable. Of course, there was no telling the damage done to the library. As Meg reached the table, Jake rose.

"Jake, you remember our treasurer, Megan Connor?"

"Of course, Mrs. Connor, the librarian. I remember your eyes—the golden brown of fine cognac." When Meg reached out to shake his proffered hand, Jake's enveloped hers.

Meg actually blushed when her hand stayed folded in the bigger man's; a small bird held delicately in his large mitt. Speechless, Thea leaned back in her chair. *Holy fuchsia!* Then, another commotion at the door snagged her attention.

"Hey, Mom, look! It's Dr. Hayes!" Before she could stop him, her son leapt up, grabbed his pack, and went to greet the man who had specifically requested minimum contact.

Thea pushed back her chair and got up mumbling, "I'll be right back."

By the time she reached her son, the four adults at the display counter surrounded him. "Excuse me," she said to a towering male back. When the back failed to move, she tapped a shoulder. "Uh, excuse me?"

The man, a blonde and bearded colossus, turned and met

her regard with curious blue eyes. Others in the group turned as one to look at her, then. Thea glanced at everyone but her tenant, who stood directly across from her. A petite woman at eye level with Alex continued with their private chat. He pulled a sheet of paper from his pack, which the two studied.

"Alex, come back to our table." If it had been a few years ago, she could have held out her hand for his formerly pudgy grip. Now she just lifted her eyebrows and hoped his training held.

"Aw, Mom. . ."

Oh, well.

"March, mister." He moved then, even though his slouching walk resembled more amble than stride. She watched him go back to the table before turning to the group. "Sorry about the interruption."

The dark haired woman Alex had been talking with smiled. "Can't stop the wind from blowing. Challie Hummingbird." She held out a square hand.

Thea accepted the invitation. "Thea MacTavish. Welcome to Potshot." All the while, she roasted beneath her houseguest's glower. Well, that was his problem.

"So your son tells me you're putting up my cousin? Or should I say putting up *with* Youngwolf?" Challie turned toward Dr. Hayes with an eyebrow raised.

Thea laughed at that, since it so closely reflected her thoughts. She met *Youngwolf's* gloomy look. Surprisingly, she saw chagrin on his face. "Yes. Dr. Hayes is my very own accidental lodger," she said.

"*Dr. Hayes*, is it? So Bram's being stuffy again, is he?" boomed the blonde giant. He stuck out a hand the size of a ham. "J. D., here. I'm the forester in this motley crew."

A shorter, more compact man with huge shoulders stepped forward, "Ian Collins, ma'am. Smoke-eater."

Challie laughed. "That translates into 'fireman'. And I'm

62

Youngwolf's token civil."

"Civil?" Thea asked.

"Civil engineer," Hayes filled in. "Or as I think of her, the woman who has trouble keeping a civil tongue in her head."

The group hooted and hissed at that, although Thea saw it was all in fun.

"Well," she said, "I really didn't mean to interrupt. I just wanted to save you from my offspring. Good-bye, *Dr.* Hayes." She flashed her nemesis a wicked grin then left amid more good-natured ribbing.

As she got back to her table, she found Alex concentrating on the last scone and refusing to meet her gaze. Meg and Jake stood. "Hey, you're not leaving yet, are you? I thought we needed to work out the conditions of the agreement."

Meg gave her a blinding smile and patted her hand. "Never mind, dear. Jake and I have worked out most of the details already. We've already begun receiving donated lumber. The rest of the particulars will take care of themselves."

"But. . ." Thea started.

Jake nodded toward her. "We'll take our leave of you, then, Thea. I'll be at the hot springs bright and early tomorrow morning. Alex offered to help me—hope you don't mind." He ruffled her son's head. To her surprise, Alex accepted from Jake what he rejected from her.

"See you at eight, Mr. Seeker," said her son.

When Meg placed her fingers over Jake's forearm as they left, Thea gave into her impulse and collapsed onto her chair. Alex regarded her solemnly, then said, "I think they've got the hots for each other," before returning his full attention to the last bites of cake.

Thea watched Meg and Jake walk across the street, looking more like a loving couple than two people who had met for the second time today. Late afternoon sun slanted down Main Street and picked up the red highlights in Meg's hair and the blue tint of Jake's. As they passed from view, Thea forced herself to relax, enjoying vivid details of her town until a loud stage whisper from behind warned her of what was coming.

"Loosen up, Youngwolf," came Challie's voice. "Now go over there and make nice with your pretty landlady. We'll meet you at the hotel afterward."

Blood rushed to Thea's face. "Alex? Why don't you run down to the grocery store and pick up some tortillas for dinner tonight."

"Great! Tacos." He held out his hand for money.

Thea gave him a five, then said, "Fifty cents for you." He blew out of the bakery, barely avoiding the grant crew at the door. She watched him run as far as the corner before the expected interruption came.

"Uh, excuse me, Thea?" She looked up into PhD Hayes' eyes. It was like sinking into a drowning pool. "Mind if I sit?"

"Yes, I do. But go ahead anyway."

He sank with a wide-legged manly stance onto the ice cream parlor-style chair, dwarfing it. Thea wondered if his entire wardrobe consisted of faded chambray shirts and form fitting jeans. Of course, if she looked as good in this style as he did, she would probably wear them everywhere, too.

He cleared his voice, folded his hands onto the table. Even his hands were beautiful. "Sorry about my crew. Once they get the bit between their teeth, there's no stopping them."

She shrugged. "I appreciate honest interest from visitors. It's what separates the tourist from the explorer."

"Yes, well. That's why I'm here; as an explorer I suppose." He pushed a hand through wavy hair, which made Thea aware of how long it was in the back, nearly as long as her slice-top crop had been before the fire. It suited him as well as his clothes.

She sat up and leaned toward him, tired of his games. "Look, Dr. Hayes, I've got dinner to fix, clothes to wash, and bills to pay. Can you please get to the point?"

He winced at the 'Dr. Hayes'. "Challie told me to loosen up. So we could start with you calling me Bram."

"That's what all this is about? Well, that's just cozy. You can call me 'Thea' and I'll call you 'Bram'. As long as we follow your rules and stay out of each other's way. Is that right?" She stood.

His long look made her ashamed of her flash of anger. He said, "Actually, I also wanted to ask about that wolf your son wanted Challie to identify."

The starch slipped right out of her. She folded onto her chair. "What wolf?"

He shrugged. "He had a picture of one, probably a copy made at the library. But since it was black-and-white and poor quality, it was hard to identify." He sat back, a perplexed look on his face.

"The strange thing is, we did see sign of something on the ridge today. It was too big to be a coyote. Could have been a big stray dog, but. . ."

The door whipped open hard enough to bounce against the doorstop. Thirteen-year-old Sherman Peabody ran into the shop, sliding to a stop at the counter. "Mister! Missus! You gotta see. A fire's started in the foothills."

A brief second later, the fire alarms at the station started screaming. Sherman pivoted and noticed his best friend's mother. "Miz Mac. Where's Alex?" Sweaty faced and rosy cheeked, the boy looked around as though Alex would reappear at any moment.

"At the grocery store. But Sherman, where exactly is the fire?"

"Can't tell. Saw smoke from up at the hot springs. It looked like it was between your house and the valley. Down in the gully where the creek runs." He took one look at her stricken face and said, "I'll go find Alex."

Thea froze until bulky Mister Bodeen trotted from behind his counter, evidently heading toward the fire station. Bram's voice broke through her study. "My crew will help. We're all experienced fire fighters. Who mans your fire department?" She just looked at him. "Thea? I asked who staffs your fire department?"

"It's all volunteer," she said. As if to make herself understand, she turned toward the big plate glass window. Pick-up trucks and cars sped toward the station at one end of the street. Hulon Peabody dashed out of his place, tossing an outdoor coat over his dress shirt and bow tie as he ran. Sy with Deputy Dwaine roared by in their squad car.

"I need to get back home. Start putting water on the roof." Galvanized, she headed for the door. Bram caught her arm.

"Wait, I'll take you in my truck." When she stared blankly at him, he said, "No use involving both vehicles. And I've got fire fighting gear in the back."

She nodded.

"All right, but we have to wait for Alex."

They headed out the door and toward the side parking area. Already, Thea smelled the stinging odor of smoke. The light haze grew heavier toward the valley. It definitely had started to thicken in the direction of her house. The fire truck's shrill siren announced it moments before the engine zoomed past. Luckily, Alex and Sherman already waited by her dilapidated Honda. Bram's crew started gathering around his truck.

He went to them. "I'm taking Thea and her son back to the house. You report to the fire station. If things look disorganized, Ian, you take charge." A nod came from the career fire fighter. "Now go. And, Challie, I want you to check back with me by cell phone on the hour. If things don't look too dicey at Thea's, I'll join you."

"Sure, cuz."

Bram motioned to Thea and the boys. "Let's go."

66

Chapter Five

In the dawn light, a solitary Bram walked the smoldering ruin of sagebrush steppe, kicking at charred tufts as he went. Sun colored the burn haze an orange uncomfortably reminiscent of flames. Still, being alone suited him. He preferred walking off the fire's effect before facing others. Residual adrenalin combined with his history of loss, making fire's aftermath difficult. Bram occupied his mind by heading toward the center of the night's maelstrom, where he looked for clues of what had started the blaze.

Looking for hot spots, Challie passed him on her own circuit. "Your fire demon riding you, cuz?"

"The usual."

"She's one jealous mistress, Youngwolf." Challie claimed his obsession with the element kept him from a normal life—whatever *normal* meant. However, he never gave in to the compulsion gracefully and never by choice.

Residual smoke and fog swallowed her up, leaving Bram momentarily panicked over her loss. Fire always took those he loved. "Challie? Hummingbird?"

"Here, Youngwolf," came her disembodied voice.

Rational thought and a hefty dose of shame took over. "Never mind. A false lead."

As his boot connected with another clump, the clink of metal-on-metal caught his attention. He bent to investigate. His gut told him he had found the fire's center—and that an arsonist had set it. Bram sifted carefully through debris until he found casings of two—no three—high-powered rifle bullets. Except for these, he intended to leave the area intact, hoping Ian would be able to detect the arson's methodology. Scrutinizing a wider circle around the area Bram saw another incongruous mass about fifteen yards away, near the edges of the miasma. Pocketing the casings, he strode toward the smoldering pile, stopping when he recognized the carcass of a coyote. The nauseating smell of charred meat and bone roiled his belly.

Bram judged the distance to clear the fire zone and decided any coyote worth its salt would have outrun this slow-moving fire, fed by lush spring growth. A few acres to the east and the critter could have hopped the creek. On a southern heading, it could have escaped to the valley below. Either route would have saved its life. The spent shells clinked in his pocket as he fleshed out a scenario.

A rifle propelled bullets too fast to spend much time in soft tissues or do much damage at this range—unless a slug hit a vital organ or shattered bone. No way could this critter have been considered a threat to the arsonist. It was not in a coyote's nature to attack when it could sidle away. Neither was the animal slaughtered for a bounty. No. This shooter killed out of pure meanness.

"Ian?" he called, surprised anew at the hoarseness of his voice. He coughed. Smoke played hell with lungs.

Bram watched the fire inspector and closet-inventor trot from behind the water tender and head toward him. Ian's face showed the same sooty smudges Bram expected to find on his.

At the other man's questioning gaze, Bram asked, "You brought a couple of sniffers this trip, didn't you?"

Ian gave him an embarrassed grin. "I like to tinker with them. Brought my fire modeling program on the laptop, too."

"I want you to see something."

Ian's regard sharpened as Bram walked him to the probable

site of ignition. Ian crouched over the incongruous pile of ash and debris, too ordered for this natural setting. Looking up at Bram, he grunted. "Looks like another arson."

"Yep. Get your stuff and let's see what you pick up. I think I'm going to call it a night and grab a little shut-eye. How 'bout you let the rest of the crew know we're meeting at two o'clock at the hot springs." He yawned and stretched until his joints popped.

"Sure enough, boss."

At Ian's keen look, Bram said, "And get some sleep. You'll be no good to me dead on your feet."

"Sure, sure."

"When shoats fly," muttered Bram as he headed toward his rig. Along the way, he nodded to the man whose water tender had been first on the scene. "Good job."

From the cab of his truck, the man wiped his sooty face with an equally filthy rag. "Any time, *Chief,*" he drawled, his eyes hard and lip curled.

Bram halted and met the guy stare-for-stare until the racist's gaze wavered. Bram waited as the man started his rig and pulled away. It proved a hollow victory as he heaved himself into his truck. At Thea's place, fatigue caused Bram to eye his backseat and considered the efficacy of sleeping in his truck. Deciding against it, he paused wearily to stretch muscles no longer used to the shovel-and-bucket mode of fire fighting. Now at nearly seven in the morning, he guessed the sun had been up for a little over an hour. He was getting too old for this shit.

In the glow of eastern sunlight, Thea's house looked more homey than rundown. Residual smoke imbued the early morning light with an apricot glow. The tired white paint on the main body of the house looked like peaches and cream. The faded green of the steps, porch, and front door drew his tired gaze in a restful sort of way. He had nearly woven his way to those welcoming steps when he remembered the three wilted plants salvaged from the fire zone. As he trudged back to his rig, the front door of the house burst open. Thea's boy and his friend exploded into the morning. Their excited voices and the slam of the door behind them brought him back around.

"Hey, Doc," came Alex's exuberant greeting. "Sherm and me, we watched you guys fight the fire through Mom's binoculars."

Bram moved toward his truck as the boys caught up with him, gamboling like pups. "Didn't know you could see it from here."

"Oh, we climbed the birch out back," piped Sherman.

"Sherm! You promised! If Mom finds out, she'll ground me for life."

Both boys looked up at Bram. He held up his hand, boy-scout style. "Your secret's safe with me, *hombres*."

"Jeez, you should see your eyes, Doc. Red as chili peppers," said Alex. "Whew! You stink, too."

"His eyes look more like my mom's strawberry jam," said the bigger boy. "Come on, Alex, let's go to the bakery. Bet Missus will give us free doughnuts if we tell her about the fire. Then we can go over to our club. Dad'll get the cook to fix us some eggs and sausage. We can eat with the rest of the fire fighters."

"Think we can grab some eats to take to the hot springs?" asked Alex.

"Sure," shrugged his friend, eyes focused down the road.

Alex turned unclouded eyes up to Bram. "I'm helping Jake. We're going to build this way-cool health spa, then the whole town will get rich. I'm getting a mountain bike with my share."

"That's great," Bram mumbled. Everything started going fuzzy around the edges.

70

"You should come with us, Dr. Hayes. Mom always has the cook set-up a great buffet after fires. Just like last time."

"Thanks, but not this time. I just want to hit the sack."

"Okay, but you don't know what you're missing. Come on, Alex. All the good stuff will be gone." The bulky boy started walking.

Still Alex hesitated for a minute, evidently waging war with his stomach. His stomach won. "Well, see ya, Doc."

He trotted after his friend a few steps before turning around and jogging backwards. "Watch out for Mom. The ladies in town were here. She stayed up all night. Now she's really acting weird." He pivoted and sprinted after Sherman, catching him in seconds.

Bram shook his head at their energy. "Oh, to be thirteen again and immortal."

His tired mind drifted, reminding him that both his mother and twin had been alive when he was Alex's age. At fourteen, he had learned just how mortal they all were. He dropped his forehead against the cool metal of his truck and tried to push the barrage of memories away.

The door opened again and Thea's voice, flowing like fresh water, dissolved his connection with the past. "Bram? You all right?"

She didn't wait for his reply, but rushed down the stairs and into the tangerine light. Tired as he was, he leaned against the truck and watched her advance, barefoot in baggy and rolled up jeans, carelessly anchored at her hips with a red cord. Her bright green top, a stretchy little thing that left a patch of smooth midriff showing, charted the sweet topography of her breasts and the geodesic curve of her ribs into her waist. The sight of this gypsy goddess made him suddenly lightheaded. Too little food and sleep, he decided as he bent his head toward his knees, bracing his arms there.

"Oh, fuchsia! You're having another attack, aren't you?"

An arm slipped around his shoulders. Cool fingers touched his forehead. "It's a good thing this condition doesn't hit until *after* the fire's out."

He groaned, then with a mighty effort, he straightened. "It's not a 'condition'. I'm just tired. And hungry."

"I can do something about the hunger. How much did the fire burn?"

"About fifty acres of rabbit brush and snakeweed. Luckily, it started in a relatively open area at the edge of the valley. Place's still wet from snowmelt. Moving up the slope as it did, we couldn't have contained it if it'd reached the scrub pines. The northern and eastern edges came up against the creek."

"What a relief." Eyes that brought to mind a mossy bed in the forest met his gaze. "Your eyes. . .you look terrible." Her nostrils quivered as her eyes widened. "Why don't you hop into the shower while I fix some breakfast. Come on." She still hadn't removed her arm from his shoulders.

"I've got something in the truck."

"It can wait," and she urged him toward the house.

"No, it really can't," he said.

She released her loose hold. "Oh, fuchsia!"

He smiled at that, but opened his door anyway and took the wrapped bundle out along with his empty thermos. He held the burlap-covered package toward her. She took it, albeit reluctantly. With a ginger touch here and there, she flipped one corner back to reveal a tangle of wilted stems and roots. She looked up at him with eyebrows raised.

"I noticed your herb garden and all the wildflowers. You seem to have a green thumb. Thought maybe you could save these. If I'm not mistaken, those are *Centaurium namophilum*." He started again toward the house and she fell into step with him.

"Well, that certainly clears things up," came her wry reply.

"That's scientific jargon for 'spring-loving centaury'.

They're a threatened species. Until now, they've only been seen in Nye County along the Amargosa River." He opened the door, stepping aside for her to enter first.

"No kidding? How do you know so much about Nye County, Nevada? I thought you lived in Oklahoma." She turned to face him, then closed the door by the simple expediency of leaning into it. Head tilted and back supported by the door, Thea looked more approachable than Bram had even seen her.

"I did my dissertation on endangered species in Nye County," he managed before becoming distracted by her actions.

As she gently stroked the stems of the plants, Bram noticed how her lashes laid curving shadows across her cheeks. She had a pretty mouth, too, as full on the bottom as it was on top. The shade reminded him of cherries off Grandfather's tree; ruby-colored fruit with sweet dark flesh. She lifted her gaze to meet his study.

"Fuchsia, here I am going on about some wilted plant and you're dead on your feet. Get that shower. I'll be in the kitchen."

"Right." He could definitely use a cleaning, although a car wash might be more expedient. Maybe it wouldn't hurt to follow with a cool rinse. He needed to snap himself out of this sudden preoccupation with his landlady. Bram trudged down the hall, while she bounded toward the kitchen.

So this was Thea being 'weird'. . .kids!

After he soaped himself and rinsed three times, the water started getting cool. *Just what the doctor ordered.* A fluffy towel in yet another jewel bright color made drying his body a pleasure. Then he realized his mistake: no robe and no clean clothes. The way he had been reacting to his landlady, he'd be damned if he would go traipsing around in this too small towel.

73

He cracked the door open. "Uh, Thea? I didn't grab anything to put on. Could you. . ."

She came into view, a spatula in hand. The smell of bacon made his stomach rumble. "My robe's hanging on the back of the door. It'll do in a pinch." A billow of smoke wafted from the kitchen. "Oops! Better get back in there. Don't want another stove fire." She disappeared.

He looked behind the door, where a bright purple robe hung. He groaned. It would probably cover Thea from neck-to-ankle, but for him, much less. At least it was one of those unisex designs in heavy terry cloth instead of some frilly girl thing. He gingerly prodded his pile of soot stained clothes. No way. As he slipped into her robe, the scent of honeysuckle drifted to him. He tugged the sash tight around his ribs, far above his waist. While the robe overlapped pretty well from there down, it gaped open over his chest. It didn't matter so much that his forearms and calves weren't covered; it would clothe him enough to get downstairs. He started down the hall before Thea's voice stopped him.

"Well, that's not so bad. Come on in. Breakfast's on the table."

He turned. "I thought I'd throw some clothes on first."

"Nonsense. Your breakfast will get cold. Besides, amethyst suits you." A brigand's smile accompanied her assessment. She headed in to the kitchen.

"Well, in that case," he took another hitch on the tie belt and followed.

Sunlight flooded the dining nook. He seated himself, back to the window, in hopes of giving his aching eyes a rest. That gave him a full view of Thea, which proved neither cool water nor exhaustion neutralized his bizarre reaction to her. Damned if her vagabond style wasn't starting to look good to him. Too good. That little peek of midriff began preying on his weary mind. As she brought two steaming mugs of coffee over to the

74

table, his gaze kept returning to tantalizing glimpses of warm olive flesh. When she plopped his coffee down in front of him, he jerked with a guilty start.

"Don't worry, it's only decaf. As punchy as you are, I wouldn't think of caffeinated anything." She settled across from him and her gaze dropped to his untouched food.

"You're being very civil, Thea. I take it that means I'm no longer *persona non grata*." He tucked into his scrambled eggs with gusto.

She shrugged. "Actually, around these parts, I'm considered a standard of civility. You've been one of my few exceptions. For now, I'll only admit to gratitude toward a man who went hand-to-hand with last night's fire. Or maybe I'm too lazy to carry a grudge."

"Lazy isn't a word I'd use." He sipped his coffee, obviously instant. "Have anything stronger to put in this?" He asked more to gain some distance from his response than out of any real desire for it.

She froze mid-sip. Her expressive face became a study. "I, ah, I don't keep any alcohol in the house." He watched with great interest as the blood left her face, then rushed back. Her eyes looked haunted.

"It's all right. I guess if I had a kid as precocious as yours, I'd think twice about that myself." He studiously forked up another bite of breakfast.

Other women in his life would have rushed in now with inconsequential tidbits about their day, or night in this case. Not Thea. He appreciated her quiet. Funny how it made him feel like a welcome part of this household instead of an intruder.

"Why *do* you react to fire the way you do?"

She caught him off guard. That's probably why he responded so honestly. He put down his fork and met her bottomless gaze. "I'm hardwired, I guess. Fire's stolen a lot

75

from me. When I battle fire, I'm dealing with my revulsion of it. Once I've won, memory takes over."

She nodded and, somehow, Bram knew she understood. Maybe it was the carefully prepared bacon and eggs that did it, maybe it was his bone deep fatigue, maybe it was the compassion shining in her eyes. Whatever it was, he continued, "I lost my mother and twin brother to fire when I was fourteen. A colleague died of smoke inhalation three years ago. I *have* to fight fires."

"Or be consumed," she said. The pulse in her neck jumped; the fine bones in her hands, as they curved around her cup, shone white. "Or be consumed," she repeated in a whisper.

Bram reached out then. If he had thought about it, he never would have done so. His much larger hands enclosed hers, then cradled them. "I didn't mean to stir up ghosts."

"Not your fault; everybody has them."

Bram's throat closed around words he wanted to ask. No reason to dig into this woman's life out of plain curiosity, he told himself. Some things went beyond casual interest. He suspected whatever brought such desolation to her eyes fell into that category. Besides, he didn't cotton to revisiting the conditions of his stay. Instead, he said, "I saw Alex and his buddy heading for town. Your boy mentioned working on the spa. He was pretty near jumping out of his skin at the idea."

A smile softened her face. She raised her cup to her mouth, effectively breaking away from Bram's hold. He stifled the sense of loss and brought his hands back to where they belonged—on his side of the table. After a sip of brew, she said, "The spa's Potshot's claim to fame. That and the mud baths. We started building last year. The fire, the one you fought your first night, destroyed all our framing."

Now she leaned forward and excitement lit her face. The change made him catch his breath. "But I found some merchants in Reno and Carson City to donate the wood we lost. I'll make it up to them when the insurance company pays us. Thank goodness the rest of the raw lumber hadn't been delivered or we'd be sunk."

"So this is a community effort?"

"Absolutely. An investment in our future with all participants sharing in stock options. Luckily the fire didn't affect everything we've done. We excavated and poured cement for three hot pools along with a cooler one for swimming, too, and laid out infrastructure. Now Jake's framing the changing rooms and spa from my design."

"You drew the building plans?" *Althea MacTavish was full of surprises.*

"Don't look so astonished, Bram. The county blessed them, for a hefty fee of course. I was really pleased with the results before the fire wiped everything out. We're trying hard to keep buildings very natural looking and low-key. Funny to think some of my architecture classes came in handy after all."

He sat back against the window seat. "I thought you were a self-taught artist who did graphics design. I didn't realize-"

"That I had a degree? Yep, a Masters in Fine Arts. Not even worth a cup of coffee at Harrah's Club, although Hulon will usually spot me a pot of tea."

He flushed. "Sorry for sounding so high-and-mighty."

"Well, condescending maybe, but your apology's accepted."

Had he just apologized to the prickly Thea MacTavish? *Maybe shoats can fly.* "Guess I've been real lucky. I worked in my chosen field since before I got my degrees."

Interest sparkled in her eyes. "Really? As an intern fire guy?"

It was his turn to grin and flex his fingers as memory overtook him. "Try a pick-and-shovel hired hand for the BLM."

77

Thea smiled, "Sounds like a waste of a good mind to me. For myself, I worked full time in Reno as a graphics designer at Visual Perceptions until four months ago. I sold two paintings, then. Jarvis, who owns a gallery in San Francisco, made noises about a one-woman show this fall or winter. Since I'd been putting money into my painter's relief fund for the last decade, I decided to dip into it."

"You have a relief fund for painters? Sounds like house painters down on their luck should be thanking their lucky stars."

A sheepish expression covered her face. "Not really. It's a separate account from Alex's college fund and I'm the painter who needed relief. So I took a sabbatical to try painting full time. Jarvis'll be in the area this June to look at the work I've finished. That'll decide him on whether I'm ready or not." Her voice shook. Like a pot low on water, she ran out of steam.

Bram recognized a make-or-break situation when he heard one. "Think you'll be ready?"

"I don't know. With having to start construction all over again…and now Derek's here for God knows what. Plus Alex keeps getting into one scrape after another. . ." She straightened her shoulders on the last. "Guess I'll just do what has to be done. At least with the town meeting tonight, Salinger will lay his cards on the table. Some of his cards anyway. It isn't in his nature to be too forthright."

"He definitely has a hidden agenda."

"Probably an entire deck up his Pierre Cardin sleeves." She fixed him with her limpid gaze before getting flustered. "Look at us, sitting here talking when what you really need is some sleep. Can I get you anything else?"

"No. Thanks for breakfast, though. You're a better cook than your son implies."

She laughed, exposing a long length of smooth neck. Bram shivered at the sight and the ache in his belly returned. "That's

78

because I won't let him live on hot dogs with occasional forays into mac and cheese." When he stood and lifted his empty plate, she waved him off. "I'll take care of that. You get to bed. And take that carafe of water with you. You're probably parched from last night."

He took the water, a glass, and Thea's robe downstairs, then shut the vertical blinds over both sliding door and windows. He nearly fell into bed, pausing only for a moment to loosen her robe and let it drop onto the bed.

Which explained his erotic dreams. He awoke to the scent of Thea. In his sleep, he had somehow dragged her robe up to his face, where he burrowed into it.

At just shy of seven that evening, Bram and his band of merry firefighters walked from the hotel to the steepled church. Challie insisted. She figured the townspeople would be more amenable to any changes the grant project recommended if they got to know the team members better. A town meeting offered just such an opportunity. In areas of social correctness, Bram nearly always listened to his cousin. If his ulterior reason centered on learning what Thea's nemesis, Derek Salinger, planned, he did not enlighten the Hummingbird, who like her namesake, had a tendency to insert her beak in the sticky stuff.

As they neared the front of the church, J. D. laughed out loud, then pointed, "You've got to love these small towns. Read that announcement board, will ya."

Beneath the usual call to service and the times for the town meeting, an inspirational line had been written. It read:

REMEMBER IN PRAYER THE MANY
WHO ARE SICK OF OUR CHURCH AND COMMUNITY

They were still chuckling as they entered, following the posted signs to the basement. Meg Connor, the librarian and council treasurer, shepherded them toward the front of the room where they settled into folding chairs.

From what Bram could tell, it looked like a good turnout. Participants filled most seating space while discussion groups milled around in the aisles. Two groups of kids, roughly divided into boys and girls, horsed around in the back, as far as possible from the scrutiny of their parents. Bram saw Alex's bright face at the center of the boys. Bram perused the crowd, not admitting whom he hoped to see until his gaze fell on Thea. She sat in the front row next to a craggy older man who Bram remembered from the bakery. His landlady looked different tonight. It took a few minutes for him to figure out why.

Dressed in a long, silky looking tunic and snug leggings the color of good Burgundy, Thea seemed both taller and more elegant. A chain with an artsy pendant hung around her neck, nestled between her breasts. One toe of her brocade heels tapped nervously. Her face looked more vivid, too, and even more exotic with her high cheekbones and almond-shaped eyes.

Bram suspected her frequent glances toward the back of the room were not entirely due to her offspring. When a commotion at the door cleared and Derek Salinger entered with his entourage, he knew. A number of volunteer fire fighters, veterans of last night's fray, started queuing near Bram's group, talking about the fire. Bram lost sight of both Thea and her adversary.

A vibrant older woman, who introduced herself as Mayor Letty Donaldson, called the meeting to order. After the usual preliminaries, she invited Bram to introduce his team amid copious thanks for their help with both the spa and brush fire.

Then, she asked, "Sy, do you have any idea what caused

these fires?"

The sheriff stood, hat in hand. "Well, Letty, I'm no authority. But we have a profusion of what I'd call experts here. What do you think, Bram?" Sy's shrewd gaze settled on him.

He had been afraid of this. So much for a quiet investigation conducted by Ian and Challie. He stood. "Unfortunately, on this last fire, we found evidence that points to arson."

The uproar his words started had the mayor banging her gavel and shouting, "Order!"

When the commotion subsided, the mayor fixed her regard on him. "And what makes you think this was arson?"

He shrugged and looked at Ian. "We found a smoldering pile of rags at the point of origin. Our electronic gear picked up a carbon-based accelerant. We'll know more when we get the lab results."

Again a din erupted and again the mayor brought the meeting to order. She fixed Bram in her sights. "And when, pray tell, were you planning on letting us know of this?"

He cleared his throat. "I'd intended to tell the sheriff this morning, but he left before I could. Then I slept the day away. However, I did have Ian, who's our career fire fighter and inspector, do the usual work-up. He deals with arson on a regular basis. Ian was going to report to the sheriff after the meeting."

He met her gaze calmly. "We don't want to start a panic. It often works in favor of the investigation to keep some of the facts from the public. Any further details can be given to you by either us or your sheriff."

Her eyes hooded much like a falcon's, belying her congenial image. "Good thinking, young man. Sy, I'm sure you'll report the findings to me. In private."

With the sheriff's promise to do just that, she said, "Now,

we have an update from Thea MacTavish about our spa. Thea, why don't you come up here so every one can see and hear you."

A smattering of applause carried Thea to the platform. She pulled a large poster board from behind the podium and propped it up on a paint-splattered easel, then turned to face the room. "As you all know, I'm heading the committee for Potshot's hot springs improvement."

A much louder ovation followed and a gruff male voice called, "Get that capital flowing, girl!"

She laughed and as she had earlier in the day, transfixed Bram with the smooth expanse of exposed neck. "What's wrong, Bud? Isn't Letty's pay as mayor rich enough for your blood?"

That brought a roar of laughter from the crowd. Apparently, being mayor of Potshot included little financial benefit. Only an edgy glance toward the door betrayed her concern over what Salinger had in store. Bram admired her audacity.

"Anyway, I wanted you all to know that we have a contractor, Mr. Jake Seeker, working on construction now. He expects to have the entire complex finished by the first of June; well ahead of our June 14th opening. The framing lumber we lost to the fire has been replaced through donations. As you know, the fire's still under investigation, which means we won't be paid for our losses until the inspector has ruled out arson by owners."

"That'll take some doing, girl. Doesn't everyone in Potshot and most in Eden Valley have a stake in the spa?"

"I know. That's why it's so important that you cooperate with the insurance inspector. Then we can use the settlement money to hire some help for Mr. Seeker."

She turned to Seeker and said, "Jake, will you stand up so everyone who hasn't met you can see who you are?"

First Bram admired her generous welcome of the man, then he appreciated the way her tunic moved against her body. Shoats and razorbacks, he enjoyed watching her way too much. Beside him, Challie nudged him and whispered, "So she's just a landlady, huh, Youngwolf? You're practically licking your lips."

He spared a scowl for her before intoning, "She's not my type."

Their exchange made them miss some of what Thea said, because then the lights went out and columns of figures were projected onto the white wall behind her.

"As you can see from Meg's forecasts, we'll be looking at a healthy payback on our investment in just one year. Letty and I already have all of our advertising in place. The second wave will be in newspapers between Reno and Sacramento next week. A couple of magazine ads hit the stands this month.

"Lights, please."

She returned to the center of the stage. "Now, Jessica Moran, who's handling hotel reservations, will update us on how we're doing."

Instead of going back to her place by the old guy, Thea settled onto the seat in front of Bram, now vacated by a young woman with a baby. Before the mother headed for the platform, she handed her child to Thea. Bram sat in a prime location to see the transformation that came over Thea's face as she took the baby into her arms. Joy, adoration, and a vulnerable sweetness lit her face with a mellow glow. For some reason, that expression started his gut clenching as though he'd been side-kicked by a mule. He wondered anew how much smoke he had inhaled during last night's exertions and its effect on his brain.

Once she sat, he watched as she bowed her head over the baby. The cropped ends of her hair met at her nape leaving the skin below it open to his scrutiny. His lips tingled in response. He heard nothing of what the woman at the podium said, until she finished speaking. Then a commotion started at the back of the room and rippled forward.

An agonized male voice cried out, "Jessie, when're you gonna come back home?"

The room went silent and necks craned to look at the man standing at the end of a row. Bram recognized him as the driver and owner of the water tender at last night's blaze. Evidently, the bigot suffered from relationship problems. *Big surprise.*

Sy, already standing near the immediate wall, started toward the man. "Now, Zechariah, this isn't the place to be airing your private affairs. 'Sides, your divorce was finalized four months ago."

The man ignored the sheriff's words. He moved toward the front of the room where Sy intercepted him. From the list to his walk and the glazed look on his face, Bram guessed the man had been drinking.

The lawman held his hands before him in a placating manner. "You know you're not allowed within hollering distance of Jessie. She has a restraining order out on you. I'll enforce it if I have to."

"Jessie!" the man howled in an inhuman way. He rammed the sheriff. "You son-of-a-bitch. You're not keeping me from my wife." The man took a swing at the larger man.

The sheriff moved with a speed that did credit to such a big man. In a flash he blocked the other man's roundhouse and gripped him from behind. The deputy moved to stand between them and the forming throng. Bram really looked at the crowd.

The sheriff rattled off some names that meant nothing to Bram. A number of hard-bitten men moved out of the pack and put hands on their comrade. Bram had not seen a more

84

implacable, closed-looking group of people since the lynch mob went after his uncle on the reservation three decades earlier. He looked around to find Thea on her feet. She held the baby protectively close in one arm with the other around Jessica's shoulder.

Her gaze flicked toward him when he asked, "Who are they?"

She leaned forward and licked her lips. "Paramilitary survivalists. From the valley."

By the time he had swung back to them, the majority of valley dwellers had moved toward the exit, forcing their confederate with them. Once the group passed out of the room, a collective sigh rose from the remaining citizens. A buzz started and continued to build in volume until Letty smacked her gavel against the podium.

Thea settled in front of Bram again with the young mother taking a seat beside her.

"Sorry about that, folks. Thank you, Thea and Jessie, for your update."

"The last bit of business tonight is a presentation by Mr. Salinger of Salinger Enterprises. He came to me too late to put his presentation on the written agenda. Seems he didn't want unwarranted speculation to cloud his appearance. Mr. Salinger?

The hackles on Bram's neck rose as the sophisticated man strolled to the front of the room. Salinger's mocking glance at Thea barely concealed his all-too-male interest. Bram sat taller, unaware that he had clenched his fists until Challie's cooler hand covered his.

"Down, boy," she teased, but when he met her gaze, he saw concern there, too.

At that moment, a well-groomed assistant rolled a rumbling cart toward the front. The cloth draped over the top sported Salinger's silver emblem and gave a flavor of grandeur to the proceedings. Once the pushcart stopped, the assistant activated some kind of hydraulic lift that canted the top while leaving the front flush. With a flourish, Salinger yanked the cover off to reveal a lighted model of Salinger Enterprises' concept of the new and improved Potshot and its posh hot springs.

"Now I'd like to present what I hope will be Salinger Enterprises' newest gem in their crown of luxury spas. Ladies and gentlemen, may I present RICOCHET SPRINGS AND SPA!"

Thea sprang to her feet. "No!"

Around them, voices raised in confusion. Someone called, "Now, listen here Mister, you can't just waltz in and take over. We're shareholders." Supporters of that stance uttered their agreement. The robust wail of Jessica Moran's baby added to the hubbub.

Mayor Letty's attempt at order failed and the tumult overwhelmed Thea's pleas, too. Pressing forward to get a better look, another contingent breached the line around Salinger. Over the bobbing heads, Bram caught the panicked look on Thea's face before she was swept into a voracious eddy of humanity.

Chapter Six

The day after Salinger's slick bid for control of Potshot's future, what seemed an endless torrent of cut flowers began arriving at Thea's home. By two weeks, the rumbling drone of florist vans triggered a startling response in her: rage. This morning's driver was new, so when he presented her with another extravagant bouquet, she tried again. "What if I don't want to take delivery of these flowers?"

The poor guy gawked, then stammered, "But they're paid for."

"Still, what if I refuse to accept them?" Her bare foot began tapping a wild tattoo.

He scratched his balding head beneath the stiff cap. "Well, I'm contracted to make the delivery, ma'am. These're really expensive flowers." As though that made all the difference.

"Fine. Leave them, then. I hope you realize you're participating in the foulest kind of bribery."

Thea's signature gouged the register. As the delivery guy made a mad dash to his van, she clenched her jaws in an effort not to toss the arrangement after him. The image pleased her, though.

No doubt, this was not exactly the reaction Derek Salinger anticipated, which meant he still underestimated his opponent. Anyone else would probably gasp at the floral beauty, then spend long minutes going on about the delectable pastels of miniature birds-of-paradise, proteases, gingers, and orchids. That was exactly what Meg had done with the first of

Salinger's bouquets when Thea gave it to her.

By afternoon, Thea finished painting for the day, so she filled the back of her car with two days worth of bouquets, then drove into Potshot. As usual, the library was her first stop. The two women met in the back room where Meg took her lunch. Piles of books under repair shared a table with a rainforest of exotic plants.

Her friend stooped to bury her face in the flowers, then she snapped back up. "Not again! There's no scent! All this beauty and no fragrance. How extremely vexing."

Thea laughed, perhaps for the first time since the last town meeting. "Don't take it personally, Meg. They're probably the best that money can buy. Just like Derek, actually. What he lacks in substance he certainly tries to compensate for in looks and money." Her brittle tone brought her friend closer.

"To think this man fathered your sweet Alex. I wish my belief system allowed me to turn vigilante and take out the trash. The man obviously has stones of brass. Surely, he wouldn't miss them in the least. The pure cowardice of the man stuns me! Especially after hounding you to sign away any claims over Alex's paternity." Meg put an arm around Thea's shoulders and urged her into a chair. She sniffed, "I still think you should have taken his money, though. Obviously he has enough to burn."

The librarian poured a cup of tea from the pot warming on a hot plate, and passed it to Thea. "Drink up, my dear. It'll do you good."

Thea sipped, then said, "In retrospect, I know I should have accepted his payoff, especially when I think of all the things I could do for Alex. . . but at the time, it felt like blood money, tainted beyond redemption. Just like these beautiful, sterile flowers."

Meg leaned forward and stroked a wisp of hair from Thea's forehead. "You were just a young lass and certainly in no state to be making such hard choices."

"Drunk, Meg, and high. That was my *state*."

Meg gave her a stern look. "You got help for that before your babe was damaged. Many a mother has wallowed in her alcoholic stupor, then claimed horror at what her habit did to her wee one as she hefted another bottle. You're made of sterner stuff than you give yourself credit for, Althea. You finished your schooling when many another would have let self-pity rule."

"Well, I'm indulging in a bit now."

Her friend sat down and continued, "Snap out of it. Think of what you've accomplished. You've done well by Alex, let no one tell you otherwise. No amount of money could have brought about what you have. It is no good pining for the road not taken."

"No. No, it isn't." Thea tipped the cup back and finished off her tea. With a forced briskness, she stood. "I'd better be off, Meg, I still have three more deliveries to make."

"I suppose you'll be lobbying this afternoon for our gentler version of the hot springs, then?"

She groaned. "Don't remind me. We only have six weeks until the final vote. It's like treading barefoot over rice paper. Have you seen the avid expressions on our neighbors' faces when Salinger Enterprises is mentioned? No telling how the people in the valley will vote on Letty's special ballot either."

"Can't be helped, my dear. I've been working on our long-term projections of what the town will see in returns compared to the lump sum proffered by Salinger. I'm sure it will show that maintaining ownership benefits us. Most of our fellow citizens recognize the difference between pyrite and gold." She smiled her Cheshire cat's grin.

"They don't call it Fools' Gold for nothing," Thea muttered.

Meg kissed her cheek and said, "Don't worry. And I think

you're wise having Jake build through this crisis. I went to see his progress this morning. The man's an absolute wizard. Only a little over two weeks on the job and he and his new helpers have accomplished an amazing amount. It will be much more difficult to tear down what he's built with the sight of it firmly before one and all."

"So he's as good with his hands as we hoped?" asked Thea, feeling a much needed lightness at her friend's words.

"Now, dear, it's too early for me to tell about that," teased Meg, her lips tilting in another cat-like grin. "But he's a fine craftsman and a survivor to boot. I'll be having you and Alex over to dinner with Jake and me this week. I'll let you know when."

"Yoo-hoo, Megan Connors? Where have you gotten yourself off to now?" A disembodied voice drifted through the stacks.

Meg frowned. "Oh, dear. It's Sissy, back for more books on the rich and the famous. Busybody that she is, she'll pester me for specifics about the new bouquets. Last time she was in, she actually had the nerve to ask how I can afford to display hundred-dollar bouquets on my salary."

Thea studied the flowers, wishing anew she could use them for barter. "A hundred dollars each? That's what a pair and a half of Alex's favorite running shoes cost. What did you tell her?"

With a wry glance at Thea, she said, "Why that they're worth at least $200.00 each and that they came from a male admirer."

"Meg!"

"It's partially true, even if the flowers weren't for me."

Thea grimaced. "And Salinger's no admirer."

"True, but I can't very well tell Sissy they're from a manipulative sociopath, now can I? Now shoo." With that, Meg bustled toward the front of the library, the newest floral arrangement in her hands.

Sissy's voice drifted through the bookshelves. "Why Megan Connor, you sly puss, not another bouquet from your mysterious *inamorato*?"

"Yes, Sissy. They're very Harrison Ford, don't you think?"

Thea's eyes rolled as she headed for the back door, shutting it behind her. With a profound sigh, she got into her car to make a run over to Bodeen's bakery and deli.

After a long afternoon of urging friends and acquaintances to stay with their original plans for the hot springs, she noticed Salinger Enterprises had set up a temporary office in the space slotted for Potshot's new Chamber of Commerce. When she walked by, she observed that the model hot springs and mud baths figured prominently in the front window. Two workers busied themselves lining the walls with other display boards, all showing glossy examples of Salinger Enterprises' lavish developments. Those visions kept flashing through her mind as she drove home.

Discouraged as she was by the lukewarm reception from some townspeople, she hardly registered the luxury sedan parked under the aspen as she pulled into the driveway. When she recognized her mother's car, she met the beady-eyed stare of a magpie perched on a speckled branch.

"Great! Why today, Mother?" she asked of the bird. That one, of course, only fluffed his black and white plumage before sinking lower onto the branch. She resolved to have Alex with her before going into the house, a level of cowardice to which she seldom stooped. With a glance at her watch, she realized it would be just minutes before her son's bus dropped him at the bottom of their drive.

Thea decided to wait around a bend in the driveway so that Alex would not suffer the embarrassment of having his mother meet the bus. Having been the ongoing recipient of Alexander's Total Immersion Technique for Parental Training, she reiterated Rule Number 1: No public displays of affection. As she meandered down the road, she startled an animal from a thicket of sagebrush. By the time she turned, whatever it was had dropped into the arroyo that paralleled the drive. The critter sounded pretty big, too. On a hunch, she climbed the crumbling bank to higher ground and peered at the ground around the brush. The alkaline soil showed deep hollows where the creature's feet had broken the crusty surface, then a straight trail to the edge of the gully. No distinguishing feature made these tracks any more identifiable than hundreds of other surface dimples.

Thea sighed in exasperation. "Woman, you're seeing a wolf behind every bush now. It was probably an overgrown bunny anyway." She quelled the thought that jackrabbits rarely hopped in such a straight line.

Just then the rattling roar of the school bus warned of her son's arrival. She skittered down the bank as backpack draped over one arm and head bent toward the ground, Alex pelted along. When his bright glance spotted her, the excitement on his face faded. His cool reception found its way to where she stored all other hurts—her squishy heart.

He dropped from a jog to a determined walk. "Now what did I do?"

Thea smiled at that. "Nothing, sport. I just thought we'd walk to the house together. I've been gone all afternoon. Just got back, in fact." She fell in beside him.

"Doing hot springs stuff again?" His limpid gaze caught hers.

"Yep."

They walked a few strides, then he said, "I guess everybody really liked that guy's ideas for the hot springs, huh?"

That guy. His father. "Some did. Others realize what a negative impact Saling. . .his proposal could have on our community."

"Uh-huh." Alex halted and looked up at her. His chin took on the mutinous cast he got when their bearings diverged. "Look, Mom, I really need to do something before I come up to the house. I'll meet you there, okay?"

For a moment, Thea studied her offspring. Other than a fidget or two, he gave nothing away. "Well, I didn't tell you, but we have a surprise visitor. Grandma's here."

"Oh, man! What does she want?"

While his words mirrored her thoughts exactly, she said, "Now, Alex. She's your grandma and she loves you."

He crossed his arms around his ribs. "All right, already. I'll be up in a minute."

Thea turned away, albeit reluctantly, then strode the rest of the way home. She squelched a niggling urge to hide in the bushes and see what Alex did, then shuddered to think of how that would impact his self-esteem if he caught her there. Why, he could end up as a counter jockey at a fast-food restaurant for life, traceable to The Bush Episode. Wasn't anything about parenting straightforward?

As she got closer to the door, she slowed to an amble, hoping Alex would catch up with her and provide necessary distraction when she greeted her mother. Without thinking about it, Thea straightened her usual attire: baggy jeans secured today by a bright tie and a tee shirt washed in hot water so many times that it now hit just above her navel. She was glad she had put a bra on earlier, though, in preparation for going to town.

Finally, she teetered at her front door. The sound of a vehicle coming up the drive allowed her to stall for a few more moments. Probably another delivery of flowers, she decided, although it was nearly five o'clock. Evidently, a delivery day was never done. When Bram's Land Rover drove into view, a rush of blood heated her face, fueled no doubt by erotic dreams from last night. Salinger's ruthless assault had shifted her view of Bram from vague foe to budding ally.

"Yet another sign that you've been too long at sea, my girl. But, hey, the gang's all here." She waited while Bram got out of his vehicle. Alex popped out of the passenger side, all smiles again.

"My own child, a traitor," she muttered, then skipped down the steps to meet them.

"Look, Mom, Bram's here early. I'm going to help him carry groceries." Alex jogged toward the man.

Bram, whose head showed above the roof of his rig, moved to the back of the truck, which he opened. He proceeded to load Alex' skinny arms with a muslin bag overflowing with produce. Thea sauntered over to them, passing Alex as he headed the other way.

Keep it casual. "I, ah, thought we still needed to work out a kitchen schedule."

"That was over two weeks ago," Bram said, giving her an impenetrable look. He slipped the perennial list from his shirt pocket. Thea glanced at it. In legible and firm writing, he had sketched a chart of his proposed cooking times. He said, "This is dinner. I thought I'd cook. And *you* were going to write up a rental contact for me. At least for tonight, I'm claiming the kitchen through squatter's rights."

He handed her a bag, dangling it by the straps as though to lure her. Without thinking, she looped the handles over one arm. "That rental agreement keeps coming back to haunt me. I'm not crazy about this fixed kind of approach. Can't we keep things more flexible?" As he closed the back of his rig, then picked up the remaining bags, she fell into stride beside him. "I mean, what if this arrangement doesn't work out for you? Never mind me, owner of the kitchen-in-question."

94

Again that slanting look and an almost smile. "Oh, I think the arrangement will do. However, you wanted your privacy and a written agreement will ensure that."

"You said you didn't want to get involved." She stopped, her exasperation with him surfacing in her voice.

He did smile then, a sexy ice cream-licking grin. "Relax, Thea. It's just dinner."

As she studied him where he stood one step above her on the landing, she wondered. In the slanting rays of late afternoon, his eyes held effervescent lights. The arresting planes of his face and relaxed mouth made her clutch the groceries to her midriff. No telling how much permanent damage the sight of that strong pulse at the juncture of his collarbones would do to her mental state. The raven's wing curve of his hair over his collar made her yearn to run her fingers through the strands. Fuchsia, she was in *dire* straits. Thankfully, the door whipped open. Thea dragged her gaze from the man and met the brittle jade green of her mother's eyes.

"Oh, hello, Mother. What brings you to the slums?" Thea took the opportunity to close the distance between her and Bram, then passed him and walked into the house. Even so she caught a whiff of his cedar scent. The aroma brought the hairs on her arms to attention. She kissed one of her mother's smooth cheeks in passing, thankful for Mother's expensive perfume, which easily trounced *eau de Bram*.

Amarantha's corrected and pampered nose quivered a bit at the nostrils. Her flawless skin positively glowed, probably helped along by the enhanced golden highlights in her well-coiffed hair. "What do you think, Althea? I wanted to meet the strange man who has taken up residence with my daughter." She pinioned Bram with her regard.

Thea offered Bram an apologetic look. "Mother, meet *Dr. Bramden Youngwolf Hayes, my *lodger*. Bram, this is my mother, Amarantha MacTavish-Seeger." She headed for the kitchen, barely listening as Bram got sucked into Amarantha's Vortex of Social Exchange.

Alex stood at one counter, the mother lode of his bag strewn across the surface. "Mom, what's *fetakine*?"

She settled her bags on another counter, then took the package from Alex. "That's pronounced *fetoocheenee*, sweets. It's a glorified macaroni."

"Not the way I prepare it," broke in Bram's voice from behind her.

"Oh?" she quipped.

"Uh-huh. Mine's a plateful of heaven."

How to deal with this new and relaxed Bramden Hayes presented a quandary. She looked at her son. "Time for homework, child-of-mine. You can have your peanut butter and jelly sandwich with milk at your desk."

"Oh, Mo-o-om."

"Your snack's in the fridge. Now skedaddle." She ruffled her offspring's hair as he trudged by, only to have him pull away with a black look. "And give your grandma a proper hello on the way."

Once he left, Thea concentrated her attention on Mother, posed to display her svelte figure to wonderful advantage. To give her credit, Thea suspected her mother only did this out of a lifetime's habit. It still made her feel like a grubby ten-year-old in the presence of royalty.

"So, did Sissy the Snoop call you about Dr. Hayes or do you have faster modes of gathering intelligence now?" she asked her mother.

"Darling, you know I protect my sources." Amarantha sashayed into the kitchen.

"It *was* Sissy, then. She's such a turncoat."

Her mother's gaze dropped to regard Thea's clothing. "I do wish you'd have come to Sacramento, or better yet, to San

96

Francisco with me this winter. I'm sure you would have liked some of the spring fashions."

"I told you, I'm on a tight budget right now. Besides, I like my threads."

Amarantha sniffed, then said to Bram, who busied himself with unpacking his provisions. "You'd never know it by looking at my daughter, but she left a promising career as a graphics designer to paint science fiction scenes."

"It's a sabbatical, Mom. And I paint fantasy, not science fiction."

Her mother went on, "I kept running into your besieged employer at any number of black-tie events this winter. He didn't look well, rather peaked and thin. You didn't tell me that you turned down his offer of part-ownership."

"Thomas and I talk on the phone nearly every week since I started my sabbatical. He does sound tired, but he's always been thin. And I didn't have the funds to buy into the business at the time. Thomas deserves better than to be tied into a slow payment schedule. It wouldn't have been fair to him."

Her mother sent a searching glance her way. "You could always come to me for a loan. If you'd just let me help—"

"Not now, Mother."

She sniffed. "How could you have traded away such an impressive opportunity for *this*, Althea? I just don't know what you could have been thinking. Do you know she's been reduced to bartering paintings for groceries and God-only-knows what else?" Again, her mother directed her question to Bram.

"They're murals, Mother. Besides, it's not like I'm selling my body."

Mother continued, "You must have seen her frescos in town. They're everywhere; on the grocery store, on the bakery, even on the library. Casting pearls before swine."

"Watch it, Mother, your pretentiousness is showing. It

probably won't help to remind you that the barter system works for me. And the one I did for the library? That was an outright gift. God knows Meg does her share of community service."

Amarantha shivered delicately. "Wall paintings—with your talent."

Thea felt Bram's scrutiny. She forced her hands to stillness when all of a sudden she wanted to fidget like a child, then faced him. "So just what is this heavenly delight you're planning for dinner?"

"Dinner? I thought he was your tenant."

Bram continued taking packages out of bags, leaving some items on the counter, placing vegetables in the sink, and putting others in the refrigerator. In quick succession, he snatched a number of ingredients while listing them. "Artichoke, prosciutto, and sun-dried tomato fettuccine. A favorite Mediterranean dish."

Amarantha tilted her head. "You've been to the Med?"

Bram stilled. "A friend taught me how to make this."

"A woman friend?"

Thea bit her tongue to keep from blurting, 'Mother!'

His guarded look met Thea's as he said to her mother, "She was a close friend. Lisa died three years ago. She was killed in a wildfire."

Amarantha's perfect mouth formed an 'O'. Bram returned to his task as Thea sagged into a counter, thankful for its support. The horror of his loss hit her solar plexus, making it hard to breathe. How many ghosts did this man carry with him?

He recovered more quickly. Thea noticed how easily he juggled all the ingredients. She definitely wanted to paint the man's hands, even if he did have some precarious ideas about what constituted noninvolvement. Then she picked up one of two bottles on the counter, hoping beyond hope that they were not what they appeared to be.

"Sparkling cider," she read with relief. She met his gaze, inexplicably grateful for his thoughtfulness. "What a wonderful idea."

"My, my. A gourmet cook no less," said her mother. Her avid look, as it passed between Thea and Bram, raised her daughter's hackles.

"It's just dinner, Mother. Relax." She ignored Bram's grin.

"Please feel free to stay, Mrs. Seeger. There'll be plenty for everyone."

"Amarantha, please, Dr. Hayes. Or should I say Dr. Youngwolf-Hayes?" She sauntered over to the counter beside Bram as he started washing an unusual assortment of vegetables. Once there, she leaned gracefully against the counter, a Lauren Bacall study in insouciance. "In what field did you gain your doctorate, if I might ask?"

"He's a glorified fireman, Mom," said Thea, an '*oh, no*' second before she wished she had kept her mouth shut.

Bram shot her another of his inscrutable looks. "Well, more of a civil engineer with heavy overtones of environmental engineering. I'm here in Potshot in my capacity as a fire safety engineer for the University of Oklahoma. I head a grant study team."

"How long does your study extend?" asked Amarantha.

"Through next fall anyway. We might be able to get an extension, but won't know until September."

"And you'll be staying with my daughter until then?"

"Only until the hotel is refurbished. Two of my team are there now." Bram finished washing the vegetables, then dried his hands and draped the towel over one shoulder. "You don't live in Potshot?"

Her mother shuddered theatrically. "Heavens no—"

"What can I do to help?" Thea interrupted.

Bram eyed her doubtfully, then handed her a couple of

shallots. "These need to be finely minced."

"I think I can handle a sharp knife," she said, injecting some tartness into her voice. Then muttered, "If I can find a sharp knife."

Amarantha plunged in with, "I have a residence with a stunning view of Reno. Unlike my daughter, I prefer the security of a gated community, especially since my husband passed away four years ago." Her mother inspected her immaculate nails.

"Never mind about how barricaded neighborhoods lead to the disintegration of entire communities," added Thea. She lifted a knife and eyed the nicked cutting edge, then tossed it back into the drawer.

"As you can tell, it's just one of the many things upon which my daughter and I disagree."

"Yes, Thea does have strong opinions," Bram concurred. Thea stifled a groan as he and her mother headed toward becoming downright chummy.

She moved reluctantly when he shifted her aside to find a knife. Evidently he had no more luck than she did in finding one honed to his liking. He excused himself, saying something about having a sharpening stone in his truck. Thea waited in a barely arrested state of ire until she heard the front door close behind Bram.

"What could you possibly be thinking of, Mother? This man is my tenant; a virtual stranger and you're practically inviting him into family issues. Besides talking about me as though I wasn't standing right here." She crossed her arms and tapped a toe while her mother popped a tomato chunk into her perfectly painted mouth.

"Oh, nonsense, Althea. We're hardly dragging out family skeletons. Besides, it never hurts to get an outside opinion. I believe you need to regain your perspective. He is a professional after all." She smiled a barracuda's grin.

100

"A fire safety professional. He knows nothing about the art world," Thea ground from between clenched teeth.

"I dare say. Still. . ." her mother trailed off as the front door opened, then closed. "He's quite good-looking, isn't he?"

"I hadn't noticed," Thea lied.

Bram returned with a hand-length rectangular object and a squeeze bottle. "Mind if I make a space at your table? Your knives really could use an edge."

Thea rounded the corner of her kitchen only to find two more floral arrangements taking up the entire surface of her dining room table.

She groaned. Her mother said, "Oh, those arrived while I was here." Amarantha sauntered over to read the cards. She glanced curiously between Bram and her daughter, "It's the strangest thing. These are from a 'Derek Salinger'. 'With love', no less. Who's Derek?"

"Some developer trying to get into my good graces." Thea all but lunged to snatch the cards from the plants, then tossed them in the paper-recycling bin.

"Well, he certainly has expensive taste in flowers. They're quite elegant, although I do prefer ones with a fragrance myself," said Mom.

Thea lifted one arrangement and headed toward the living room. "Mother, why don't you grab the other one and bring it in here. It's in the way."

She glanced at Bram as she left, by now used to the frown on his face. He had worn the same expression since the flowers began arriving. By the time they had removed the unwanted flowers and returned, the man sat at the table. A motley pile of kitchen knives perched before him as he alternately oiled and rubbed the blades across the whetting stone in front of him.

He glanced up as she returned. "Nice flowers."

"All pastels with no scent." She frowned.

101

He smiled.

"Do you think Alexander would like me to help him with his homework?" asked her mother.

All in all, it made for a long evening.

After Thea kissed her mother goodbye, then tucked Alex in, she decided to sneak out for a long soak at the hot springs. She grabbed a towel and flashlight, then slipped out the back of her darkened house.

The waning moon shed enough light that she skipped the flashlight after all. The whoosh of wings above signaled a nighthawk on the hunt. Rustling in the brush sounded like warm and fuzzy nighthawk snacks. It was still cool enough that she felt confident no rattlers would be soaking up radiant heat along the trail. Even so, she wriggled into her hiking boots, just in case. She hopped the stones across the creek, then followed a private path to the springs.

Her mind tripped and raced over all that had occurred over this last couple of weeks. The spa fire, Derek's initial salvo followed by his worrisome absence, Alex's wolf sighting, the brushfire, Mother's visit, Bram. *Bram.* His presence had started a strange domino effect on her inner balance that did not bode well. Worse yet, his proximity changed the whole feel of her home.

His scent, subtle as it was, remained long after he left an area. This morning she caught a whiff of cedar in both kitchen and bathroom. When she showered, she found one dark hair, too thick to be hers, clinging to her shower curtain. It established an intimacy with him somehow. That didn't even begin to touch on the effect he had on her when they were in the same room. Hormonal surges, be damned. Erotic dreams or not, she refused to succumb.

The hamster wheel of thoughts made the twenty-five

minute walk to the hot springs pass in a flash. A lingering odor of charred wood overlaid the heady resin of new-cut lumber. She turned on her flashlight. Sometimes snakes curled up on the hot rocks here, but she saw no sign of reptiles. Dark watermarks showed where other Potshot residents had availed themselves of the springs earlier. Low-lying skeletons of buildings squatted where only ruin had been a few weeks ago. When she had more time, she promised herself again to come up during daylight.

Blessed peace, she thought as she climbed the stepped trail to the highest pool. From here she could see the warm glow from Potshot throughout summer when the air and water temperatures more closely matched. Tonight, with the hot steam and cold air clashing, all she saw was a gradual lightening against fog. Most residents considered this pool a privacy lagoon and chose to soak *au naturale*. Tonight, Thea wanted nothing between herself and the healing waters.

Bubbling waters masked night sounds. Steam curled thickly into the surrounding air. These springs remained blissfully low in sulfur compounds, so when Thea took a deep breath, pine and sage filled her lungs. In no time at all, she shucked her clothes and waded into the now smooth-bottomed pool, a result of a terraforming project. With a sigh, she sank onto a ledge created to allow soakers to keep their heads comfortably above water.

She lay her head against a rolled hand towel and let the air out of her lungs in a slow exhalation. "This is the life."

"Thea?" A disembodied voice issued from the swirling mists.

With a yelp, she sprang up and hot water lapped her chest. "Oh, fuchsia! Bram? Is that you? I thought I was alone." With a muttered oath, she abruptly sat.

He swam out of the haze in a surge of water. His head formed from the vapor in a primordial way that made her

103

catch her breath. "Sorry. Didn't mean to startle you. The steam's so thick I couldn't see who it was."

He stood, exposed to his lower ribs, before finding a spot on a ledge nearer to Thea. She noticed the sculpted form of his upper body in the moonlight, then studiously avoided looking below the waterline. She figured it was too dark to see whether he wore trunks anyway. However, just the thought of Bram in the same pool with her raised the temperature of the water a few degrees.

He said, "I'm afraid you've caught me. I've made a habit of these late night soaks. The night of the fire was the only one I missed."

She forced herself to relax enough to sink further into the water. With fumbling hands, Thea found her submerged towel on the ledge, wringing it out before stuffing it behind her head. She would just outwait the man before getting out. Certainly darkness and steam provided enough privacy for both of them.

Which sounded great in theory. But Thea could not seem to move past the phase of 'naked-in-a-pool-with-Bram' to relaxation. She wiggled and sighed, but remained jumpy as a frog over boiling water. Finally, she said, "You know, I guess I just wasn't in the right mental state for doing this tonight." She judged the mist thick enough to conceal her once she rose out of the pool anyway. Still she waited.

He said, "Wasn't quite the relaxing evening I thought it would be."

"Mother," Thea replied. "There's no such thing as restful around her. I hope you didn't take everything she said as gospel. She's cushioned from reality by financial abundance."

"So you're saying she doesn't have to worry about money," he paraphrased.

Thea moaned. "It never fails. I'm around her for more than an hour and I even start to talk like her. Sorry."

His low, sexy chuckle centered a slow ache in her abdomen. She closed her eyes. *Don't you start now*, she told her body, evidently to no avail.

"I don't know, Thea. I enjoyed listening to her talk about your childhood escapades."

Thea did groan then. "At least I never burned down a sheepherders' shack." She wished her words back the moment they left her mouth. She tried for subterfuge. "So, how are you coming on solving the arson fires? Sy says your team's been especially helpful. Unlike our insurance company."

His silence threatened to drown her in her own anxiety. "If you're asking if I think your son had anything to do with either fire, the answer's no."

Her locked arms loosened, dunking her to her chin before she recovered. "How did you know?"

"That you were worried about Alex's possible involvement?" The water swished with his shrug. "I guess it was a combination of things; your reaction to his adventures with the magnifying glass, his. . .ah. . .assertions of independence and your response. Come on, Thea, you love your son and want to protect him. It's obvious."

She swallowed the hot lump growing in her throat. "You forgot to mention how many Potshot residents eyed my son at the town meeting. Tongues have been working overtime since then, too. I might as well get him a tee shirt that says, 'Blame me. I did it'."

Again, that quiet strength surged between them. "I didn't notice."

"Oh, you just don't know Alex, Bram. For the last few years, his shenanigans have kept our community in a constant state of turmoil." Rivulets of sweat stung her eyes. "At different times, he's had the entire town convinced that they were under siege by an abominable snowman and a miner's ghost. Now it looks like he's working on a werewolf theory. That fire at the shack was neatly sandwiched between Sasquatch and the phantom miner."

"He's an active kid all right. But Thea, Alex doesn't fit the profile of an arsonist. Besides, Jake Seeker collaborated his story on the spa fire."

"Jake Seeker spoke up for Alex? Why am I just hearing this from you?"

"Probably because I happened to be in the Sheriff's office today when Jake dropped off his deposition. Evidently he was the one who Alex saw at the fire."

"Why didn't Alex recognize him?"

Bram slid closer until he was no more than a foot away. "I couldn't tell you. Your son's blessed with an active imagination, but there's no maliciousness in him. I'm still not sure that his wolf story's pure fancy either. We've seen signs of a big predator on the mountain. Alex seemed pretty sure of himself last time we talked about it."

Thea took her rolled towel and blotted at her eyes and face. "And when was that?"

"Today as we were coming up the drive. He told me that he'd just put out some food for his wolf." When she didn't say anything, he continued, "Your son's an enterprising youngster. It sounds like he's getting double portions of school lunch, one for himself and one for his wolf buddy."

"We don't have any wolves around here," she said. "We *do* have feral dogs and coyotes, though. When one of them starts coming too close, I worry about rabies. I don't like the thought of Alex feeding it—whatever it is. What if it decides Alex looks like a tasty snack?" Adrenalin sang through her blood, making the idea of relaxation ludicrous.

"Could be time to track Alex's critter. Relocation would certainly be a viable choice if we find a wolf."

Thea tried to ignore the warmth that his 'we' instilled.

Bram cleared his throat. "If it is a wolf, it's not indigenous.

With the bizarre behaviors some animals adopt when faced with habitat destruction, you really never know who might be showing up for dinner."

"Or who might be dinner either. Great! So the chances are good that my son's communing with a savage carnivore." With that she stood, momentarily forgetting about her nude state. The water lapping above her breasts reminded her. She sank lower.

"Uh, Bram, I'm not sure how you're attired, but I need some privacy so I can get out."

A much longer silence stretched between them. His voice, when it came, sounded somewhat hoarse. "Oh. All right. How about if you give me a call when you're dressed. I'll walk you back down the mountain."

"Sure. Sounds like you could use a glass of that sparkling cider you brought for dinner, too. You have to watch these hot springs, they'll dry you out in no time."

As she waded toward the edge, she thought she heard him say, "Dehydration's not the problem." It made no sense so she filed it under general nonsense.

Once at the edge of the pool, she glanced behind, then held out a hand. Steam effectively obscured her hand from two feet away, so she figured she would be safe from Bram's view. Even so, she draped her minuscule towel for maximum coverage and hustled for her larger wrap as soon as she got out, then snagged her clothes and headed for a convenient rock. After a quick dry, she wrestled into her clothes, the process hindered by damp skin.

Finished, she called, "Okay, Bram. I'm decent. You can come out now." She hung back from the edge, toweling her short hair with a semi-dry corner.

When Bram arose from the vapor-shrouded pool, it called to mind the mythical birth of a god. First his water-laden head came up, shedding silvery water, then his sculpted torso.

Moonlight played sweet games of hide-and-seek, highlighting his peaks and shadowing his valleys. When he stood before her, clad in a pair of disreputable looking cutoffs that hung low on his hips and high on his thighs, Thea gasped for air, all too aware that she had held her breath during his entire ascent. When he reached toward her, then over her shoulder, she thanked the night for its cover of darkness, especially after he hefted a towel and boots from the rock ledge near her head. It had been too easy to lean toward him in that brief moment between longing and intent.

He made quick work of drying himself, then knelt to lace up his boots. Standing he said, "Ready?"

She managed a nod.

The walk down the mountain passed in a blur for Thea. Night air barely slowed her racing pulse or cooled her heated skin. For she had to admit to what she felt for Bram in the moonlight: unrequited lust. *Fuchsia!* What had she let herself in for now? It gave puny comfort to think he felt nothing of the sort for her. *She* lived in this wanton body full time, not him. So as she walked, she tried to outpace her body's appetites. Even huge inhalations of night air barely helped. All too soon, they reached the creek, then the back porch.

"How about if I get us a glass of something cold. Why don't you wait here? Cool down a little." She could have kicked herself. If anyone needed to chill, she was that person.

With the refrigerator open, she fanned the door a few times, welcoming the frigid air before pulling out the opened bottle of cider and a pitcher of orange juice. She needed time to revive her commonsense, yet it took only moments to pour two glasses. Light from the kitchen barely illuminated the man's form where he half sat on the porch rail with his towel around his neck. He stood when she came out, accepting the orange juice.

"Sure you don't want cider?" she asked. "I'm afraid only

one more glass was left."

"No thanks." He took a long swig of orange juice, giving Thea a profile view of his neck and chest as he swallowed. She shivered as gooseflesh covered her arms and chest.

Bram misinterpreted. "You're cold. Let's go into the house." He led the way. Rather than set him straight, Thea followed.

He set his glass on the table and Thea flicked on the overhead lights. As she turned back to him, she saw his bare back for the first time.

"Oh, my God. What happened?" She closed the distance between them without thought. Now she traced the damaged area covering an entire shoulder blade with her fingertips. Thinner scars crisscrossed the obvious burn and trailed to a point on his lower back.

Bram froze at her words, then stayed rigid in a half crouch midway to sitting. He winced.

She withdrew her hand immediately. "I'm so sorry; I didn't mean to hurt you."

With a soul deep sigh, he finished sitting. "You didn't. It doesn't hurt anymore."

She studied the scars again. The upper part looked as though his flesh had melted, then reformed into a waxen consistency. "Fuchsia, this must have hurt like hell."

He draped his towel to cover it more completely. "It's ugly all right." Bleak darkness stole the light from his eyes.

She searched his face, feeling her way through the shroud that descended with her stupid response. "I'm sorry I reacted that way. I. . .it just surprised me."

He nodded. "You took it better than some."

She sat in the chair facing him. "I recognize burn scars. But those other ones. . ."

He took a gulp of juice. His eyes looked at her, then through her. "After my mother and brother were killed—I went a little wild. You live in a small town. You know that once you get a reputation, everything bad that happens within a certain radius of your stomping grounds comes back at you. Whether you deserve it or not." His hands, strangely inert, settled on the table where they bracketed his glass of juice.

"A couple of white folks lived a few miles off the reservation. Kept a smokehouse filled to brimming with meat poached from the Rez. When the smokehouse was raided, I was the one they took after." His look sharpened a bit then as he focused on her. Thea did what she wanted and cupped his hand in hers.

"There I was, a skinny unkempt Indian kid—roaring into trouble like a wildfire eats grass. Just over fifteen years old, full of piss and vinegar. Neither strong enough nor smart enough to run when I had the chance. Decided to beard the old racist in his den.

"Old man Mims was a mean old son-of-a-gun, Betty Mims wasn't much better. Between them, they had me belly-strapped to the trunk of an old black walnut faster than a shoat can clear a wallow. Beat me with his rodeo belt buckle to within an inch of my life. Had that same belt around my neck for a lynching from that tree just about the time my grandfather came around the bend in his old pickup. Luckily, he'd brought reinforcements."

Thea consciously relaxed her hands from squeezing his. "Oh, Bram."

"Grandfather had them charged with aggravated assault, battery and attempted lynching. The Mims said they just wanted to scare me, teach the dirty Injun boy a lesson about stealing. Fine upstanding citizens that they were, they were acquitted of all charges."

Thea didn't even realize she was crying until a tear hit her bare arm and rolled down toward their clenched hands.

Bram leaned forward then, reaching toward her face with

110

his free hand. "Hey, you told me only onions made you cry."

"Must be a delayed reaction—from your pasta."

He cupped her face with one hand while his thumb wiped away the wetness on first one cheek, then the other. She broke. "Damn the Mims, Bram. Damn them to hell."

"What if I tell you it was the best thing that ever happened to me?"

She shook her head. "You're nuts to think I'd believe that."

His chuckle turned into a raucous laugh, laden with humor just the same. "Smart woman. But it did turn me around. I quit wasting my life, finished the Rez school, and went on to college. I don't know if I would've left the path of self destruction on my own."

She nodded. "Sometimes it takes a glimpse of death to make a person choose life."

He cocked his head as though listening for the echo behind her words, but he said nothing.

Thea sniffed, nervously now, and said, "How about some more juice?" She reached for his nearly empty glass.

His warm hand closed around hers. Bram fixed her with an implacable gaze. "I don't want pity, Thea."

She grinned at that. "It's only orange juice, Bram."

After a startled look, his mouth curved into a reluctant smile.

Chapter Seven

Bram studied the slope leading to Potshot as Ian pointed out aspects the engineer already knew. Ponderosa pines grew out of a foot's depth of duff, which acted like an accelerant when mixed with flame. Succulents amid the dry needles barely slowed a wildfire. And if flame reached the town's manmade structures, the blaze would light up the sky all the way to Reno. From this vantage, Bram saw only fuel.

"I recommend putting barriers up here." He poked his index finger at the topographical map of the vista spread out before them. "Then here, and here."

Ian nodded. "The town's risk is greatest from those directions."

"Prevailing winds and uphill terrain. The townspeople'll have to get involved. These're pretty big changes. Especially here." Bram pointed out the hot springs area. From their vantage, they viewed new construction proceeding at a rapid rate. Jake Seeker was proving a man of his word.

The fire inspector forced air out of his lungs. "If that slick developer buys the town out, anything we do could be for naught. Did you get a look at the guy's plans? Self-sustaining, they're not."

Bram grunted. "You, my friend, are obviously unaware of Potshot's other force of nature. My landlady, Thea MacTavish. I can't see her going quietly into any corral constructed by Salinger. It's personal for her. She won't give up."

"She probably won't like our options for the town, either.

Removing trees, relocating access roads and terracing could be construed as pretty intrusive."

"They're better than total devastation."

"No arguments there."

"Thanks for your input, Ian. It's good to know we're on the same track."

"Anytime, boss."

"How's the modeling coming?"

Ian cracked his knuckles as though limbering them for the computer keyboard. "Between Challie and me, we'll have the program area-specific by the end of the week."

"Good. I'll want it converted into presentation format."

"No sweat. It'll be up-and-running before the next council meeting." The other man's attention wandered and Bram followed Ian's line of sight to snag on Challie, where she and J.D. surveyed a new access road that would double as a firebreak.

"We done here, Bram?"

He recognized Ian's eagerness to join the others. Bram admitted, too, that he had been surly as a badger lately. Gone was their easy camaraderie from earlier projects.

"Sure. Thanks again." He watched his friend stretch into a ground-eating stride, making a beeline for Challie. Bram turned away, allowing his gaze to range over Potshot and from there, southeast to Thea's place—the crux of his surliness.

Nestled as it was against the gully's bank, the house remained hidden. Even so, the newly acquired ache in his groin intensified. "Shoats and razorbacks, now geography's giving me a hard on," he muttered and returned his gaze to Potshot, which only served to remind him of Salinger's plans.

He rolled his shoulders, but to no avail. For the first time since choosing his career, Bram had trouble staying focused on a project. Thea's subtle charms and the mire of Potshot's ordeal with Salinger Enterprises were diverting attention best directed toward fire safety issues. *Shoats*, but Bram truly detested bullies.

Salinger's attempted hostile takeover paled beside the man's attack against Thea. That outraged Bram most, and on levels other than the most obvious one. Why his landlady's problems troubled him at all. . .

Challie's voice announced her arrival. "Youngwolf, I hope you're not planning to blindside Thea with our plans like that developer did."

If looks could speak, Challie's tongue would cleave to her palate. No such luck.

"I mean it, cuz. She flashed to steam while that Salinger guy was speaking. You know we need the townies on our side. No matter how much grant money we have, which *is* finite, without their support, we won't be able to make any difference at all."

Bram just looked at her. She shook her head. "*Men*! I'm telling you, Youngwolf, you need to get Thea on our side before we broach this with the council. Especially now that the meeting's been moved up."

Bram rubbed the burn scar on his forearm. He knew it was psychological, but it always ached when faced with slippery human challenges. Yes, his cousin definitely had a point. Thea needed to know. Still, why him?

"Hell, Hummingbird. I don't know where you get the idea that I have any influence with Thea. I know it's stupid to isolate her from the process, but every time I talk to her. . .well, our talk always goes south. It's like trying to herd Grandfather's pigs. Those critters were too smart for their own good."

Challie patted his shoulder in a comforting manner. "That bad, huh?"

"What's that supposed to mean?"

"You only call me Hummingbird when you're feeling

about thirteen-years-old. But don't worry, cuz, I'm sure you'll find a way. Maybe you should just spill your guts in hopes that your landlady takes pity on you. She strikes me as a woman of empathy."

He shook his head. With ironic chagrin, he said, "I've told Thea more about my past than any outsider needs to know. Still don't know how it happened. Besides I'm not so sure our process will go more smoothly by involving her. Thea has a way of getting the bit between her teeth. Still, I'd like to get as many townspeople involved as possible."

"The earlier the better."

He looked at the verdant patina over the foothills and valley. It took little imagination to visualize the landscape parched by the blistering heat of summer. For a moment, he envisioned the place black and smoldering. Lifeless.

Yes, Hummingbird was right. He needed to enlist Thea's help. *Shoats and razorbacks.*

Bram saw Thea reflected in the window as he stood in front of Salinger Enterprises. Her image superimposed over a placard announcing a 'gala' for the following evening. Hosted by the big bad wolf himself. Looking at the slick models, an obvious attempt to court votes, left a bad taste in Bram's mouth. His response became more visceral once he recognized Thea's silhouette.

She advanced until she stood beside him, wafting the scent of sun-drenched honeysuckle before her. "Hiya, boarder."

He slipped an appreciative glance over the top of her head, where she sported a voluminous bandanna, then to her cardinal red tee-shirt and her slouch jeans, held up today by a multi-colored cord. For some reason, her dazzling appearance no longer had the jarring effect it once did. In fact, he actually looked forward to seeing what outlandish color combinations

115

she might don next. He definitely savored the hint of skin that showed along her taut abdomen. To think he had been in the equivalent of a hot tub with her. *Thea naked.*

"Doesn't it just make you sick?" she asked. Her gesture took in the glossy rendition of Potshot's future before she began gnawing on a newly ragged cuticle. Catching herself at it, she glanced his way and stopped. "He's not to be trusted, you know. Salinger's sneaky, brutal and only in this for his own gain.

"Still, I wish I could have afforded all the bells and whistles for my presentation. Maybe then half of Potshot wouldn't be seeing dollar signs flashing in front of their eyes. This flashiness makes it tougher to envision a nourishing environment that will support their children and grandbabies."

"Sustainable," he said as he dragged his gaze back to the window display.

"What?"

"Sustainable living. That's what this model lacks."

"Well, supporting our way of life is definitely what I'm going for." She looped her arm through his, turning him away from the display and urging him down the street, all in the same movement. Her mischievous look drew him. "I, ah, noticed you installed a couple of alarms in the house. Smoke from Alex's attempt at breakfast set the upstairs one off this morning. Had to use the broom handle to reset it, sort of *piñata* style. I hope I didn't break anything."

Bram glanced down at her. "I'll check it when I get back tonight."

"Thanks. For installing the detectors, I mean. It was a very . . .*sustaining* thing to do."

He fixed his gaze down the street, where Potshot's tree shaded park showed some activity. A Fish & Wildlife truck dumped a tank of water into Boondoggle Pond as he watched. Probably fingerlings, Bram decided, although the reason eluded him.

"I installed the alarms out of self-preservation, Thea. Remember, I've seen you in action. Unfortunately, it sounds like your son's taking after you."

"Low blow, Bram. But it's too late to save your reputation on this one. You're just a caring kind of guy. It was bound to come out sooner or later."

Bram shrugged his shoulders to relieve sudden tension as she continued. "Right now, I'm on my way to the library. You're welcome to join me if you'd like."

He pointedly looked at their intertwined arms. "I have a choice?"

She laughed, the early evening sun glinting off of her eyes and fine boned face. "Oh, I'm sure you could break free if you wanted to."

He didn't want to, though. Which explained why he walked arm-in-arm with Althea MacTavish, civil disobedience personified, into a library filled with people. Mainly females, from what Bram could see and hear, all of whom turned to regard them as they came through the door.

Mayor Letty called out, "About time, Thea."

Another female voice said, "I can certainly see what took her so long," amid murmurous laughter from at least a dozen women's throats. Bram fought hard and unsuccessfully to keep blood from rushing to his face.

Thea chose to disengage. "Sorry. Alex's bus was late. But I'm here now. Time to roll up our sleeves and get to work."

Bram decided to wander through the stacks, hoping for both composure and an inkling of how to bring Thea on board for his proposed changes. In the biographies, he found a tome on Catherine the Great as Thea marshaled her forces for their fight against Salinger. In economics, he unearthed a book by the Beardstown ladies while Meg explained the fiscal effects of selling out to Salinger. When Letty stood up to admonish her troops, Bram wandered into the classics where he discovered Sophocles' version of *Antigone*. Such coincidences made him jittery as a hog at a slaughterhouse. The idea of this group of women conspiring against his grant team did not bode well.

By then, he decided to slink toward the door for a covert escape. His hopes dashed as Thea's clear voice sang out, "Oh, Bram, could you wait? We're just wrapping up."

So much for a clean getaway. He waited only half the time he expected. Thea swept over to him much like a wave breaking the surf. Her damnable perfume heralded her arrival. As he tried to hold the door for her, they got tangled over whose arm would hold the door and whose shoulder should push the portal open. She ended with her back pressed to his chest in a move that left Bram breathless and dizzy. It was all he could do to follow her down the two stairs to sidewalk level.

". . .and that's what we'll do," she finished.

He managed, "What's that perfume you're wearing?"

She gave him a look of pity, possibly based on his male inability to focus on the crisis at hand. "I'm not wearing perfume." But that fragrance. . .

"Watch out!" she cried and saved him from ramming the public mailbox.

The near miss cleared his mind. He said, "I'm going to grab something for dinner before heading back to the house."

"Oh, nonsense. After all that food you bought earlier this week? Why not let me fix dinner for you? Consider it compensation for having to deal with my mother the other night."

Bram struggled manfully with an excuse, but ended smiling weakly into her wide grin. "What're we having?"

"Black bean and rice tacos," and with a nod she set a brisk pace toward her car. His stomach whined like a starved puppy

118

as he caught up with her.

"No meat?"

She just grinned. At the car he faced one of Thea's mythical wonders arrayed along the outer wall of the grocery store. She said, "Perceval and the Fisher King," with a soft, almost shy smile. "I like Perceval filled with genuine awe rather than the fool some would have him."

At Bram's blank look, she continued, "You must know something about Perceval? The young knight of Arthurian legend? He became Grail-keeper in my favorite version." Her focus shifted subtly and she said, "I do wish he could have done more for the Fisher King, though."

The guy probably just needed a steak, Bram decided. He asked, "Why?"

Her expression held deep sadness. "No one should have to suffer as he did. But enough already. So, how does dinner sound?" With a shake of her head, she brightened.

Bram grappled with disappointment, but as he looked into Thea's face, tacos sounded better than any London broil. "Count me in."

Along the way to his rig, he noticed the main billboard over the local gambling joint announced Salinger's party. He quelled his unease by reminding himself that it was not his problem.

After a dinner that satisfied much more than expected, which said something about his assumptions, Bram settled himself onto the twig-type sofa in the front room. Before completely relaxing, he studied the joints of the couch, held together by wrapped plant fiber. Alex plunked down beside him.

"Man, flowers everywhere," the boy exclaimed in disgust.

"You can say that again." He added his glare to Alex's. Earlier Bram had helped Thea carry three more flower arrangements into the living room, designated holding area until she transported them to people in town. He refused to acknowledge why the sight of those expensive blooms pissed him off so much.

Thea strolled in with a bamboo tray holding an Asian looking pot and three mugs. She set it on the coffee table. "The ever present apple spice tea. Alex and I used to share a mug almost every night until last fall."

"The autumn of my affliction," explained Alex.

Bram's confusion must have shown on his face, because Thea appended with, "That's what Meg calls the stage when young people start reacting to their hormones. She's really very forward thinking, you know. She says that when you're raised an Irish Catholic, everything equates with sin. According to Meg, hormones are the biochemical basis for sin."

As Bram glanced askance at Alex, the boy shrugged, "Don't look at me. I don't know what any of that means." Alex twirled a knuckle-sized clump of honey onto his spoon before depositing the entire mass into his steaming cup.

Thea met Bram's gaze with a smiling intimacy suggesting warm summer nights. It was enough to give an independent man waking nightmares. So if he took his first gulp of tea too fast, then burned his tongue, it made sense. He manfully kept from spewing the contents as Thea ran into the kitchen, returning a moment later with a dripping ice cube in hand.

"Come on, fire safety guy. Open up. You know the cold will minimize damage." When he balked, she snipped, "My hands are clean."

For some reason, he complied and opened his mouth like a baby bird. But when Thea slid the cube onto his tongue, when their gazes tangled in an odd familiarity that kept springing up at times like this, he forgot all about the burn. Her fingers brushed his lips and an electric jolt raced along his neuron pathway to his belly and below. In a totally unconscious

120

move, she sucked the melted drops from her fingertips. One droplet got away from her sweetly pink tongue and quivered at the corner of her mouth.

The boy said, "I was hoping you'd help me with my science project, Bram."

Thank goodness for Alex. In another moment, Bram might have hauled Thea across his lap to sip the renegade water bead from her lips. He dragged his gaze from Thea's lush mouth and centered on Alex. It took an inordinate amount of energy to do so, though.

He crushed ice with his teeth and swallowed before responding. "You want my help with a science project?"

"Yep. I want to make a model, kind of like the one that guy has for our hot springs, only not so Bambi looking."

"Bambi?" Bram asked.

"A girl in Alex's English class. She wears lots of pink and lace. Poor kid even sports heels," Thea supplied.

"She paints her fingernails, too. Yuk! So what do you say, Doc?"

"I'm pretty busy. . ."

The boy took his ambivalence as a go-ahead. "I want to show how you're going to rip out all the trees and plants around Potshot, then makes these giant steps down to Eden Valley."

"Terraces," Bram clarified. Thea squeaked and Bram found himself looking into her widened eyes.

"Yep. That's what Ian called them. He said you'd be bringing in all kinds of earthmovers. Bet Potshot won't even look the same when you're done. Me and the guys can't wait. Nothing ever goes on around here *that* . . ." Alex's voice tapered off as he picked up on the tension flowing from his mother. ". . .cool."

"Alex, why don't you take your tea into your room and finish your homework." Thea's voice brooked no room for argument and Alex, smart boy that he was, picked up his mug with a muffled, "Later, Doc" to Bram. Bram wished he could go to his room, too.

Explosive silence filled the space between them. Thea finally detonated. "Terraces? Ripping out all the shrubs and trees around Potshot? When were you thinking of telling the council?"

Bram held his hands palm up. "We're cementing our plans this week."

"Cementing? As in, these are the plans, now live with them?" She whipped around and started pacing back and forth. Her hands moved in sharp actions that went with her words. "You know why we're fighting Derek's development. He plans to change Potshot into a superficial tourist trap. It isn't just that he's slime or that he ruins everything he touches. It's because we want to keep Potshot as it is. You're the one who said it, Bram. Sustainable."

She stopped in the middle of the room and faced him squarely. "Where will Potshot be once you've done what you want?"

"Safe from wildfire."

"Safe? You can't really believe that. There's no such thing as safe." Her body looked taut enough to snap in two.

He pushed both hands through his hair. "Look, I intended to talk with you about this. Tonight, even. But not like this."

"Like what?"

He gestured toward her. "You're angry and acting—"

"Betrayed? Deceived? You bet I am, Mister! Oh, *excuse me*, Doctor Youngwolf Hayes, *PhD*. And don't even pretend to know how I'm feeling." Her moist gaze brimmed. She crossed her arms, then waged a private war on her emotions. The sheen left her eyes, overtaken by battle's light.

"Well, buddy, you're here on our sufferance. We did not agree to any of your changes when we invited you here."

He cleared his throat. "That's not entirely true, Thea."

She backed away from him, feeling around for the chair behind her. Once her knees came up against it, she sank onto it. "What are you saying?"

"In our contract, Potshot agreed to our terms, which includes abiding by our findings. Right now Best Science points toward extensive environmental suppression methods. Those consist of sculpting slopes, removal of fuel from around dwellings, and building new access roads that double as firebreaks."

She wrung her hands. "We thought you meant to add sprinkler systems, wind breaks, and fire resistant building materials. In fact, when we bought the lumber for the spa, we did so with that in mind."

He studied the anguish on her face and deflected a sharp pang at having caused it. "We couldn't have been more specific without studying the area firsthand. We needed more detailed information. Computer programs and geographic information systems don't give all the   necessary facts."

Her fixed stare, which clung to his for some redeeming message, transferred to the night dark window. Bram followed her gaze to find the two of them reflected there; tragic figures beyond touching distance. Loss hit him like a mule kick to his gut.

"You have to give us some say in this, Bram." Her voice sounded distant as her regard settled on him. "This is our home. These birches, poplars, the aspens and pines you call fuel and talk about chopping down are our trees. They're our heritage and that of our children and theirs. I know every hollow and ravine on this side of the mountain. My son knows them, too. You're talking about destroying our countryside, our link to those who came before us."

Bram leaned forward, willing her to see what he did. "But Thea, we're not offering destruction. We're conferring salvation. If a monster wildfire like the one that occurred just under a hundred years ago sweeps up that valley and onto this mountain, then God help you all. You and your son and friends'll be so much tinder for the beast." He searched her face for capitulation, but saw none.

"Our surveys and data tell us you're due. We chose Potshot because we felt we could make the biggest difference here with available funds."

She shook her head. "You don't get it, do you?"

"Get what?"

"If you transform the character of a place, it stops being home. The synergy we have here in Potshot? If you mess with it, we'll fall apart. We'll lose our sense of community. Our roots will shrivel and die. That's what I'm afraid you're proposing."

She leaned forward, her elbows rested on her knees. "A fire, I know that's bad. Of course we'll do what we need to do to protect lives. But if buildings are lost, we'd rebuild. That's what community does. And you might as well know, I'll fight you all the way if your proposal looks like it'll ruin what we have here."

She stood and said, "I don't have anything more to say about it now. It's been a long day. Good night."

"I'm talking about saving lives."

"Are you? Is that really what you're trying to do? Or is that the convenient excuse that you use to give your personal demons full rein?" Her searching gaze stole his novel sense of belonging.

When she left, he wondered how his profound intent to protect the residents of Potshot could leave him feeling like an assassin. He recognized this emptiness as an old companion, much like the burn scars on his back and arm. But the hole gaped more than it had before he met Thea.

After a long day on Ricochet Mountain, prefaced by a morning on the phone with local contractors, Bram did not want to go to Salinger's gathering. He knew Ian and Challie could deliver the verdict of his team's findings. In honesty, he wasn't crazy about facing Thea after last night's debacle, but Hummingbird persisted. Besides, Bram refused to give into cowardly impulses. So here he was, decked out in a tweed sports jacket, vest, and chinos with his favorite tee shirt next to his skin.

Even the latest saying on the signboard outside the church failed to puncture his dark mood, although it practically ruptured J. D. It proclaimed:

THURSDAY NIGHT: POTLUCK SUPPER. PRAYER
AND MEDICATION TO FOLLOW.

A lavish display of wealth transformed the church basement and Tuesday bingo parlor. Music, lighting, even a plush rug had been added along with cleverly-placed partitions depicting the crown jewels of Salinger's projects. An extravagant smorgasbord traversed one wall. Citizens queued beside it. Children wormed their way into the dessert section using guerilla tactics, miraculously leaving the adults standing.

Bram's restless gaze failed to locate the person he most wanted to see. Instead, he settled his regard on the animated Derek Salinger and the maelstrom around him. Just the sight of that golden boy brought Bram's hackles to attention.

A tuxedo clad waiter stopped in front of Bram with a tray of fluted champagne glasses. He snagged one off the tray and gulped it. Then Thea and her contingent made their entrance.

Dressed as she had been at the town meeting, Thea looked dynamic in true red. Her split-sided tunic and snug leggings made him think of Xanadu; her provocative face recalled the woman of the misty hot springs. Had that only been a few nights ago? He took a step toward her, then stopped. The last person she would want to see right now was Bram. He saw the determined lift to her chin as Salinger came into her sights. Well, maybe he wasn't the *last* one on her list. Small comfort.

He watched Salinger make eye contact with Thea. Then smooth as a sidewinder, the man sauntered toward her. Bram, too, started meandering toward Thea. Why this weird protectiveness toward Thea kept cropping up, he refused to question. He knew a poisonous reptile when he saw one. Once Bram got nearer to Thea, he positioned himself behind the women buzzing around her. They served as cover while the latest scene unfolded. Meanwhile, Derek Salinger slid lethally through the space between them.

The blond man captured one of Thea's hands, placing her in the position of making a public scene to disengage. Bram wondered if he was the only one who saw how tendons in her delicate hand and wrist strained against this incursion into her personal space. He barely kept himself from responding physically. Shaking Salinger by the scruff like the bad animal he was appealed to Bram's baser instincts.

"Thea, sweetheart, why am I not surprised to see you here tonight? And with reinforcements, too." The man swept his mocking gaze over her friends and neighbors. Turning his gaze on Bram, Salinger forced Thea's hand toward his mouth where he appeared to kiss her tight-fisted knuckles. Only Bram saw that he, in fact, nipped her hand with his too white teeth.

Bram pushed closer as Thea whipped her hand away from the man, who finally broke eye contact with Bram. Color stained her cheeks as she snapped, "I see your dog-and-pony show's in full swing, Salinger. Still think you can buy the support of Potshot?"

126

Derek smiled again. He moved closer, pushing Bram's restraint to the breaking point and effectively cutting her off from her friends. "Ah, Thea, still the idealist. How can the good people of Potshot forego an offer of this caliber? Tut, tut, sweetheart, and here I thought you'd grown beyond such petty concerns. I want us to find some middle ground, truly I do. Haven't you enjoyed the bouquets I've been sending?"

Bram surprised himself, finding that he now stood at Thea's side, having missed the transition between wanting-to-be-there and acting-on-impulse. She slid him a wide-eyed look before saying, "Whoever you hired as your lackey has impeccable taste. I can't say I'm fond of pastels, though. And I always prefer my flowers with scent."

She curved her hands around Bram's closest arm and said to him, "Shall we find our seats?"

The trembling in her fingers transmitted through their contact. He offered an untouched flute of champagne to her. She declined with a violent shake of her head and he set the glass on a passing tray. They seated themselves near the front.

"I guess I should thank you for your intervention," she said in a low voice just after the mayor called the meeting to order, asking for additions to new business.

Thea's lack of enthusiasm made it clear she viewed him as the lesser of evils. "I expected your friend, Meg, to guard your flank better."

"She's still putting the finishing touches on our financial report." With another look at him, she said, "How did you. . ."

Directly behind her a man stood to be heard, interrupting her words. "See here, Mayor. I think we've got us a big problem with coyotes. Broke into my chicken coop last night and cleaned out all but one hen. My oldest, toughest bird's all that's left. Scared her so bad, I don't expect to get any eggs for a month of Sundays."

Thea snapped to rigid attention and craned her neck to

127

see who spoke. No sooner did that man state his problem than another guy farther back stood, and a few others, too. Amid reports of missing cats, a smashed bunny hutch and a goose gone astray, Bram's gaze followed Thea's, landing on a curiously still Alex near the door; an ashen-faced Alex at that.

Bram heard the last person say, "Damn, Letty, if I didn't know better, I'd say this was a feral dog. It's a might bigger and badder than any coyote I've ever run across; wily, too, with paws as big as platters. What if it starts seeing babies like Jessica's here as a snack?" The young mother in question brought her baby closer to her chest.

While the mayor reassured everyone present that she would contact the proper wildlife authorities to look into it, Bram saw Alex slip from the room. In the close seating arrangements, he felt Thea gather herself to rise, only to sink back onto her seat. Bram met her anguished expression and did the only thing he could think of: he curled his hand around hers where they lay clenched on her lap. When she gave him a searching look, he squeezed her hands gently.

The vote for Salinger's spa followed. At the request of someone from the valley, Mayor Letty passed out papers and pencils rather than take a show of hands. Afterward, she asked both the Sheriff and Deputy to gather the informal ballots. Those two disappeared behind an artist's depiction of what Potshot could be with Derek at the helm. Looking at the slick likeness made Bram grind his teeth. He figured Thea's response to be exponentially greater and wondered how she could contain her emotion behind her composed face. The bright spots of color on her cheeks along with her glassy eyes betrayed her turmoil. That and her icy fingers curled beneath his.

Bram reluctantly surrendered his seat for his presentation. At the front of the room he met Ian and Challie. His cousin hung and draped storyboards with her usual efficiency while

128

Ian adjusted the screen for computer projections. Gazing over the crowd, Bram's regard snagged on Thea time and again. Her hollow-eyed visage made him want to apologize publicly for giving this demonstration now. Taking a deep breath, he fixed on what he was here for: making the community of Potshot as fireproof as he and his team could.

After reviewing the topography that made Potshot so vulnerable to wildfire, followed by the cyclic history of blazes in the region, Bram launched into proposed solutions. Using a pointer and an aerial view, he showed the planned changes as Ian bracketed them with his computer presentation. By the end of his talk, he heard the ping of the metal spring from a pen as it bounced on the floor after Mrs. Moran twisted its barrel to the breaking point. In fact, Zechariah's mother looked none too pleased with his intentions. Another long moment passed before anyone responded to Bram's call for questions.

"If you relocate that northern access road, it'll be right in my front yard," quavered Bud Donaldson Senior's voice.

His remark opened a floodgate of debate.

"But those silver birches have been on my land since my great granddad planted them," and "How can you limit defensible space only to my house? What about my fields and livestock?"

Questions built in intensity and volume until a wall of sound blended individual voices into a roar similar to a fire's howl. Letty stood and banged her gavel for a few minutes before the sheriff retrieved his megaphone from his patrol car and brought the meeting back to order. Letty gave everyone a long moment to reseat himself or herself, but not long enough for the murmurs to build to the earlier din.

The Mayor's eagle eye settled on Bram for a heartbeat, before ranging back over her neighbors and friends. "Well, folks, it looks like we're getting one surprise after another tonight. I'd say we all need to take a deeper look into what Dr. Hayes proposes before making any decisions. I'm sure we can come to some agreement with these folks. After all, we're all on the same side." She turned to her husband, Bud, and gave him a warm and loving smile.

Riffling through papers on the table before her, she cleared her throat. "Looks like we'll have to wait for resolution on the Salinger matter, too. Sy and Dwaine counted and recounted the votes." Her hooded eyes swept the room, settling for a long and poignant moment on Thea's taut face and shoulders. A slight smile softened the older woman's stern mouth.

"Turns out we're short of a majority for setting Mr. Salinger's plans into motion. Unfortunately, the margin's close enough that we'll have to fall back to our original agreement with him. That means another vote at next month's meeting."

Another month of Salinger's special kind of persuasion. Bram practically groaned out loud.

He watched Salinger, where the man stood to one side of the room as one of his aides whispered something in his ear. Both laughed. Salinger's relaxed mode negated this as a win for Thea. If Bram had not seen the flash of tension on the man's face just seconds earlier, he would have thought this setback meant nothing to Salinger. However, he had seen the rage and suspected he knew to whom it would be directed.

Just before Letty postponed further business for another night, Meg bustled in with a sheaf of papers. She left them at the door, then waved to the mayor who nodded. "Looks like Meg's got more information about the spa, too. You can pick up copies for yourselves on your way out the door." With that, the meeting ended.

A veritable horde thronged forward to speak with Bram. He answered all questions as fully and honestly as he could before leaving them to Ian and his handouts. By then, Thea

130

was nowhere in sight, so Bram decided to head on home.

Of course, it could not be that easy. The sheriff called out to him as he strode toward his vehicle. In deference to the older man, Bram waited on the sidewalk outside the darkened bakery while Sy caught up with him. The two men nodded to each other and Bram asked, "Mind if we talk and walk?"

"Works for me."

They took a few strides before Sy said, "I usually try to give folks the benefit of a doubt, son. But as I was running some routine checks on our arsonist, I got back some disturbing information from Claremore, Oklahoma."

"I wondered how long that would take." Bram had unraveled Sy Benton's pretense at being a hick within minutes of meeting the man. Now, he said nothing more and waited for Sy to reveal his hand.

"I've grown up with most of the folks locally. Know their foibles and their strengths. Amazing the things you learn about people during a Fourth of July picnic or two. You and yours, well, I don't know you that well." Sy paused for a few steps, but not to catch his breath.

Bram waited.

"Seems the prime suspect in our arson cases might be a man who had some trouble as a fifteen-year-old orphan kid off the Cherokee reservation. The Claremore Sheriff thought maybe this boy decided to take revenge on some white folks who did some serious damage to him. Mulish youngster supposedly set fire to their smoke shack. Got real lucky with that little escapade, though, since those folks, obviously feeling contrite about how they'd beat this kid just short of meeting his maker, dropped the investigation. Guess these citizens, Benjamin and Betty Mims, pulled up stakes and put more distance between them and the reservation shortly after that." Sy led the way to Bram's Land Rover, then halted beside it.

"Was hoping you might shed some light on this story."
Sy's regard probed Bram's face beneath the illumination from
the streetlight.

Bram met the older man's gaze and said, "About that
smokehouse fire, all I know is hearsay, Sheriff. The boy's
mother and twin brother had been killed two years earlier
in a fire. In fact, he'd been burned pretty badly trying to get
them all out of the house. It seems like a stretch that the same
boy would be setting fires after that kind of event, don't you
think?"

Sy made much about pulling a toothpick out of his chest
pocket and probing his front teeth.

"That may well be, son. But human nature being as
perverse as it is, who knows? The youngster might have had
a strange tendency *toward* fire instead of *away* from it. Like a
moth to flame."

After another searing look at Bram, the Sheriff clapped
him on his shoulders and said, "Well, I'd best be getting back
to the church. My April will be fretting over where I got
myself to. See you around, son." As he turned away, he added,
"I've been hankering to see just what you grant folks do all
day. Maybe I'll be up sometime for the grand tour.

"Oh, and thanks for those shell casings from the last fire.
May help to corner the varmint responsible. Or not."

"Anytime, Sheriff," Bram said. It took discipline to calmly
fit his key into the ignition, then drive sedately from the lot.
Home, he told himself before catching the incongruity.

Home. Funny how quickly that feeling centered on Thea's
place. Hell, he had even started appreciating the sound of
wind in her chimes. Not to mention the primal colors he
considered too vivid at first. Such thoughts brought him up the
winding road to Thea's. He left his driver's side window open
to let in the full-bodied scent of sage. The full moon gave the
road a silvery finish that made he feel he drove along the

132

surface of a river.

The same moon illuminated the lethal shape of Derek Salinger's car, parked catawampus behind Thea's. As Bram's shoulders tightened, he wondered if Salinger had intentionally blocked Thea's escape route with his vehicle. Slamming the door as he leapt from his own haphazardly parked truck, he worked hard to contain his fury. As he strode toward the house, Bram used every technique his grandfather had taught him about conquering anger. He turned ice-cold as he approached the house and the furious voices near the front door.

". . .my son! You signed the papers, too." Thea's husky voice nearly spit out the words.

"Yes. But those papers said nothing about me deciding to claim my rights as his father," countered Salinger.

"Father! Try *sperm donor*."

"Maybe so. But now I'm ready to exercise my rights as a father unless. . ."

"Unless I submit to your plans for Potshot? Over my dead body." The timbre of Thea's voice gave a sense of finality to her words. It made Bram shiver, even enclosed by his icy rage as he was.

Soft-footed, Bram stepped into the yellow circle of light surrounding the entryway. His presence at Salinger's back became known only when Thea's flickering gaze announced it. She nodded to him with a stiff jerk of her head, "Bram."

Salinger whirled around, just short of a panicked spin. Practically nose-to-nose then, it was the other man who stepped back. "What the hell! Can't you see we're having a private conversation here?"

"You want this guy here, Thea?" Bram asked, all the while fixing the blond man in his sights.

"No. No, I don't."

Bram barely nodded. "You heard her. Leave."

133

"Now wait just a minute. . ."

Even though the two men stood at a height, Bram reached out and ever so gently grasped Salinger by the lapels before lifting him enough to bring him closer. "The lady said leave."

The man's hands closed around Bram's wrists in a futile attempt to loosen his hold. When that didn't work, Salinger must have realized how absurd he looked, dangling like a rubber chicken from a pole. Ridiculous was just what Bram had been going for, too, knowing how this guy would never stomach such an image.

Salinger went still and with a deadly glint in his eyes, he said, "Enough. I'm going."

Bram released him with such alacrity that the man staggered before catching his balance. Salinger shrugged his silk jacket back onto his shoulders and shot his cuffs before turning toward Thea. "We're not finished with this. Not by a long shot."

He shouldered by Bram on his way down the steps. Bram didn't bother watching Salinger. He recognized an enemy's retreat when he saw it. Instead he focused on Thea's face, where the strain of the last few hours made for sunken cheeks and eyes. Her normally full mouth thinned and tucked into a downward curve.

Her regard remained glued on Salinger until his car roared down the drive, then she lifted her chin and met Bram's look. "Thanks."

Bram shrugged. "What are tenants for?"

"Indeed." A grim smile touched her lips.

When she started down the stairs, Bram said, "Whoa. Where are you off to now?"

Seemingly reluctant, Thea paused outside the light's range. With a deep exhalation she said, "Alex isn't home. His friends said he took off midway through the meeting."

Bram spun on his heels and caught up with her in two

strides as she headed for the path around the house. She made no comment about his company, but moved over to share the stone walk. Bram took that as consent. They crossed the creek and went halfway to the baths before she spoke.

"I'm used to fighting my own battles, Bram."

They walked a few paces before he said, "Me, too. But turning down help against a bully is pure stupidity. I don't see you as stupid, Thea."

"That's something, I suppose." She sighed and stopped. "Why? Why are you helping me like this? I'm dead set against your proposal for Potshot. You're doing this—helping me—won't change my mind."

He halted, hearing frustration beneath her tirade. After a moment, he said, "I'd never use your problems for my own gain. I got involved because I wanted to, because it was the right thing to do. I have a Grandfather who'd disown me for less."

Admitting his involvement made him feel exposed, even shy before her. Those feelings conflicted with his urge to lean forward and test the softness of her mouth with his. Instead, he held himself rigid under her scrutiny. He thanked all the Beings for the cover of darkness. Although the full moon gave its own illumination, it obscured facial expressions.

She hesitated, then nodded and began walking again. He fell in behind her. It took about twenty minutes to reach the pools at the pace Thea set. Once they got there, she called out to her son. On the second summons, two dark forms, one tall and the other much shorter, broke away from the new construction to one side of the first pool.

A gravelly-voiced man broke the stalemate. "Over here, Thea."

"Jake? Is that you?" she asked.

"None other." The two shadow forms walked closer and met Thea and Bram midway toward the pool. The shorter figure resolved itself into Alex.

"Me and the boy were having a little heart-to-heart before I escorted him down to your place. Sorry to worry you."

Thea put her hands on Alex's shoulders as she peered into his face. "You scared the devil out of me, Alex. Don't ever do this again."

He hung his head. "Well, I'm sorry I scared you. But none of this would've happened if you'd believe me about Zorro."

"Zorro?" his mother asked.

"My wolf." Alex lifted his chin in a gesture Bram associated with Thea at her fighting best. The boy sounded as contrite as a fox with a hen in his mouth.

Chapter Eight

Thea's nemesis, the specter of Derek Salinger, invaded her refuge. Edgy and out-of-sorts, she wandered toward her son's room, noticing ominous darkness in places where she usually found comfort. Even the ordinary act of tucking Alex into bed felt strange.

The reading light by her son's bed cast her adrift in the surrounding gloom. She leaned across his island of a bed and smoothed the coverlet over him, barely restraining herself from cuddling Alex close, burying her face in his mussed hair. From experience, she knew to expect scents of sunshine and sage. The active boy smell might erase the lingering unpleasantness of Derek's expensive cologne along with phantom odors of stale beer and fermented grapes, vomit and cigarettes. She straightened from kissing her sleeping son. Her silhouette leapt from coverlet to wall, making her jump.

"Spooked by your own shadow. Shame on you, Thea MacTavish," she murmured, wanting to laugh it off along with the ugly memories haunting her. She ached to linger by her son's bed and ensure his safety. Instead, she recognized her own cowardice in the deceit of turning toward her child for comfort. As Thea waded through his clothes, she stopped herself from prolonging her time in the room by picking up after Alex. She switched off the light.

Once in the hallway, the clatter of stoneware drew her. "Oh, boy, what now?"

Having a man knocking about her home frazzled her

nerves. At the kitchen door, she amended that thought. Before her stood a man with the unlikely family name of 'Youngwolf'. *Fuchsia,* but his name suited him, too. Like a wolf, he exuded poise and competence, regardless of his surroundings. The shadows nipping at her heels receded in his presence.

As usual, Bram did the unexpected, setting two mugs of steaming tea on the counter. "You're just full of surprises. No man's ever made tea for me before. I hope this doesn't amount to fraternizing with the enemy."

"I'm not your enemy, Thea."

She edged nearer and bent to inhale the aroma; apple cinnamon, her favorite. Were none of her rituals safe from this meddlesome guy? His woodsy scent wafted to her, setting off a thrill not unlike the steep descent of a roller coaster. *Not now*, she warned her body.

Yet, Thea remained so newly awakened to carnal possibilities that she felt raw. In defense, she removed bags from both cups and plopped them into the compost tub beneath her sink. She dribbled honey into her mug and started for the back door. A glance over her shoulder gave her a view of Bram, leaning casually against the counter. "Join me?"

"Sure."

Speed and grace, Bram Youngwolf Hayes moved like his namesake. She held her breath until he reached her side, then gulped fresh air like a miner too long in the hole. If he found anything odd in his landlady's tendency to gasp around him, he didn't mention it. How could she feel so safe yet so precarious around this man? Thea eased into the blessed anonymity of the porch, using darkness to cloak her confusion.

"I'll get the light," he said.

"No, don't. Please. I prefer moonlight."

So they settled on the top step, hip-to-hip, knee-to-knee. As the teacup's warmth penetrated Thea's chilly hands, Bram's body heat permeated her entire right side. It felt good, this sharing of warmth. Primal and necessary, even life-sustaining. Yet another assault on her well-armored heart. That Bram appreciated the elemental allure of silence appealed to her.

Relative silence, she corrected. For here on this spring night, any number of nocturnal critters scurried and stalked about their business. As Thea watched, uncanny eyes caught moonlight in their depths, glittering deep within underbrush. Considering her day, the mountain's nightlife should have felt more hostile, a glut of lions-and-tigers-and-bears, oh, my! But with this man at her side, she basked in Bram's restful companionship until moonlight resolved the landscape into a monochrome, varying shades of charcoal punctuated by muted silver. Persistent scents of sun-heated sages and mint saturated the air.

She said, "It's easy to forget how rich the world can be without color."

"From your house and what you wear, I figured you're pretty keen on color."

Thea shifted a little, uncomfortable beneath his scrutiny—and his insight. "Actually, when I first started sketching, charcoal was my favorite medium. I still like to play with it, stark as it can be. Like this landscape."

"Huh. Well, I suppose I'm partial to moonlight myself." They sipped. A high-pitched blast echoed overhead as a bat flashed across the moon's face.

Thea's delight bubbled into laughter. "See that strong, steady flight? Probably one of the brown bats I've seen roosting in an old pine upslope of us. Lightning clobbered the tree the summer my stepfather struck it rich in uranium. The year I turned sixteen." She sighed. "I got caught skinny-dipping with the valley kids that day. My mother grounded me for life."

"For life, huh? Doesn't seem to have slowed you down a whole lot."

"If that was an obscure reference to my headstrong nature, it's a fact that punishment never works on me. Poor Mother and Charles."

Bram chuckled, sending an intense and sensual frisson down her spine. He said, "I can appreciate your come-hell-or-high water attitude, Thea. Done that myself. It's the skinny-dipping I'm stuck on." His voice roughened toward the end.

She leaned forward, trying without success to read his expression. The recent memory of being naked-in-the-hot-springs with Bram made her flush. She wondered if his memory of the incident flashed his blood to a rolling boil, too. *Best to defuse that right now*. The last thing her revived libido needed was any more fuel. She had begun to think she suffered from early symptoms of spontaneous combustion herself. "Was that prurient interest, Bram? Or scientific curiosity?"

"Why, I'm motivated by pure science, Thea. Specific gravity in a heat sink and all."

"I see. Prurient then."

"Absolutely. Although I do find myself most interested in your pigheadedness. Specifically in how it's probably gotten you into more trouble than a shoat in quicksand."

"A shoat being a baby pig?"

"More of a newly weaned piglet, but let's just stick to the subject. About your pigheadedness. . ."

"I'm game, if you'll agree to table any discussions about your proposed changes to Potshot. I'd much rather talk philosophy, Bram."

"I'm all ears."

Other than his earlobes, which definitely held promise, Thea considered that an exaggeration. Especially after seeing him in wet cut-offs, hung low on his hips. Thankful again for the cover of darkness, she dragged her attention away from her sizzling inner vision of Bram unclad. "Okay. Values. So, are you a big accumulator of material goods?"

"Not big, no. I like nice things. A good efficient vehicle, a clean living space, warm in winter and cool in summer. Have to admit, I do appreciate my gadgets, which I suppose you could blame on my scientific turn of mind and all. But I suppose, no, I'm not big on hoarding. Can get to be a burden, lugging stuff around. Or worrying about it when I'm away, which I am. A lot."

His last admission clanged a warning. The smooth lip of the cup drew her fingers into an endless caress. The earthenware was warm and satiny—like Bram's skin. Her mind leapt from the thought like a startled deer. "So you're a traveling kind of guy. Here today, gone tomorrow."

"You make me sound like an old Fuller Brush man. In fact I'm a scientist, Thea, and I go where my science takes me. I'm also not by nature easily distracted, which means you owe me."

"Owe you?"

"An explanation. Are you a mad stasher, a died-in-the-wool capitalist?"

She considered. "I do like to have extra paints and canvases on hand. And I usually buy food in quantity, at least ever since having Alex. But I don't think I'm a crazed consumer, which isn't to say it wouldn't be fun to have extra money socked away for, oh—new sneakers for Alex. I don't do name brands, though. No one has ever died from lack of brand name clothing—at least I don't think so."

"Take my word for it; no one has." His voice held a smile.

She regarded him, an impenetrable shadow with moon's silver playing over his cheekbones and straight nose. "I just hope this lean time doesn't become a pivotal chapter in my son's life. You know, the one he tells his psychiatrist about after living an unfulfilled life."

"Alex is an intelligent kid. He won't hold this against you."
His rich voice coiled around her.

"That's sweet of you to say, Bram. Yet again, there goes
your tough-guy reputation. But what you're really hearing
is guilt. Things're stretched now because of my decision to
paint. Poor Alex. At least I have my career-in-waiting. In case
I'm as delusional as I sometimes think I am about my abilities
as an artist."

"You? Delusional? I don't think so. Definitely quirky."

"Quirky?" she countered.

He shrugged. "It's not like Alex goes hungry or unclothed.
I've never seen anyone so eager to explore his environment. A
kid's got to be well-grounded to do that."

Thea squashed down old sadness as an animal shrieked in
the distance.

"Raccoons fighting," she whispered.

Resting her chin on a fist, she said, "I want so much
for Alex, Bram. To instill in him a sense of adventure and
hopefulness with enough courage and self-esteem to follow
where his path takes him. So many people get worn down and
accept the dregs. I mean, look at my mother. For her, Charles
represented a material success she believed that she'd never
reach on her own."

"What about your dad?"

"Like Alex, I was a natural child. Mom says my father
went MIA in Vietnam just before the withdrawal; she claims
she wouldn't have married him anyway." She pondered that
for a few moments. "I guess the man didn't submit to her
ideas of the good life."

Bram gulped tea before saying, "A lot of people don't
cotton to scraping by. No fault in that. I wouldn't live on the
Rez for anything, though I do like to help out when and where
I can."

142

"I get that, but my mother's answer to everything is money. She always aspired to bigger and greater things than Potshot had to offer. I don't follow her ethics, but I can accept them. As long as they're not pushed in my face too often. Her last big decision was to convert her concrete driveway to marble. Evidently, you can't park your Bentley on ordinary concrete. Can you imagine?" She laughed to cover the hitch in her voice. "She set up trusts for me and Alex, which I haven't dipped into. Yet."

"Why? What're you afraid of?"

"Selling out, I guess. Let's just say I've seen how money corrupts. Besides, I want my life to be my own."

"Beholden to no one," Bram supplied.

"Exactly."

Again, quiet reigned. Farther up Ricochet Mountain, a rockslide crashed and echoed. Both of them sat straighter, looking toward the peak through the gloaming.

"That sounds like Jackrabbit Slip, about a mile up and east. It's always rearranging itself."

"Wild place you've got yourself here, Thea. Makes my condo in Norman, Oklahoma appear downright tame."

"The mountain's always changing. It's one of the I things I love about living here."

Time wove a shining filament between them until Bram spoke. "It's tough choosing such a different path from your parent. My grandfather's a member of the Keetoowah Society. They follow traditional Cherokee ways. The Band's predominantly full bloods. You can just imagine how well I fit into that."

She tried to see his face, got a sense of solidness and calm. "That prophesy fulfillment thing can be an easy trap."

He laughed. "You'd be surprised. Grandfather calls me 'Searcher'. Always looking over the next horizon. But my brother Eric loved the old ways. One of my cousins, Jay Eagle of the Stilway branch, took him under his wing—no pun intended. With Grandfather's blessing, of course."

"Was that a good thing?"

"For my brother it was. Jay's still involved in the WhitePath Foundation, teaching Cherokee language, keeping it living and vital. He's ten years older than me. Ten years older than my twin would have been."

His voice rang hollow and Thea gripped her mug harder to keep from reaching out to him. "Would have been?"

"Eric died. A ceremonial fire that got away from him."

She did touch him then. Her fingers curled around his forearm as she tried to ignore his heat and tensile strength while offering comfort. "I'm so sorry, Bram. I've heard that twins are even closer than other siblings."

His stillness made her ache. "Not a day passes when I don't miss him. But other than looks, we weren't that similar. Eric followed the old ways, a member of AIM."

"AIM?"

"American Indian Movement. By the time Jay inserted himself into my brother's life, Grandfather had just about accepted our mixed blood. He also believed that we could still be saved from further disgrace by learning Cherokee ways."

"And you didn't."

"I'm a scientist. I've followed where my curiosity and inclinations led, not necessarily where my grandfather wanted."

Thea scuffed her bare feet on the step. "Boy, does that sound familiar. Mother won't stop trying to bring me back into the fold either." She tried for lightness, failing miserably as she withdrew her hand from his arm. After a moment, she smiled into the darkness. Her battle with her mother was so old and inconsequential compared to the death of a sibling. In truth, the conflict with mother barely caused a twinge anymore.

144

Bram's hand covered hers, where she gripped her knee. His touch felt alive and full of promise. . . . "You've found your own way, Thea. You live a full, rich life."

"And you're not ready to go screaming into the night from all the craziness?" She asked.

His hand curled around hers as she turned her palm up to accommodate him. His cup met the porch step with a hollow clunk. Something swirled in the dark around them, smoky and hot. Mouth dry, Thea recognized passion.

Bram's voice brimmed with it. "You're so alive."

She swallowed hard. "And you're not?" When he withdrew his hand from hers, she recaptured it.

He said, "Instead of folding up, you attack. An unscrupulous developer and blackmailer; even. . ."

When he hesitated, she nudged him. "Even?" She could barely see his face in the natural lighting: strong brow ridge, shadowed eyes, slanted cheekbones, firm mouth and chin.

"Even drawing a line in the sand against me. Fighting to save your community. I don't know too many people who'd give a shoat's snout about that." He paused, this time leaning closer to her face in the silvery light. His eyes reflected the moon's glow, his lips beckoned. "Thea, why can't you agree to my proposal?"

"I'm willing to negotiate. Are you?"

He laughed, full-throated and long. "You just won't give up. Didn't your mother teach you the art of subterfuge?"

Before she could answer, he leaned forward and, capturing her face in his free hand, he brushed his lips against her forehead. He shifted to rest his forehead against hers. "Can't you see I only want to protect you and Potshot?"

He rubbed his cheek against first one side of her face, then the other. Apple-spiced breath glanced off her cheek and ear. Shivers stole down her arms at the barely perceptible scratch of whiskers against her skin.

"I think you want to, Bram—I really do." His lips skimmed the curve of her chin along her jaw to her ear. She gasped, gripping his hand harder. "But—but I don't think—you're seeing—the balance you need—to have in the process."

His lips came within a heartbeat of hers. She let loose her heavy mug, which rolled with a *thunk* to the next step. Thea lifted her hand to his face. "Oh, fuchsia, Bram! Will you just kiss me?" She pulled his head toward hers so he would neither argue nor retreat again.

And oh, my. What a kiss.

By the time they parted for air, she sprawled halfway across his lap. One of his arms looped around her ribs, while the other supported her upper back as his fingers stroked— stroked her neck. Exquisite.

She relaxed her hold and loosely coiled her arms around his middle; that taut, firm middle she had covertly watched from Day One. As their breathing normalized, somewhat, Thea lolled her head against Bram's shoulder. From this perspective, moonlight struck lush glints off his hair and eyes. She sat like that until she gathered enough resolve from her seemingly boneless body to scoot over and sit on the step.

She finally said, "Wow, tell me you didn't see that coming?"

"I didn't. What's next?"

Luscious shivers. Thea leaned forward to retrieve her fallen cup, cradling the unbroken crockery between her palms, mostly to keep her treacherous hands occupied. "This is not a good idea, Bram."

"You thought so a moment ago."

"You're supposed to agree with me." At his silence, she faced him. "Bram? Tell me that you don't think this is a good idea."

He reached out to stroke a lock of hair off her cheekbone. "Can't do that, Thea. Feels too good not to be right."

"Great." She turned away and studied the moonscape. "Well, it's too much for me."

"How so?"

Mental bricks built a wall separating her from her body's yearning. She named each one. "First I'm trying to assess this feral wolf who's bonded with my child. Then, there's Salinger's move to wrest custody of my son from me. Let's not even talk about Derek's campaign to turn Potshot into Disneyland-with-a-Vengeance. That doesn't touch on getting the spa built before summer, when, I might add, my paintings have to be done." She paused for an enormous breath. "Now I have to fight my own body's attempt to make me into your sex slave."

His hand kept doing this delicious rubbing thing along her neck and upper back. "Sex slave? I can live with that. You know, I'd like a beer. I've a six-pack in my rig. Get you one?"

Beer. Just one—she shot him a harried look. "Thanks. Thanks a lot. Now I can add staying sober to the list." With that she clambered to her feet and headed into the dark house.

Bram followed her inside. Once at the sink, she flicked the light on and started scrubbing her abused mug with excessive force. Bram firmly, but gently, took the cup from her before turning off the water.

"Thea?" When he leaned down to see her face, she silently cursed the shorn hair that gave her no cover from his intense look. "We're going to talk."

"About?"

"We could start with staying sober."

She scrunched her eyes closed. "You have no idea."

"That's right. So help me out."

Charged silence. "Why? What ever happened to your staying out of my personal life? You know, the Youngwolf Hayes' *Rules of Detachment*?"

"I changed my mind."

147

"What if I haven't?"

"Oh, you've changed all right."

"What on earth gives you that idea?"

"This." He pulled her close and lowered his mouth to hers, let his lips do the talking. Inquisitive, warm, and devouring all at once, his kiss enticed her into compromise, softened her defenses and won her over to his side.

She pulled away, but in a languorous way. "All right." Then, less breathlessly, "All right. You're probably the only one in town who doesn't know anyway." Even then, she could barely bring herself to begin.

Thea let him maneuver her toward the living room. Bram stopped in front of the couch and pressed her to sit. Settling beside her, he sat close enough so that she breathed in his woodsy scent as his body heat curled around her. She clasped her hands between her knees.

"Well, to make a long story short, I'm a recovering alcoholic. Fourteen years on the wagon." She turned to him on the last, expecting to see a look of distaste on his face. It wasn't there. Only an aspect of waiting, open and nonjudgmental, met her gaze.

When the silence spun into a longer thread, he said, "I'm hardly a stranger to alcoholism, Thea. On the Rez, it's endemic."

"Well, it's a big deal in Potshot. Just not done. Especially when you're a girl who starts drinking at thirteen."

"I've known younger."

"Fuchsia, you're making this too easy, Bram."

"I didn't know it was supposed to be hard." He brushed his lips against her forehead and she closed her eyes.

"It started on the sly. You know, refilling depleted decanters with water. Mother and Charles put my weird mood swings down to hormones. Sheer youth gave me great resistance to hangovers, but I was a mess. I drank more and

148

more all the way through high school." She opened her eyes, staring into his, fierce and honest as a hawk.

"Yet you got through high school."

"Surprised me, too. I even managed to get my associates degree through an integrated program with the university, then graduated early on top of that. When I went away to college, I did really well on the entrance exams and skipped even more basics."

"You did this all under the influence. I'm impressed."

"Don't be. That was when I first really tried to get my drinking under control. I finished my bachelor's in a year, which I guess gives you an idea of how much I loved my art. I still drank socially, though. I liked the easy chemical high, the not having to work within myself to feel good."

"Yet you're sober now, Thea. Fourteen years says a lot about who you are."

She turned away from him, caught more in the past than present. "Derek Salinger came into my life during my first year into my master's program. He needed a tutor."

Thea's laugh sounded like a raven's caw. She swallowed hard. "A tutor. Anyway, I needed the cash and he had plenty of that. With him came the party life. At nineteen years old, I was out drinking all night, then back in class the next day. Since I was in the master's program, it was easy to make up for lost time by pulling occasional all-nighters. Again, blessed youth, but my work began to suffer. Actually, that's a huge understatement. My work became nonexistent."

Coming to her feet, she walked toward the dark window, barely noticing the reflected interior of her house. "That really scared me. So I told Derek he'd have to find another tutor. He refused. Said he'd fallen hard and couldn't live without me. Couldn't live without me—and yet he lives."

Bram's strong arms wrapped around her. His solid chest touched her back as she said, "I, ah, I guess I was infatuated with him or at least with the idea of love. Too screwed up to know any better. He did the whole courtship thing. Flowers, expensive gifts, the best booze money could buy. Still, I didn't want to go to bed with him. If that doesn't validate intuition, I don't know what does." Old bitterness colored her words.

"You pulled out of your nose dive, though," he said, pulling her more firmly into his embrace.

It felt so good to be held like this. So right. "Meg became my advisor. Helped me get into a program. Without her I don't know how I'd have made it."

"You did it, though." Thea relaxed, sinking into the man's strength until he said, "I don't want to let go of you. But if we do much more of this, I won't go to my bed. It'll be yours or nothing. I don't think that's a good choice right now." Regret deepened his voice.

He led her toward the couch. "So let's compromise. How 'bout we sit on the couch for a while. Just until you're okay and I'm ready to let you go." He kissed the top of her head.

Her reluctance to release him felt solid as any wall. She followed him onto the sofa, gravitating toward him. Bram pulled the afghan from the back and draped it over them. Thea leaned into his chest and his heartbeat soothed her. His scent reminded her of the forest in high summer, when sun freed the scent of resins. His chambray shirt felt soft against her cheek as she watched natural light transform the parquet floor into an illusive moonlit stream. Bram's breath became the wind in the pines. She closed her eyes, just for a moment.

Thea awoke to the echo of the front door closing. A blanket pillowed her face. Where the knitted cotton remained warm from his body, she smelled Bram. She struggled to sit in a room tinted apricot by morning sunlight. The roar of Bram's rig coming to life brought her to her feet and she stumbled to

150

the window only to see his vehicle disappear around the bend.

Wrapped in the afghan, Thea mumbled, "Great. I just spent the night on my couch with my tenant." She couldn't quell her contentment, though. Never mind her head-to-toe blush at their remembered kisses.

Thank goodness for Alex, she decided, as he scuffled into the hallway. "What's for breakfast, Mom?"

"How about pancakes?"

"And blueberry syrup?"

"Why not?"

"And bacon?"

"Don't push your luck, buddy." She even got a kiss and hug before he remembered his hands-off policy and hustled back into the bedroom to dress for school.

An hour later she parked in the lot below the spa. It took long minutes for her to register what she saw as she crawled out of her Honda. Pivoting slowly to take in the tent city crouching like a mushroom patch just above the spa parking lot, she tried to get her bearings. Winter camouflage fabric did nothing to disguise the temporary housing. She glanced at two Honey Buckets before letting her regard settle on the changing rooms' new roof. Thea wondered if she had pulled a Rip Van Winkle and slept away more than a night on Bram's brawny chest.

Meg walked into view. "Althea! I'm so glad you decided to stop by and see our progress. I honestly could not describe to you how much of a difference our new crew has made."

"Whoa, Meg! Where'd all these people come from? Do they know how little we can afford to pay them?" She met her friend at the trailhead.

Meg stepped briskly onto the path, pea gravel crunching underfoot. "Of course. Give me some credit."

Thea lunged to catch up. "But I count twelve tents. How—no, *where,* did you find that many workers willing to work practically *gratis*?"

"Why in Reno and Carson City, just as we discussed. Jake knew quite a few citizens who were more than willing to lend a hand. In fact, we had the devil of a time winnowing the interested parties into a small enough crew. I must say, I felt terrible employing only the few we have."

That stopped Thea cold. "Really. Who are they, then? Those tents look military. Don't tell me you got the National Guard to help?"

Meg continued up the hill in her methodical way. "Not the National Guard, no."

Again Thea hurried to catch her. "Not migrant workers, I hope. If you'll remember, we decided early on not to take advantage of immigrants."

Meg's serene profile gave nothing away. "We've plenty of diversity, that's for certain."

"Are you being purposely obtuse, Meg? You are. Well, just stop right now and let's put all our cards on the table." Thea planted herself firmly in front of her friend.

"Oh, Althea, you do have a tendency toward theatrics. You're so steadfast most of the time, I forget about your artistic tendencies." Still, Meg's face took on a rosy hue and Thea knew the exuberant color came neither from exertion nor the morning sun.

The younger woman crossed her arms and started tapping her foot.

Meg's chin lifted as she walked around her. Thea threw up her hands in defeat. "Please Meg. Just tell me. How bad can it be?"

Meg's face lit up with her enthusiasm. "It's not bad at all, my dear. They're homeless vets! I'm so excited about this. You know we've always bemoaned the fact that so many people live on the streets in our cities. And now, we actually get to do something concrete about it." Whatever the librarian

152

saw on Thea's face made her pick up the pace. "You've been so busy lately, I didn't want to stress you further. So when Jake offered his suggestion, I researched the viability and now—now we have our labor force."

Thea stopped when Meg did, which gave them both a clear view of the new construction. If Salinger had his way, his plans would eradicate this progress. To calm herself, she inhaled saw-heated wood and pine scent. Her gaze wandered over the building, gratified by the elegant sweep of the structure. Sounds of power tools and hammers overlaid her heart's rhythm. She wondered if somewhere on the mountain, Bram heard what she did. The thought gave her a sense of immediate connection and recalled their kisses. Closing her eyes, she relived the evening until a solid baritone rose in song, weaving into the cacophony. She opened her eyes.

"That sounds like opera."

"From *Carmen*, I believe. Our electrician has a wonderful voice, doesn't he? And the woman who plasters and does the dry wall has a lovely soprano."

Thea ran her hands through her hair, stopping along the way to massage her tight scalp. "Please tell me our insurance covers them?"

"No problem, my dear. Despite the insurance company's unwillingness to settle our arson losses, we're fully covered for anyone on-site."

"Unless we have another arson," Thea said. "Meg, are these people—capable of making decisions about employment? I mean are they. . ."

Meg gave her a humorous look. "Crazy? No more than you and me. They're mostly coping with symptoms of posttraumatic stress disorder, which makes them marginal, I suppose. Jake and I *are* ensuring that the ones who need medication have it."

"So they're not forced labor. I mean, Jake didn't strong-arm them into working for us and drag them up here against their will. . ."

Meg's laughter interrupted her. "Althea, you've such a dry wit. That Jake might force anyone against his or her will—I don't think so. But why don't you come and meet them? Ask them any questions you might have."

Following Meg's lead, Thea spent the next hour doing just that. She met the electrician, the plumber, the cabinetmaker, a cement mason, and a tile setter. The drywall worker, she of the fine soprano voice, had temporarily stepped out. What Thea learned about their work experience knotted her belly. For each of them came from careers no further away from the streets than Thea herself. A former CEO, a professor, a mother, a cellist. *Butcher, baker, candlestick maker*, she finished in a nonsensical rhyme that did little to ease personal concerns.

"We're all just a month or two away from the streets, aren't we, Meg?"

"If that," her friend agreed.

"None of the crew seems particularly set on one task."

"Yes, they're willing to lend a hand to any colleague in need. No task too menial—or too lofty."

Glancing up, Thea noted three men—oops, make that two men and one woman—in the rafters. She winced. "Better them than me." The only one who gave her pause was the electrician, who sported head-to-toe tattoos. Or so Thea suspected, since the man was clad in coveralls and a T-shirt.

Meg noticed her preoccupation. "Our professor of anthropology. Couldn't get tenure, wouldn't you know? He has some lovely tribal tattoos, many from New Guinea evidently." Meg and Thea wound down their tour with Jake in tow. On higher ground, Thea beheld Ricochet Hot Springs and Mud Baths from a bird's-eye view. She settled on a convenient rock, folding her arms around her knees. Her

154

gaze ranged upward, hoping for an illicit glimpse of Bram. Catching herself, she focused on the project at hand.

"Are they getting enough to eat?" She asked.

Jake chuckled. "Kind of a lean bunch, eh? But we're being wined-and-dined. Between the Bodeens and Peabody's club, Meg keeps our larder full."

"Certainly. To be truthful, my dear, Jake and I decided it might be best to limit interaction between our citizens and the workforce. At least in the beginning."

"That makes sense." Thea captured Jake's dark-eyed gaze. "Over time, I suppose we can counter any misconceptions our neighbors might have."

Jake's eyes narrowed a little. "From the Illustrated Man on down, none of these folks present any danger, Thea. They're unfortunates, fallen on tough times." He turned away, stuffing his hands into jean pockets while he surveyed his domain. "These folks're all artisans—and veterans looking for a fresh start. Just like the bulk of humanity. Might surprise you to know this group represents four wars-worth of cannon fodder: Vietnam, the Gulf Wars, and even one old-timer from Korea."

"Jake, I didn't mean to put you on the defensive. It's just that Potshot's a small town with a village mentality. The residents aren't used to homeless people. They may be fearful of what they don't understand. And with our recent bout of arson fires, it would be easy to blame outsiders."

The older man nodded. "And I suppose some of my crew have obsessions and compulsions the good people of Potshot wouldn't be entirely comfortable with. But these folks do good work. All for a cot and three squares a day. No alcohol. No drugs except those prescribed by a doctor."

Thea rubbed her forehead against her knees. "I'm sorry, Jake. Meg. But even I feel uneasy when confronted with people who live so close to the edge. I'm not so far removed from the streets as I'd like, especially right now."

"You're not the only one, my dear." Meg dropped an arm over her shoulders.

She took a deep breath, which felt like the first in over an hour. "The craftsmanship is exceptional. They're doing a great job."

"That they are," Jake agreed

She got to her feet. "Meg, what do you say we put together a bazaar at the Church. We could ease our neighbors into this more gently that way. Besides, it looks to me like our workers could use other choices in clothing. Unless body art counts as attire."

Meg giggled, covering her mouth like a girl. When she could, she said, "Sounds like a grand idea, Althea. I'll discuss it with the minister."

Jake nodded. "Ladies, I'd best be heading back to work. We're right on schedule and I want to keep us going that way."

Before he walked more than a few steps, Thea said, "Thank you, Jake. For everything. This spa means a lot to Potshot and Eden Valley."

His inscrutable gaze met hers. "Means a lot to all of us, Thea."

To Thea's right, a piercingly sweet call announced a diving kestrel as it swooped for a kill. The nimble hawk missed its strike and flashed into the sun. Thea followed its progress and by the time she turned back, Jake was striding down the hill. She rubbed her arms.

"Boy, did I come across as a bigot or what?"

"Not really, just a woman close to the precipice. And honestly, Thea, doesn't the spa fairly take your breath away?"

Her smile widened. "It does. Even better than I'd hoped and it looks like we'll meet our opening date after all."

"I'm sure of it. Has that scoundrel Salinger been in further contact with you?"

Thea let out a long breath. "He stopped by last night and caused a scene. He's threatening to sue for custody." She gulped a heavy stone of dread before continuing. "Of course, if I support his plans for the spa, that all goes away."

Meg slid an arm around her ribs and squeezed. "He won't get away with any of his shenanigans, Thea. We'll see to that."

Thea managed a nod as Meg asked, "Now to move into warmer climes, how is your stint as landlady progressing?"

Blood flooded Thea's face. "Well enough, I suppose." *Oh, and Meg, did you know I'm leaning toward becoming my tenant's sex-slave?*

Her friend chuckled, making Thea wonder if she spoke aloud after all. "I just realized what an evil laugh you have, Meg."

"Oh, come now, there's nothing evil about biology in action."

"Unless you're caught in the equivalent of a riptide," Thea muttered.

"That's why we have hormones, dear. Otherwise the species would dwindle to nothing and then where would we be?"

"Extinct?" Thea looked with longing down the mountain.

Meg's curious regard practically scorched. "You needn't sound so buoyed by such a dire event. Now tell me what your problem is with the braw laddie." Evidently ready for a long heart-to-heart, Meg settled onto the rock vacated by Thea.

Well, why not. Thea plunked down beside her. "You mean aside from Bram's harrowing plans for Potshot?"

Meg waved a negligent hand. "Completely surmountable from my perspective."

"Really? How so?"

"He's a man craving a connection, Althea. You're a woman with her fingers on the pulse of our community. I know he's only a man, dear, but who better to awaken him to the soul of Potshot than you?"

Thea sighed. "I thought you had a solution."

"I do. And once you put your fine mind to the task, I'm sure you'll see what I mean." Meg slipped an arm through hers. "For now, though, I'm dying to hear about the other—barriers—he presents to your peace of mind."

"Well, to start with, he's unpredictable. And stubborn. Oh, and self-righteous. Probably worst of all, he's *gorgeous*."

"He is that, my dear."

"I suppose the thing that's most annoying is. . ."

"Yes?"

"Oh, Meg, I *like* him. I really like him."

Meg squeezed her arm. "Now that does present a problem."

Thea only nodded.

After a time, Meg said, "I admit, I expected more in the way of comings and goings, the way you blushed earlier."

Thea avoided her friend's gaze. In a small voice, she said, "As usual, you're right. Last night, he—he kissed me."

Silence greeted her proclamation, so she continued. "I mean, 'kiss' doesn't even begin to describe it. One moment I was sitting on the back steps, just talking; the next I was lounging across his lap. I don't even remember getting there. I've turned into a lap slut!" The last came out as a wail.

Meg's shoulder jerked against her. *I've driven my best friend to tears of sympathy*. However, when Thea met Meg's regard, she saw a face brimming with laughter.

"Meg, you traitor."

The librarian moved from repressed laughter to hoots. After what seemed an eon she finally lowered the decibel level to a soft chuckle as she wiped tears from her eyes. Thea planted her chin in her palms and ignored the outburst.

Finally Meg wrapped an arm around her. "Oh, Thea,

158

loosen up."

Thea gave her a quelling look only to see Meg's merriment building again. "Don't you dare . . ."

All to no avail. Meg's laughter rang down the mountainside. Her friend's hilarity aside, Thea wondered if Bram held the cure for what Derek Salinger had done to her fourteen years ago.

Chapter Nine

The imminence of summer weighed in with lengthening days. As Thea painted the final brush stroke on the canvas, Meg's advice clicked into place. Maybe this happened because her block to painting heroes had shredded like wind-blown fog or perhaps it was due to the late May sunlight that boogied its way through her windows. Either way, her course became obvious.

Thea resolved to teach Bram her artist's trick of seeing the underpinnings. She would make clear to him the bones upon which Potshot's flesh hung—the granite beneath the town's alpine meadows and resinous pines. Then he would see her home not as a tiny hamlet clinging precariously to Ricochet Mountain, but as a living organism. Thea intended to bring Bram into her world.

Of course, his connection would be more casual than hers. Potshot could never be to him the essential mental compass it was for her, especially after a week like the last one. For Bram, Potshot would become an entity worth maintaining. Regret dimmed her vision when she realized how much less satisfying Bram's experience would be than hers.

She washed her face and traded paint-stained garb for a clean T-shirt and jeans. Off to town she went, her little Honda purring along as she sang along with the Dixie Chicks on the radio. Her first stop was the Sheriff's office. Thea rapped her knuckles on the door, walking in as April Benton packed away the final lunch dishes.

"You spoil Sy beyond all belief," Thea teased. Smells of coffee, yeasty bread, and tomato-based Italian herbs filled the air, making Thea's empty belly groan.

"Woman knows a good thing when she's got it." Sy grinned at his wife and gave Thea a wink.

"It's more likely he doesn't eat worth beans if I don't feed him," groused April.

Sy's big hands settled over his wife's broad shoulders, made strong by running a grocery from her wheelchair. He gave her neck a few deep rubs before leaning down to kiss her. Their lips clung, their affection for each other still strong after thirty-seven years of marriage, all but seven of those years with April in a wheelchair. A poignant twinge nicked Thea's vitals. She wanted to blame it on hunger, but honesty won. Love in action sometimes had that effect on her.

After Sy stowed the lunch basket under the chair, April wheeled toward the door.

"See you at the reading circle tomorrow, Thea. I picked a doozy this time: a love story with lots of hot sex, a mysterious stranger, and overlapping past lives. Oooowee. You're gonna love it."

Once the door shut behind the woman's chair, Thea faced Sy.

"What can I do you for?" he asked, hands on hips and a smile on his face.

"Well, there are a couple of things and now I'm not sure where to begin."

"How about taking a seat? Coffee?" At her negative response, he poured a cup for himself before settling into his own chair. "Have at it, Thea."

"Okay. First, I need to let you know that Alex told me about a wolf. Evidently, he's been feeding it for a month or so. He's even named it, Sy. Zorro. I didn't say anything earlier because, well, you know Alex and his imagination."

"Don't we all. So, you've seen this wolf?" His sharp-eyed look practically pinned her to the chair.

She hesitated. "Not really, but the grant people have seen what they think is wolf sign on the mountain."

"Humph. Well, that might be a lead worth following. There're a few people purely pissed about losing their pets and laying hens. Got a call in to a buddy at Fish and Wildlife, too. He's due back from leave this week. Best you keep Alex away from this critter."

"Tell me about it." The mere thought of her son feeding a wild animal tripped her heart into a fierce castanet rhythm. She put a hand over her chest.

"You know, Thea, if it's a wolf we've got, I'd really like to have professionals deal with the critter. Don't like to see it killed by some hothead who let's his gun do his thinking for him. Enough of those in the valley as is." He gulped a swallow of coffee.

"How 'bout I come out to talk with Alex about it today? Warn the boy off. Maybe that'll reinforce whatever you say. Can't say I'm crazy about him getting so close to a wild animal."

"Me either. I just hope you can catch it before it's blamed for any more mischief. Did Letty find her cat?"

"Not that I've heard of."

She stared glumly at her knee until the sheriff said, "You've got more than the wolf on your mind. Don't make me work for it."

"Well, I was wondering, if someone wanted a restraining order against a guy, what would be required?"

Sy sat forward then, putting his coffee cup down with a clunk. "Has this nameless person been pestering you?"

She sat forward, meeting Sy's steely gray eyes with her gaze. She took a deep breath and plunged in. "Actually, it's more complicated than that. Derek Salinger and I have some personal history, Sy. I don't want to get into specifics, but he's been over to my place twice. Thank goodness Bram was around or. . ."

"Or?" Sy's rapid-fire question brooked no delay.

"Or it might have gotten uglier than it already is. I swear I came within a heartbeat of bashing Salinger both times." She offered a rueful grin.

"Thea MacTavish, I can't believe you'd wallop anyone, even that arrogant peacock."

"Well, like I said, Salinger and I share some history. But he's threatening me now and I don't want him near me—especially on my property."

"If he's trying to coerce you, I can do something about that. What was the nature of his threat?" His clear eyes allowed her no deceit.

"He may try to take Alex away from me."

Sy digested that before sitting back in his chair with a *whoosh!* "He's made no threat of personal injury to you, though?"

Thea thanked him silently for not voicing the obvious connection. His scrutiny told her that he knew, though. "Sy, anyone who threatens my son, threatens me. You know that."

He blew air from pursed lips, an exhalation full of annoyance. "Thea, the law doesn't give me the right to restrain a man from contacting his son, no matter how scarce the fella's made himself over the last thirteen years. That's for the courts to decide. But I can do something for you if the man's making a nuisance of himself. Especially if you think you're physically at risk." The glint in his eyes warned her to think carefully about her next words.

"Yes, that's what Salinger's become. A nuisance. And think of the risk I'd be in if I cave into my wicked nature and smack the man silly. Now that I think about it, maybe he's the one who needs a restraining order. Not that *I'd* pursue *him*. The further away the better."

"That's still pretty flimsy, Thea. Anything else?"

She gnawed her bottom lip and her gaze clung to his steady one. Trump. "He was violent before—with me and other women. Meg can back me up on this, even though I never lodged a formal complaint. I don't think anyone else did either. There's too much money and too many lawyers behind the Salinger name." *Would the past forever haunt her?*

Sy sat back in his chair. "He hurt you."

"I came to terms with the episode a long time ago. Self-defense classes helped nearly as much as getting sober." *Oh, Alex, my sweet boy.*

"Son-of-a—but no one took legal action?" He kneaded the loose skin of his neck with one hand. "Well, I'll get that order for you, Thea. Wish it was more than a paper tiger."

"Thanks, Sy."

"And you'll let me know if he so much as makes eye contact?"

"You bet."

He stared out the window. "What kind of a crazy world is this?"

"One where I can go to my local sheriff, ask for help, and actually get it."

He nodded once. "That you can. Now, you had something else on your mind?"

Broaching this topic moved her away from the abyss and she gave a deep sigh. "About the fires? I know you've been doing background checks on people who may be connected."

"April's been flapping her jaw, has she?" Sy shook his head, but his soft smile gave Thea room to maneuver.

"It's just that I was wondering if your investigation covered Salinger. I mean, he and his staff got here around the time the fires started, too. Who'd be more likely to want to keep Potshot off balance than a group trying to get townsfolk to yield to their demands?" She spoke so quickly she had to pause for breath.

Sy rocked his chair. The creaking sound prickled Thea's already frazzled nerves. Scents of aged leather and Old Spice tickled her nose. "Been working this over, have you?"

She nodded, leaning forward even more. "We could really use that insurance money. Besides, if you found the culprit, the loose talk about Alex would be put to rest. And—"

He raised his eyebrows.

"Sy, wouldn't it be worth it to do a deep search of Salinger's ethical standards and work practices in the process? Why is he so intent on our little hot springs anyway? From my experience with this creep, nothing's too low for him when he really wants something. Besides, the man rarely lets you know what he wants until the trap's sprung." With a deep breath, she settled into her seat.

Sy swung his chair to-and fro, studying her. "Could do that. We have discretionary funds for just such inquiries." Sy's feet came to the floor as he bent toward her and placed a big paw of a hand over her fingers where they twisted together on his desk. "But I won't let this become a witch hunt, Thea, no matter how much that smooth city boy grates in my craw or how much he hurt you in the past." Their gazes tangled and held until she nodded.

"I'd expect no less, Sy."

"Good." He came to his feet with startling grace. "Well, I've got my rounds to make now. So unless you have anything else?"

She stood, too. "Thanks for your time. I appreciate that you listened."

He walked her to the door. "So how's the other wolf situation? Dr. Youngwolf Hayes?"

Caught by surprise, Thea felt hot blood flood her cheeks. "F-fine."

Sy's eyebrows practically met his receding hairline. A huge grin covered his face. "Oh? So that's how it is. Hope you remember I was the one to introduce you two. Makes me first in line to give away the bride."

Which stopped her in her tracks. "Puh-lease," she said in Alex's best exasperation mode. "I just haven't thrown him out of my house yet, that's all. You heard his crazy plans for Potshot."

"Uh-huh."

She refused to dignify his knowing look. Instead, she marched through the door he held for her, then strode toward the library. She had wolves to research. Besides, she hoped to pry Meg out of the library long enough to go to the spa. Thea burned to see what progress Jake and his motley crew had made.

On Main Street, whiffs of grilled meats and baking pastries vied for her attention. A good crowd parked headlights-in along the sidewalks fronting the bakery. Hulon's parking lot was filled to bursting as well. As she crossed the street, Thea noticed with relief the closed sign on Guinevere's Hair Salon. Maybe Jessie would be able to cover for Meg at the library. A horn honked and Thea waved as Dwaine pulled up beside her in the patrol car, window down.

"Don't you ever use the cross walks, Thea?"

She grinned and leaned into his window, noting the rifle strapped upright near Dwaine's right hand and the grill between front and back. "We only have three and none are convenient. Cool wheels, Dwaine."

He actually blushed, his obvious pleasure making Thea want to giggle. "Yeah, well, with the expected influx of tourists, not to mention potential perps, we've upgraded."

"Looks good. Real big city."

"So where're you off to?"

She straightened as another resident pulled around them,

offering a toot in greeting.

Gesturing vaguely toward the library, Thea said, "Thought I'd see if Meg wanted to go to the spa and do a progress check. I think Jessie's there today."

"Jessie's at the library?" Dwaine's mud brown eyes positively glowed.

"And baby Phoebe. They go most Mondays, now. Jessie enjoys helping Meg. I think it gives her and Phoebe a chance to mingle with other mommies and toddlers during the children's reading hour."

Thea could tell from the deputy's intent gaze that he was still digesting the fact of Jessie-at-the-library. She said, "If Jessie will tackle librarian duties, maybe Meg'll join me. We need to deliver lunch to Jake's crew along with some tools he requested from the hardware store."

"Well, could be I can give Jessie a hand. That baby carrier has to slow even her down. Maybe this could count as my contribution to the spa and all."

"Not to mention all those little 'perps'. Your presence could come in handy."

"Aw Thea, they're just kids." He grinned, his square jaw, shaven head, and big ears making him look like a high school quarterback, despite his late 20-odd years. Thea found him endearing.

She offered, "I'm making a batch of lasagna with your venison burger this week. How about if I make a pan for you, too?"

"Never been known to turn down lasagna. That's right nice of you, Thea. Can I give you a lift?"

"It's only a couple of blocks."

"Well, I do believe I'll meet you there." As Thea headed for the sidewalk, he said, "And you take care around Jake's people. They seem like a harmless bunch, real good workers. But you're a single mom. Don't want any of the men getting fresh with you or anything."

No mention of the construction crew's interesting history or propensity to wear tattoos and little else. Yet another reason Thea loved this town. "Don't worry, Dwaine. If I have any problem, I'll call you." She waved him away, walking the remaining distance in the time it took the deputy to drive there and park.

Less than an hour later, Thea and Meg rounded the last curve up the recently paved road to the spa. Three vehicles belonging to Bram and his crew were parked in the lot.

"I wonder what they're doing here?" Thea mused as she pulled her car into the pristine parking area. "Looks like Hulon must have donated the paint for the parking slots." It glowed the same lime green as the Bar and Grill.

She and Meg parceled out picnic and building supplies from Thea's trunk as Alex dashed down the steps. "Hiya, Mom. Auntie Meg."

"Why aren't you in school?" Thea asked.

"You signed the form, Mom. Remember? We got an early out so the teachers could do grades."

She rubbed her forehead. "Oh, that's right."

He wore a belt-and-loop combination that Jake must have rigged for him so he could carry tools around his hips, too. This contraption proudly sported a folding measuring tape and a screwdriver. Thea worried a little about the latter. When Alex was only four years old, he had removed every screw from all the doorknobs in the house. Thea had the devil of a time getting him out of the bathroom, where he trapped himself.

She handed her son a basket. "How was school today?"

"Good. We got to choose subjects for our biology paper. I chose wolves."

"Now there's a surprise," she said.

He started swinging the open basket in wide loops around

168

one arm. "Look, I can hang it upside down, but nothing falls out." Her son did just that while Thea sucked air to keep from yelling 'Stop!'

Meg smiled, sporting a tranquil look Thea envied. "Lovely, Alex. That's centrifugal force in action, dear heart. It's the same force that let's you ride the corkscrew roller coaster at the fair without falling on your head."

Thea said nothing, merely retrieved the basket from her progeny and handed him new hand tools. He stuffed those that fit into various loops and pouches suspended from his belt, then gripped the last one, a small planer, in one hand.

"Did ya see the fire guys? They've been around the back of the hot springs all morning. Bram says they're going to make the new health spa safe from wildfire."

Thea clutched her picnic basket tighter. "Oh, he did, did he?"

Something in her voice penetrated even Alex's consciousness. Bright blue eyes caught her in their crossbeams. "I'm not supposed to tell you the details. It's a surprise."

"I'll bet."

They trudged up ten steps to the first and main level of buildings. The tent city looked well maintained with what Thea could only assume resembled military precision. As she walked under the roof overhang, she inhaled the resinous scent of raw pine. Even the special fireproof siding, their primary building material, smelled good. Scrutiny of the construction site showed her what an excellent choice Jake had been. She loved the natural feel to the place already. The din of hammers, saws, and voices raised in communication or song greeted her.

Alex skittered by both her and Meg, evidently fueled by his excitement over the latest tools. Thea used her hand to shade her eyes against the mid-afternoon sun all the while looking upslope. There above the mud baths stood Bram, outlined by backlight as he held conference with Ian.

He looked like a giant from where she stood: tall, ruggedly built and unreachable. Thea needed only a glimpse to remind her of their kiss. Just the thought of that riotous bliss made her breathe faster. Oh, why, oh, why had she rambled on about her past?

"Holy fuchsia, I've really let that guy get under my skin." She lowered her hand and trailed after Meg, following the sound of voices.

She found Meg fussing over Jake, who stood with a canteen in one hand and a hammer in the other. His craggy face looked even more worn than usual. Erratic highlights stained each cheekbone.

Meg fussed, "You're driving yourself too hard."

"Now, Nutmeg—" the man started.

Nutmeg? Thea repeated to herself.

The librarian, evidently looking for support, latched onto Thea. "This man's burning-up with fever, Althea. Please help me knock some sense into his thick head. I've already explained that he needs to take care of himself, otherwise he'll be laid low even longer."

Thea headed toward the rangy man, plunked down her basket, then reached up to feel his forehead. "You're pretty hot, Jake. We don't want you on the job when you're sick. Why don't you let *Nutmeg* take you back to her place and look after you."

Neither noticed her use of Meg's new diminutive. Instead Jake said, "Now, Thea, you know the more I have done by the time the next vote comes around. . ."

"Yes, I know. But from what I can see, you're way ahead of schedule. Besides, your crew will continue to work. And Jake," she pivoted slowly before facing him again, "It's absolutely beautiful. Just as I envisioned it. No, *better*."

170

"Let me show you. . ." he began.

Meg cut through his words. "Oh, no you don't. You're going home with me now. I have a stack of books in the car that I know you'll enjoy. I planned on making a nice kettle of chicken soup anyway." As she spoke, she began drawing him along in her wake. She peeked around his lanky frame to catch Thea's eye. "Alex can show Thea how to clean up for the day, can't you, dear heart?"

"Sure, Auntie Meg." He looked positively thrilled with the idea.

Jake said, "Just put the tools in the chest, son. Leave it unlocked for my crew."

"Yes, sir."

Yes sir? Thea eyed Alex doubtfully and nearly checked his forehead for fever.

Meg maneuvered Jake to the top stair, then called, "Thea, I'll need to take your car. I can get it back here within the hour."

"Don't bother, Meg. I think Alex and I can catch a ride with Bram. If not, we'll take the trail home and leave the baskets for tomorrow."

"Well, all right, dear. I'll call tonight and let you know how our patient's doing." Thea watched until first Meg's head dipped below view, then Jake's.

Alex snagged her hand in his. "Come on, Mom. I'll show you how Jake likes to put his things away." So for the next fifteen minutes, that was what they did. Thea glimpsed a novel side to her son.

Alex kept getting sidetracked by projects 'he and Jake' worked together. But it was the reverence with which he put away the tools that really made her heart-proud. The older man was a great influence on her son; a gift she could not have predicted.

The way the construction people treated her and especially

her son eased her worries, too. They thanked her for the provisions and, after washing up, settled into lunch according to their personalities. Some ate together, others found privacy. Alex bloomed under their attention and Thea even received a wink from the doctor of anthropology. She decided not to report it to Dwaine, though.

Toward the end of their clean-up operations, Bram strode into the central work area, evidently following the workers' directions. "Hi, Alex."

She whipped around to see him, blaming her sudden light-headedness both on her speed of movement and on last eating over six hours earlier.

"Thea! I was hoping you were still here, but when I saw your car pull away. . ."

"Jake's got the flu. We're putting away his tools," piped Alex.

Thea tore her gaze away from the vital man in front of her, then pushed herself off the workbench that had supported her through the dizzy spell. "Meg took Jake home in my car. We're just finishing up now," she said, then carefully lowered the lid over Jake's tool chest. She turned much more slowly to face Bram, surprised to catch him gazing at her with an unfathomable look.

They stood like deer stunned by oncoming lights until Alex yanked on her hand. "Mom, I'm starved."

She jerked her gaze from Bram and said, "Well, you're in luck, partner. I brought more food than we can possibly eat." With a nervous glance at Bram, she asked, "Want to join us? There's enough here to feed Meg and Jake."

"Sure. We're finished for the day."

"Cool," said Alex. "That means we can work some more on my science project."

Bram dropped a casual hand on the boy's shoulder, an action in which his mother no longer indulged. Too many

172

shrugs of rejection could do that to a person. Evidently, what was okay for Bram was not okay for Mom. Sadness filled her at the thought. It must have made her move too slowly.

"Come on, Mom. Let's eat," Alex prodded.

Bram's smile made Thea's toes curl. "How about if I take the big basket and Alex takes the little one. You, Thea, can lead us to the best place for a picnic."

"That's easy," piped Alex. "We used to come up here a lot, huh, Mom?"

Her son's voice grounded her. "Yes. Yes, we did," she answered. Enough musing about hunky fire safety engineers with eyes that picked up mahogany highlights in the sun. She sashayed out of the work area and tackled the rustic steps leading to the deer trail.

Two hundred feet over the hot springs and mud baths, although only a fraction of the way up the mountain, Thea stopped. She pivoted slowly and took in the view. Conical crowns of Ponderosa pines covered with dark green needles topped trunks of furrowed bark, which made the tree so resistant to fire damage. Farther down the slope, she saw where the park-like expanse gave way to greasewood, and rabbit- and sagebrush, still green in mid spring. Yellow daisies and ice plants rooted among the pines. Potshot was hidden by the mountain's shoulder. A slight haze hung over the valley. The hum and flutter of insects and birds, the scurry of chipmunks and lizards had subsided. In the quiet, air swirled through the branches with a surge like distant surf. She inhaled the volatile fragrance of vanilla from Ponderosa bark as Bram and Alex breached the ledge.

Only slightly breathless, Bram slanted her a look filled with humor. "You set a good pace, Thea."

She grinned. "I didn't have anything to carry."

Alex plunked himself down and began sorting through the smaller basket. "Scones! And apple cider."

Thea whisked the booty out of his grasp. "Sorry, sport. Sweets after nourishment."

Bram set his basket down on the rock outcropping, which provided nearly bench-like seats. Thea thrust the dessert basket into his arms. "Guard this, will you?"

"You trust me?"

"I want to," she countered, knowing her response went much deeper than the task warranted.

She doled out the main fare, enumerating each choice. "Roast beef on sourdough," snatched by Bram, "turkey with raspberry jam on Russian rye; chicken salad on whole wheat; lots of vegetables with cream cheese on wheat," which she set aside for herself. "And," with a glance at her somewhat deflated son, "Missus' famous *piroshky*."

With a glad cry, Alex seized the last and dug into the savory roll filled with meat and cabbage, one of the ways Thea knew of getting her offspring to eat vegetables without complaint. She retrieved the individual cider bottles from Bram, and after distributing them, settled beside her son. Bram moved the basket from her other side and sat there. His exotic scent of incense cedar infused the air. Bram's nearness made Thea positively giddy.

She took a big bite of her sandwich. Alex, who had been struggling with his bottle cap, leaned across her lap. "Bram, could you open this, please?"

"Sure." The man proceeded to show Alex, much to his delight, how to open recalcitrant bottles using a sharp rock ledge.

That would have been fine, except Bram angled across Thea's lap to return the opened bottle to Alex. She might have believed herself hypersensitive to the man, until he sent her a glint from two inches away. The look fanned carefully banked embers into a firestorm. Good thing she had already swallowed or she would have choked. After a gulp of cider, she braved another bite, now fueled more by her need for a smokescreen than hunger.

Alex and Bram talked around her. Mostly her son chattered about all his favorite places along the mountain: a shallow indentation here; a hollowed tree there. "I almost got to where Zorro lives last Saturday. After it rained? I followed his tracks."

Thea nearly strangled on her fright. Bram put a hand over her forearm, signaling her to silence with his look. He said to Alex, "You'll have to show me where you lost the trail. I'd like to see if I can track him to his den."

Her son, who bolted his last bite, traced a grubby index finger in the dirt. "Well, I don't know. . ."

"Remember when I told you I have a friend who works with endangered species? Well, I talked with him this morning and he's really interested in meeting your wolf."

Alex gave him a measuring look. "You said he wouldn't hurt Zorro."

Bram got up, moving to hunker down in front of her son. "I told you he's an expert in wolf recapture-and-release. That's all he'd want to do, Alex. It's important to him that your wolf finds a good home in a natural setting. Zorro *is* a wild animal."

The emphasis Bram placed on the last made Thea glad she had kept her mouth shut. Going postal about her son's wolf would have ended in another blind canyon of silence, which was categorically not a favored experience.

"He's my friend." Alex's eyes glistened with a definite sheen.

Bram gripped the boy's shoulder in commiseration. "I know, buddy. And because you're his friend, it's important to make sure he lives where he can be happiest. That would be in his native setting."

Alex gulped manfully. "I know." Finally his gaze moved to

175

his mother.

"I'm sure Bram's right, Alex. Think of how you'd feel if you had to live somewhere you felt uncomfortable and didn't know how to act. Where you couldn't be yourself."

"Like Grandma's? Everything in her house is breakable and costs too much."

Thea suppressed a grin. "Kind of like that."

Bram slid his hands off the boy's shoulders and stood, making a play of stretching. Thea enjoyed every moment of it. "Hey, Thea, how 'bout some of those scones I spy peeking out of that basket?" His warm regard dared her to hide her interest.

He and Alex argued amiably about how to divide up the various fruit fillings. Then they set about eating every crumb. Shortly after finishing, at Bram's urging, Alex headed down the mountain, taking the trail for home and homework.

Thea was still reeling when she asked, "How did you do that?"

"What?" Bram asked as he settled beside her, only closer than before.

"Get my child to run down the mountain to do homework."

"Oh, that. I'll tell you if you give me a written tenant's contract. Maybe throw in some television time and fresh wildflowers in my room every day. Some quality time on the veranda—just you, me, a couple mugs of tea. Then whatever comes up. . ."

Sensual memory flooded her, making her breathless and woozy. "That's blackmail."

"I suppose some would see it that way. I see it as an opportunity not to be wasted." His heated breath tickled her ear, sent voluptuous shivers from her neck to the base of her spine.

"Just the facts, Dr. Hayes." She studied her clasped hands.

"Not nearly as much fun, but if you insist."

176

"I do." She met his lush regard.

His gaze lingered on her mouth. "Too bad. Well, when Alex decided I was going to help him with his project, I set up some rules. One was that he has to finish his regular homework first." His regard lazily traced her chin line to her eyes.

"Stop that," she said in a breathless rush.

"Stop what?"

"Stop looking at me like that."

He gave her a crooked little smile. "All right."

The few inches between them disappeared as he covered her lips with his.

Chapter Ten

With each breath, Bram inhaled Thea's honeysuckle sweetness, which only added to the heat growing inside him. Their kiss prolonged into another—then another. He broke away first, gratified to find Thea lolling across his lap. Her contours fit him better than old jeans. Of course if his jeans were this sexy, they would be a lot less comfortable and he'd never be able to wear them in public. As Bram zeroed in on another taste of Thea's cherry pie lips, she said something his desire-fused senses declined to translate.

"What?"

She sighed. "Wildfire."

The welcome in her gaze distracted him. "Your eyes," he said, but he leaned toward her mouth.

"Wildfire, Bram. That's what your kisses do to me. Sweep through me, burning everything else away until all I am is flame. Full of these little fire eddies."

He slid a hand over her midriff, could feel a quiver from deep inside of her. Snuggling her closer, he supported her back. "Firewhirls. Like dust devils on blistering desert sand except they're made of fire." He inhaled her essence, knowing exactly what she meant.

"You're the fire expert. Just how long do these firewhirls last?"

"No more'n a minute. The bad news is they're quick. Faster than you can run."

"Great," she said as she struggled upright. He helped her

178

stand, directly in opposition to his body's wishes. "So they don't last long, but I can't outrun them."

Oddly, she refrained from immediately packing the baskets. Instead, Thea settled down beside him and took a deep breath. He stretched his legs and tried to ignore the ache in his groin, a futile gambit.

"I hope you're right about the not-lasting-long part anyway," she said.

He opened his mouth to protest. How could she belittle this passion between them? The wolf inside him howled his frustration. Bram snapped his mouth shut. He planned on being here a matter of months. That definitely did not equate with happily-ever-after. Not to mention the fight he expected to have on his hands once the team started making physical changes to Potshot.

"Sy's looking into getting a restraining order against Salinger."

The guy's name worked better than ice water, Bram decided. "Good. It's long overdue."

"I suppose." She gave him a sidelong look. "And since we're on the topic of biological fathers, I haven't heard one word about *your* dad, Bram. Just your grandfather."

Thea spoke as though her choice of subjects was routine rather than intrusive. Still. "That's because I never knew my father. He was an Army major. Had been invited to lecture, then teach at the University of Central Oklahoma. Grandfather raised me."

"And?" Her gaze refused to let him off that easily.

"My father was transferred after two years and Mom didn't hear anything for a month, then learned through one of his buddies that he'd been killed in a training exercise." Thea's long fingers covered his hand. "Evidently a vehicle rolled over on him. His friend said that he'd intended to come back for my mother. And for us." The thought no longer had the power

179

to hurt—too much.

He shrugged. "Who really knows? My brother and I were born seven months after he died."

"Your mother never located his family?"

"Never tried as far as I know."

"And you've never attempted to find out about them either?"

"Let it go, Thea. I have."

She rested her head on his shoulder and looped an arm through his. They sat like that while shadows crept down the mountain. Voices drifted from below; townsfolk who had come to the hot springs to socialize and unwind from the day. Birds started feeding in the coolness of late afternoon. One flyer gave a cry that sounded like *whip-three-beers*, with an emphasis on the high middle note.

"Flycatcher," offered Thea. The staccato rhythm of a woodpecker as it searched a trunk for burrowing insects sounded behind and above them.

Bram stroked Thea's palm. He said, "This feels pretty good."

"It *is* good, isn't it?" Thea gave his hand a squeeze. "Still, I need to head on home. Alex will be wondering where I am. Besides he's probably raring to go on his science project." She gifted him with a smuggler's grin. "Oh, and I told Meg I'd catch a ride home with you."

"I see how you are," he teased. But his gaze snagged on that mysterious hollow at the base of her throat. He watched her pulse hop into double-time.

"Bram, you've got to stop doing that."

"I know." So he forced his eyes closed, only opening them as he surged to his feet. Thea hopped up beside him, not giving him a chance to pull her up and probably back into his arms.

As they tidied up the area, Bram felt drenched in Essence

180

of Thea. Her scent, her wit, her deep forest eyes called to him. Somehow he kept his gaze to himself—mostly. Then, each with a basket in hand, they started back down the mountain. As they strolled past the three hot spring lagoons and nearer to the swimming pool, voices lifted in greeting.

Thea whispered under her breath, "Don't stop or we'll be here for hours. Just wave, smile and keep moving. Unless you want to get into endless discussions about your project or Salinger's plans."

Bram picked up his pace to the truck. The next thing he knew, they were on the road home. *Home*, he mused. Interesting how that word kept cropping up when he thought of Thea's place. *Less than five months left to the grant,* he reminded himself. Not very long at all to call a place *home*.

Besides, his grandfather kept intruding on his thoughts. The old man was always hell on guys who made implicit promises to women without any intent of carrying through. If the woman was a mother and sole support of a family, Grandfather grew even more adamant. Once Bram learned about his own father, he had wondered how much those circumstances shaped Grandfather's ideology.

Now he wondered what constituted an implicit promise. One kiss? Two? But he balked at calling what passed between him and Thea simple kisses; that was like comparing candlelight to a firestorm.

Bram parked in front of the house only to realize no word had passed between them the entire way. When he slanted a glance in Thea's direction, she looked perfectly relaxed with their silence. Since this fell outside of Bram's previous experience with women, he sat there for a long moment until Thea let herself out.

She grabbed one of the baskets before moving toward the front door, then turned to call, "You staying in there all night?"

181

He caught up with her at the door. "Okay, now you're doing it," he said.

"Doing what?" she countered, pushing the door open. "Alex, we're home, honey." She leaned down to slip the shoes from her feet.

He shut the door behind them, taking much longer than she did to pull off his boots and socks. By that time he hurried to catch up with her. In the kitchen, he said, "You submerge yourself in silence."

She gave him a confused look. "I'm not sure what you're trying to say, Bram, but hold that thought." She left him at the counter and paced away from the kitchen and down the hall. "Alex?"

The whisper of bare feet against the parquet floor heralded her arrival again as she passed him on her way to the back door. "Alex?"

A faint "Shhhhh," issued from the gully formed by the creek. For some reason Thea went absolutely still. Then, she slipped on the laceless tennis shoes she kept by the back door and headed down the path to the creek. Bram followed.

An entirely new set of flowers bloomed along the path to the creek, replacing those that had thrived over a month ago. Evidently, like Thea, these plants flourished in the dry climate. He walked between carpets of blue larkspur and pink corydalis. Maroon peony with yellow centers made nodding acquaintance along the trail.

He only noticed these in passing while Thea disappeared into the ravine. Since his feet were bare and tender, Bram walked more tentatively. He paused at the top of the bank, freezing at what met his view.

In a tableau below him, Thea had halted between what looked to be a Mexican Gray wolf and Alex, who squatted barefoot in the creek. The boy seemed to realize that now was not the time to move. The wolf glanced quickly at Bram as the man came into range, but returned its golden-eyed scrutiny to the woman, who now stood closest to him.

As long from head-to-haunches as Bram was tall, the black wolf would have weighed over ninety pounds if he had been eating regularly. Hunting without a pack could hollow a wolf out, even with domesticated chickens, cats, and dogs supplementing his diet. Three capes of fur covered the animal's back and stood out clearly against his gauntness. His head sank between his shoulders where he leveled his muzzle toward Thea's chest like a weapon. Bram recognized the early stages of either hunting stance or defensive mode. A chill brought the hairs along Bram's nape and arms to full attention.

After about thirty seconds going on three hours, while no one moved, the wolf's head lifted. Even though the animal did not look relaxed enough to start panting, he appeared more curious than defensive. Bram took his first deep breath.

In a low chanting voice whose cadence spoke of Cherokee storytellers, Bram said, "Alex, I don't think you're in danger, but I want you to listen to everything I say. Move as slow as you can. Come to your feet, then just stand there. Don't say anything. That's right, so slowly that you don't make any ripples in the water. Good, good. We don't want to frighten our guest and make him do something he'll regret later." The boy, whose teeth had started clicking together in a staccato beat, did just as Bram told him.

"Thea," Bram started, but she gave him a sharp look without moving her head.

With teeth clenched, she managed to say, "I'm not going anywhere until Alex is with you."

Again in a low singsong, Bram said, "Okay. Just keep your gaze lowered like that and don't look the wolf in his eyes. Alex, start moving toward me. If I say stop, you freeze right where you are. All right now. Move."

Bram, while keeping his gaze on the wolf, fell into a song he had learned from his mother. The boy started toward him. The wolf actually began panting, even though his golden stare shifted between Thea, Alex, and Bram with unnerving regularity. Bram figured that from Thea's vantage, the wolf's teeth must loom even larger than they did from here.

Midway up the bank, Alex stubbed a toe on a rock. He jerked to a stop without uttering a sound, but his uncontrolled movement echoed in the snap of the wolf's jaws. Intelligent, feral eyes fixed on the boy. Bram squatted slowly, extending his arms until the boy's hands reached him. With a smooth movement, he pulled Alex into his arms. The boy clung with wiry strength to Bram's neck as the man stood. Icy feet and hands clasped him like a baby possum grips its mother.

"Now you, Thea. Move as easy as you can. No," he soothed with his voice, "Don't look him in the eyes. We don't want him to think you're challenging him. That's right, darlin', keep it leisurely, a walk in the park. Watch that rock to your left. There you go." Sweat trickled down Bram's side and pooled in the small of his back. "Come on, you're almost home, that's it. . ."

With Alex grasped in one arm, Bram clasped Thea's outstretched hand and pulled her up the bank. He folded her toward his chest as his knees grew wobbly with relief. Alex let go his strangle hold of Bram's neck and hugged his mother, too.

They all looked at the wolf, whose panting brought his emaciated torso into sharp relief.

"Poor guy. He looks half starved," Thea said. The wolf cocked his head at her words.

"He is," Bram agreed. He filled his lungs and let go with, "Now get!"

The wolf stiffened to full attention. Thea and Alex jerked in his arms before snuggling closer. At another time, Bram

184

would have reveled in the closeness.

"Get!" Bram yelled. The wolf whirled away, taking a few lunging strides up the trail before settling into a lope. His flag of a tail nodded in farewell as he rounded a corner.

Relinquishing her frantic hold on her son, Thea sank onto the dirt at Bram's feet. "Whew! That was way too close."

"I'll say." Bram joined her, setting Alex on his feet beside him.

The boy continued standing. "Zorro wouldn't really have hurt us, would he?"

Bram caught the flutter in the boy's voice. "Well, Alex, he's one hungry looking wolf. And he's far from home. You've taught him to come to you for food and that's just what he did. It's hard to know how an animal like that will react under the circumstances."

Alex's gaze dipped to the ground. "I was getting rocks from the creek for my science project. Next thing I knew, he was standing there. I - I didn't have anything to feed him."

Thea tugged on her son's wrists. For once, the boy responded to her as she chafed his wrists and hands. Thea said, "I know you were trying to help him, Alex, but now it's time to bring in people who know what wolves need."

The boy's chin firmed. "They'll hurt him."

"They won't, honey. Remember what Bram said? They'll probably just move him to a place where he can live with others of his kind. This isn't his home. He's lost and confused here." She turned to face Bram, her look full of appeal.

Like he could resist, so Bram jumped in with, "Your mom's right, son. We need to bring in the wolf experts on this. That fellow looked like a Mexican Gray to me. They're an Endangered Species. I don't have a clue as to how he got here, but I know this breed of wolf usually lives in the chaparral desert. He's starving and probably lonely, too."

Alex gulped on the last, then turned his dirt-streaked face

185

in the direction the wolf had gone. "I don't know where he lives, though. Jake says—he thinks he might know." He glanced at his mom.

Thea frowned. "That's odd."

"Why?" asked Bram.

"I didn't think Jake'd been around here long enough to know the mountain that well."

Alex said, "He knows all kinds of stuff about Potshot. He's shown me some pretty cool places already. I can show you some of them if you want. A couple of them are secret, though." His innocent look took in both his mother and Bram

Bram smiled at the resilience of youth. "Sounds good, partner." Thea still had a crease between her brows, so Bram said, "How about if you two give me a hand in the kitchen. I was thinking steak fajitas for dinner."

"Sure!" crowed Alex. He took off for the house at a run, his callused feet scattering pea-sized gravel along the path.

As the sliding door reached the end of its track with a bang, Thea winced. "Alex, take it easy, honey. You'll derail that thing again." But the boy, like a gust, was long gone.

Bram stood, helping Thea to her feet. Her gaze clung to him. "Just how much danger were we in back there?"

He rubbed the scar along his forearm. "Not too much, I suspect. However, as hungry and defensive as the wolf was, I didn't want to take any chances."

She placed a hand on his chest. "You were great. Thanks."

With a gesture completely foreign to him, he lifted her fingers and kissed them. "Anytime." Her eyes went all soft, the green of a shadowed trout pond. He came within a heartbeat of kissing her.

Alex hollered from the back door. "C'mon, you guys, I'm starved."

Thea tugged away, looking confused as a cat in a mud puddle. "You've got to quit doing that, Bram."

186

"Me!"

She slipped her hand through his crooked arm and pulled him through the door. Then, while Thea had a low, but intense, phone conversation about the wolf with the Sheriff, Bram and Alex enjoyed free-run of the kitchen. Afterward the place definitely looked worse for use, but Bram decided the fajitas turned out great. Once the food was gone, Alex disappeared into his room for homework, while Bram, against Thea's expressed wish, helped her clean the kitchen. Her mobile face took on a remote look.

Maybe that was what prompted him to say, "In summer, the Rez kids would sneak off to the waterhole every chance we got. Our favorite one was in public lands. We'd go through a couple of barbed wire fences, meander between grazing Longhorns, then traipse along rivulets under the willows. Tribe elders were always warning us off, trying to scare us with tales of quick sand, which were true by the way. That only whetted our appetites."

"Of course," Thea took the platter from his hands before submerging it in rinse water.

"They worried most that the Rez kids would mix it up with the townies." He finished washing the last dish and let the stopper out of the sink before leaning his backside against the counter.

Thea deftly stacked the last plate in the rack and swirled her fingers through the remaining rinse water. "So, there was a lack of acceptance between the reservation kids and the townspeople?"

"The usual white and nonwhite garbage, but it never became an issue at the swimming hole. Granted, we stayed pretty much segregated. No real problems, though. In fact, when we showed up with homemade skimmers, the townies became downright friendly."

"Skimmers?"

"These round cutouts from old plywood. We'd toss them onto the shallows and surf across the riffles."

They exchanged smiles. Thea said, "I'll bet the adults who worried the most were the same ones who played at the waterhole when they were kids."

Bram thought about that for a moment. "Why would that be?"

She tossed him the damp towel, which he caught. "Oh, come on, Bram. Parents will do almost anything to keep their children from making the same mistakes they did."

He raised his eyebrows. "Guess you'd know."

"About parenting? Or misspent youth?"

When Thea got her dander up, Bram knew to duck. "You're the parent here, Thea."

"Thanks, I think, but my mother's the shining example of this particular trait. Since I was born out of wedlock, she was determined I'd never succumb. So when I got pregnant with Alex, you can imagine the homecoming. Not that I made a cognitive choice to have a baby."

The hollowness in her voice struck him. "How so?"

"Maybe I'll tell you some time."

Bram recognized a cave worth exploring when he saw one, and Thea's unspoken tale lured him the same way. "*Now* works for me."

Her gaze slid away from his. "Right now, I'd rather deconstruct my mother. Tea?"

"I'm fine."

She led the way to the back porch. Bram watched as she weighed sitting on the steps against choosing more conventional seats. With an opaque glance at him, she folded onto a wicker chair. He took the one across from her, disappointed that she chose distance when they could be sharing body heat. *Aw, hell, and maybe more kisses, too.* Both of them stared across the back acreage, Bram straining to see if a wolf lurked in the gloaming.

She shuddered. "The visual of that hungry wolf within pouncing range of Alex will haunt me forever."

Thus stating his sentiments—except that the visual of Thea within striking distance scored high on his list, too. He said, "The sheriff's on it now."

"I know. I gave him the name of your contact, too."

"Good. Time to play wait-and-see, then. Besides, I'd rather talk about you." In the diffused light between day and night, Thea's skin looked soft as sun-heated velvet, her mouth the bruised color of ripe plums. Her trim curves fit right into the moldable cushions of the chair as she gnawed her lower lip.

"Oh, that's right. I promised to psychoanalyze Mother. Since my education's in art, this could be a novel experience."

Nice avoidance tactic, Thea. "You said Amarantha wasn't happy about Alex."

She shifted, tucking one leg beneath her and dangling the other over the seat edge. Like mini-chimes, her earrings tinkled when she moved. "No, Mother loves Alex, but she saw my pregnancy and unwed state as a repeat of her mistakes. I guess you could say she never allowed herself to see the positives."

"Positives? There're too many unwed mothers on the Rez. From what I've seen, these girls are trapped in lives with slim-to-none choices and piddling economics. What mother would choose that for her daughter?"

"Not mine, that's for sure. But she did set a good example to live by. She got pregnant, chose to keep me, then did the best she could." A rosy hue stained her cheeks. "I mean, even though we're not on the same wavelength now, I know she loves me. She made decisions in her life based on what she thought would be best for me. Because of what she accomplished, I realized I could raise Alex on my own. I'm stronger for it."

When she stopped, he prompted, "What about your stepfather?"

She reached overhead in a stretch, drawing Bram's regard down her body to her breasts and taut midriff peaking from between T-shirt and waistband. His mouth went dry and blood rushed to his belly and below. Good thing there was some physical distance between them or he would have Thea across his lap again in no time flat.

"Poor Charles. Even as a kid, I could tell that Mother wasn't passionate about him. As I got older, I saw what they had. He gave us financial security; she gave him entree into circles that called for a beautiful and cultured woman willing to play hostess. He even adopted me to please her. Of course, I dropped his name during my bout with terminal teenage defiance. Still I just can't get past the feeling that. . ." Now she looked fully at him. "Well, that she gave up some of the most important parts of herself to become Charles' wife."

Bram took a deep breath. "It was her choice, Thea."

"I know, I know. But she settled for security over passion. It was one of those things I felt guilty about for a long time. As though my existence pushed my mother to make that choice. I know better now, but the remorse still catches me unaware, if I'm tired or blue enough."

She draped both arms over the rests and the warm floral fragrance Bram identified as Thea wafted over to him. *Think of something else*, he told himself. "Don't you know anything about your real father?"

Arms akimbo, she pushed herself deeper into the chair and grimaced. "Not much more than you do, I suppose. Just that he went to Vietnam and never came back. Mother always skirted the issue. It became a source of contention. I wanted to know more and she refused to tell."

Alex popped out of the kitchen. "I'm done with my homework, Bram. Want to work on my science project?"

Anything was better than tormenting himself over a woman he should not want. "Sure. You know where we stored the supplies? Why don't you run down to my room and pull everything out. I'll be down in a minute."

The boy spun around and ran into the house. "Whew! Doesn't he ever slow down?" Bram asked.

"Only when he's sleeping," came Thea's wry answer.

She unfolded from the chair and sauntered into the kitchen, where she put together a plate of cookies and a pitcher of milk. Bram tried to stay out of her way and found himself studying the fade pattern on her jeans. The kitchen grew a lot warmer.

"You know, Bram, Alex gave me strict instructions not to peek until you're done. So you'd better take this snack with you." Her smile looked a little forced as he accepted the tray.

"I'm sure he didn't mean it the way it sounded."

She shook her head. "Sure he did. He wants to do some male bonding, and I'm practicing letting go in degrees. I just wish. . ."

Tray in hand, he waited for her to finish. "What?" he finally asked.

"I wish he'd bond with someone who lives here in Potshot. No offense, Bram, but you're about as transient as they come."

That truth made his diaphragm contract as though kicked. He managed to say, "I know. It's tough."

This time there was no smile in her eyes when she said, "Tell me about it."

Early one morning a week later, Bram slogged through subalpine woods trying to keep up with a man nearly twice his age, although he looked much older. The wiry back of Jake Seeker, obviously recovered from his bout with the flu, posed a challenge to Bram as he tried to move through the woods with the same expertise and speed. An hour into their hike, they emerged on a ridge overlooking both Eden Valley and Potshot. Jake paused for what he called a breather, even though Bram was the only one who needed it.

When he finally caught his breath enough to speak again, the younger man asked, "Where'd you learn to move like that?"

Jake took a swig from his canteen, then handed it over to Bram. "Courtesy of the United States government, son."

"My grandfather taught me to hunt. I always thought he was the best there was. You're better."

The older man took a snowy white cloth from his rear pocket and swept the fine film of sweat from his brow and neck. "Survival's the best teacher." He turned his craggy head toward the north face of the slope, then pointed. "See that overhang? About a mile up and over? That's where I suspect our wolf has made his lair."

They had already checked two other places that Jake picked as definite maybes. He had also said that this would be the best choice.

"How'd you get to know this area so well, Jake? You've been here about the same amount of time I have. My crew and I have been all over this mountain, but I've seen more new area with you today than I did the first two weeks."

Jake grew as still as the towering Ponderosas, then shrugged. The gesture looked strained to Bram's eye. "Spent my childhood hereabouts. Did a lot of camping, fishing and hunting."

Bram's interest peaked. "Really? Why doesn't anyone recognize you?"

Jake gave a dry chuckle. "Why, son, people see exactly what they expect to see. I'm no more than an old, shell-shocked war vet. Most folks wouldn't believe me if I told them I was once young or good-looking." His fathomless gaze settled on Bram. "Why I suppose that in certain parts of this great country, you'd be pegged as a no-count Injun, even in these days of heightened social awareness."

Bram's muscles tightened at the man's words, but Jake went on, "But in other places, you're both Native American and the Great Spirit personified." Again that dry laugh. "Have to admit, neither description gives one iota of insight into who you really are, now does it? So I like to take each person as they are, and hope for the same in return. Personal history's just that. It might be interesting, but it really doesn't tell you more about the guy in front of you than what your five or maybe six senses are already saying."

With that, the man took off again, leaving Bram to follow as best he could. The physical activity dissolved tension, so by the time Jake came to a halt again, Bram felt relaxed and mostly in agreement with what the old guy said. This time, Jake stopped at a rocky outcrop that towered above the overhang of interest. They shimmied up the highest boulder, granite heated to just short of discomfort by morning sun nearing summer solstice.

He followed Jake's example and crawled to the apex. Once there, Bram was glad of their precaution. For over the lip of rock and across a clearing, they could see three wolf pups playing amid sunflecks at the cave-like entrance to the overhang. Whining, growling, and yelping, they tumbled over each other. Their color varied from silvery to black. A large gray female lounged across the opening of the cave, her long pink tongue lolling in rhythm to her pants. The black male was nowhere in sight.

Bram fumbled with the binoculars hanging from his neck before raising them to his eyes. The pups looked well fed with round bellies taut under woolly fur. Not so the female. Her ribs looked even more cadaverous than her mate's and

193

her fur lacked luster, appearing dull gray instead of silvery in the sunlight. The wolf's eyes held tawny, intelligent lights, though, and her lips curved in a definite lupine smile as she watched over her offspring. Bram turned his head toward Jake, started to speak only to squelch the impulse when the man held an index finger to his lips. Jake signaled him to go down the rock. They scooted as quietly as possible until Jake stopped.

The old guy talked low without making the whispery sound that carries so well. "Pups must be about a month old or they wouldn't be out of the lair. Small litter. Still on milk, too. Ma's not doing too well."

Bram nodded. "Something's wrong with one of her front legs. The knee angle looks off kilter."

Jake blew out a long sigh. "Damn."

The pups joined their voices in a yipping joyful sound. The two men crawled back to their former lookout.

The black male had returned from his hunting foray. The pups lunged around him, staging mock fights that Bram knew would establish hierarchy among them in the next weeks. The male nosed his offspring with affection, but kept moving toward his mate. Once he came even with her, he nuzzled her. She licked his jaws. To Bram's surprise, the black regurgitated food onto the ground in front of her. She gulped it while lying down.

The men slid off the rock. Bram said, "I've never seen anything like that before."

"Not with adults. That's how pups're fed. She must be in worse shape than we thought."

The men pondered that until Jake said, "Pups'll be needing meat soon. The male won't be able to provide for them and the female, too."

Bram nodded. "I contacted my friend again last night. He and another biologist from Blue Range Wolf Recovery will be here by week's end. They'll coordinate with Sy's Fish and Wildlife contact. I'll call again tonight with the latest information and maybe he can push things forward."

Jake gave a sharp nod. "Better be heading out. Don't want that male to catch us this close to his den. Might push him into doing something stupid."

They left as quickly and quietly as possible. Still, when Jake paused one ridge over, they looked back to find the black wolf perched on the same rock where they'd been only twenty minutes earlier. He faced their way. The wolf's alert stance left no doubt in Bram's mind about whose territory this was. He turned to follow Jake's receding back. Their swift pace put maximum distance between themselves and the adroit predator. An hour or so later, they reached the hot springs.

Jake led Bram into his work area, where they washed up. The man pulled out a picnic basket crammed with food. With a restrained glance at Bram, he gestured to the tool chest opposite him. "Take a seat, son. As you can see, Nutmeg's trying to fatten me up. You can give me a hand with this. She needs to know how much I appreciate her efforts."

The brimming basket reminded Bram of Thea's and his outing a week ago. They had been tiptoeing around each other ever since. With Bram's confirmed status as a transient out in the open, he tried to leave as light an imprint on her daily life as possible. Of course, that did not stop Alex from spending several evenings with him in the basement while they worked on the boy's science project. Somehow they kept ending up in the living room sharing tea with Alex's mother, who now chose to remain physically, if not mentally, distant.

Jake broke into Bram's thoughts. "You have to be fine-tuned into the female psyche lest you get caught in the currents."

"You a mind reader, Jake?" Bram took a huge bite of his chicken salad sandwich. It helped to cover his disquiet at

Jake's new direction.

Jake swallowed and continued. "For instance, I'd be a fool to accept this food from Nutmeg without realizing what my response must be."

Bram gulped. "Response?"

Jake took another bite and let Bram's concern gnaw away at his already ragged control. "Seems to me that by accepting her food, I'm also taking on certain responsibilities. So I ask her if there's anything she needs at the grocery store. I help with dishes and even prepare a meal for both of us whenever she allows me into her kitchen. 'Course, that only deals with material obligation."

"You mean there's more?" Bram had relaxed as Jake rattled off the list of things to do in payment for food. After all, he did all those things for Thea. However, Jake's last remark siphoned off any relief.

"Sure there is." Jake gave Bram a roguish look as he held up a home-baked berry tart. "You don't think a woman's showing off her culinary skills just to get some help with the groceries? Nope. She's giving you a taste of the bliss you could have. Just like the scent coming off a salmon egg tempts a trout to bite that hook. Only she trolls with homemade pies and savory stews."

Bram felt the urge to touch his mouth for the inevitable hook scars at that point. Only with the greatest will did he keep his hands on his lunch and his face blank.

"Scary, huh?" Jake asked.

Okay, maybe his face showed more than he thought. Bram did the manly thing and grunted assent.

"Except that if you want what the lady's offering, it isn't scary at all." The older man took a moment to lick fingers made sticky from fruit filling.

"Even though Nutmeg's years younger than me, age isn't such an obstacle as you get older. Of course, she and I seem to connect at a level that makes all this guesswork unnecessary. You might say that we've been looking for each other all our lives. We just needed to recognize that fact." He pulled out an apple, and liberating his buck knife from his belt, he proceeded to quarter, then core the fruit.

Jake offered him a chunk. Bram shook his head, "No thanks. So you and Meg connected. That fast?"

"That we did. We're still in the courtship stage; don't want to cheat each other of the fun. We both know where we're going." Jake crunched a bite of apple and swallowed before remarking, "You know, folks say you and Althea have something special going on, too."

Bram sipped, then choked on the water. Jake gave him a friendly thump or two between the shoulder blades. When Bram stopped sputtering, the older man said, "Of course, it's a little more complicated for you two, with the boy and all. Fine boy, Alex. Seems to like you well enough, too, from what he says."

"What folks?" asked Bram. At Jake's puzzled look, he added, "You know, the ones who're talking."

"Oh, them. Why, I'd say probably everyone in Potshot who's been close enough to see the sparks coming off you two. Some're more anxious about it than others. Wanting to know what your aim is." Jake wiped his hands on a napkin before adding, "Nobody in Potshot wants to see Althea hurt again."

"People know what happened between Thea and Sal..." he blurted, barely stopping from making Thea's deep secret, common knowledge.

"It's a small town, my friend. We try to take care of our own in these parts," this relative newcomer said.

It did not sound too menacing, not when Jake seemed so sorrowful. "I'm only staying through summer, Jake." Somehow, it came across as hollow to Bram as it must have to the other man.

"That's hardly insurmountable, son."

"And Thea's not likely to appreciate our final plans for Potshot. She's adamant about keeping things as they are, even when changes are for the betterment of this entire mountain system."

Jake just looked at him, so he continued, "All right! So Thea and I combust with proximity. It's hormonal, nothing to base a relationship on. Besides, she's really not my type." Bram forcibly shut his mouth.

"Your type being?" prompted Jake.

"It's always been statuesque, bottled blondes with just enough brains to get them through the night."

"Sounds like a pretty tedious diet to me."

Jake's assessment deflated Bram. He slumped, forearms draped over his lap. "Yes, I guess it was. In fact, I don't know what I'm doing where Thea's concerned. I mean, I think we're behaving all right. You know, maintaining the proper tenant/ landlady relationship. Next thing I know, she's draped over my lap and we've been kissing for I don't know how long."

The thunderous expression on Jake's face seemed all out of proportion to what Bram said, but it did make Bram sit up and take notice. As quickly as the ominous look appeared, it slipped away. The other man offered a blinding grin before breaking into a great belly laugh. When Jake slapped his knees, then stood, Bram just sat there, totally confused over what had transpired.

"So that's how it is." Jake thumped Bram's back. "You're all right, son. Now, I'd better get back to what this town pays me to do. And so should you."

Still a bit dazed, Bram dragged himself to his Rover. He drove in this bemused state into Potshot, where he had promised to pick up some equipment before meeting the group that afternoon. As he passed the library, the sheriff's car careened out of the back parking lot, nearly barreling into him before skidding to a stop. When Sy recognized him, the big man got out of the squad car and stalked to Bram's window.

"Just the guy I wanted to see," said the sheriff. "Got a minute?"

"Sure."

"I need your opinion on this."

Bram parked his vehicle along the roadside. Sy met him at his door, then led the way to the lot behind the library.

"It seems that our firestarter decided the library might make a nice blaze. Meg needed something out of the storage shed. She found what looks to be the makings for another fire."

When Bram gave him a sharp look, the sheriff only nodded. "Looks like the same *modus operandi* as the last two."

Chapter Eleven

Thea spied Bram and ducked out of sight before he saw her. Since Kissing Incidents I and II, her composure around the man resembled unset gelatin. Thus, she chose to linger over old Mrs. Moran, who had been in the library when Meg found evidence of the fire setting. Ma Moran, light-headed and dizzy since tottering out to see what Meg had unearthed, moaned. Cantankerous at best, the woman sat with her head between her knees as Thea absently patted her back. Like a circus terrier leaping through flaming hoops, Thea's mind jumped from Bram to the new proof of arson and back again.

"Hello, Thea."

Bram's rich voice caused her to straighten so quickly that she felt woozy, too. The man reached out and steadied her. The heated imprint of his fingers on her shoulder made her lean toward him instead of away, as she knew she should. Still, she congratulated herself on not throwing herself at the man in a fit of rash passion. When the sun lit his eyes like that. . .

"Whoa! You all right?" Bram moved closer until his distinctive scent swept over her. She plunked down right next to old lady Moran.

"It's okay. I'm just. . .I just went vertical too quickly. Low blood pressure," she lied. In fact, she expected her blood pressure would shoot the mercury right out the end of the calibrated tube.

Bram squatted in front of her. "Looks like this scare is

taking its toll on everyone." He shifted his impenetrable gaze to Mrs. Moran and gave Thea a chance to catch her breath, a breath filled with Bram.

"How're you doing, ma'am?" he asked.

Thea turned to find Ma Moran white as sun-bleached sand. "You're not doing well at all," Thea stated. She took the woman's cold hands in hers and started chafing them. "Fuchsia, Bram, maybe you should let Sy know that we need Dwaine over here. He was at the library earlier with Jessie. Plus he's a trained paramedic."

"No, no. I don't want that," Mrs. Moran fluttered. She grew more agitated, trying to stand. Bram supported her shoulders, only to be swatted away like a nuisance fly. "Leave me alone. Get your redskin hands off me. Leave me alone!"

When Bram released her, she swayed for a moment before getting herself underway. Thea watched as the woman wobbled a few steps, then righted herself. Her vile mutters continued.

Thea straightened then, too. "Boy, you never know where prejudice will raise its ugly head. I'd say she's immune to your charms, Bram." *Wish I were.*

"Humph," was all he said.

"Poor thing looks like she could use some help. Jessie says Ma Moran's been going off the deep end for a long time now. It's gotten worse since Jessie left Zechariah. That man refuses to take his mother in to see Doc. Still, I don't remember her being such a bigot."

They watched until Mrs. Moran went around the far end of the fence. When Bram started toward the shed, no more than a glorified lean-to at the southern corner of the library, Thea stayed beside him, drawn along like iron to a magnet. The jittery crowd made way for Bram as he approached, which meant that both of them crowded into the open shed where he stopped. The stench of accelerant filled Thea's nose and burned her sinuses.

Bram hunkered down by a heap of newspaper and fabric strips. Various cleaning supplies filled two shelves above the saturated mound. The rag end of the library mop had been enlisted as fuel, too.

With Sy wedged next to Bram, Thea leaned over his shoulder to catch what the engineer said. "It looks like the same method, Sheriff."

Sy nodded. "Appears to be an organized crime scene anyway. Definite planning, premeditation and conscious effort, I'd say, and hidden to avoid detection. Perpetrator was probably waiting until nightfall to torch it."

Thea shivered. Somehow, her response communicated itself to Bram, for he cocked his head toward her. Their gazes tangled. He grasped her hand and stood.

"Looks like you might want to set up a watch program here in town, Sheriff," he said. His hand gripped hers more strongly. Not that Thea was gnawing off her paw to get away. If anything, she drew courage from his touch.

Sy nodded yet again. "Other than catching the varmint, a neighborhood patrol seems like the only way we're going to keep this individual from burning Potshot down around our ears."

Dwaine leaned over Thea's shoulder. "I got that list of bystanders, Sy."

"Good." The older man's gaze cut to the people standing around him and settled on the local pharmacist. "Sissy, why don't you let Hulon know that I need him over at the office. Pronto. And folks, I'd appreciate it if you'd all keep what you saw here today to yourselves." His gaze swept the rest of the group.

A woman with a mission, Sissy bustled away. Sy grimaced and swept the hat from his head. "Damn poor luck having Sissy Peabody here. She'll have the whole town riled up by suppertime."

Thea said, "I'm betting everyone will know long before then. My mother knows what I'm having for dinner before I do half the time."

Bram grinned at her. It melted what little resistance she had left. He asked, "Mrs. Peabody's that good, is she?"

"Better, I'd guess," Sy inserted.

The crowd dispersed as Sy and his deputy took pictures of the crime scene, then started cleaning up the mess. Bram stayed, too, holding Thea captive by his presence. Finally, she broke away; remaining in Bram's orbit weakened her promise to herself. Simply, she had to maintain distance. That or cave into her craven hunger. So, she headed toward the bakery only to be hailed by the postmistress.

Thea learned that Sissy had already been there. They discussed the latest incident before the woman handed over a certified letter she had been unable to deliver earlier that day. After Thea signed for it, she decided to open it right then, guessing that the stiff envelope held her contract with the art dealer. Afterward, she remembered having no sense of imminent doom.

Thea wished she had waited. She wished she had never signed for it. She wished Derek Salinger off the face of the earth.

After working her way through the legalese, she realized that she was being ordered to present her son to some laboratory in Reno where a sample for DNA analysis would be taken; a sample that would establish Derek's paternal rights.

Later Thea would wonder how she ended up behind the library, standing in front of Bram. Now she stared at him as he pried the letter out of her hands. He bent his head to read. When he raised his gaze to hers, the compassion she saw there made her eyes sting and throat ache. He drew her into his arms and held her for a long time while she conquered her tears. Finally, she wriggled from his embrace.

"I'm sorry, Bram. You're not my own private wailing wall." She tried to move away, but his hands gently caged her shoulders.

"No apologies, Thea. We all turn to those we need."

She regarded him. "I wish you hadn't put it that way."

"Don't I know it."

She sniffed, saying, "I'm going to Meg's to wash up. Alex takes unmerciful advantage of weakness and I'm meeting him soon." Thea searched his face for any sign of disgust, the kind she was feeling for herself right now.

He touched her cheek with a stroke of his fingers. "I need to get with my crew, too, as soon as the Sheriff's done with me here. We're having a work meeting tonight. Dinner at Peabody's. Why don't you bring Alex down and join us there. My treat."

She glanced away, then back. "I can't do that, Bram. We keep teasing ourselves about where this affinity of ours is going. I don't want Alex reading more into it than he already has."

Sadness became Bram's predominant expression. It went so deep that Thea gripped her hands to keep from reaching out to him. He nodded. "You're the Mom."

They walked together as far as the sidewalk. He said, "Take care," and took a few steps backward, his regard holding her in place. It was only after he turned and headed into the library that she found the strength to move toward Meg's.

Later that night, Thea reminded herself that she could only accept Derek's newest assault, not change the underlying facts. She sat on her back porch, sipping tea and basking in moon glow. Another night, she might have hiked up to the hot springs for a soak, but with the firestarter at large, she dared not leave her sleeping son even for that short time. So now she restated the litany that she had been running through since kissing Alex goodnight.

Derek was Alex's biological father and Alex had to be told.

Her latest painting needed to be finished, then framed.

Alex's wolf family needed to be captured and transported to a better place.

Bram occupied a permanent lodging in her heart and mind.

Of course, the tedious recital sometimes fell into a different order. Nor did each item take up the same amount of worry time. How to tell Alex about his father and how to keep Bram at a physical distance actually made up the bulk of her maudlin thoughts. She snorted to herself; sappy indeed. At this rate, the next thing she'd be telling herself would be how much she needed a drink.

That helped her shake off the mood somewhat, if not the very real problems she faced. A rustling in the brush along the creek grew more rhythmic even as she told herself that. She stayed still and listened as the dull thud of footsteps became clear. Not the wolf, then, unless he now wore boots. Before long Bram's head, torso, then whole body came into view. She had a fairly good view of the man as he came closer. What a sight he was.

Wearing his disreputable cutoffs and obviously fresh from the hot springs, Bram's body took on a luminosity Thea usually associated with moon sheen. His bent head kept her from seeing more than hollows of his eyes along with the strong lines of his cheek and chin, but she had no trouble at all in viewing the rest of him. Moonlight played lovingly over wide shoulders, along his collarbone and on the peaks of his chest, arms, and even stomach ridges. All else was thrown into deep relief. As it had been the first time she had seen him when he shifted from the mists at the springs, he seemed more mythic hero than mortal.

Bram's boots scrunched on the pea gravel along the path and made her aware of how near he had advanced. She swallowed hard and said, "Hey, tenant."

He slowed, but did not stop. With a bounding stride he leapt up the steps to her side, snatching away her breath. He kneeled in front of where she sat on the shabby wicker chair. Taking her cup from suddenly nerveless hands, he set it down before drawing her to his chest.

Heat from his body wrapped around her as his arms enveloped her. She slipped from her seat to kneel between his bent knees. He smelled of the sage and lavender growing along the walkway. Seemingly of their own volition, her arms enfolded his lush strength. Powerful muscle seared the chill from her bare arms. Their mouths met and Thea spun—spun out of control. His mouth tasted of wild mint. She drank of him, alpine water warmed by sun. They exchanged no words. None needed to be spoken.

Woman.

Man.

They complemented each other perfectly. Her body responded to Bram's as parched desert welcomes rain. She budded much like sage flowered, feeling suddenly fragrant and beautiful. Gentle but insistent, he caressed her in ways that gave maximum pleasure. Bram's touch suspended gravity. She lost her sense of up and down.

Sprawled on the rag-rug that covered the slats of the porch, she finally became aware of where she stopped and he started. His head lay on her abdomen along the bare space between tee shirt and jeans. Bram's hands bracketed her hips. Thea pushed her fingers deep into the thick hair along the back of his head, curling her fingers around his nape. There below his ears, the heavy thud of his pulse beat counterpoint to hers. The harsh sounds of their breaths wove harmoniously into other night sounds.

He rubbed his face, slightly raspy, against her skin, then inched up until he lay alongside her. One of his hands, fiery with pounding blood, flexed over her stomach. The other propped up his head as he studied her.

"This isn't going to work, Thea. I can't stay away from you."

"Me either. Away from you, I mean." She turned her head, barely making out his profile in the darkness. "I promise myself that nothing more will happen and then. . ."

"Then, this," he finished.

"Yes. This." Again his face lowered to hers and, God help her, she lifted hers to meet him. Their lips met in hungry resolution. Heat-for-heat until he pulled away, then flopped over onto his back beside her. He gripped her hand in a hold that should have been painful, but was not.

More night sounds and breathing flowed over her. As the yip of coyotes lifted into the air, the low peal of a wolf silenced them. Into the uncanny quiet, each of Bram's inhalations found answer in hers.

"Challie told me that three more rooms at the hotel should be finished by next week. I think I'd better take one of them." He rolled his head so that he faced her.

Could the rending sensation in her chest possibly be her heart? "That might be best."

"I don't want to go."

She swallowed hard. Silence.

He sat and draped his arms over bent knees. "Neither do I want to make your life any tougher than it is. Alex's science project will be finished before I leave."

"I appreciate that." She sat, too. The heat between them flared even without touching.

"I know having Alex tested is going to be hard on you."

"You have no idea."

"You're right. So tell me. Why are you so mulish about Salinger's claim of paternity? I'd think you'd be glad for the financial support. That deadbeat can obviously afford it."

Thea tasted blood from her bitten lip. "You don't know everything, Bram."

He leaned into her and his look scorched. "As you keep saying. Tell me, Thea. Why are you so opposed to Salinger's paternity claim?"

She leaned back, letting her arms support her. "You're the most trying man."

"I know."

With a weighty sigh, she let go. "You remember when I told you about becoming Derek's tutor? In college?"

"Uh-huh."

"Well, one night—one night he took me up in a company plane. One with a bedroom suite." Old anger and pain, dry as dust, coated her mouth and throat. *Do I really want to tell this man everything?*

He kissed her temple and warmed her to her toes. "And?"

An alignment occurred deep within and decided her. "When the pilot announced that the plane was one mile up and holding, Derek. . . Well, he went nuts. Didn't even get me drunk first. Oh, as usual, I had a good buzz on, but I could still see everything, feel everything." She blinked in response to the tactile memories.

"Thea?"

"He raped me. When I didn't cooperate, he slugged me a few times for good measure. I tell myself I'm over that part now. It's just that having him around again. . .his threats to take Alex from me. I can't—I *will not* let that happen." She shook off the heated swell of tears before they spilled onto her cheeks.

"Come here, Thea."

208

The comfort Bram offered proved too much for her then. She turned into his arms and gripped his waist with her arms. Face against his chest, she took comfort in his strong heartbeat. His hands soothed her back and shoulders in long slow circles. He offered nonsense sounds in his grandfather's language. They sat that way for a long time.

Against his chest, she murmured, "Alex was conceived that night. Before I realized I was pregnant, I'd sworn off the booze. It made me easy prey to predators like Salinger. I committed myself to being a lucid and focused artist, too. Believe it or not, that helped me to deal with the rape. By then, my scholarship was in jeopardy, so I was seeing an advisor on an augmented schedule."

"Your mother?"

"I couldn't tell her. She'd have told Charles and it really would have hit the fan then. Besides, I'd gotten myself into the mess."

"You had to have someone. When I think of you alone—"

"Meg was there for me. She's been my mentor since my year as an undergraduate. But when all this came down, well, she became the mom I'd always wanted. And a friend. She's the only one besides Derek who knows the circumstances of Alex's conception. Meg's offered to put out a hit on him and believe me, the visual works. Now you know, too."

"You didn't go to the police?" Oklahoma tinged his flat voice; anger and menace fused in a dangerous heat.

"Derek Salinger's daddy owns a good part of San Francisco. They'd never have believed me, a drunken scholarship student on probation."

"And that bastard Salinger got away scot-free."

She leaned away from him. "You might want to watch how you use the term 'bastard' around here. Alex is second generation after all."

"Aw, Thea."

"That was a joke, Bram. Pretty feeble, I guess."

"What about when Derek realized you were pregnant?"

"I mostly saw him at a distance after that—surrounded by his bootlicking buddies. Later I heard how he bragged about his conquests, members of Salinger's Mile High Club, of which I was the charter member. Meg wanted all of us to band together in a class action suit against the scum. It just didn't seem worth it by then, not in my third trimester. I wanted it behind me."

"Son-of-a-bitch."

Thea decided she never wanted to be on the wrong side of his fury. "He is that. He was smart enough to run to his daddy's lawyers, though. In exchange for natal care, hospital expenses, and one year of pediatric care, I signed papers relinquishing any future claim I could make against him. He came back at the end of that time with more papers to sign and an offer of cash. I signed all right, but I didn't take his blood money."

She studied the shadowed face of her companion. "I'd do it again. In a heartbeat, if it would keep Alex safe."

Bram's face, even in darkness, looked implacable. "Salinger seems to believe he has a hold over you."

Thea froze, barely containing the rage that threatened to overcome her. "He may believe that. But I'll never ever let him get his grimy paws on my son."

"I don't like the idea of you fighting Salinger alone."

She pulled away with more reluctance than she liked. "Meg's always been there for me. It's just that now. . ."

"Her and Seeker," he said.

"Yes. They seem to have bonded."

He stroked her nape while unspoken words swirled into the dark.

"About Seeker, Thea. He told me he grew up around here. I didn't get the feeling that anyone else knew that. I thought you should know, though."

She considered that for a while. "That's odd. Yet Jake's really good with Alex. Fuchsia, who am I kidding? The man fits in everywhere. So I suppose if he wants to keep his past to himself, it won't do any harm."

'Harm' dangled and drooped in the air between them.

"What about us, Thea?"

She squeezed her lids shut and clenched her hands together. "You're here through September, Bram, plus we keep ending up on opposite sides of your plans for Potshot. There is no us."

On the mountain another coyote gave throat to his loneliness and from across Eden Valley, another voice answered. This time, the wolf remained silent.

Bram leaned toward her and pressed his face against hers. "Oh, Thea," mingled their breaths. All in a rush, he stood and disappeared into the house.

Thea's throat ached with her desire to howl into the night. Instead, she wiped moisture from her face. His tears or hers, who shed them, really didn't matter.

Chapter Twelve

June heat shimmered off the granite rocks surrounding the wolves' lair. Ears pricked and head raised, the male stared toward the blind. *It was almost as though the wolf sensed the humans hidden there*, Thea decided as she peered through binoculars. Sun-heated pine and granite dust filled her nose while across the distance, mock battle growls of Zorro's pups teased her ears. The clever hunter lowered his head then, triggered by cues beyond Thea's awareness. Flowing into a ground-eating trot, he headed for the hidden trap. Bram was in that concealment along with two biologists and a veterinarian. The thought tripped Thea's heart into double-time. Safe within her own cover, she gnawed her lip.

Compressed air escaped the wolf-threatened blind with a *whoosh!* A tranquilizer dart smacked into the black's hindquarters, where it quivered like a crazed bird-of-prey. Thea recoiled as if her flank had been thumped instead of Zorro's. With a yelp and a twisting leap, the wolf bit the dart, pulling it out with his teeth. He shook the projectile hard enough to break its plastic back. Thea gulped an involuntary protest.

Fuchsia, but she was glad Meg had the Alex Watch this morning. She would not choose to have her son witness this sad, but necessary, deed.

"Sweet," said Dwaine. He lowered the sites of his high-powered rifle, loaded as a deadly backup measure.

"Hardly," Thea replied. Like her, the deputy lurked in

the shadows of a rocky slab, out of easy visual reach of the wolves. Still, Bram had warned her that Zorro's lupine sense of smell could find them.

The ambush rushed toward its conclusion. Somehow the wolf's now silent effort tainted this conspiracy of man against nature even more. Zorro looked like anything but The Big Bad Wolf as the drug stole his dexterity. Thea covered her mouth to keep from giving voice to his heroic struggle. How could the wolf know they intended no harm? To him, he and his family were under attack from an unseen enemy. Bushwhacked. Even as she thought that, Zorro staggered toward his mate, who fearlessly tried to stand on her mangled front leg. The female gave an imperative growling bark. In wolf language, it must have meant 'Come now!' since her pups headed for her at breakneck speed.

Rocks sliding behind Thea drew her away from the distressing sight. What she saw caused her heart to stutter. "Alex!"

But her son ignored her as he raced toward the clearing. Jaw clenched, he pelted around boulders and pines. She tried to head him off, but he dodged both her and Dwaine, veering toward the wolves. Only three strangers and Bram stood between her son and the slashing teeth of two angry wolves.

She must have cried out then. Bram stepped from cover and turned toward her. In that inimitable way of his, he assessed the situation, then dashed toward Alex, who ran blind with tears glazing his face. Bram caught her son in his arms, swinging around upon impact and holding Alex against his side. Thea sprinted toward them. In the time it took to reach them, the shooter got off two more shots. *Whap, whap!*

She did not see whether they hit their mark. Sliding to a stop beside Bram, she captured Alex's chin in one hand, steadying herself with an arm around the man. "Alex! Stop thrashing! Look at me. Look at me!"

He stopped struggling and his reddened eyes finally met her gaze. "You lied to me. I hate you!"

"Honey, they're not hurting Zorro. Those're tranquilizers, just like Bram told you. The wolves will only sleep for awhile."

Alex whipped his face toward Bram. "That's right, Alex. And Zorro's mate is in bad shape. She needs surgery. By the time the vet's finished with her, she'll be good as new."

The boy leaned around Bram's shoulder, his gaze unerring. "Let me go."

"You'll stay with us, then," Bram said, his tone brooking no nonsense.

Alex gave a curt nod, but his lips trembled. Bram released him and Thea wrapped her arms around her ribs to keep from reaching for her son. He stood, twisting his hands together. The bones of his shoulders moved in sharp relief beneath his snug T-shirt and his nape looked vulnerable and boyish. But the look in his eyes when he glanced at her showed the man he would become.

"I need to get closer."

Bram laid a hand on one shoulder. "Watch the biologists, Alex. They'll give a thumbs-up when it's safe."

Alex's jaw set in a mutinous cast, but he stayed. Both adult wolves were down now. In the clearing, one man delved into oversized packs while two women, one the shooter, checked the wolves' vital signs. The pups nuzzled their mother's face and belly in obvious confusion. They showed no fear of the humans, only puppy skittishness.

The markswoman straightened and signaled. Alex jerked as though shocked and sprang into a ground-eating lope. Bram and Thea followed more slowly. Jake and Sy appeared from a stony outcrop above, both men slinging rifles. A belated chill shook her. If the sedatives had not done the job, Alex would have witnessed bloody and tragic death today.

All parties converged at the overhang. Dwaine nodded to the markswoman. "Nice shooting."

Her frizzy red hair had escaped its twist. She stroked Zorro's shoulder. "These're fine specimens."

"He's not a specimen. His name is Zorro." Thea hardly recognized her son's resolute voice.

The biologist gauged Alex with a glance. "You're the one who found the black, then. Good job. He'll be right as rain with regular feeding. We're unbelievably lucky to find a wild and viable mated pair. How's the female?"

"She'll be able to use her leg once we reset it and she heals. Looks like she got caught in a trap," said her partner, the veterinarian.

Sy and Jake joined them, both men cutting troubled glances at Alex.

"I thought you were keeping Nutmeg company, son," Jake said.

Alex held himself stiff with arms crossed in a punishing grip. "I wanted to say goodbye."

The older man sent Thea a perplexed look and she shrugged.

Meanwhile, the other biologist dragged a sling carrier to where the wolves lay. As he and the redhead lifted the male, the wolf's head lolled and his tongue protruded. He looked dead. A sob escaped Alex, then, and Thea wrapped her arms around him.

"He'll be fine, honey. He's in a deep sleep and can't control his movement."

Her son chewed his lip. When he knelt to coax a pup toward him, the redhead said, "Better not. We don't want the pups getting too comfortable around humans. It'll put them at greater risk once we release them into the recovery area."

The pups were so sweet, Thea could understand her son's response. Blue eyes with hints of gold along with densely

215

furred bodies, they drew her, too.

"Where're you taking them?" Alex asked.

"The Blue Range area in Arizona, where we have a breeding program for endangered Mexican Gray wolves. Once they're strong enough and the mother's recovered, we'll release them into the Apache or Gila National Forests."

"What made them endangered?" Thea asked.

The redhead answered. "The usual stuff: guns and poison. Wolves sometimes eat cattle. Ranchers sprinkle poison on the carcasses."

Alex gulped. "But won't my wolves be killed, too?"

The man answered, "We'll do our best to see that doesn't happen. The areas we're releasing them into don't have cattle and support enough natural prey to keep them fat and sassy. Now if you'll stand back, we have some work to do before the anesthesia wears off."

Late afternoon sun bounced luminous rays off the hot spring pools by the time they completed the grueling walk down the mountain. Sage and dust filled Thea's sinuses. She and Alex watched the burdened slings lift to deposit the still unconscious adult wolves into trucks. The pups rolled out of carriers into the containment with their mother. A quick glimpse of them gamboling around her prone form was all Thea got before the sliding door closed. She stood with her son as the trucks pulled out of the hot springs' parking lot. Dejection oozed off Alex as Bram ambled over to them.

"That went well. My friend will keep me posted, Alex. I'll let you know how Zorro's family does."

Alex glared at him. Tears spilled over onto his cheeks. "I hate you, too. Leave me alone." He pivoted and ran after the departing trucks.

Bram stepped back as though struck and Thea laid a comforting hand over his arm. "I'm sorry, Bram. Once Alex calms down, he'll regret his words. I know he didn't mean them."

"Oh yes he did. And I don't blame him." He pulled away from her light touch, then walked toward his rig.

Torn, Thea hesitated before tracing her son's path. Much as she hated to admit it, the dejection in Bram's voice and posture haunted her. Besides the man's intrusive plans for Potshot, he had 'Temporary' written all over him. She could not afford the energy necessary to sustain such a tenuous relationship, no matter how her hormones looped-the-loop in his presence. More to the point, Alex needed his mother.

By the time she caught up with her son and they headed home, Bram had packed and moved to the hotel.

After finding Bram gone, Thea went through the motions. Alex refused to talk to her, preferring the solitude of his room. The quiet she usually appreciated turned oppressive. Like sucking on a sore tooth, Thea wandered the basement room. Bram had left the space too neat for her taste, even going so far as to vacuum the area rug into patterns. Pillows lined up like soldiers on the bed, the curtains hung stiffly at attention, and his used sheets had been stuffed in pillowcases for washing. A harsh laugh escaped her then; Bram had not intended the geometry—it was simply his nature. Thea left everything as it was except the sheets. Those she pulled from the case before burying her face in the folds. Bram's scent lingered, lifeless and distant rather than warmed by his body heat. She wondered if she would be able to wash the linens until all traces of the man disappeared.

Still, the flow of life persisted. Tonight the returns on the special ballot would be announced followed by the final council vote for the hot springs. Thea dressed carefully, knowing she did so for Bram rather than the meeting. She swung by Alex's room before leaving. His living space looked impossibly neat; a holdover from Bram's science project rules. Thea wondered how long this vestige would remain.

"You're sure you don't want to go with me?"

Her son's eyes looked swollen and his blond hair swept back from his forehead in a haphazard way. A book lay face down on his bed. "I'm going with Ian. He promised to pick me up. We need his truck for my project."

She hesitated, then heeded his need for space. "I made sandwiches. They're in the fridge. You can have an apple or orange. If you'd like to make chocolate milk, you can."

"He's gone, isn't he?"

She bit her lip as the hollow ache washed over her anew. "Yes."

Alex picked at a hole in his jeans and for once, Thea let him. "We always knew he'd go," he said in a diminished voice.

Thea walked to her son and kissed his forehead. He offered no resistance. "Bram's still at the hotel, sport, if you want to talk with him."

"Fat chance."

At the sheriff's request, she met Sy at his office before going to the church; one more activity intended to distract her from the hole left by Bram's departure. Sy set a cup of coffee on his desk, then shuffled stacked paper.

"You're looking a little peaked, Thea. Sure you want to do this now?"

She dragged her flagging attention back to him. "Why not."

He studied her for a long moment before leaning into his chair. "Was glad to see that everything went so well with Alex's wolves. That boy got a might upset when they tranquillized the adults, though. I'm sincerely glad Bram was there to explain the situation."

"Yes. He promised Alex that he'd keep him posted on the

218

wolves' progress."

"That female's leg was pretty badly damaged. Hope they can fix her up." Sy rocked a little in his chair.

"The biologist said it looked like she'd gotten caught in a trap. They expected a full recovery."

"Those pups sure were cute little guys. Can purely see why some folks would want to take them home, raise them like dogs."

She finally smiled. "They were adorable little rascals. I had to remind both myself and Alex that they're wild critters. Those little ones would never be content as domestic animals."

"I heard tell that Bram moved into the hotel."

Thea leaned forward. "Sy, you didn't ask me to come down here to discuss the wolves or Bramden Hayes. You'll make us late for the town meeting."

He grinned, as though he got the response he wanted. Just what that was, he left Thea to wonder. Sy went on, "Just visiting, Thea. No need to get your fur up."

He bent his head to the papers on his desk. "I got some information back on that little project we started a few weeks back." His glint penetrated her blue funk.

"Seems our boy Salinger got himself into a fix in Russia late last year. Turned out to be public knowledge actually, just not something any of us here in Potshot took much notice of." He pushed a faxed newspaper clipping toward her.

Thea glanced at the banner headline: *A Capitalist's Nightmare* it read. Before she could examine more than a few lines, Sy continued.

"Seems that Salinger took a big chunk of his corporate holdings and dumped them into a Western-style hotel in Moscow. The funds he used came through improper channels. Sounds like the Golden Boy lived the high life there, too— drugs, parties, girls. He's what I'd call an Ugly American."

219

Thea gave up reading the article until later. "And?"

"The Chechen mafia caught up with him. To give Salinger credit, the hotel looked like a good moneymaking deal. Any other place and it probably would've been, but Russia isn't exactly Potshot, now is it?

"We can only hope."

"After another hotel owner, this one from Oklahoma, was killed by local thugs, Salinger sold cheap and came home with his tail between his legs."

Sy studied another paper on his desk, then glanced back at her. "Sorry, Thea, can't let you see this. It's more along the lines of confidential information. What it basically says is that this flop follows a long string of failures. When young Salinger came home, his daddy tore his son a new butt hole. Guess young Derek's on the equivalent of a tight rein, to say the least."

Thea sat back in her chair with a *whoosh!* Suddenly, everything fell into place: Derek showing up here out of the blue; his active courting of her vote; his attempted blackmail to make her buckle under his demands. Now Thea, for the first time, had ammunition to use against him. "So he's trying to prove himself to Daddy? That's what this is all about."

"I figure there's piles of money involved, too."

"Derek's inheritance?"

"Can't say for sure. Seems likely, though."

While Thea mulled that over, Sy slid another paper toward her. "Here's the preliminary paperwork for that restraining order you wanted. You'll probably have to show up in court, too."

Instead of taking it, she stood, the newspaper article in hand. "I may want that later, Sy. Right now, I need to speak with Salinger before the meeting starts."

Sy stopped her with, "Now, Thea, some of this only works as hearsay. . ."

220

"I know, Sy. I'll treat what you've said as rumor." She strode toward the door.

Sy said, "And one more thing. The timing of the first and second fires doesn't coincide with Salinger's presence here. He has firm alibis."

Thea waved that off. "More's the pity. I didn't really think he'd done the deeds. Still, you did need to check out the lead, didn't you?"

He chuckled. "That I did, Thea, that I did."

"Now, Sy, if you don't let me out of here, I really will miss an ideal opportunity." She just about closed the door, when she thought of something else and popped her head inside. "Why don't you and April come for dinner Friday night?"

"I'll check with the boss and see what she says. You wouldn't, by any chance, be making your famous venison lasagna, would you?"

"Might be. I still have some burger left from Dwaine's last deer." She let the door close and headed toward the church, where cars already packed the lot for the meeting.

When she saw lights in Salinger's display space, she changed course. 'Bearding the lion in his cave' appealed to her and damn the restraining order. What she had in mind would make that paper tiger obsolete anyway. The door was ajar, but she knocked. Three aids surrounded Derek and when they all turned to look at her, she fixed her gaze on the blond man.

"I need to talk to you. Alone would be best," she said.

He smiled that shark's grin perfected on her and other unsuspecting females, then shooed his contingent out. They all grabbed some portion of display before trooping from the building. All of them gave her sidelong glances. Thea waited until the last one exited and closed the door firmly behind her.

Derek, of course, took the opportunity to move closer than she liked, forcing her to tilt her head back. "Thea, sweetheart, this is such an unexpected pleasure."

"More than you know." She stepped around him, stopping when she reached the room's center. He hitched one elegant flank on a corner of a table; the picture of urbane charm.

"To what do I owe this visit? I suppose it's too much too ask for complete capitulation?" He stared at her breasts for a second too long. It left her feeling in need of a scrub brush and long soak in the tub.

She forced herself to close the distance between them, then presented him with the press article she held. "Actually, I've recently been made aware of just what—ah—shaky ground your corporation's on." Before he could take the sheet of paper from her hand, she stepped back. "Tsk, tsk, Derek. A string of business failures capped by the fiasco in Moscow? And now you want to take the lion's share of our little venture into hand. I don't think so."

He crossed his arms over his chest. A slight frown creased the skin between his brows.

"We've continued to build our version of the spa right where you intend to develop. That means you'd have to tear down all our hard work. Do you really think the good folk of Potshot would let you do that? Or place their future on the quaking sands of your offshoot company? Especially once they understand that you're on the equivalent of business probation."

A smirk covered his face. "You won't be able to convince them of that before the final vote, sweetheart. Frankly, your information's come just a tad too late."

She cocked her head at him and hoped the tremor from her racing blood would not give her away. "Oh, you're probably right, but I wasn't going to tell them. You are."

His eyes narrowed. "Sweet Thea, are you sure you haven't been drinking?"

That put steel in her spine. She positively stalked him.

"Oh, no, Derek. Not a drop. But if I'm forced to make a statement, I'll also include some little known facts about your despicable past. About how you raped me and other young women. How you left your own child and his mother high-and-dry. I'll tell them about how you came back to us, not to give fatherly support to your 13-year-old son, but to blackmail me into acquiescing to your plans. I'll tell them about your string of business failures and ask them if they really want to hang their faith and future hopes on you." She shook with rage now, standing in front of him.

"I'll have you in the slammer for defamation of character."

She laughed to cover the thrill of fear. "You don't have enough character to defame. Besides, the damage would be done as soon as I spoke."

Although he continued to sit, she noted his clenched jaw and white face. In a low voice, she asked, "How do you think they'd vote?"

He sprang to his feet quick as a striking snake; so fast that she took an involuntary step back, but no more. She refused to give him any sense of victory. His next words hit her like blasts from six inches away. "You little *bitch*. As though you'd tell them any of that. You wouldn't risk losing your status as queen bee in this little backwater."

She craned her head back and spat, "Try me!"

He raised his fist, frozen at the top of its arc as the door slammed open behind him. "Better lower that hand, Salinger. You've got a witness to your violence now. Thea, step away from him." Bram's voice, edged in honed steel, cut through the tension.

Thea indulged in a long look into her opponent's eyes before shifting away from him. He lowered his hand, shrugging his shoulders to adjust his suit. He did not fool her for a minute. White brackets around his mouth and shrunken pupils warned her of undiminished rage.

"This is not over between us. Not by a long shot," he ground out between clenched teeth.

He pivoted on the balls of his feet and stalked from the room. When Bram made no move to budge from his path, Derek's lips thinned as he stepped around the man. He left the door open behind him. Once the angry staccato of his footsteps faded, Thea surrendered to her body's reaction. Adrenaline raced through her system until even her teeth started chattering.

Bram came to her between one shudder and the next, or so it seemed to her. She practically launched herself at him. His arms wrapped around her, holding her close enough to hear his heart surge. "What possessed you to meet that polecat alone? And on his stamping ground? He almost hit you. I'd have torn him limb-from-limb if he had. Almost did anyway. Would have been purely my pleasure." His breath fanned the hair over her forehead. She loved that tinge of Oklahoma in his voice.

Between shivers, she managed, "You never would've sunk to his level."

His hands framed her face. "Don't be so sure. And don't you ever, ever do anything that pig-headed again." Unlike Derek's, Bram's pupils looked huge.

"I know I shouldn't have. Really I do. But there just wasn't time for a better approach." She laughed as a bubble of joy spilled over the aftereffects of anxiety. "Fuchsia, Bram! I think he's going to back down. At least as far as the hot springs goes."

She caught her lower lip in her teeth. If only the mire of custody over Alex could be resolved so easily. For now—

Now! "What time is it?" she asked, breaking his comforting hold on her shoulders. She glimpsed the clock on the wall. "Come on, Bram! The meeting's already started."

They exited the building in a rush, breaking into a run

when they hit the street, then hurried through the church door without slowing. They entered the basement meeting room breathless, but in time to see Derek take the podium. Thea tried to compose herself. If Derek balked at withdrawing from Potshot, she would be forced to carry through on her threat. Just the thought of baring her soul in public sent freezing rivulets through her abdomen. Nevertheless, if that was what she had to do. . .

". . .with great regret that I'm informing Potshot of my decision not to progress any further with our plans for the health spa."

A roar of disbelief filled the room. Thea stood in the perfect position to see the shocked expressions on the faces of Derek's aides. As the clamor died down, he said, "After doing more in-depth research, we didn't see the kind of profit margin that would make this a good opportunity for Salinger Enterprises. With so many better projects. . ."

"Liar," she muttered.

Bram slid an arm around her shoulder and whispered, "It doesn't matter."

Amazingly enough, it really didn't. Any damage done to the townspeople's belief in their hot spring's potential could be assuaged. Once the local economy took a leap upward, Derek's words would be recognized for the fabrication they were. Thea leaned into the heat and strength of the man beside her and let Salinger's words wash over her unheeded.

As Derek and his assistants formed a phalanx and headed toward the door, Letty Donaldson took the podium and called for a fifteen-minute break before moving onto the other business scheduled for the evening. People swirled from their seats, clotting the aisles to discuss this latest development. Derek and his group converged at the door where Thea and Bram stood.

For a long minute, Derek met her stony gaze, then

motioned for his people to go first. With a false charm that remained intact in spite of the fury bubbling up in his eyes, he leaned toward her.

Thea stiffened. She felt Bram bunch in reaction and said to him, "It's all right, Bram." Bram stepped back.

Derek's hot breath brushed her cheek as he leaned toward her ear. "You will live to regret this, sweetheart. The boy's mine." He dipped down to lick her neck from collar bone to jaw.

She jerked from him. Before she could spit out her disgust, and her fear for what he threatened, he smiled and walked through the door. Bram started after him, obviously unaware of what had transpired, but knowing that somehow Salinger had wounded her. Thea clutched his arm.

"No. Nothing you do or say can change anything," she said through lips gone stiff with dread.

He looked like he wanted to argue with her, but a group of Potshot's residents descended. As friends and neighbors inundated her with questions, Thea locked her anxiety into a tight compartment. She would take it out later, over and over again, to pick her worries apart in excruciating detail. But not now. Not now.

After an interminable break during which Thea realigned the possibilities for the spa in terms of what had taken place, the mayor called the meeting to order. Without looking, Thea felt Bram leave her side. His departure left her bereft as Letty introduced the university team.

Thea edged toward the front with Meg and Jake, where they had saved a seat for her. She settled between them and Jessica Moran. The lights dimmed, leaving only the ones at the front to illuminate the grant team. The draped tray holding Alex's science project served as a centerpiece.

Alex and Bram had invited her for a private viewing the day before, but a summons from Sy had postponed it. She would see Alex's project for the first time tonight along with the rest of Potshot residents. As Bram began speaking about his mission, Thea's concentration frayed. She barely registered how her gaze lingered on Bram or how his proximity gave her a deep sense of peace even amid the internal turmoil. Even so, she divided her gazing time between the man and Alex.

Her son sat on one end of the front row between best buddies Sherman and Keith. Although somewhat subdued, Alex looked much recovered from the wolf debacle. Her attention kept straying to him, but not because the boys wriggled and whispered in counterpoint to Bram's voice. No, Thea just needed the reassurance that her son's presence gave her. She would have to tell him about his father soon, before they trekked to Reno, where some stranger would take a sample from her son; a sample that would forevermore tie him to Derek Salinger. She shuddered.

Alex sprang from his seat. Evidently, the unveiling was about to take place. The gathered adults chuckled indulgently as Sherman gave him a helpful shove. Her son's gaze searched for and found hers in the crowd. She smiled, letting her pride shine. With a few skipping steps, Alex walked to the tray, where with Ian's help, he pulled the cover from his model. Even though the scale was too small to be seen from more than four rows back, the crowd broke into spontaneous applause.

Letty's voice blared over the loudspeakers, "Don't worry folks, you'll all have a chance to see Alex's handiwork after Dr. Hayes gives his talk. And Alex asked me to remind you not to touch it, since he still has the science fair to get through."

Alex's cheeks grew rosy and he ducked the same way he might to avoid a motherly kiss. Thea's eyes burned as her son returned to his seat. She noticed how he avoided Bram's overtures.

The slide show began. As Bram introduced one point after another, one change after another, Thea wondered how she would ever survive the cold filling her. "Defensible space. . .remove all vegetation. . .prescribed burns. . .terraces and other slope sculpting. . .findings from the Sierra Nevada Ecosystem Study. . .auto-suppression. . .rebuild access roads. . ."

Bram went on and on. Nothing made sense to Thea except that he expected Potshot to make sweeping changes. Voices raised in uncertainty during the question period gradually penetrated her turmoil. The clock on the wall behind Bram told Thea that only twenty-five minutes had passed as she sank into despondency. A few rows back, Hulon Peabody stood and asked something about defensible space in Potshot proper.

Bram said, "That will mean sprinkler systems, fire resistant roofs and other building materials plus attachments to wells and pools."

The last brought a roar of laughter. Someone, it sounded like Bud Donaldson, called out, "Nobody has a swimming pool here, Dr. Hayes. That's what the springs're for."

Bram nodded. "I know that. But should anyone choose to install a pool in the future, those provisions will need to be included."

Another murmur of acceptance. Thea jumped to her feet. "What's wrong with all of you? Can't you see what he's proposing?" She looked around, vaguely aware of Jessie and Meg's hands on her arms, urging her to sit.

"He's telling you that Potshot won't ever be the same again. It'll be a completely different place from what we want, from what we all chose when we decided to live here!"

Letty's voice interrupted. "Now, Thea, you're out of order, dear. I believe Bud had the floor."

Thea swung around, only to snare Bram in her gaze. "You can't do this, Bram. Not for some irrational response to a catastrophe that may never occur. Not to purge your own ghosts."

His eyes, so full of empathy and another emotion, deep and warm and beautiful, held her gaze. "This has nothing to do with whim, Thea." His gaze broke free and swept the room.

"This area's overdue for a conflagration the likes of which is only seen every hundred years. Your time is up. That's why we chose your community in the first place. That's why you invited us here. These changes will save lives. Your lives." He met her gaze again and held it.

He said, "Ian, start the film."

"Bram, are you sure. . ." the other man began.

"Start the film, Ian. These people need to know the aftereffects of wildfire. Then they can decide for themselves."

The lights dimmed and the film started. Thea sank onto her chair, perched on the front edge. A more polished and distant Bram, as narrator, filled her view. Then first person accounts of wildfire's horror issued from the screen. Dead and mutilated animals; gutted communities arrayed against beatific views of what they had been before the fire. Scientists, including Dr. Bramden Youngwolf Hayes, explained how they came too late to their catastrophic predictions. The screen's horror mesmerized her.

Even with irrefutable evidence, Thea could not get beyond feeling coerced and ensnared by Bram. He had deceived her into trusting him, then done what he intended all along. He ambushed her with eyes the shade of a kestrel hawk's, hands that gave joy, a mouth that freed her from past hurts.

Or maybe she had it wrong. Bram had never wavered from his purpose. Perhaps Thea had seduced herself into this predicament.

As credits rolled, she stood, working her way to the aisle.

She left the room. Leaden, she forced herself up the stairs. Another person bowled into her as she headed toward the double doors leading from the church. Thea reached out without thinking and steadied the woman, who turned out to be old Mrs. Moran. The woman's eyes showed white around the rims as she tried unsuccessfully to speak. Her clawed hands dug into Thea's upper arms with surprising strength.

"What is it?" Thea asked.

When the woman's mouth finally shaped the sound she wanted, it emerged as a whistle of empty air. Chilling fear claimed Thea for the second time that night.

"What?" she demanded of the older woman, practically shaking her now.

"Fire!" came out as an eerie trill. The woman marshaled a breath and screamed, "Fire!"

Chapter Thirteen

Bram slumped at the curb in front of the charred remains of Salinger's storefront. His post-fire reaction hit him—every bit as bad as usual. Luckily, the dizziness and shakes were over now. He watched Moran's tanker truck pull away, heading toward Peabody's where the fire crew would enjoy yet another much-deserved breakfast. Jake's construction gang mingled with the tired throng. In the predawn, they looked just like any other resident of Potshot and made Bram feel like the odd-man-out.

Bram scrubbed his face with hands blackened by soot. No doubt his actions added to what must be a haggard exterior. He grinned, picturing the story Alex would weave if the boy could see him now. Bram would be some fantastic creature like Alex's miner's ghost or abominable snowman or werewolf. The smile slipped. Like Thea, the kid would probably see a water skimmer, an insect that never broke surface tension and skipped along water without dipping below the surface.

Discontent ate Bram's satisfaction at overcoming the fire. He turned to peruse the remnants of the building, as though to prove to himself that he had accomplished something in the night. First light made the wreckage both clearer and more terrible. How they had managed to keep the devastation from Jessica Moran's hair salon on one side and Donaldson's remodeled emporium on the other. . . Bram almost believed small miracles did occur. Almost.

Except that he knew that if he dug into the wreckage as Ian and Challie were doing now, he would unearth a slew of scientific evidence in support of why they had been able to suppress this fire. Sometimes even *he* got tired of the mundane explanations. Sometimes he needed to believe in higher powers. Sometimes he wanted to trust in what he couldn't quantify and go with his gut feeling. Explore squishy emotions.

Thea.

Sy joined him to hand over a canteen. Bram took a long swig of cold water from the town's community wells before giving it back. Charcoal filled in the lines of the other man's face, aging him a good ten years in the process.

"You look like hell, Benton."

"Kiss my ass, Youngwolf."

Bram grinned, then scowled. However this fire had started, and he would bet good money that it had been arson—and he intended to get to the bottom of it. If a vengeful Salinger had anything to do with it, well, he'd enjoy watching how Sy played that out.

He swiveled around to see how Ian and Challie were doing. Toward the back of the dismal room, they stood knee-deep in debris from the fire. Smoldering remains of Salinger's glossy displays curled around Ian's fireproof coveralls. As Bram watched, the fireman leaned into Challie and planted a kiss on her sooty nose. Hummingbird slanted into the kiss until it became a deep meeting of mouths.

So that's how the winds blow. Bram greeted the discovery with much less enthusiasm than he would have a day before. He pivoted around and said to Sy, "I guess we'll know more about how this one started once Challie and Ian finish their analysis."

Sy hooted at that. "Could be a while, partner, human nature being what it is." Bram gave him a crooked grin before

232

the other man clapped him on the back and stood. "C'mon, young'un. Hulon's delivered quite a spread. I feel like I've got a raccoon gnawing at my gizzard."

Bram matched the older man's stride. As they walked, Sy said, "Got to tell you, Bram, this fire business has given me a few sleepless nights even when we aren't actually fighting the stuff. I'd love to pin this on Salinger's tail, but it just doesn't fit the man's profile. Not that I won't enjoy putting the guy in the hot seat for a time. Especially since he's been putting Thea through the ringer."

The worry nibbling at Bram became full-fledged apprehension. He pushed hands through gritty hair. "I don't know what to tell you, Sy. Maybe we'll be closer to a resolution after my crew sifts through what's left."

"And maybe not," added the sheriff.

Bram had nothing to say to that. Instead he held the door into the casino for Sy. Once in the restaurant of Peabody's gambling joint, odors of smoke and sweat combined with more pleasant aromas of bacon, fried eggs, cinnamon rolls, and coffee. Bram searched the room until his gaze snagged on Thea. She stood behind the long buffet table, ladling out food to a line of hungry fire fighters. Her silky pantsuit from the night before glimmered an emerald green amid dark blotches of sooty men. Her face looked paler than usual and her tip-tilted eyes dominated her face. Yet seeing her settled Bram into an unfamiliar peace.

She greeted the man standing in front of her. After a brief grin, her gaze ranged the room, first passing, then snapping back to Bram. Tension around her eyes eased and a relieved smile lit her face. Muscles bunched in his chest, already tight from a night of hard labor. He sucked in a deep breath, the first in a long time. Had Thea moved beyond her anger with him? Maybe now she saw how vulnerable Potshot was to fire.

Sy clapped him on the back for the second time in five

233

minutes. "Hooey! Looks like I'm not the only one looking forward to a hero's welcome. Well, come on, son. Doesn't do to keep Althea MacTavish waiting." The sheriff started toward the men's room, where they could wash up before eating.

A quick scrub, then Bram stumbled back into the queue. The line finally brought him opposite Thea. Their gazes clung, then she looked him over quickly, saying, "No new battle scars, I hope?" The tremor in her voice told him more than she might have intended. Blood moved into her face as she avoided his gaze.

"Not a one. Your little fire department's shaping up real well under Ian's direction. Jake's people lent a hand, too." About that time, he realized how heavy his plate had grown beneath Thea's ministrations. He glanced down to find it half filled with bacon. "Whoa, Thea. Let's save some for the guys behind me."

On that, her cheeks positively glowed. "Oh, fuchsia! Look what I've done. I must be more tired than I thought." She applied her tongs and slid much of the bacon back into the warming dish.

"You look real good this morning," he said before hurrying onto the next tray. Sometimes compliments put Thea in slash-and-burn mode. This time her sidelong look conveyed shyness.

After downing a quart of orange juice and emptying two full plates of food, he wanted to crawl back to his hotel room and into bed. Instead, he lingered until Meg escorted a group of children, Alex among them, into the restaurant before turning them loose on the leftover food. The kids swarmed the tables like locusts, their bright chatter piercing even Bram's blanket of exhaustion.

He watched as Thea, finished with her volunteer duties, nabbed a pot of hot water, a mug, and a tea bag, then joined her son along with about five other kids. A wave of discouragement rolled over Bram. Was it so hard for the woman to seek him out now and then? He mustered the grit to leave just as Thea picked up her pot and mug to head his way. A rush of elation hit.

I'm on a roller coaster, he decided as he hurried to clear a place for her. She settled beside him.

"I thought you'd be gone by now, Bram," she said with a gleaming cat-eyed look.

He leaned over to speak softly in her ear. "That why you're so happy to see me?"

She rewarded him with a rose pink blush. Even over his own stink, he smelled her scent. He played the thief, carrying away Essence of Thea and banking it for later.

Thea took a long drink of her tea, then grimaced, although she continued to cradle the cup between fine-boned hands. She said, "All these fires are driving the townsfolk into full acceptance of your plan."

He cocked his head toward her, listening hard for what she meant.

With another glint at him, she said, "I mean, they wouldn't be quite so open to it if the image of total destruction wasn't hanging over them."

"If you think I have anything to do with these fires..."

She let go of her cup with one hand long enough to wave in dismissal. "Of course not. Don't be silly. It's just that. ..well, it seems to me that if we could find out who the firestarter is, the town would view your proposal with clearer eyes." She nodded to herself and took another sip.

Glacial ice formed in Bram's gut. "Thea, you're not thinking of involving yourself in this, are you? Because if you are, I'm telling you this arsonist is not someone who wants to be caught. Firestarters can get violent when trapped."

"You'd know more about that than I would. I'm just saying that we need this behind us. Then we can concentrate on making changes without losing the soul of Potshot." She turned toward him, catching him in her high beams.

"You believe that?"

"Absolutely." She tipped her cup and finished her drink. With a clunk of finality, she set the mug on the table before standing. He struggled to his feet, too. She met his gaze, laying a hand over his heart.

"I'll do whatever I have to do to preserve the character of Potshot, Bram."

"And what do you think I'm trying to do?" he asked. Anguish made his voice harsh.

"I know we live in an area prone to fire, but I suspect you're trying to put your ghosts to rest—at any cost. Don't you think you're exaggerating the danger we're in to do that?"

She leaned forward and up, her mouth skimming his cheek and setting off a chain reaction of delight. He turned his face to capture her lips, but she eluded him.

"I'm so sorry we're on opposing sides here, Bram." She turned to go.

He caught her arm. "Thea, I'm trying to save lives."

She bowed her head, but refused to meet his eyes. "I know you think you are."

Bram crawled out of a sleep that bordered on comatose. A gilded evening greeted him along with a hefty dose of the stink of curing paint. He stretched hard, grimacing as the faint odor of smoke billowed from his sheets—that after a long shower punctuated by two scrubbings. The irony hit. In his profession, he usually did not small like a chimneysweep. After all, he *prevented* fires.

Since coming to Potshot, he'd seen more field action than he had in the last fifteen years. He preferred his dealings with fire to stay distant, even academic. Recently, life kept getting in Bram's face with annoying frequency. The fires, Thea, the arsonist, Alex, the wolf family, Salinger; all contributed to a free-falling sensation in his gut.

Favoring action over introspection, Bram bounced out of bed. In quick order, he pulled on clean jeans and ordered room service. As he settled at his work desk, actually a glorified table, he watched through the window facing the main drag as Bud Jr. made tracks from the hotel to Peabody's, then undoubtedly to the deli/bakery. He grinned. Supper would be hot and fresh.

Bram powered up his laptop. By the time the expected knock came, he had accessed all his messages and responded to most. He called, "Door's open, Bud."

A voice drifted through the door, "It's me, Dr. Hayes."

"Alex?" Bram swiveled his chair. He paced to the door, then pulled it open.

Sure enough, it was Thea's son. The solemn expression looked foreign on Alex's face.

"Come on in. Your timing's good. I just finished going through my messages and chow'll be here in a few minutes."

Alex followed him in, plunking onto the unmade bed. In typical kid fashion, the boy bounced a few extra times, testing the mattress for its potential as a trampoline. Bram settled more sedately into his chair.

"I've had some good news about your wolf family." Bram waited for the boy's gaze to return to him. Alex finished his perusal of the room and its contents in a flash.

"Yeah? Sweet."

"The female came through reconstructive surgery very well. Her leg'll probably recover completely."

The surprising gravity of the boy's regard propelled him onward. "In fact, the biologists've been exploring the wolf release area for open territory. They'll be freed next spring, when the female's fully healed."

"Won't the puppies be, you know, too tame by then?"

Bram smiled, glad to see the boy had taken so much away from this experience. "The Blue Range area of Arizona was developed specifically to reestablish Mexican Gray wolves. It's the biologists' job to study them. They've set up the surroundings to minimize human contact and maximize a natural environment. Then they teach others how to make a better fit for wolves."

"That's fly."

When Alex started swinging his legs while picking at frayed patches on his jeans' knees, Bram realized that the boy's main reason for calling on him had yet to be broached. He asked, "How's the competition shaping up for your science project?"

Alex stopped dangling his legs and leaned forward. "We laid out our projects in the gym today. So far, nobody else's looks as good as mine."

He slumped back on his elbows. "It'd be awesome to win the grand prize. I'd be able to go to science camp this summer. And with the gift certificate, I could get Mom something really great for her birthday. Even have money left over."

He collapsed his arms and sprawled onto the bed, hands over his head. "But I probably won't win. Some of the big kids have really good displays. Ninth graders are such buttheads."

Bram tried to think of a response. But another detail had caught his attention. "So it's your mom's birthday?"

"Yep. Next Tuesday. 'Course that art guy from San Francisco will be here. He wants her paintings for a show or something. She'll probably be too busy for a party."

The boy left off his study of the ceiling and turned his head toward Bram. "Why'd you move out?"

From the intensity in Alex's eyes, Bram realized they had finally reached the crux. "I told you before I left. The hotel

238

finished my room."

The boy just looked at him.

Bram angled forward, forearms braced on spread knees and hands loosely linked. "I didn't leave because I don't like you or your mom, Alex. I like you both. A lot."

Alex examined Bram's face before saying, "I thought you really liked Mom. I mean, I *saw* you, you know, *with* her."

Bram's blood branded his cheekbones. This was not just any kid; he was the son of the woman Bram'd been *with*. "You're talking about when I kissed your mom."

It was the boy's turn to blush. "Yeah, I guess."

Feelings Bram still needed to resolve blindsided him. He barely restrained himself from leaping to his feet, prowling the room, and howling like Alex's black wolf. "Well, son, I do feel more than *like* for both you and your mom. But Alex, I'm only here through September. It's not fair, I mean it wouldn't be fair to. . ."

Alex rolled up, his face and body teetering on the edge of excitement. "Hey, I saw you. I mean you were really sucking face. Don't you have to *love* a girl to do that?"

His expression nearly startled a laugh from Bram. He squelched it with a mighty effort. What a question! And what a trap. So Bram said, "I don't intend to stay any longer than the project runs. It wouldn't be right to pretend otherwise."

Alex's face turned a deep red. Anger sparked in the boy's eyes. He bounded off the bed and headed for the door, all in a rush. As he yanked open the door, he stopped just long enough to turn tear-laden eyes on Bram, "You're a wuss, you know that? And I still hate you!"

The heavy door resisted Alex's attempt to bang it shut and closed behind him with a staid whooshing sound. Bram scrubbed his eyes with his hands, feeling like a grade-A louse. Too honest to ignore just how badly he had failed Alex, he dragged himself up and drifted into the bathroom where he doused his face in cool water. Afterward, he stared at his image in the mirror, then swiped a wet hand over the surface, leaving a dripping and blurred copy of himself.

"You are a wuss, Hayes."

When supper came, he let Bud Jr. set it up on the oak tray allocated to him once Bram converted the table into his office. Bram stood by as everything was settled to Bud Junior's satisfaction. When the man, who looked to be close to Bram's thirty-five years, hesitated before leaving the room, Bram asked, "How's it going?"

The man gave Bram a direct look out of eyes that drooped at the corners. "Well, there's some talk. Since I can't abide malicious rumor, I figure you should know about it."

"Oh?" Supper had lost its appeal anyway.

"That slick guy, Salinger, was letting it be known around town that you got into some trouble as a kid. Seems like you started a fire or two back in your home state." Again that steady gaze.

Bram let loose the long exhalation that had been building from the moment he heard the word *rumor*. How could he explain the truth to this decent man; a man worried about the fires threatening both his community and his way of life? When a straightforward account eluded him, he said, "That's why they're called malicious rumors. They're meant to hurt."

The other man frowned, obviously unwilling to let the subject drop, but realizing that he would get no more from his hotel guest. Instead, he said, "Some pretty vicious gossip's circulating about the old guy, Jacob Seeger, too."

"You mean *Seeker*. Jake Seeker," corrected Bram.

The other man's chin firmed. "I like the man myself. Sure as hell can't see harassing a decorated veteran. The guy's only trying to get his life back. He's no arsonist."

On that note Bud Jr. left. Bram ambled to the casement near his worktable. He wished these renovated windows opened. Yet even without fresh air and street sounds, he stood there long enough for shadows to fill the street; long enough to ache for a young boy on the brink of manhood. He knew only too well how rash mistakes could change the course of a young man's life. Bram returned to work and ignored his congealing meal.

The next afternoon, he accompanied Ian to the sheriff's office to give Sy their fire report. Frustration gave his footsteps a staccato sound. This report would disappoint Sy as much as the last one. Not only did the findings fail to shed light on the culprit, they also fueled the circulating gossip.

The two men entered the office, only to find a contingent of townspeople surrounding a harried Sy. To Bram's eyes, the sheriff looked like a raccoon treed by a pack of hounds. When the outside door closed behind Bram, the assembly around Sy turned as one to confront the two men. Sissy Peabody's scrutiny fell on Bram and her lips compressed and nearly vanished. He steeled himself for what came next.

"Just the folks I wanted to see," Sy said as he waded through the throng, reaching for the report as though for a lifeline.

He flashed Bram a warning to keep quiet. Then the older man moseyed back to his desk as though he had not a care in the world. After he seated himself, he fixed a stern look on the crowd around his coffee mess. "Ladies and gentlemen, if you'll excuse us, we've got some business to attend to."

The sheriff faced down Sissy, earning even more respect from Bram. When the group passed Bram, the woman gave an audible sniff, as though something rotten had been dragged into the room without her say. Bram waited until the door closed behind them before seating himself in one of the chairs near Sy's desk. Ian sprawled onto the one across from Bram.

241

Sy looked at Bram and let out an exasperated sigh. "Damn, son! You sure as hell don't make it easy on an old coot trying to maintain some sanity in this town."

The sheriff lowered his gaze to peruse the report. He went through it slowly once, then paged back through it quickly, obviously looking for particular information. Bram knew what he wanted and wished he had been able to deliver. The sheriff tossed it onto the cluttered desk.

"No help there. It says that the fire probably smoldered for quite a while before igniting," Sy stated.

Ian nodded. "The arsonist didn't use the same kind of accelerant he used last time. As the report says, it took hours to take off."

"Wait a minute, are you saying we're dealing with a different mode of operation, another arsonist?"

Ian glanced at Bram before saying, "I don't think so, Sheriff. I think our arsonist just refined his technique."

Bram rubbed his chin and jumped in with, "I was there just before the town meeting. I didn't smell anything. Since the fire was set in a utility closet, it was probably undetectable until it flashed."

"Well, shit just keeps hitting the fan, does it?" Sy leaned forward, his gaze intent on Bram. "Just what were you doing there? Anyone with you?"

Ian said, "You can't possibly believe that *Bram*. . ."

The sheriff held up a hand. His regard stayed on Bram. "Son, just tell me what you were doing there."

For a brief second, Bram felt fifteen; a half-breed troublemaker in over his head. He shook it off. "I walked by and saw Thea inside. With Salinger. He was going to hit her. I got involved."

Sy's steady gaze pinned him to the chair. Bram finished with, "I left for the church with Thea."

Finally, the sheriff relaxed in his chair. He contemplated

242

the window facing the alley alongside the jail. After a time, he looked back at them and said, "Well, it's good to know there's some light in this mess. Got any gut feelings about this? Something you can't put down on paper?"

Ian glanced at Bram, who nodded for the firefighter to continue. "Still looks like a one-person show to us. And the arsonist screwed up this time. The fire didn't burn hot enough to wipe out as much evidence at its source."

"And?" prompted the sheriff.

Ian continued. "We sent a couple samples to our lab at the University and should have the results in a day or two. But what's struck us, all of us, is what's missing."

"And that is?"

Bram finished. "No smell of accelerant."

Ian jumped in again. "If my hunch turns out to be true, then we're dealing with someone who knows enough chemistry to use an oxidizer with an organic to make a slow smoldering fire."

Sy pondered that. "Got any other leads that aren't leads?"

Neither Bram nor Ian answered.

The sheriff rocked forward and his feet slapped the floor. "Well, thanks for your time and help with this, gents. Looks like I'm going to have to do what the voters put me in office to do—solve a crime or two."

Bram got up and headed for the door, holding it open for Ian. He considered hanging back and having a few private words with Sy. Instead, the sheriff outflanked him and said, "So, Dr. Bramden Hayes, maybe you could be more specific. Tell me why I shouldn't haul your butt in for suspicion of arson?"

Bram's attempt to keep his shoulder and neck muscles loose failed miserably. He told Ian, "I'll catch up with you later."

He turned to the sheriff, who now stood close enough that

Bram could see white whiskers mixed in with darker ones on his normally close-shaven face. "I thought we'd covered this before."

"Not to my satisfaction," countered the sheriff.

"Walk with me?" asked Bram. When the sheriff's eyes narrowed, he added, "I'll answer all your questions." Sy nodded, then fell into step as they headed back toward the hotel where he hoped to find a fax from the University.

"Why don't you start with how your twin brother and mother were killed in a fire that you managed to escape unscathed." Even expecting it, Sy's first question wounded him.

"Unscathed? With second and third degree burns on my arms and back?"

The sheriff had the decency to look uncomfortable. "I need the facts, Bram."

The acid in Bram's catalytic response burned, but he swallowed and said, "Are you familiar with any Native American ceremonies, Sheriff?"

"Can't say that I am."

"Well, my brother knew just enough to get himself killed. You see, we're half-white, half-Cherokee, but our grandfather belongs to both the Keetoowah Society and United Keetoowah Band. What that means is that he places a lot of weight on being a traditional, full-blooded Cherokee." He paused as they waited to cross Main Street.

As Bram stepped onto the cross walk, Sy beside him, he continued. "More than anything in the world, my brother wanted to prove himself worthy. He wanted to be all Cherokee. You see, that's kind of a loophole in Native American traditions. You don't always have to be pure Indian to be a Blood, you just have to act like one."

They passed the deli. The fragrance of fresh bread hardly penetrated Bram's senses. "Eric decided to fast his way toward a spirit vision, helping it along with a sweat bath. He constructed a lean-to against our house, built a fire, and sat inside waiting for his spirit guide to show him the way. But the fast must have weakened him—probably not enough fluids. He—he must've collapsed."

They reached the hotel, but Bram leaned against the railing on the back porch. From here the downward slope of the ground increased until the landscape abruptly descended into the valley below.

"Our house was old; in poor repair. It was early morning, a couple of hours past midnight, when the flame broke through the back wall into our mother's bedroom. I awoke to the sound of fire eating it's way through the house.

"Have you ever heard fire? I mean really listened to its howl when it finds prey?" He glanced at the white face of the man beside him.

"Can't say I have, son."

"I woke up choking, disoriented. My brother's bed was empty. Somehow, I made my way to my mother's room. I crawled. No air.

"She looked like she was still sleeping, peaceful and pretty. The flames hadn't even touched her bed. At that time, I knew nothing about smoke inhalation or asphyxiation. So I wrapped her in blankets and dragged her out of the room, then out of the house."

Bram rubbed the scar on his forearm hard enough to draw beads of blood. "She was already dead. My brother's remains. . ." He swallowed, but the swelling in his throat made for difficult speech. "Well, there wasn't much left of my brother."

"That's enough, Bram."

"I don't even remember getting burned. Isn't that strange? I don't even. . ."

"I said that's enough, son."

Bram blinked hard a few times. Finally he focused on the

sheriff's face, on the look in the older man's eyes. He forced the next words past a difficult place in his throat. "Before you ask about the smokehouse fire, I do know who set it. You'll have to believe me when I say that I didn't find out until after the fact. Tempers between the townies and the Rez ran hot that summer. When the Mims beat me for my supposed theft, it became another rallying point for dissidents."

The sheriff looked toward the valley. "I appreciate your honesty, Bram. Know it wasn't easy. Real sorry you had to dredge up such hard memories, but I had to be sure about you."

"And are you?"

The sheriff gave him a nod. "About 99.9% sure. Can't ask for more than that. I like you, son. That could be seen as a disadvantage in my position. As an officer of the law, it's my job to scrutinize any and all suspects. Now, I just hope we can put this behind us."

"So do I, Sy." Bram started for the back entrance to the hotel.

"Why don't you let me buy you a cup of coffee and a piece of pie over at Bodeen's," the sheriff offered.

The rawness of internal wounds made Bram ache for seclusion. However, when he met Sy's regard, he could see that the older man had suffered through the retelling, too. For some reason, it mattered to Bram that he and the sheriff move beyond this. It would be so easy to let resistance become a wall that separated them. Bram aimed to keep him as a friend.

He said, "Sure, just let me check my faxes and I'll be right down."

Fifteen minutes later, Bram tucked into a slice of strawberry rhubarb pie while Sy hummed over his cobbler. "No one, *no one* including my momma, God rest her soul, makes peach cobbler like the Missus," Sy said between bites.

Bram nodded as the tart pie filled his mouth. Instead of

246

talking, he savored the taste while watching the ebb and flow of patrons along the street. With the warmer days of June, Mister had brought out his collection of picnic tables. Each one sported an umbrella. From the hotel, the sidewalk cafe had looked like a flotilla of sailboats. The freshening breeze even made the canvas flap like sails in the wind.

Bram inhaled the late afternoon smells of Potshot. Aromas of grilled chicken and onion floated from Peabody's to mix with yeasty fragrances from the delicatessen. A sage and pine bouquet reminded him of the forest's proximity to the town and the sagebrush dotting the valley. Over it all hung the scorched smell from the gutted area across the way.

Quick as thought, Bram circled back to his earlier conjecture. "You know, Sy, our arsonist's probably a local. More important, the frequency's escalating."

Sy grunted. "Hate to think of someone I know causing such mischief. We've been lucky so far. I live in unholy fear of someone being hurt by all this. If you've got a fix on the perp, you might want to spit it out."

Bram shook his head. "I don't know your neighbors like you do. You'll want to look hard at anyone who profits from these fires. Could be financial, could be as obscure as a gain in social status."

"I suppose it's too much to hope for good old insanity? The idea of cold-blooded planning pretty near freezes my blood."

"I wonder about that angle myself, but the scenes have too much continuity. The firestarter may be a psychotic, but I'm no shrink."

Both men sank into gloomy study. Only when Thea's old Honda rattled past them on its way to the parking area did Bram snap out of his bleak analysis.

In the time it took for a rust-colored kestrel to cut a swathe through a cloud of emergent insects, Thea and Alex rounded the corner. Thea looked good enough to eat in one of those

247

jewel colored tee shirts she favored with baggy jeans anchored to her hips with a bright scarf. Bram gathered his scattered reason before she caught him in the act of salivating.

Her smile faltered when she saw him, only brightening as she wove through other diners toward their table. "Well, hey, you two. Does April know you're ruining your appetite for dinner, Sy?" Her impish look flustered the sheriff not at all.

"Now, Thea, you'd best not be carrying tales. I'd hate to dig into my arsenal of stories about some of your youthful transgressions."

She slid a shining gaze toward Bram. "Don't listen to him. He'll say anything for his cobbler."

Sy asked, "So what brings you and Alex to town this fine evening?"

The glance she gave Bram harbored more secrets than answers. "We're celebrating. Alex's science project won best-of-show."

As congratulations filled the air, Alex sidled closer to Bram. In an undertone, he said, "I didn't mean what I said. You know, when I said I hated you."

Before Bram could respond, Thea snaked out one-handed to curl an arm around the boy's shoulders. "Why don't you run in and see what looks good? I'll join you in a minute."

Alex left with alacrity, leaving Bram to deal with not being hated. It seemed the boy still considered him a wuss, though. *Ouch.*

Thea said, "My mother's meeting us here. I thought the deli might make for neutral territory."

Sy sucked on a toothpick, then asked, "Amarantha still fussing over your leave-of-absence from Visual Perceptions?"

"Yep."

Bram said, "Alex mentioned you have an art dealer coming up next week."

She moaned. "Don't remind me. I should be home framing

as we speak."

Sy nodded to a place behind Thea. "Looks like the gang's all here."

Bram and Thea followed the direction of his regard to find Meg and Jake strolling the sidewalk. Bram noticed how the sheriff's eyes narrowed as he scrutinized the new arrivals. Well, not Meg actually. Sy's measured look centered directly on the man at the librarian's side, one Jake Seeker. Amid the festive greetings, the sheriff's intense regard of Jake seemed to penetrate only Bram's consciousness. As the latecomers sauntered into the deli to place their orders, Bram waited for the sheriff to speak.

When the man continued to fiddle around with his toothpick instead, Bram said, "Jake's relatively new in town."

Sy smiled, a grin that seemed fueled by some inner amusement. "Not as new as you might think."

"Your arsonist might have had some background in explosives, courtesy of Uncle Sam," Bram mentioned.

Sy stared into the distance. "You know, I did my stint for Uncle Sam, son. Some of us took the long way home."

The staccato sound of high heels on cement announced Amarantha MacTavish-Seeger. Both men turned to watch the woman approach. Dressed with an elegance that would have put the late Princess Grace of Monaco to shame, Amarantha glided toward their table carrying one of those ridiculous purses that could maybe hold a large handful of birdseed.

"Son, hold onto your horse. We're about to see some fireworks," Sy warned before Thea's mother reached their table.

Amarantha smiled graciously at her subjects. "Sy. Dr. Hayes."

Bram nodded. Sy grinned and said, "Amarantha."

Thea's mother raised an eyebrow. "I saw that disreputable car my daughter insists on driving parked alongside the delicatessen. Am I to assume Althea and Alexander are inside?"

The door from the deli opened. Thea and Alex frolicked out first, followed closely by Meg. Jake, as official doorman, took up the rear. Amarantha obviously took her cue from where the men's gazes went and turned toward the new party.

Sy called, "Look who joined us."

Thea hesitated, her wide gaze fixing on Bram before tripping toward her mother. As she stepped forward to greet the woman, her mother froze in position like a pole-axed calf. After that, everything happened so quickly, it took some time for Bram to sort it all out.

Amarantha said something like, "Jacob? Jacob Seeger?"

Jake came forward with what Bram could only call resignation. "Hello, 'Mantha."

Sy started to stand, saying, "Now, Amarantha. . ."

Before the sheriff could intervene, Amarantha swung an arm back and delivered a roundhouse to Jake's face that should have brought the man to his knees. More interesting yet, Bram knew the man could have dodged the blow. Instead, the old guy just took it. Amarantha's purse left an angry imprint on his cheek. By then, everyone was milling around like refugees from a burning barn.

Thea's mother yelled, "You son-of-a-bitch, Jacob Seeger! Where the hell have you been?"

Grasping her mother's arm, Thea said, "What's going on here?"

"Thea, I'd like you to meet your father," Amarantha said.

Chapter Fourteen

I really want a drink. Better make it a double. Thea practically tasted her chosen poison. The visualization appalled and frightened her in equal parts. Vowing to attend a meeting in Reno later, she dragged herself from the perilous image.

For now, Thea practiced a name, if only in her mind. *Jacob Seeger*. Otherwise known as Jake Seeker. Not a huge leap, but his alias fit him better. Yet according to her mother's hysterical disclosure, this man, this long-lost veteran of an Asian war, was brother to Thea's stepfather Charles, father to Thea herself, and grandfather to Thea's son. *How convoluted.*

Father, she tried, letting the foreign sound roll across her tongue.

Thea clenched her arms tighter over her chest, then released her hold a fraction when dizziness struck. A grim smile curved her lips. How would those present react if she fell to the floor in a self-induced faint? Still, her collapse would be the least bizarre scenario to occur today.

Eerily removed from herself, Thea sensed a buildup of magma-like anger as she observed the tableau in Meg's living room. The librarian's home seemed anything but cozy at the moment. Towering waves of silence buffeted the occupants. A shudder overtook her. *What other novel and unwanted truths might be forthcoming when the firestorm leaped the barriers?*

Sy stood sentinel by Thea's mother where she had crumpled dramatically onto Meg's favorite chair. Under her daughter's jaundiced gaze, Amarantha shrugged the afghan off her shoulders. Thea suspected that since her mother could not reject Jake, she discarded the throw instead. No doubt, the sheriff stayed to protect Jake from Amarantha. Mother looked capable of any number of violent acts.

Artistically applied blush on her mother's cheekbones stood out as twin maps of her fury. Her hair resembled sea-tossed kelp, radically different from her smooth French twist. In white knuckled hands, Amarantha still clutched her bejeweled purse, her main weapon of choice after she had flailed Jake, *Jacob*, with her arsenal of succinct and odious words. She now contented herself with aiming her baleful glare at her former lover.

Thea's gaze ping-ponged from her mother to him. *Jacob Seeger*, she repeated. Her biological father. The man looked more cadaverous than usual as Meg pressed an ice pack against his ravaged face. The bleeding had finally stopped, but from what Thea saw of the split skin over his cheekbone, he needed stitches. Bloody gauze filled a wastepaper basket near the librarian's feet.

Just a typical Seeger family reunion.

The pressure building in her chest burst free. Thea swallowed with an audible gulp, then spoke. "Just when were you going to let me in on your little secret?" she asked the man on the couch. Her voice shook with effort, but, *fuchsia and indigo blue*, what did he expect? Thank goodness Bram had kept Alex with him and out of this pathetic clattering of family skeletons. She wished herself with them, too.

"Thea, I'm so sorry about this. I hoped we'd get to know each other better first. You have to understand, I didn't know about you. At least not till a couple of years ago." The man's voice creaked with effort. His gaze went first to Meg, then to the sheriff. Those two sent darting looks in her direction.

Thea pushed herself off the wall, which had been her sole

support for too long. "Meg? Sy? You knew! You both knew and didn't say anything?" Her voice choked as heat flooded her and broke the crust saving her from deeper feeling.

"*Damn* you. My *friends*. How could you?"

Meg came to her, trying to enclose her within the comfort of her arms. When Thea jerked away, Meg gripped her elbows instead and said, "I only learned of the connection two days ago. I promised Jacob time—"

"Time? There will never be enough time to deal with this," Amarantha spat, her voice brittle.

The man on the couch said, "It's been longer than you know."

The misery in his voice subdued Thea's hurt enough to ask, "What do you mean?"

He took a deep breath before meeting her gaze. "I've been living on this mountain for the last four years."

Silence hit, a subsonic drum stroke. He maintained eye contact. "Lived like a sick animal, scrabbling around for food, shelter, pelts to keep me warm. I took to thieving. A shirt off a clothesline, shoes off a porch. Three years ago. . ." Meg slipped an arm around Thea's waist. The librarian had obviously heard this before.

"I saw you and your boy hiking on Ricochet Mountain. There was no mistaking you for mine. I knew. . .knew that your mother had married my brother. But Charlie had a childhood disease in his teens. Couldn't father children, the Doc said. So I knew. I knew.

"After that, I kept an eye out for the boy. Scared the bejeebers out of him a couple of times, when I wasn't quick or careful enough. Truth is, I wasn't quite in my right mind."

Incidents clicked into place. "The ghost of Penny Ante Mine," said Thea.

"Bigfoot," added Sy.

Realization dealt her another blow and she groaned. "I

didn't believe Alex."

"None of us did, Thea," said Sy.

Thea fixed each person with a look, until she settled on her mother. "I don't need to deal with this right now. In fact, I'm a grown woman and don't need a daddy at all. Why don't you work it all out? I'm going to find my son."

She left, unable to extricate herself from Meg without an injured glance. Walking from the house on her own two feet galvanized her. Thea saw Bram and Alex sitting at the deli and headed toward them, keeping her eyes fixed on her destination so the looks and whispers along the way would not penetrate her fragile calm. The faces of her two men, yes, *her two men*, promised refuge from the tempest whirling within her.

Something must have leaked from her demeanor, though, wrath or hurt or maybe just plain confusion. As she came within fifteen feet of her son and Bram, the man slapped a ten onto the table and gave Alex the keys to his truck.

"Go on over to my rig, Alex. Clear off the seats for you and your mom. We'll be right over."

Alex trotted to her and wrapped his skinny arms around her waist for a brief hug before running toward Bram's Land Rover. His unsolicited affection nearly undid her.

"Come on, Thea. Let me get you home," Bram said.

"My car. . ."

"Don't worry about that right now." He put an arm around her shoulders and steered her toward his vehicle.

It hit at that moment, a flash of such utter clarity that colors brightened, tiny sounds pealed like bells, and Bram's scent completely filled her senses. Self-knowledge lodged like an arrow in the place her softest emotions dwelled. She staggered like the drunkest of drunks.

Thea had read about this effect and scoffed. Even pitied those who believed the old adage. *Truth is, love can knock the starch out of a person. Fuchsia and indigo blue!* Bram evidently thought she needed a higher order of assistance. He lifted and carried her, Althea MacTavish, who was really no lightweight, all the way to his truck.

"Mom?"

Thea tried to reassure her son, but what could she say? *I've been overcome by love for this man* had a nice ring to it, but that was not her way. Besides, this was also the man adamant about changing Potshot.

Bram said, "Don't worry, Alex. Your mom's a little dizzy. She'll be okay, son, just give her some space." Thea nearly laughed aloud at his pedestrian diagnosis—except she thought she might yowl. What did this heroic man know about her predicament anyway?

Bram placed her gently onto the front passenger seat, then carefully pushed her head toward her knees. "Just dangle your head. That's it, darlin'. You're shocky is all. Deep breaths now. That's real good."

His warm hand curved over the back of her neck and sent tingles down her spine. "Indigo blue, this on top of everything else."

"You're on overload, Thea. You'll feel better in no time."

"Mom? Why did Grandma hit Jake like that?"

Thea sat up, meeting Bram's dark gaze, lingering in that private place for a brief moment. She twisted toward her son. "You really like Jake, don't you, Alex?"

Alex treated this like a trick question. "Yeah. So?"

"How would you like him as a Grandfather?"

Alex's mouth dropped open a little. "No shit? That's *too* cool. He's going to marry Grandma? But I thought he liked Auntie Meg…"

Thea laughed, while all she wanted was to cry.

She sat beside Alex on the back steps after talking until

her words ran dry. Beside her, Alex felt taut enough to break. "You mean that wussy developer guy is really my *father*?"

"No, he's not your father. He forced himself on me not out of love, but because—because—"

"He's a deviant asshole."

She sighed. "I suppose. What I meant is that being a father means participating in your child's life and…"

"So he didn't even want me?" The mutinous cast to Alex's face could not conceal his hurt.

Thea put an arm around his slumped shoulders. "Oh, honey, he never knew you. That's his huge loss. The fact is, *I* didn't want him in our lives and he used that to his advantage. He was despicable and corrupt even then."

"So now he's making me get this blood test just so he can take me away from you."

"That's what he believes will happen. The lawyers I've spoken with tell me that the judge will listen to what you want, though. After all, judges try to rule in favor of a child's best interest."

His back straightened. "Well, I don't want anything to do with that jerk. And I'll tell the judge so."

Thea considered the prerequisite meetings with psychologists, lawyers and child advocates, then rubbed his knotted shoulders. "You know what? You don't have to decide anything right now. I just thought you should know what was going on."

In an abrupt move, Alex clamped her in a stranglehold. "I love you, Mom."

Squeezing her eyes shut against the sudden heat there, she said, "And I love you, Alexander MacTavish. I promise that we'll get through this."

He released her and stood, obviously trying for nonchalance. "You know, I'm like totally starved."

She curbed a smile. "Then have the rest of the lasagna.

256

It just needs to be heated up—" As she started to rise, Alex pressed her down.

"Hey, Mom, I *do* know how to work the microwave."

"Then go to it. Oh, and there's salad and garlic bread left, too."

"Yeah, yeah," floated behind him as he went through the sliding door.

Instead of the sound of the door closing, though, Bram's voice asked, "Mind if I join you, Thea?"

She twisted toward him, acutely aware of how ragged she felt both inside and out. "Do so at your own risk."

Alex's head popped back out the door. "Hey, Mom, Bram brought takeout Chinese food. Can I have that instead?"

"When did you find time?"

Bram shrugged. "While you two were talking, I made another run to town. Hulon's special tonight is Chinese, so I brought it back." He turned to her son, "Have at it, Alex, but leave some for your mom."

"Will do. And thanks." The *whoosh* of the door acted as an exclamation point.

Bram lowered himself beside her, then handed her a water-beaded glass. "Mrs. Bodeen's lemonade. She thought you could use some cooling off."

Ice clinked as she sipped. "Ah, that's just right. It's also good to know the Potshot Express hasn't faltered. How bad is the talk?"

She caught a brief flash of his teeth before gravity won. "Let's see. Salinger, 0, Thea 50. Amarantha and Jake are in a dead heat, though."

With a long drawn out breath, Thea reveled in the quiet of dusk. Bram sat beside her as they sipped lemonade. The door opened. "Yo, Mom. I'm heading to my room. You guys want anything?"

A glance at Bram and Thea said, "We're good. Brush your

teeth before you go to bed and I'll tuck you in later."

"Jeez, I'm thirteen years old."

"You're still not old enough to mess with a mother's prerogative. Oh, and turn out the lights."

"'Night." The door closed yet again.

She flexed bare toes against the worn step, then noticed Bram still wore his boots. He usually left them at the door, which meant he must be frazzled. After a time, he asked, "You okay?"

"Ummm." A cricket chirped, joined an instant later by a veritable chorus. Thea smiled, feeling weightless and free in the aftermath. If one man could come back from the dead, maybe another might be persuaded to stay.

"Alex sounded excited about Jake being his granddad."

"That's one of us anyway. I'm too old for a father-figure."

"Jake's all right."

"He's not exactly a poster-boy for responsible fatherhood."

"Vietnam messed him up pretty bad, Thea."

"It looks like Vietnam did a number on all of us. Still, I'm glad Alex is taking this craziness in stride." *Better than his mother.*

"The kid sure didn't cotton to the idea of Salinger as a his daddy, though."

Something in Bram's voice focused Thea's attention. He sounded—"You're glad!"

"Huh?"

"I swear, you sounded almost elated just now."

"About what?"

"Alex. And his obvious distaste about having Derek as his father," she clarified.

"More than distaste, Thea. I'd say Alex was downright pissed-off."

Thea leaned forward until she peered into his face. Moonlight gave her little to go on, though. "There it was again—in your voice."

Silence stretched between them before he said, "Alex doesn't need a deadbeat for a role model. He needs a man willing to participate in his life."

"Ah," she said, but continued to watch Bram's shadowed features.

"Quit that."

"What?"

"Looking at me like that."

Thea moved forward until her breath fanned his face and neck. She took the glass of lemonade from him and set it beside hers on the step. Ice tinkled intimately.

"Damn it, Thea. You'd push a saint to his breaking point."

"*You're* most definitely no *saint*."

Bram closed the distance between them and covered her lips with his. Thea purred under the onslaught of his mouth, warm and eager on hers. When he drew away for air, she stood, but only long enough to straddle his lap. He groaned.

"Thea, I'm not made of stone."

She flexed and rubbed against him. "Oh, I don't know. You appear to be rock solid to me."

His mouth recaptured hers.

It makes such a difference when you approach an obstacle without ambivalence. Especially with a man teetering on the edge of self-discovery. Those were her last coherent thoughts for a long while.

When he skimmed his fingers beneath her tee shirt, she arched toward him. For some reason, he stopped then, hot hands framing her back below her shoulder blades. The enveloping touch made her feel petite and delicate, a novel sensation for Thea. Their strident breathing filled the night.

"Thea, I want you. But not here."

"What do you have in mind? Alex is asleep."

"Don't be so sure," he muttered. He slipped his hands

from her shirt, much to her disappointment, then leaned back and snagged the old throw off her willow chair. Tossing the coverlet over one shoulder, he arose. His shoulder impacted on Thea's midriff halfway through his ascent as he lifted her, belly down.

"Whoa! Bram, this isn't nec. . ."

"Not now, Thea."

With his unyielding fingers splayed beneath the edge of her cutoffs, he cupped one hand over her bottom. He stroked her from there to the sensitive backs of her knees. His actions started a body quake, making her glad of his full support. With one arm around her knees, he anchored her onto his shoulder.

When he hit his stride, Thea squirmed and giggled until he let her ride him piggybacked. With her arms around his shoulders and legs clenching his waist, she pressed her cheek against the flex and contraction of his back muscles beneath the chambray shirt. Down the creek bank, then up the other side he carried her. A synergistic mix of crushed mint and Bram's cedar scent filled her nose. Instead of going toward the hot springs, he veered onto another moonlit trail. An owl winged from a nearby tree. At a clearing within a stand of Ponderosa pines, she slipped off his back. His breathing, fast and hard from lugging her uphill, did not keep him from pulling her into his arms and kissing the breath right out of her, too.

The damp fragrance of his skin called to her. She teased his buttons open, then slipped her hands inside his shirt. His nipples hardened instantly, and she followed her fingers' path with her mouth.

Bram closed his arms almost convulsively around her. "This is it, Thea. Your last chance to say no."

She lick-kissed him to his collarbone, the highest she could reach without rolling onto tiptoes. "Now why would I do

260

that?" she murmured against his pulse.

"Oh, Thea," he whispered. He framed her face with his hands and kissed her long and deep, just the way she liked it.

While she reeled from their kiss, Bram yanked the throw from his shoulder and tossed it onto the ground over a bed of mustang clover. Compacted herb scents permeated the night air. As Bram lowered her onto the blanket, she realized how comfortable a bed of clover could be—under the right circumstances.

Bram alighted beside her. Her head fit comfortably in the crook of one arm as he brushed hair from her forehead with feathery strokes. "You're so beautiful, Thea."

"It's the moonlight."

He chuckled, "No, it's you."

Bram kissed her again.

And again.

The cool air of early summer whispered over her skin when he peeled off her shirt, shorts, and panties. Stalking the progression of discarded clothing, he laved kisses over her summits and vales, warming her air-cooled skin to feverish heat. She worked frantically to extract him from his clothes, an approach that went more smoothly once he pulled his boots off. Helter-skelter, Thea flung his shirt, then his jeans, and finally his jockey shorts into the night. Which meant that at the moment of truth, Bram hastily tracked down his pants to get a condom from his wallet.

Their giggles rang off a granite overhang up the slope from them. An eon later, or so it seemed to Thea, Bram scrambled back to her on their nubby blanket.

"You don't make things easy, Thea."

"Life's tough," she whispered while nibbling along his jaw toward an ear lobe. "Luckily, it's punctuated by moments of perfection."

"Like this." He traced her body from shoulder to thigh,

261

his pleasure-giving hands sending joyous cascades along her nerve endings. She seized one of his hands and pressed it against her point of greatest heat, where hot blood coiled heavily and expectantly.

"You're scorching me to cinders, Bram. I can't take any more foreplay."

She pushed him onto his back and straddled him for the second time that night. Being naked changed everything. *Skin.* So much sensitive skin. She rubbed her body lengthwise along his, then sheathed him slowly, igniting him by degrees.

Wildfire flared, racing through both of them. The firestorm transformed muscle, sinew, and blood into liquid fire. Each movement, each murmur kindled the heat. Thea's fire blazed with Bram's until nothing separated them. They became flame together, reducing to ashes all that came before this moment.

In the aftermath, Thea sprawled over Bram, both of them gasping and shuddering. No margin existed between where her damp-sleek skin left off and his began. Her breath and his mated. Her heartbeat and his filled her ears with distant booming, reminiscent of individual explosions along an avalanche slope. A landslide of emotion tumbled through her, laying waste to any remaining barriers. Her tears mingled with their sweat, pooling in the hollow between his chest muscles until they overran the borders. Bram, stroking her neck-to-back-to-bottom, hesitated.

"Thea?" He located her face with his fingers; fingers that gave extraordinary pleasure. "Darlin'? You crying?"

Oklahoma sat heavily in his voice. He slipped her to one side and onto her back. She curled away from him and he cuddled around her spoon fashion, his arms enclosing her.

"Did I hurt you? Oh, Thea, you had me so hot for you, so wild. . ."

"No. No you didn't hurt me. It was just too much. Too good. Too perfect, that's all." *Shattered, I'm shattered.*

262

He moved, if possible, even closer. "Let me hold you. That's all you need. Been needing this kind of touch a damn sight too long from what I can tell."

Bram pulled the blanket's edge over them, making her feel snug, even cherished. Time drifted. The heavens shifted and she napped.

Before leaving later that night, he made love to her with such thoroughness that she needed time to recuperate again. In the moon's blush, Thea sprawled in languorous abandon, while Bram sprinted down the mountain for her shoes. A bat swooped upward, feasting from an insect swarm high above Thea's nest. Wings flashed before the nocturnal hunter swept from her view. The bat's joyful motion spurred Thea to sit. As she did, a delicious sense of well being swept over her. Bram's tenderness boded well for them. He couldn't possibly leave in September when he carried such a depth of emotion. Not when she loved him, too.

She stood and did a little jig around the moon bright clearing, gathering her clothes as she went. Thea wriggled into her cutoffs, stuffing panties into a back pocket. Bram returned as she pulled her tee shirt over her head. She turned to him, feeling shy and more vulnerable than she liked. In the glow of his flashlight, his eyes sparkled.

"Hey," she said.

Dropping her shoes onto the clover, he laughed, then lifted her by her waist and whirled her around. "I feel great. Fabulous! *Spectacular*!" He shouted the last.

When he stopped spinning, Bram brought her against him for a leisurely slide down his body. As her toes touched the ground, her knees buckled. She would have kept going if he had let her.

"Whoa, now." He held her close to his chest, her chin tilted toward his face. Bending his head, he kissed her nose before ravishing her sensitive mouth. Breaking away he said, "How

263

'bout I escort you home? I'll fix us a late night supper of biscuits and gravy with eggs. Maybe some of that Canadian bacon Alex likes so much."

"You didn't wake him, I hope."

"I kept a low profile, darlin'. Alex was dealt a big hand today. Thought you'd want to tell him about us yourself."

Us. Warmth uncurled in her belly. "That was thoughtful. Thanks."

They kept within touching distance all the way home. Actually, they took few steps without kissing. Thea found that if she teetered on top of his boots, she could reach his mouth with only a little stretch. They reached the house to find all the lights on and Alex, fully dressed, waiting at the back porch.

"Where were you guys?"

The shadows under his wide blue eyes made Thea pause on the top step, a deep chill overtaking her satiated warmth. She leaned toward her son, "What's wrong, honey?"

The whole story emerged. With a quick look at the pile of rags bundled under one edge of the back porch, she called Sy at home. Bram squelched her first reaction, to hop into her car with Alex and head for town. Only Bram's presence, strong and sure, kept her there until Sy, with Dwaine riding shotgun, barreled into her driveway. The dust barely settled before Ian and Challie, in their vehicle, pulled up behind them.

The newcomers studied the fuel under the porch before trooping into Thea's kitchen. Sy seated Alex on a dining room chair, then hunkered in front of him. Her son clenched an untouched glass of orange juice.

"Now, Alex, start from the beginning. I want you to tell me everything that transpired."

Alex looked at his mother. Thea nodded and fought to control her rage and fear. Hearing the story for a second time still made her quake.

"I was sleeping. But I rolled over on my headset, and it,

264

like cricked my ear. So I woke up." Alex glanced at Thea, obviously wondering if she would make a big deal out of his going to sleep with his headphones on. When she didn't, he continued. "I was really thirsty, so I went to the kitchen to get something to drink. That's when I heard the noise. From outside on the back porch."

"What kind of a noise, Alex?" prompted the sheriff when the boy balked.

Alex's hands twisted in his lap. It broke Thea's heart to see him do that. She clamped her arms to her sides, not wanting to distract her son with mothering he may or may not want. When Bram stepped over and put a hand on the boy's shoulder, Alex looked up with what could only be gratitude.

He went on with his recitation. "You know, a scuffing kind of sound. I thought it was a raccoon. Sometimes they come up to the porch and mess things up. So I got two pans out of the cabinet, like we do when we want to scare deer or raccoons off. I didn't turn the light on, 'cause it's always better to surprise them."

"Good thinking, son," said the sheriff.

Alex only looked at him. "I slid the door open, but when I looked out, I didn't see anything. Not at first. That's when the monster stood up." His voice rose with a trill of fear.

Sy cut a look at Thea. "The monster?"

Her son wound his tee shirt into a twist so tight that it unwound like a whirligig when he let go. "I guess it'd bent over to push the rags under the porch."

The sheriff nodded. "Seems likely. What did it look like, son?"

"Worse than the ghost and Bigfoot. It had this wild hair that glowed silver. Its face was all shriveled and crazy looking with holes where it's eyes should've been. It scared me so bad, I must've made a sound. 'Cause next thing I knew, it was looking right at me."

"Then what happened, Alex?" the sheriff prompted.

The whites of his eyes showed as they darted from Bram to her. "I thought it was going to come after me. So I threw a pot at it. Mom's best saucepan, the nonstick one. Didn't hit it though. Not with that pan, anyway. Then it started running away. Well, not really running. It sort of stumbled along. So I threw the other pot and hit it, but it kept on going."

Sy covered the boy's hands with his much bigger ones. "You did fine, son. Then what did you do?"

"I ran back to Mom's room, but she wasn't there. So I ran downstairs. I forgot Bram'd moved to the hotel." Fat tears gathered in the corners of his eyes. He wiped them away with the back of one arm.

"I thought the monster got Mom. I wanted to call you, Sheriff, but I know how grouchy you get when you're tired."

Sy looked flustered at that. "Well, son, this isn't the same as when you saw the ghost in Penny Ante Mine. What did you do then?"

"I got Mom's biggest frying pan, turned on all the lights and waited by the back door. Sort of hidden in the shadows, just in case the thing came back for me. Then Mom and Bram got home. I'm sorry I didn't do better."

That broke her. With each word that passed her son's lips, a cold stone of fear settled within her. What if Alex had continued to sleep? What if the arsonist had realized only a boy stood between him and holocaust? *What if?*

All the while, she had been rolling around in the woods with Dr. Bramden Youngwolf Hayes like a bitch in heat. Some Mother she had turned out to be. Would she ever forgive herself?

Thea stepped toward her son, replacing Bram's hands with hers. "You did nothing wrong, Alex. In fact, you were very brave. I'm sorry I wasn't here for you when you needed me." Her voice cracked and Alex patted her hands.

266

She shot a glint at Bram, who urged her and Alex into the living room and onto the couch. He kissed her forehead and tucked a quilt around them before going back into the kitchen. Thea cuddled her son close and listened to the hushed intensity of conversation buzzing from the kitchen. Ian and Challie wandered into the front room to say good-bye. The fireman squatted in front of Alex.

"You're a real champ, Alex. It takes a lot of courage to stand your ground like that, bud." He shook Alex's hand.

Challie bent toward Thea and put her smooth cheek against hers. "Don't be so hard on yourself," she whispered before leaving.

Sy ambled in shortly afterward with Dwaine tagging along behind him. "I'm not sure I want you staying up here by yourself, Thea. Why don't you consider moving into the hotel until we catch this guy?"

She looked hard into his eyes, searching for the condemnation she felt for herself. Only his caring and unease met her regard. "Thanks, Sy, I'll consider it."

Sy studied Alex for a time. "You did real good, son. Can see you're growing into a fine young man. Thea, why don't you walk me to the door?"

With a glance, he motioned with his chin. She wanted to inhabit the blanket cocoon, but dragged herself to her feet. Sy would only ask if he had something for her ears only.

At the door, the sheriff lowered his voice and said, "Don't want to alarm you, Thea, but Alex is the only one who's seen this guy."

It took a moment for the impact of what he said to sink into her. "You think Alex's in danger."

Sy took off his cowboy hat, then resettled it.

Dwaine's regard drilled into her. She searched both men's faces. They tried for the detached looks of law enforcers, but failed when the concern of friends won. She shook her head.

"But he didn't really *see* anything. All he saw was this ghoul. That's hardly enough for recognition."

Dwaine clarified it for her. "The firestarter doesn't know that. He believes Alex can identify him."

"You think hard about moving into town now," Sy added.

"Don't worry about your place, Thea. I can come up and stay here." The deputy's offer brought the first warmth since coming home that morning.

"I will. Thank you both for getting here so quickly."

After she closed the door behind them, she pressed her forehead against the resilient wood. Only when Bram's hands closed over her shoulders did she become aware of his presence. He pulled her back into his chest, enclosing her within his arms. It felt so good, so right. She struggled out of his loose hold, glancing toward the couch where she had left her son.

"Out like a light," Bram confirmed.

"I need to talk with you." Thea marched past the man, heading for her bedroom. On second thought, she turned into her studio instead. Even now she needed no reminder of her and Bram naked together. *Especially now*. She spun around and waited, toe tapping, for Bram to follow. Hair tousled from their night together, eyes drooping a bit from lack of sleep, he looked like ice cream on a hot summer day. She crossed her arms over her chest.

"Don't you see where my lo. . .my passion for you has gotten me? My absence put my son in danger. He could have been killed."

Bram's gaze searched her face as he reached toward her cheek. She dodged his touch. He dropped his hand back to his side. "But he wasn't, Thea. What happened to Alex last night was bad luck. He handled the situation, and now *you* have to handle it. We have more evidence now, even a description of the culprit once Sy sorts fact from fancy. And what we did last night? Well, that was everything two adults can ever hope for. And more."

If she expected him to understand, she was wrong. "Don't you see, Bram? I had no business being with you when I knew that arsonist was out there. I let my feelings override commonsense. My actions endangered my child. I can't let that happen again."

"Thea—"

"No! Let me finish. It's more than the situation with Alex. You're still intent on changing Potshot. Worst yet, I made a mistake going with you last night. I thought I could do this, but I can't. I can't jeopardize my life or my community for a temporary relationship no matter how much I've come to care for you. I've worked too hard for balance. Please don't make this any harder than it already is."

Thea pushed by him and out the door. In the bathroom, the cold water she slapped onto her face helped a little. Her chest burned with repressed emotion. With love. She heard Bram's truck start, then the receding sound of his engine. Thankful beyond belief that Bram had not pressed his plea, she trekked back to where her son slept on the couch. He looked exposed and helpless as a newborn. With great care, Thea tucked the comforter around his bony shoulders. His body made the slightest of mounds beneath the blanket. After brewing a cup of tea, she settled into the rocker across from her son and watched him breathe.

Deep within, the woman who had bloomed in Bram's arms wept and threw herself against the double-edged constraints of motherhood and of protector to her community.

Chapter Fifteen

"Why're you ticked off at Bram, Mom?" Alex asked as they drove down the mountain into Potshot.

She glanced in her mirror at the hulking Land Rover pacing her car. "What makes you think I'm angry?"

"You hardly said anything to him. And he was being really nice. He's even helping us move our stuff to town."

She sighed. "I'm not mad. Just tired."

Whap! Alex released his safety belt and bounced onto his knees to face backward. He waved with such enthusiasm it was a wonder his shoulder didn't dislocate. In her rearview mirror, she saw Bram wave back. A delicious quiver shimmied up and down her spine before settling like Jell-O in her lower abdomen. Even from here, she craved the man.

She wiped an absurd grin off her face. "Alex. Seatbelt, please."

Her son plopped down and pulled the safety belt to its maximum extension, then released it to twang back into its holder. At least the seatbelts worked. Judging from the rattles and shudders each time she turned the key in the ignition, her car was on its last wheel. She refused to look at the odometer anymore; all those zeros, and the indicator had turned over once already. From her perspective, it was an event worth celebrating whenever the Honda started.

"Alexander!"

He yanked the strap across his chest and clicked it into place. "So how long do we get to stay at the hotel?"

"That depends."

"I think it'll be fun. Bram and Ian and Challie and the rest're all there, too. Don't you think it'll be fun?"

'Fun' definitely was not the word she would choose. *Frustrating* and *agonizing* worked for her, but definitely not *fun*. "Sure, honey."

"We'll get to eat out all the time. That'll be great."

"It sure will." Thea barely suppressed a moan. Vivid recall of the low-to-nonexistent balance in her checkbook and credit card account flashed. She pictured the careful stacks of completed paintings in Bram's truck and a litany of 'oh, please let them sell…' began.

They pulled into town and maneuvered into the parking area behind the hotel. Bud Senior, who had been sitting in the glider on the veranda, caught up with them as she cut the engine. He was pretty spry for a old guy with a cane. Bud propped himself on the window she could no longer close, since the mechanism in the door had failed yesterday.

"Althea."

"Hiya, Bud. What's up?"

Bram pulled into the space beside hers. Bud decided to wait for the other man before resuming. As Bram joined them, she watched the play of muscle and tendon beneath Bram's chambray shirt and—*fuchsia help her*—his worn jeans. Sensual memory nearly overwhelmed her. When she glanced at Bram's face, his heated gaze told her she had been observed. *Caught in a lustful response—how embarrassing.* Hot blood flooded her chest and face. Clearly immune to the byplay, the older man fixed Alex in his bleary-eyed stare.

"Hear you're a regular hero, son."

Alex's cheeks turned a fiery red. Bud swung his faded baby blues to her. "Dwaine says you can stay at his place instead of here, Thea. Thought it might help with your finances and all. Be glad to have you stay at the hotel, though. In exchange for that mural you promised to paint alongside the hotel. It's just that we don't have any facilities for cooking in the rooms."

Again Thea's face warmed. *Shrinking assets hurt.* "Dwaine's place might be better. Thanks for the offer, though, Bud."

Alex leaned across her lap and said to Bram, "Dwaine's place is really cool. He's got horns and heads all over his walls. Wait till you see his guns."

Thea promised herself to make Dwaine lock each and every one up before she let Alex loose. Interrupting before her son went into great and loving detail about Dwaine's collection, she said, "I think I'll head over there now. Thanks, Bud. Say hello to Letty and Bud Junior for me."

Bud fumbled in his chest pocket. "Oh, I almost forgot. Looks like your old boss couldn't get a hold of you at your place, so he called the sheriff."

"My answering machine's on the blink."

"No matter. Sy knew you'd be stopping by." He handed her a scrawled message.

Thea frowned at the cryptic note. 'IMPORTANT YOU CALL THOMAS AT ST. MARY'S HOSPITAL IN RENO'. She glanced at the room and phone numbers, then clutched the paper. Her chest tightened and the gnawing sensation in her belly intensified.

Bud handed her the house key, then lingered to wave them out of the lot. Bram followed. One leavening moment occurred as Thea drove by the church, where the sign read:

THE LADIES OF THE CHURCH HAVE CAST OFF
CLOTHING OF EVERY KIND.
THEY CAN BE SEEN
IN THE CHURCH BASEMENT SATURDAY.

"Why're you laughing Mom?"

So I don't cry? "It looks like we may get a bigger turnout

272

than expected at our rummage sale."

"I don't see what's so funny about that."

Concern over Thomas dampened her sense of fun and she shrugged. "I'll explain later."

Alex huffed, "You always say that."

Once at Dwaine's, they began unpacking both vehicles. Thea fussed over her paintings, covered and ready for transport. Try as she might to do otherwise, she found herself staring at Bram and thinking impure thoughts.

"Everything okay, Thea?" he asked in passing.

"Anything but," she muttered.

Wedging a draped canvas between hands and hip, he stopped in front of her. Flustered, she said, "I was just checking to make sure the paintings remained covered."

Not that she worried about damage during the move. Nothing that simple. Instead, she fretted that Bram would see her last three paintings. Once he saw those, he would realize how often, and in what depths, he had invaded her mind and heart. *That wouldn't do. No, it wouldn't do at all.*

"Not to worry. I'm treating them like day-old kittens." He tilted forward and planted a whisper of a kiss on her mouth. By the time she recovered, Bram was halfway to Dwaine's extra bedroom, where the paintings would be stored. He called, "Let me know when I can see your work."

"How about when black becomes my color of choice?" He was too far away to hear. *If* the gallery chose to display her paintings in September, Bram would be Oklahoma bound.

After they unloaded, Bram invited the MacTavishes to a fire demonstration. Alex wriggled like an eager puppy and Thea acquiesced. "Just give me a few minutes. I need to make a call."

She escaped to the kitchen. As she punched the multitude of numbers off her card into the phone, her anxiety level rose. Her call was transferred to Thomas' room, but the phone rang and rang until a nurse answered. Thomas was sleeping. The woman told her that Mr. Sakamura's condition was very grave. Once Thea wrote down the visiting hours, limited due to his illness, she went to join Bram and Alex.

What she saw gave her pause. She kept to the shadows of the doorway where she observed them without intruding. Bram stood in the gaping door of his truck while a glowing Alex sat in the driver's seat. The man talked the boy through the shift pattern.

"You've got to keep the clutch in, Alex, or the gears will catch and jam."

"Bad news?"

"The worst. You'd leave pieces of your transmission from here to Oklahoma."

"No shit."

"Yep."

Alex shifted through all the gears, lifting and lowering his left leg as he let the clutch in and out. Bram must have adjusted the seat to Alex's leg length. "Good job, partner. Real smooth."

Alex beamed. "So can we try it with the engine running?"

Bram glanced toward Thea's hiding place and she stepped into view. Bram winked and said, "Maybe later, buddy. Here comes your mom."

Alex hopped from the vehicle. Thea's upbeat façade cracked like shale when she saw her son imitate the man's wide-legged stance. *Bram's departure will blast holes the size of bomb craters in both of us.*

Bram studied her face. "What's wrong, darlin'?"

"My friend's ill. He's in a hospital in Reno."

"I'm sorry to hear that." He found a knot in her shoulder and started massaging. Thea leaned into his touch instead of away, as she should. *Fuchsia!*

"Who?" piped Alex.

274

"Mr. Sakamura, honey. Thomas is the owner and my employer at Visual Perceptions," she said for Bram's benefit.

"He's always making these paper cranes and dogs for me," her son added.

As Bram moved his hand to her other shoulder, Thea said, "Origami."

"I'll drive you to Reno once I finish the demo."

"I don't know if that's a good idea, Bram." Deep and promising as vats of melted chocolate, his eyes enticed her. Bram withdrew his touch, but she swore he did so reluctantly.

"It's no problem. I'm making the trip anyway."

"Will you give me another driving lesson, Doc?"

"Could be, partner." He roughed the boy's hair and Alex canted toward him. "We'd better hightail it out of here, though, if I'm going to make my presentation on time."

When Thea aimed toward her car, Alex dragged her toward the passenger side of Bram's truck instead. Her son sat beside the man, while Thea settled onto the backseat. Alex jabbered as they drove, which left her to gather her frayed defenses and marshal her strength.

They pulled into the clearing, where the size of the turnout surprised Thea. At least two hundred people milled around—witnesses to Bram's display of combustion. Off to one side, she spotted Moran's tanker truck, where Zechariah parked in readiness for suppressing the demonstration fires.

Neither Jake, a.k.a. Jacob Seeger, nor Meg surfaced, which granted Thea a minor reprieve. From the last message left on Thea's useless answering machine, she knew Mother had gone into hiding after yesterday's debacle. Clearly Amarantha needed time to absorb the return of Jacob Seeger, too. *Good.* If Thea had to deal with anything else right now, she would implode, thus becoming the first human black hole ever. For some reason, the visual brought a smile to her face.

Which could explain why Bram, who opened her door,

might believe her to be a woman of diminished resolve.

Which could justify the silken urgency of his kiss.

Which did not exonerate her for letting him kiss her until her toes curled. *In front of what felt like the entire populations of Potshot and Eden Valley.*

Before she took issue, Bram stepped back and offered his hand in a courtly gesture. Alex looked positively ebullient as his mother slipped an arm through his icon's. She whispered, "That was cheating, Bram."

"You liked it."

She matched her step to his. "Still, it only complicates things."

He shrugged. "I don't see the difficulty, Thea. Only opportunity. Here, this's close enough."

She looked around and asked, "Close enough for what?"

"You'll be far enough from the flames to be comfortable, but close enough to see what I want you to see."

"Any closer to the proverbial flames and I'm toast."

He laughed and kissed her cheek. With a more serious expression, he said, "You're not the only one."

Thea watched him walk toward the heaped kindling as Alex tagged along. A gaggle of kids gravitated toward her son. The story of his encounter with the fire-starting phantom had obviously gained in proportion with each retelling. Her anxiety peaked until she squashed it through the simple expediency of repeating the Serenity Prayer to herself. She concentrated on the accept-what-you-cannot-change part. While Alex basked in the adulation of his peers, Thea tuned out and let her tired mind free-spin.

When Ian lit off the first pile of brush gathered from Eden Valley, the mound ignited with an explosive *whoosh!* She recoiled and yelped. Alex's crew sniggered and mocked her reaction.

Her son patted her hand. "Lay off, guys. Mom, it's all

right." The fire burned hot and fast, reducing the mass to glowing cinders in less time than she expected.

Bram hoisted his bullhorn and said, "You saw it. That's how fast the sagebrush steppe in your valley can burn. That's what we're trying to prevent."

The voices around her pealed with shrill worry. Bram's voice boomed again. "If you'll look, you can see the second pile's made up of deadfall and duff. This duff is the thick layer of decaying organic matter found throughout the forest on Ricochet Mountain and around Potshot. Remember, this fuel has not been treated with accelerant."

He nodded to Ian. The fireman kindled the next stack. Thea prepared herself, but the blast of ignition still made her jump. This time, all voices died away as the crowd watched the mound burn to embers. Only when Moran drove his truck closer to extinguish live cinders did voices raise with a stridency that drowned even Bram's amplified voice.

"Ladies. Gentlemen. Please. Can I have your attention?"

Finally, when the din settled to a dreary roar, he continued. "I know this demonstration was graphic and frightening. It was meant to be. You need to know what you're up against when it comes to wildfire. Now you can make an informed decision on how best to support my grant team and your community. Thank you for your time."

People roiled around Thea before forming into discussion groups. *You don't have to be a painter to see the bold strokes on this canvas.* When Alex urged her toward Bram, she went without resistance.

Thus she stood near him when Zechariah Moran, with a copy of *Smokechaser's Gazette* tucked under one arm, said, "Am I the only one to notice how the fires started when the university eggheads blew into town? That guy Salinger said the Injun Chief here has a history of arson back on the reservation."

Thea understood the term 'flashpoint' as she rounded on the man. "You keep a civil tongue in your head, Zechariah Moran. Every person on Bram's grant team has put his or her life on the line fighting fires with us. Bram has been in the forefront each time, in spite of personal losses that would have crushed a lesser man. With the smallest effort, even *you'd* learn a thing or two about integrity from *Dr.* Hayes."

Moran stuck out his chin while his eyes narrowed to slits. "Ah, hell, Althea, everybody knows you're sleepin'—"

Bram interrupted with a fierce, "That's enough, Moran."

The man twisted toward Bram, as though to make an issue of it. Perhaps it was the make-my-day expression on Bram's face, but Moran backed down with a muttered, "Well, someone had ought to look into all these new folks coming into Potshot. What about that old guy? What's his name? Jake Seeker. He's trouble if I ever laid eyes on it."

"Leave it alone, Zechariah," directed Sy.

In the commotion, he had joined the fray. The sheriff perused the crowd around Moran—mostly people from the valley, who gathered closer in timeless mob instinct. Sy's harsh gaze rested on one, then another, until he met all their stares.

"Investigating suspects is my job and, believe you me, I've been doing it. We have some good leads, too. But I can tell you up front that Doc Hayes and Jacob Seeger are not on my short list. Or my long list either.

"Now you all just calm down. Show's over. Go ahead and discuss how you want to vote among yourselves, but you'd best bring any proof of arson you think you might have to me. Other than that, do us all a favor and keep your noses out of this."

As the throng dispersed, Bram escorted Thea to his rig. Her limbs trembled and stomach spasmed in the aftermath. When Alex sprinted over, wanting to ride into town with Keith and Sherman, Bram countered the offer with an invitation for all of them to go into Reno. A pitch for ice cream cones sweetened his proposal. After checking with parents, the boys piled into the backseat. Sounds of their horseplay reverberated throughout the truck.

Bram inclined toward Thea's ear and, in spite of her best intentions, an immoral shiver zipped up and down her spine. He said, "Thanks."

"What for?"

He looked away as though contemplating some inner space rather than the valley below. "For standing up for me like that."

Relief buoyed her. "It didn't bruise your manly ego?"

"Hah. Very funny, MacTavish."

Filled with a helium-like element, she smiled and said, "Anytime, Hayes."

Two hours later, her cheer long gone, Thea stumbled from Thomas' bedside. Bram waited in the reception area, thumbing through a sports magazine. When he saw her, he stood.

She clung to his gaze. "He's dying, Bram."

His arms closed around her and Thea burrowed into him. Sadness too deep for easy tears rocked her. "I'm so sorry, darlin'." He slipped into what Thea called his Cherokee croon and rocked her. Given a choice, she would stay here forever.

When Thea could speak again, she asked, "Where're the boys?"

"I left them eating ice cream in my rig. Alex found my old Game Boy in the glove box."

Thea stepped away and scrubbed her face. "Your poor truck."

He shrugged. "It's a utility vehicle, Thea. Should be able to handle three boys."

Wrinkles and two dark blotches marred Bram's chambray.

"Look what I've done to your shirt."

He captured her hand and pressed it against the solid beat of his heart. "It'll wash."

Meeting his compassionate gaze, she said, "I never cry."

"I know. Only onions, right?" She gulped and nodded, and he said, "Let's get out of here."

Instead of leading her directly to the Land Rover, he relocated them to benches near cement planters. Afternoon sun cast long shadows and Thea appreciated the shade. "I hardly recognized him, Bram. Between chemo and radiation therapy, the cancer. . ." she choked.

"Why did he wait to tell you?"

She sniffed and shredded a Kleenex. "Dear man. He didn't want me to feel pressured into returning to Visual Perceptions. Or into a partnership, which I can't afford anyway."

Starting with her neck, Bram gently kneaded the muscles framing her spine. Even one-handed, his touch conferred strength and warmth. *Life.* "Sounds like a good guy."

"He is. Thomas doesn't have family and his illness forced him to sell the company. He signed the papers yesterday. Guess that means I'm out of a job. No more ambivalence about going back after all." She tried for a watery smile, but failed miserably.

Bram handed her an oversize handkerchief. After regarding the tatters left of her Kleenex, she hesitated only moments before blowing her nose. "Thanks."

"Anytime."

"Thanks, too, for being here. And for lending a hand with my paintings. I know it's making it hard to maintain our distance."

The intensity in his look caused her to sit straighter. He cupped her face and canted toward her. His regard settled on her mouth, then returned to her eyes. "Darlin', if I had my druthers, I'd be in your life and bed each and every day

280

until—"

"Until you leave in September."

Which said it all. They returned to Potshot in relative silence. On the backseat, the boys tangled in sleep like exhausted puppies.

Chapter Sixteen

Construction trucks rolled into town within days of the vote supporting Bram's plans. Sidewalks vibrated and windows rattled while residents turned out to see the cavalcade. A group of Thea's protesters tried to stop the vehicles from entering Potshot, but the massive trucks simply went around them. Now the same group waved signs across from the hotel. Oddly, Thea was nowhere in sight and Bram's hopes for reconciliation dove like a catfish for a muddy channel. At least she wasn't bodily throwing herself in front of the monster trucks.

On the other hand, with school on summer hiatus, kids were everywhere. Their artless exuberance helped to ease his misery. When Bram caught sight of Alex with his friends, he headed toward the boy.

"Hiya, Doc! Great trucks." Alex's enthusiasm made him smile.

"Look at the claw on that one!" exclaimed one of the girls. A hushed delirium of anticipation fell over them.

Bram figured it was one of the few moments he would get a word in edgewise, so he asked, "Are we still on for your mom's birthday surprise tonight, partner?"

Alex pried his gaze from the parade of colossal vehicles. "Sure. I don't think it's going to change her mind about you, though. She's clueless. Besides, that art guy's over at Dwaine's right now, looking at her stuff. That's why she couldn't show up to protest."

The last of the construction vehicles turned off Main Street and fine grit hung like gold dust in the early morning air. Afternoon heat would produce thermal ripples along the street, but for now, the waters of Boondoggle Pond prevailed and kept the air cool. All the kids but Alex stampeded after the earthmovers. As the boy hopped from foot-to-foot in an eager dance to join his friends, Bram said, "I'll bet the bulldozer driver will give you a ride if I ask him to."

The youngster looked at him with such pure joy that Bram laughed before tousling Alex's hair. He was an easy boy to love. Alex ducked, taking off at a full run. "Wait till I tell the guys," he yelled back at Bram.

Bram cupped his hands around his mouth, "Don't forget. The hotel at six sharp."

Alex waved, then cut around the corner and out of sight. As Bram swung toward his rig, he noticed old Mrs. Moran half a block away and heading toward him. With an arm in a homemade sling, she visibly wavered between either walking toward him or bolting. Skittish as she was, she high-tailed it across the street. The woman moved well for an oldster. He tried to shrug off her obvious efforts to avoid him. After all, Zechariah Moran never referred to him as anything but 'Injun Chief' and 'Redskin'. Obviously, Ma Moran's son had suckled the milk of prejudice at her breast.

He hopped into his truck. The Rover started with a roar, then he backed out and charged from the hotel parking lot with more speed than necessary. Bram conscientiously eased his foot off the accelerator. Just because an old biddy crossed the street rather than share a sidewalk with an Indian was no reason to abuse his rig. Yet, instead of heading to Jack Rabbit Ridge, where the work crew gathered, he turned right and headed toward Dwaine's place. *Ian and Challie knew the drill. They could handle heavy equipment operators.*

Two days had passed since he saw Thea; two days since

she defended him against Zechariah Moran in front of the Creator and everybody else; two days since she renewed her stand against their relationship taking its natural course. The tightening in his groin reminded him of the seventy-four hours and twenty-five minutes since they had made love. He wondered what lasting effect *that* would have on him. It was enough that Bram missed Thea with a gnawing ache.

As he pulled into Dwaine's driveway, he noticed another vehicle besides Thea's—this one a sleek town number that probably did everything but cook dinner. *Hell*, he amended, *it probably did fix supper*. The luxury car sported California plates along with deeply tinted windows. Like a predatory cat, it eased away as he approached. The automobile pulled smoothly into the circular driveway and disappeared from sight.

Bram parked next to Thea's clunker and he hopped from the truck. Studying the main door as he approached, he noted again the grainy wood etched with deer, elk, and cougar. A hunter took aim at top center. *No question about it, the deputy loved his sport*. As Bram started to knock, he realized the entry gaped open a good three inches.

His heart pounded as he pushed against the heavy door and called, "Thea? You in here?"

Just about the time he decided she had gone with the art dealer, Bram heard a strained sound from the kitchen. "Thea?"

In a few strides he plowed through the hunting lodge motif of both foyer and living room to the kitchen entrance. Head supported by her hands, Thea sat at the butcher-block table. Her delicate fingers splayed through her cropped hair as she stared at the patterned surface. Bram took the steps necessary to reach her, then hunkered down beside her, one hand on her upper back.

"Darlin'? What's wrong?"

Her dazed expression worried him. "Bram? You'll never

believe what just happened."

Anger over the dealer's tactless rejection of her work filled Bram, along with a hefty dose of compassion for Thea. "What does that guy know about art anyway? You'll find someone else to show your paintings."

The stunned look on her face gave way to hilarity. "No, you don't understand. This... *this* is what I can't believe." Her laughter took on an hysterical edge as she waved a rectangular sheet over Bram's head.

Bram seized the slip of paper and she let go without resistance. "It's a check."

"I know that!" She flung herself into his arms. Her exuberance bowled him over as she sprawled on top of him. "Can you believe it? I've never seen so many zeros before the decimal point before. And you know what? It's only a partial payment for the paintings he wants. Plus he expects I'll have commissions for future works!"

He laughed, too, before closing his arms around her. They lay there, giggling and chuckling. Finally, Thea stilled. Bram crooked his neck to look at her. A new expression that Bram identified as pure and unmitigated terror filled her face.

"Oh, *fuchsia*! What if nobody else likes my paintings? What if he changes his mind and I have to give the money back?"

Bram struggled to sit with Thea slumped against him. He bent forward and put the check on the table. From there, he worked into a cross-legged tailor's position while Thea rearranged her legs around his hips. He framed her face and kissed her forehead, her eyelids, and the corners of her mouth.

"You're fretting over something that just isn't going to happen. That man does this for a living. He's not going to throw big money around without damn good cause."

She slid her arms around him, wiggling until she circled his chest. "You think?"

He liked the way she weighted his lap and filled his arms. Things were definitely shaping up and in ways he had only fantasized about. "Damned right, I do. He's a businessman, and he's been doing this for how long?"

She squirmed, evidently to get more comfortable. Bram suppressed a groan. "At least twenty years in San Francisco. I think Jarvis started out in Boston."

"See what I mean? He'll make sure you get what's coming to you." His lips grazed her mouth.

She exhaled a beckoning scent of apple over him as he inhaled the warm fragrance so unique to Thea. She went very still. Her eyes shimmered green with lustful intent. "Just what is it that you think I have coming to me?"

"It'd be better if I showed you. Why don't you go lock the front door though first? I'll get the back one. And the blinds."

"You got it." Bram untangled from her and raced to the front of the house where he shot the bolt. When he hit the entry into the kitchen, Thea was on him like accelerant on briquettes. Legs wrapped around his hips, she closed the minuscule gap between their lips. Heat filled Bram so fast he expected to explode on the spot. He had been trained to recognize the warning signs of spontaneous combustion, though. Hungry flames licked his soul.

Her lips broke away from his. He groaned and followed, but she eluded him. In seconds, he was glad she had when her mouth found his neck, then chest. "Thea, I'm burning up, darlin'."

"Let's just get. . .some of these. . .clothes off." She peeled off his shirt, then did the same to hers.

Bram reached for the buttons of her jeans, following the progress of his fingers with his mouth. Denim pooled around her feet as he kneeled before her with his mouth over her cotton hipsters where they covered her *mons*. He supported her by cupping her buttocks. She swayed in his hold, her

286

hands in his hair.

"You're making me dizzy with desire." She removed her hands from his hair to support herself on the table behind her.

"Hold that pose."

He wrestled his own boots, jeans, and shorts off before slipping her out of her underpants. That barrier gone, he buried his face in the damp curls formerly covered by panties.

"Bram, if you had any idea. . ."

He enjoyed her little gasps of pleasure for some time before he stood and lowered her back to the table. Bringing her legs over his shoulders, he found out what a nice sturdy table Dwaine had. Its height turned out to be perfect, too.

Much later he supported himself on his elbows above her. The dampness on their skin mingled while they caught their breath. He studied her sweet face, her eyes soft as spring moss, and said, "Thea, I'm crazy in love with you, darlin'."

Her breath caught. She swallowed hard and her eyes got all misty. "Oh, Bram, I. . ."

His arms nearly buckled with the relief over facing up to his true feelings. He smiled and lick-kissed her mouth. "You always going to cry after we love each other? If so, I'm going to have to lay in a large supply of tissues."

"No, it's just that. . ."

"I know you're not happy with what I'm doing in Potshot, but we can deal with that. I have a few options you might like better…" Uneasiness, the pit viper in a lush meadow, moved through him. *Shoats and razorbacks, why didn't she just tell me that she loves me?*

The phone rang, startling them both. They laughed self-consciously as Dwaine's answering machine picked up. The message played in the background.

"What is it that has you so tongue-tied, sweetheart?"

Meg's voice sounded taut as a lasso on a calf's neck. "Thea, are you there? Please pick up."

Thea rolled onto her elbows, her attention on the machine. "It's your father. Jacob. That scoundrel Zechariah Moran assembled the equivalent of a lynch mob and went after him at the hot springs. Sy's got both Moran and Jake in lockup. Jake for his own protection. If you get this message, meet me at the jail." The connection broke with a click.

Bram rose, then helped Thea to her feet as they scrambled for their clothes. In short order, they stood face-to-face and floundered for words.

Bram finally said, "We'll take my truck."

"Not this time." She caressed his jaw and chin with the back of her hand. "We'll talk later."

He turned his face and pressed a lingering kiss onto her palm. "I'll meet you at the jail."

She nodded before leaving the kitchen. The front door shut behind her. Bram glanced around, not knowing what he was looking for, but knowing it was no longer here. His gaze seized on Thea's check. He picked it up and tucked it into a nook on the counter. Feeling lost, he stood there for a long moment.

"Love struck fool. Wishing Thea loved you won't make it happen." With a shake of his head, Bram pivoted on his heels and followed his heart out the door.

Sy kicked everyone out of his office except Bram, who waited by the coffeemaker. As hard as Bram listened, no sounds breached the interior door, which led to the jail cells. Meg and Thea were still back there with Jake while the deputy stood guard nearby. Beyond the street door, Bram heard the muffled buzz from the crowd who had attacked Jake. Like a headless rattler, the remnants continued to thrash about—all nerve and no reason. With that idiot Moran behind bars, Bram hoped the dregs would disperse soon. He rubbed his forearm,

288

the old hurt always greater at times like these. Muscle memory of hate-induced actions made the scars on his back twitch.

Bram forced his attention to Sy's words, ". . .purely poetry in motion the way Jake took down Moran. Survival's definitely what that compadre's good at. Jake's crew did real good at containing the situation, too. A lot to be said for Uncle Sam's Green Machine. Those vets knew their business." The older man took a long draw on his coffee.

"There've been times I could've benefited from a better grasp of hand-to-hand," Bram said.

The sheriff grunted in assent. "Still don't know how Amarantha got away with hitting Jake. By all rights, he should've laid her flat when she took after him. She'd never have known what hit her, that's for sure." Sy rubbed his neck. "Glad he didn't, though. I'd've hated to drag his butt to jail for that. Can't have him hitting a woman. Even Amarantha."

Bram remembered Jake's look of iron restraint. "He chose *not* to react with violence, Sy."

"Could be, son. Guess Jake figured he owed her a few licks after what he put her through. Raising Thea on her own couldn't have been all sunshine and posies for Amarantha. Lord knows, Charlie wasn't up to the task."

The inner door to the cells opened. Bram turned to meet Thea's look. She nodded to Sy. "He's got a bruise or two, but Zechariah looks a lot worse."

Sy asked, "Moran behaving himself? Sounds awful quiet."

Thea grinned. "You have to give Dwaine points for creativity. He slapped a strip of duct tape over Zech's mouth. He called it a 'muzzle order', I think."

Sy peered through the entry into the cells, then closed the door with a contented smirk. "That'll teach Moran to keep his yap shut."

"I expect he'll regret not having taken time for a closer

shave this morning," added Thea.

"Yep, could smart just a might getting that tape off."

Thea's smile fell flat as her gaze met Bram's. "You want to see my fa. . .Jake?"

Bram shook his head. "There'll be time for that later. Let him and Meg have some privacy. It's turned into one wild day, hasn't it?" He went to her, rubbing her back lightly before centering on the tightness between her shoulder blades.

She put distance between them. "I need to find Alex, Bram. He really likes Jake and I don't want him to learn of this episode from anyone else."

Sy said, "Works out pretty good, Jake being his granddad and all. I suspect Alex and the gang'll probably be up at the construction site. They took after the earthmovers like bandits this morning."

Thea winced and looked up at Bram. "That's right. Your plans are progressing right on schedule, aren't they?" With those words, she brushed by him and headed out the door.

Sy said, "Better go after her, son. I know what that look means when my April fixes it on me."

Bram steered through the door before it closed behind Thea. She presented him with her back as she strode toward her car.

"Thea! Wait."

She made no concession to his call other than to increase her speed. He jogged to catch her. "Talk to me, Thea. Why're you being so bullheaded about my project?"

Thea slanted him a look, but said nothing. When she reached her junker, he blocked her access to the driver's door with his body. She planted her feet and glared at him. "Get away from my car, Bram."

He crossed his arms. "Not until we settle this."

Her fists clenched and Bram pictured Thea taking after him like a kitten after a panther. *What was it with these MacTavish women anyway?* Instead, she spat, "I already told you why."

"Only in snatches, Thea. Just tell me the truth. What are you so scared of? Why are you so *terrified* about my project's effects on Potshot?"

Her jaw flexed. She took one step closer. "All right. I'll tell you. *I'll tell you.*"

He watched the war of emotions on her face and wondered if she would be able to do so. Abruptly, she shrank from him. Her gaze fell.

"I have a darkness in me, Bram, a waiting kind of bleakness. It tries to consume my joy in life, my confidence in myself. If I let it, it would consume everything important to me. I won't."

"Let me help, Thea."

As though deaf to his heartfelt offer, her next words raised gooseflesh on Bram's arms. "I've been there. Once. After Derek's assault. Before I realized I was pregnant, I lost myself in the dark. I didn't care about anything or anyone, least of all myself. To keep that from happening again, I keep promises to myself. No alcohol. No loss of conscious choice. Minimal self-pity. But I need clarity to resist and I have to work hard sometimes to keep myself from the precipice. I want to raise my son and respect my art." She lifted her gaze and the misery he saw there nearly brought him to his knees.

"You're not alone, sweetheart."

"Yes, I am. And I'm closer to drinking again than I've been since quitting. If I started, I don't know if I'd be able to stop. I could lose myself completely. I'd go back into that hole and never come out again. I'm not sure I could have dragged myself out of it without my son and the support of Meg. Without this community." Her regard flickered. She stepped further from him—wrapped her arms around her ribs.

"Yesterday I learned my friend and former employer is dying. Tomorrow, I take my child to Reno, where he'll be tested for a paternity that's never been in question. Derek Salinger will have the proof he needs to take my son away from me. Regardless of the restraining order or his violent behavior, Salinger's money and lawyers will twist the law in his favor. Then today, a mob attacked the man who fathered me. These are people that I'd have trusted with my life a few months ago."

Her look blazed a path to his soul. "Today, you started changing the hills and valley where I grew up. It took eons to form this landscape, you'll alter in a matter of hours. Don't you see, Bram? Since you came into Potshot, everything I've counted on has been threatened. My son, my ties to this community, the very ground I walk on. Even my hard-won faith in myself."

Her dry stare worried him. She closed her eyes and a frown puckered the skin between her eyes. "I'm so afraid, Bram, so afraid of spinning out of control. Look at my *father* for God's sake! Homeless and lost for over thirty years. Am I programmed for that behavior at a genetic level? I must be. Darkness comes knocking at my soul's door at every opportunity. If I open the door, will I be able to shut it again? Or will I be just another derelict on a city street, hiding from the failure I've become?"

Bram recognized the abyss in her vision. He had been there and back. He reacted with his gut and stepped forward, wanting to cradle her, but instead, he shook her. "Open your eyes! Damn it, open them, Thea, and take a good look at what's in front of you. You're the one who's chosen to stay off booze. You've made a good life for yourself and your son. You're strong, Thea. And this other stuff. . ." He made a wild gesture, taking in the town and mountain.

"You don't need any of it to be who you are. You're incredible and vital and powerful in your own right." Her eyes opened with a lethargy that left him cold. He said, "You're not losing anything. Not Alex, not Potshot, not yourself. Not me. Woman, look at me! Darlin', you've got my heart wrapped up in a doeskin medicine bag."

She shook her head. "I can't, right now, I just can't. It's too much. I thought I could before Alex saw the firestarter. I really believed I could, Bram. It's just too complicated. Loving a temporary man, fighting Derek's claims, watching my town disintegrate, now worrying about who might want to hurt my son…"

"You love me," he said.

"Yes! But that doesn't change anything!"

"Why, Thea, it makes all the difference."

Thea pried his hands loose and navigated around him. "I'm going to find Alex."

Before she could duck into the car, a group of boys sprinted around the sheriff's office. Bram immediately noticed Alex's absence. Keith and Sherman skidded to a halt in front of Bram, the others stacking like kindling behind them. "Dr. Hayes, are you going to get the bulldozer guy to give us a ride?" asked Sherman, his cheeks red and eyes shining.

Thea called, "Sherm? Keith? I thought Alex was with you."

The heavier boy looked around Bram. "Oh, hi Ms. Mac. Alex *was* with us. Old lady Moran made him go with her."

Thea pushed away from her car. "What? Why would Mrs. Moran want Alex to go with her?"

Sherman shrugged. "I don't know. But Alex sure didn't want to go. She had him by his ear. Made him get into her old beater pick-up. No one saw but me. I was. . .well, I kind of hid when I saw her coming. But Alex wasn't quick enough. Guess I should've said something, huh?"

Thea asked, "How long ago?" She got into her car.

He gave her a shamed look and said, "Couple of hours? I thought, well, you know, that he'd done something he shouldn't have. Like last year when we rode our bikes through her garden."

Thea looked at Bram. "You let Sy know I'm going to get Alex."

Her gaze conveyed more than her words. Recent incidents gained fresh relevance. Bram remembered seeing Mrs. Moran that morning. She looked robust. He recalled how the late morning sun caught in her loose hair, making a silver nimbus around her head. The old lady had an arm in a sling. A pot thrown by a frightened boy could cause that kind of damage. Bram yanked Thea's door open.

"You're coming with me, Thea. In my truck. I'm not taking 'no' for an answer."

Bram hustled her to his vehicle. She jumped into the passenger seat before he got to his. They buckled up, then took off, leaving a rooster tail of dust hanging in the air. The boys watched them go. Once Bram pulled onto the main drag, he handed Thea his cell phone.

"Call Sy and let him know what's going on."

"Hurry, Bram. Please hurry."

"Let me know where we're going and I'll get us there."

"Take the first left out of town. It turns into a dirt road a few miles down, but keep following it."

She punched numbers into the phone. Bram remained only peripherally aware of her conversation with Sy. Instead his brain made a blitz analysis of the facts. Snapshots of Alex rose spontaneously: Alex hanging one-armed from the birch behind Thea's place; the boy's courage when faced with a hungry wolf; the love shining from Alex's eyes when Bram gave him his first driving lesson. Bram would be damned if he let anything happen to the boy he loved.

When Thea put the phone back in its cradle, he said, "I should have figured it out before now."

"How? How could you know? And maybe we're wrong."

294

"I don't think so," he said, then swerved into a tight turn.

He accelerated around another bend, braking hard as he reached the line of vehicles headed toward Eden Valley. He recognized people from the attack on Jake.

"Hold on, Thea." He pulled into the oncoming lane and floored it. Defied by no more than a gamut of crude gestures and honking horns, Bram raced the Rover along the bumpy road. Faced with a car coming the other way, Bram dodged into the line of traffic.

That was too close. A number of vehicles still clogged the road. Along the byway, mountain pines gave way to the edges of sagebrush steppe.

With a measuring glance toward the roadside, he warned Thea, "Here we go again. Hang on." He veered his rig onto the side of the road and hit the accelerator.

The truck fishtailed a few times before settling into the terrain like a good courser. Bram steered around scrubby junipers and larger clumps of sagebrush, but ran over everything else. One false turn of the wheel and they would be nothing but mangled debris. He finally passed the last of the traffic. With a wrenching, head-to-the-roof maneuver, he jerked the truck onto the dirt road.

"Wait, Bram! Ma Moran doesn't want to be caught, right?"

"She shows no signs of remorse," Bram agreed.

"Take this next right! I have a hunch. This'll take us to her old place. Jessie and Zechariah gutted it years ago when Ma Moran moved in with them. She might not expect anyone to think of it."

"Tell Sy."

A glance showed him that Thea was not as calm as she sounded. Fine lines of strain bracketed her lips, nose, and eyes. "I'll call now. *Hurry*, Bram."

She hit redial and braced the phone against an ear. Bram concentrated on the road until Thea snugged his cell phone into its cradle. "Sy's five minutes behind us. Now tell me. Why Ma Moran?"

Seeing a straight stretch ahead, he said, "Arson-for-profit. Fires are big industry, Thea. They generate contracts for everything from bulldozers to fire crews to water tankers."

She responded with, "Moran's water tender."

"Yep. He's also a volunteer firefighter and volunteers aren't paid until they fight a fire. Mrs. Moran's got strong motivation. She's found a perfect way to create work for her son."

"But why not Moran himself? Wouldn't he be the more likely suspect? And how does she know so much about fires?" She broke off and yelled, "*Left!* Left here."

Bram hit the brakes, but loose gravel and sand caused the Rover to slide beyond the turn-off. He slammed the truck into reverse, making the left on three wheels. A hundred yards down the sagebrush-cluttered lane, they came to a singlewide. Panels of aluminum siding drooped away from the frame. Mrs. Moran's Ford had been parked haphazardly by the trailer's door. A good thing or Bram would have thought the place deserted. Both truck doors stood open. Curtains obscured every window of the trailer, too. Since this dwelling was long past inhabitable, the window coverings made Bram's suspicions soar. Just what did old Ma Moran intend to hide?

The Rover skidded. Thea leaped out and ran toward the house before Bram's truck lurched to a final halt.

"Damn it, Thea. Wait!" Bram kept his voice low, but urgent, then flung himself out his side and raced after her. "Thea! Slow down. Don't frighten her."

Somehow his warning penetrated, because she stopped just short of wrenching the door open. Bram closed the distance between them and spoke as softly as he could without whispering. "She must have heard us, but won't know I'm with you. There's probably another door in the back.

296

You knock once I'm out of sight. Act pleasant, as though nothing's wrong. Just say you needed to pick Alex up for an appointment."

"And could I drop her at the state prison?"

He kissed her hard on the lips and said, "Tell her anything to ease her suspicions. Good luck." He raced toward the closest corner.

None too soon. Before Thea could knock, the door scraped open. Instead of lurking around the corner, Bram skirted around back and found what he sought: a recessed door without a screen. He made his way to it, drew his buck knife, then tried the knob. It turned, then clicked as the tumbler caught. The mechanism sounded loud as a firecracker to him.

He pressed on the door with the greatest care. Old as it was, the weather stripping no longer sealed the frame. *A blessing.* He pushed the door open just enough to listen. When he didn't hear anything, he opened it more and peered through the crack.

Drawn curtains, no more than a collection of sagging towels and stained sheets, cast an eerie green tinge. Water damage discolored the wall panels, making the place look like a dirty fish bowl. A refrigerator, ancient and rounded looking, identified this room as the kitchen. Grimy spaces showed where other appliances had been. More importantly, Bram spied the back of a spindly chair occupied by a slim boy whose arms had been secured to the stiles with a twisted rag. The kid's sun-tipped hair and build left no question about his identity.

Alex's grubby hands twisted within the knots as he tried to find a weakness in his bonds. *Good boy*, Bram praised silently, *don't give into fear*. Another rag around Alex's head at mouth level ensured that Mrs. Moran could avoid any awkward interruptions.

Voices from the other room sounded remarkably distant,

297

which gave Bram impetus to push the door open half a foot more. Now he could see into the next room. The front entryway was offset from the rear one; both Thea and Ma Moran remained beyond sight. Bram stepped into the room.

Alex stilled, then whipped his head toward Bram. Agile young neck that he had, he managed to give Bram a three-quarter view. The boy's eyes showed white all around his pupils. Muffled grunts issued from his throat. Bram shook his head and held a finger to his mouth.

Walking the way his grandfather taught him to hunt, Bram took two strides to the boy. He changed his hold on his knife and resolved the knot as Alexander the Great had done when faced with the Gordian knot. With a *snick!* of his blade, he freed one of Alex's hands.

The low murmur from the front room changed tenor. Thea's muffled voice carried to him.

". . .that shotgun down, Mrs. Moran. Take me to my son."

Oh, hell. The old lady had a gun. That changed everything. He looped the cut cloth over the remaining knots to make it look whole before placing his hands over the boy's shoulders. He spoke low for Alex's ears only. "Stay calm. I'll handle this." He waited precious moments until Alex nodded.

Bram faded across the kitchen, slipping behind a curtained area leading to an empty pantry. Only after he took position there did Bram realize he hadn't completely closed the door. By then it was too late. Way too late.

Through a break in the curtain, he watched Thea blow into the room, giving no credence to the double-barreled shotgun aimed at her back. Icy cold washed Bram's belly. From the set of Thea's shoulders and face, Bram decided Mrs. Moran might have good reason for arming herself. Thea looked enraged enough to rip the older woman limb-from-limb. Instead she rushed to her son, slipping down onto her knees. She carefully pulled the gag free of Alex's mouth.

"Did she hurt you, honey?" She made a quick examination of her son, following the direction of her gaze with her hands.

"I'm okay," Alex croaked.

Still Thea advanced until she made sure. When she moved behind the chair to untie Alex's wrists, Ma Moran nudged Thea's shoulder with the gun barrel.

"That'll do, missy."

By then, Thea had uncovered the loose ends, but stuffed them back into hiding, all without giving away a thing. She lunged to her feet. The other woman stumbled backed as Thea whirled to face her opponent, then advanced a step toward the raised barrel. Wintry sweat trickled down Bram's spine as he prepared to launch himself from concealment.

Luckily, Thea regained her senses enough to realize she had no chance against the loaded gun. Fury sparked from her eyes. She dropped her chin and said, "Let him go."

The old woman cackled. "Always did have a lot of pluck to you, Althea. Got to give you that." The steel in the woman exposed itself as she poked Thea with the barrel. "Now why don't you just get off your high horse, girl? Won't do your boy any good to see his mama blown full of grapeshot, now would it."

Ma Moran pointed her chin at another of the vinyl-covered chairs. "Set yourself down. Once I have you tied, I'll fix us a nice cup of tea. We'll have a little chat. And don't think this bum arm slows me down none. It don't."

A cup of tea? Bram searched the bare wall where only the blackened and greasy outline of a stove remained. A Medusa's head of bare wires stuck out of the wall there. At that moment, Bram realized the true depths of the woman's insanity.

Chapter Seventeen

Taller than Thea and ropy with muscle as only an active older woman can be, Ma Moran wedged the gun against the back of the chair before turning her attention to Thea's hands. The front sight dug into the skin beneath Thea's right ear with an urgency that turned her stomach to jelly. She squeezed her eyes shut against the gruesome image of a double-barreled shotgun fired at pointblank range. The gun at her head also quelled her overt attempts to free Alex. *Hold on my sweet boy.* Cold sweat coated her forehead, oozed along Thea's sides and back.

Now would be a good time for the cavalry to arrive. Where in fuchsia is Bram, anyway?

"My man was keen on you, you know," panted Ma Moran as she tightened the knots.

"I didn't know." *What was Mrs. Moran talking about?* Ma Moran's husband Butch had drunk himself into an early grave while Thea was away at college.

"'Course, I didn't find out about it till after we was married. Guess you're lucky you never had nothing to do with Butch, Amarantha. Man had a temper that made a wolverine look friendly. Being wed to him weren't no bed of roses, believe you me."

"I'm Thea, Mrs. Moran. Amarantha's my mother." She tried to instill her voice with a sense of calm, but her voice quavered.

"Mom?" Her son's glance darted toward the older woman

in horror. Thea refrained from shaking her head, which would jiggle the barrel. She made a shushing sound instead.

Ma Moran cackled and pulled the ties hard enough to make Thea grunt. "Sorry 'bout that, Amarantha. Can't have you getting frisky. Always were all shit and splatter, weren't you? Except when you lassoed yourself that rich fella. Married the wrong Seeger, if you ask me. The other one was right pretty afore he took himself off to Vietnam. Wouldn't've minded some of that myself."

With a grunt, the woman hauled herself to her feet. The shotgun went with her. Thea let her head slump forward as relief slackened her muscles. Her head snapped backward when Ma Moran nudged Thea's chin with the barrel's front site. Crazed eyes, black as onyx, stared into hers. Thea quashed an urge to lash out with her legs. *Too much like infuriating a grizzly bear—an insane one at that.*

"All those years with Butch pretty near killed me. But I outlasted him. Now it looks like I'll outlive you, too, Miss Hoity-Toity."

"Mrs. Moran, I'm not Amarantha. I'm Thea. Why don't you let Alex go? Then we can have a nice cup of tea." Beside her, Alex started to cry, choked sobs that infused Thea with a mother's immense strength. Arctic terror, which threatened to freeze her motionless, melted beneath fury's heat.

Thea glared at Ma Moran until the woman pulled the barrel from her throat. Moran's mad gaze fixed on something behind her captives. The older woman frowned and muttered, "Now how in tarnation—" She skirted the chairs, shuffling toward an objective beyond Thea's view.

Oh, God, don't let her have seen Bram, Thea prayed.

Alex twisted his head around frantically, trying to see what the crazy woman was doing. Thea followed suit, straining her neck, nearly rigid with apprehension. But Ma Moran only shut the backdoor against a draft that must have pushed it open.

Where's Bram?

Thea needed to act before the woman tied her legs. If Bram was unable to help, then so be it. She gathered herself for a lunge, visualizing an armless tackle of the woman. Then she saw Alex's gaze darted to the pantry area adjacent to the backdoor. The hanging over the opening *could* hide a man.

The curtain exploded outward as Bram launched a rear assault of the shotgun-toting woman. The two grappled and grunted. Thea yelled, "Bram, the safety's off!"

Mrs. Moran, formidable in her lunacy, struggled for control of her gun. With an explosion, one barrel discharged, filling the ceiling over Thea's head with grapeshot. *That did it.*

Ears ringing and debris raining on them, Thea hollered, "Alex, catch yourself." Her voice sounded as though it bubbled from the deep end of a pool. *No time for that now.* She kicked her son's chair, knocking it sideways onto the floor. He arrested his fall with his free arm.

"Alex! Under the table! NOW!"

She rocked onto her feet and ran crablike toward Bram, where he tussled with the woman. As powerful as he was, Mrs. Moran broke his hold around her midsection by thumping the butt plate against his elbow. He managed to keep one hand over the trigger guard. The deranged woman twisted, presenting Thea with a view of her backside. *Looks like a target to me.* Thea swung the chair out and away from her back, putting her arms at an awkward angle, but building momentum just the same.

Her chair connected with Ma Moran, whacking the woman to her knees. Bram wrenched the gun from her hands as she fell. With another rotation, Thea collided with the woman again. This time, she hit the madwoman's upper back, which launched Ma Moran onto her face and chest. Once her nemesis collided with the ground, Thea folded over her, belly-down with the chair over them both.

Blood sang in Thea's ears and her heart beat a swift rhythm against her sternum. Beneath her, Ma Moran bucked twice before lying inert. Since the shotgun blast, Thea sensed external sounds as vibrations. She hoped the defect was only temporary.

Mrs. Moran shuddered at regular intervals, letting her know the woman still breathed. Relief bloomed; she wanted to incapacitate the woman, not kill her. *Okay, so I did harbor murderous thoughts while Alex was still in danger, but I'm past that now. Mostly.*

"Thea, you all right?" Bram sounded as though he called to her from the top of Ricochet Mountain, but Thea nodded.

He tugged her wrist ties to give notice of intent, then he cut her free. He flung the chair off her and dragged her into his arms. An outpouring of love, relief and gratitude made her knees buckle. She nestled there for less than a heartbeat before breaking free to run to her son.

Alex crouched beneath the table, where he plucked ineffectually at the remaining knots. His tear-stained face crumpled when he saw her. Thea cuddled both boy and chair before Bram interrupted and sawed through the remaining bonds. Her gaze returned again and again to Ma Moran and Thea trembled like a quaking aspen. Bound hands-to-ankles and her eyes blank and distant, the old woman sat on her haunches and rocked on the peeling linoleum. She talked to herself, too, but Thea recognized no words except:

"It ain't over yet. Not till we have our tea."

Like a cold breaker, an icy chill swept over Thea. The three survivors sat amid the carnage of Mrs. Moran's former kitchen long enough to regain a vestige of hearing. Thea inhaled the persistent odors of rancid grease and mouse droppings newly combined with the stink of cordite. Alex squirmed from the circle of their arms.

"I've got to take a leak," he muttered, then sketched a

wide circle around Mrs. Moran and scrambled toward the backdoor, evidently preferring the Great Outdoors to the trailer's nonexistent plumbing. As her son reached the door, the entry sprang open and a long arm hauled the boy from the room. In a flash, the sheriff barreled through the entryway, his revolver cocked and steady.

Bram yelled, "Sheriff! Put down your weapon!"

Thea struggled to her feet, but Bram was already halfway to the sheriff. She said, "Hey, Sy. You're a little late."

The sheriff asked, "Everyone okay here?"

Thea and Bram nodded as Sy's regard settled on Mrs. Moran. "Trussed like a Thanksgiving turkey. Hot damn! Looks like I missed all the fun." He clicked the safety on his pistol and offered them a shame-faced look. "I demolished my new cruiser on the flats. Hung the undercarriage up on a rock and ended up hitching a ride in Bodeen's pastry truck."

Thea and Bram looked at each other, then back at Sy, whose attention had strayed toward the entrance to the defunct living room. Dwaine filled the doorway in a no-nonsense stance, pistol at the ready. Florid and sweating, the baker brandished his tire iron high and skidded to a halt right behind the deputy, nearly bowling him over. Thea started to giggle. Before long she and Bram collapsed into each other in a fit of hysterical laughter.

Their hilarity died a quick death when Dwaine said, "I smell smoke."

The door bounced off the wall as Alex windmilled into the room. "The trailer's on fire!"

Bram, Alex, and Thea sprinted out the door, leaving Sy to deal with Mrs. Moran. Thea stayed on Bram's heels while he raced the perimeters of the singlewide. Where skirting gaped, smoke billowed from beneath the mobile home. Bram pried an arm off an obsolete antenna, where it lay on the ground, and raked the smoldering mass from beneath the trailer.

"Get my shovel from the Rover!"

Thea raced to comply. The entire episode lasted all of five minutes as the men stomped and flattened the cinders into dry alkaline soil. Too depleted to do more, Thea and Alex clutched each other and surveyed the damage. *So this was how Ma Moran intended to get rid of the evidence.* She refused to substitute 'evidence' with 'bodies', not when one of them would have been Alex. The men finished their fire dance and, other than Dwaine's smoking soles, none of them looked the worse for wear. Even Bram's usual reaction to fire was absent and Thea wondered what had changed.

Meanwhile, Ma Moran cackled and drooled from the back of the pastry truck. The speed of the woman's descent into madness sent another chill through Thea.

Answering Sy's call, a fire truck swung into the yard followed closely by Zechariah Moran's water tanker. The smoky dust, sirens and orchestrated activities sent Thea into overload. She enfolded her son's shoulders and retreated into bystander mode.

"Soak the underside, will you, Hulon?" Sy waved them toward the mobile home as he returned to the trailer.

Captain Peabody ordered his crew to that effect, then asked, "What on God's green earth happened here today?" He rolled his eyes at Mrs. Moran, whose son had joined her. His voice raised, Zech obviously teetered between outrage and confusion.

Bram squeezed Thea's shoulders. "Alex caught himself an arsonist."

"Old Mrs. Moran? Who'd have thought it? Looks like she's gone off the deep end, though. Good job, boy." The smoke-eater tipped his hat to the boy, who lifted his head in pride.

Toting Mrs. Moran's shotgun and another rifle, Sy joined them. Thea edged away from both weapons, bumping hard against Bram. The sheriff swung the rifle forward. "Look what I found. I'm pretty sure we'll find that those shells you recovered from the first arson fire match the bore on this thirty-thirty, Bram. I wondered where the rest of Butch's collection had gotten to. Zech had most of his pa's guns, but not these two."

"May I?" Bram accepted the rifle, and lifted it to his shoulder, sighting down the barrel. Thea gave into her anxiety and stepped back. "This scope would've made killing the coyote kid's play." He handed it back to Sy.

"Sure enough. I'm taking Mrs. Moran into Potshot in Bodeen's truck. Hate to have to ask you so soon after this unpleasant incident, but Thea, you'll need to fill out some paperwork before I release her to the hospital in Reno. You, too, Bram."

Thea's head felt too big for her neck. Even the sun looked less bright from the depths of what must be post-trauma exhaustion. "Hospital?"

"I don't have the facilities for her. She needs professional care."

Thea had no argument with that.

"We'll come by your office on our way to Thea's place," Bram offered.

"Works for me."

Bram, Thea and Alex piled into the front of the Land Rover. Despite the bucket seats, Alex draped over Thea's lap like an oversized puppy. "What's wrong with Mrs. Moran, Mom?"

She exchanged a look with Bram. "She's sick, honey."

"Will she get better?"

Thea hugged him closer and his pointy chin dug into her shoulder. "She may. But she'll never be able to hurt you again. You heard the sheriff call Reno? An ambulance will pick her up from the jail today."

"She was talking to you like she thought *you* were *Grandma*."

"I know, honey. That's part of her sickness." They passed the new squad car on the flats, where the vehicle balanced precariously over a clump of sage.

"Doesn't look good," Bram said.

Thea shivered. "Better than the alternative."

Before going to the sheriff's office, they delivered Alex to the library, where he would stay with Meg. After an hour that felt more like three, Thea straightened from Sy's desk. Sy did most of the work, asking questions, then writing Thea's responses, yet she felt drained. The sheriff clicked off the tape recorder and slid a two-page report across the desk toward her. "You'll need to sign this, Thea."

"Only two pages after all that?"

"Got all the pertinent details. We have enough evidence to prosecute and then some. That is, if Mrs. Moran's fit to stand trial, which I purely doubt."

The phone rang and Sy excused himself. After reading, then signing the report, Thea stood and tried to work the cricks out of her back and shoulders. Bram drew her to him simply by looking too good to ignore. She joined him at the coffee mess, where he filled her hand with a Styrofoam cup of Lipton's best.

"This'll be the second time you saved my cookies today," she said.

"Not exactly the birthday celebration I'd planned for you, darlin'"

She burned her mouth in surprise. "Really? You made plans?" Despite the grinding day, warmth wavered and bloomed in the region of her heart.

"Yep. Alex and me had it all figured out. Now we'll have to postpone it for a—Sy, you needed us for something more?"

Sy's grave expression made Thea's neck and shoulders

tighten to the point of pain. "Dwaine finished with the crime scene, but I'm sending him up to your place, Thea. It seems that Sherman saw Mrs. Moran coming from there when she nabbed Alex. Better to be on the safe side."

"You don't think—" Her heart pounded in time to the dull ache starting in her head.

"Now Thea, like I said, I'd rather err on the side of safety. You get cleaned up at Dwaine's and by the time you're done, he'll have finished his walk-through at your place. Bram, I'll need your statement, too."

Bram's arm tightened around her shoulders. "Can it wait till later, Sheriff? I'd like to see Thea over to Dwaine's first."

Before the sheriff answered, a sound they knew all too well split the air. "Well, hell and damnation. Thought we'd seen the end of this." Sy's official radio began to squawk in concert with the external sirens.

A fire truck roared past them as they stepped out the door. Sirens pierced the gloaming and smoke's acrid odor choked the evening air. At a break between traffic, the three of them dodged to other side of the street for a better view. Sy punched the redial on his cell phone.

Lighter than the darkening sky, white and gray smoke billowed northeast of Potshot. "Oh, no. Not the spa again," Thea wailed.

Sy said, "Not that lucky, Thea. Dwaine says it's your place."

Her knees did give out then and, except for Bram's strong arms, she would have planted her face on the sidewalk. He hustled her toward his Rover and Alex intercepted them there. Meg and Jake followed. The older man said, "Looks like Thea's house."

A curt nod and Bram said, "If you're coming with us, get in." When Thea fumbled three times to connect her seat's safety belt, Bram brushed her hands away and did it for her.

Then he kissed her.

"Hold on, darlin'."

They made the distance in half the time it usually took. She struggled from Bram's truck as the windows of her house shattered, blowing outward in an explosion of glass. To Thea's ears, the fire sounded like a live thing, ravenously devouring what she had worked so hard to build. Concealed by two fire trucks, a tangle of hoses and the frantic illumination of emergency vehicle lights, Thea had a tough time seeing her home. When she did, she was glad for Bram's support. He wrapped his arms around her from behind and she rested her head against his chest.

"It's gone, isn't it?" she asked.

Plumes of water hit the roof. "Not by a long shot. They may save most of the structure yet."

Her son stood wide-legged before her, silhouetted against the raging backdrop. Thea tugged Alex into her arms until they nested against Bram. The tension in her son's shoulders had nothing to do with physical closeness and everything to do with the devastation before them. She murmured, "We'll be able to replace nearly everything, honey. Thank goodness for your grandma's insistence on making copies of our photos and—"

If anything, Alex grew more rigid. "Grandpa's medals!"

He flung himself from her with such force that Thea gasped for air before crying, "Alex!"

Heart in her throat, she went after him, but agility and youthful speed won. From behind, Bram snatched her arms, keeping her from following. He forced her attention to him, "Thea! I'll go after Alex. You stay here. Stay here!" He pushed her into Meg's arms, reinforced by Jake's presence. Thea struggled against their hold, but to no avail.

Alex was nowhere in sight by then. Bram dashed to one of the fire trucks, digging through a compartment and donning a turnout coat and hat before racing after Alex. An ax weighted one arm, but he looked ill equipped to win against the ravening firebeast. Struggling like a feral cat against Jake's hold, Thea bit the inside of her mouth, tasting blood. Bram disappeared into the flaming maw where her door had once stood.

Meg's voice penetrated her consciousness. "Our Father, who art in heaven. . ." but Thea's entire being concentrated on the fire and the two people she loved most in the world. Something gave way in the house, crashing and sending sparks through the gaping windows. It might as well have been Thea's heart.

"It's too long. They've been in there too long."

". . .on earth as it is in heaven. . ." Meg whispered.

Unable to watch a moment longer, Thea broke from Meg's grasp. She ran a ragged course toward her burning home, leaping debris as she went. Dwaine positioned himself between her and the inferno, and she rammed into him. "I can't let you go in there, Thea."

She struggled against his hold. "Damn it, Dwaine, Alex and Bram—"

"If anyone knows what he's doing, Bram does."

"That's not enough!"

"There they are. Look."

She wrestled around to see. The blaze licking the entranceway parted and Bram's tall form resolved itself from the flames. To Thea's eyes, he looked elemental, as though he formed out of the fire. Lengths of leg and arm that could only be her son's stuck out of the coat. Bram leapt down the steps to the walkway and strode toward them, his burden more like a fragile package than a living and breathing boy. Dwaine stepped aside and Thea met Bram.

Burning herself on the snap fasteners, she grasped Alex, coat and all. Then Thea peeled the encumbrance away from

310

her son. He wriggled in her hold.

"Jeez, Mom. I'm okay, I'm okay." Alex coughed and sputtered.

Thea pulled him into her arms and squeezed him hard enough to make orange juice. *Alex's manly pride be damned—he owed her a good hug.* One wiry arm, stronger than she believed, snaked around her neck. When she could talk again, she framed his dear face and said, "If you ever scare me again like this—"

"I know, I know. Grounded for life."

"Why in the world did you run into the house like that?"

He held out a flat case, which he had cradled against his chest. "I *told* you. Grandpa's medals."

Jake's lean hand lifted them from Alex's youthful grip. "Hell in a bucket, Alex. These aren't worth your life, son."

"They were worth yours," the boy said.

Thea shook her head. "You can *both* explain this later. In the meantime, I have someone else to thank."

She gave a tremulous smile and rose. Looking up at the man who had saved her son's life for the second time that day, she flung herself into his arms, knocking the helmet off his head. "Thank you, Bram. How I'll ever be able to repay you—"

His lips met hers in a hungry kiss. When he broke away, he said, "Don't worry, darlin'. I'll think of something."

Less than an hour later, Thea, Alex and Meg perched on the open end of Bram's truck while Jake paced. All watched the progression of the fire crew's clean up. Thea's house still stood, although from what she could see, 'gutted' was too mild a word for the ruin. Yet in comparison to what she could have lost, the destruction seemed minor. Thea embraced Alex with both arms and, much to her continuing surprise, her son tolerated the display. Her gaze kept returning to Bram, who worked with the others, assessing damage and checking for hot spots.

Alex opened the container that could have cost him his life. Thea studied the contents, which looked like an assortment of military medals. With great reverence, her son lifted each decoration and named it. "Silver Star. Bronze Star. Purple Heart with a star. Commendation Medal. The Marines gave these to Grandpa, but he won't tell me why. Except for the Commendation Medal for going to war, and the Purple Heart and star for getting shot." He laid them one-by-one back into the velvet-lined box where they glinted in the Rover's interior lighting.

With eyebrows raised, Thea cleared her throat and looked at the man she now knew as her father. Darkness and emergency lighting made his bruised face look even more cadaverous. *The Morans had left more than their share of dents on her family today.*

"Since Alex put himself in jeopardy for these, maybe you can tell him what they're for. Tell *us*, Jake." *Proper names would have to do for now. 'Father' might never feel right on her tongue.*

"Don't like looking backward, Thea."

Meg stroked his closest arm, holding his hand when she reached the end. "Jacob?"

His eyes looked especially beautiful in his ruined face as he gazed at the librarian. "All right, Nutmeg."

He fixed his regard on Thea. "I was a sniper. Deadly at more than one thousand yards. Just doing what I was trained to do. They ordered me incountry in a hot area. Uncle Sam provided bullets at twenty-cents a pop; I had ninety-nine confirmed kills and over 200 probables. Our motto was 'Kill one man, terrorize a thousand'. I think the government got its money's worth. In place of my humanity, they gave me the Silver and Bronze Stars. I try to believe that I saved more lives than I took. Some days the rationale works better than

312

others."

Even Alex had nothing to say. Thea's tongue fused to the roof of her mouth. *What medal do they give a man lost from his family for over thirty years?*

Meg got to her feet and wrapped her arms around the rangy veteran. "You're home now, Jacob. That's all that matters."

Jake's face lost some of the unnatural rigidity. "Keep telling me that, Nutmeg. Maybe in a couple thousand years, I'll believe it."

Thea tried to swallow three decades of sadness as Bram drove them toward Dwaine's place. When he steered past the Sheriff's office, Thea witnessed the ambulance's arrival to take Ma Moran to Reno and St. Mary's for observation. "Bram, stop the car."

Leaving Alex with Meg and Jake, Bram and Thea joined the other bystanders. Renewed panic struck Thea as they wheeled Mrs. Moran from the jail. Bram nestled her closer to his side. "You okay?"

"I need to see this, Bram. Maybe it'll serve as closure." He feathered a kiss over her forehead.

The brawny medics treated the incapacitated woman gently, first sedating, then wrapping her in a straightjacket for transport. Zechariah Moran, looking much worse than Jake, crawled into the ambulance with his mother. Even though this woman had given Thea an amazing amount of grief, the recent fury she had harbored for Mrs. Moran evaporated. Alex was safe. She just wished the woman would quit muttering, 'It ain't over till it's over'.

Bram tightened his hold around Thea's shoulders. "She's as crazy as they come. Don't listen to her gibberish."

"It gives me the creeps. Especially now that I know what she meant."

"All the more reason not to pay her any mind."

A yawn cracked her jaw and she said, "I'm finished here.

Let's get to Dwaine's."

By the time they reached the Rover, Jake and Meg had extricated themselves from a sleeping Alex, who lounged across the backseat in exhausted abandon. Through the open door, Thea saw that he still clutched his grandfather's medals to his chest. Meg stepped forward to hug her and said, "I'm so sorry, Althea, for all your tribulations. You and Alex are more than welcome to stay with me until you sort out the muddle."

Thea kissed Meg's cheek. "Thanks, but Dwaine's staying at Sy's tonight, so we have a place. I need a space to remember that my life isn't all fire and shotguns. Let me think about your offer."

"Tomorrow will do," Meg agreed.

She faced Jake. "Thanks for being there for Alex, Jake. He needs a grandfather."

The older man nodded. "I plan on being here for him." *And for you* went unspoken.

Thea squeezed one of his work-worn hands and said, "Goodnight." It took more energy than she thought she had to crawl into the truck. She leaned her cheek against the cool window as Bram drove them to Dwaine's. A blur of images accompanied her and most of them had to do with conflagration and guns. When Bram turned off his truck's engine, a little shock hit Thea as she noticed her car still parked in the drive. Dwaine's place looked snug and hospitable—as opposed to wreathed in flame. Firsthand, she knew how much could change in twelve hours.

When she nearly fell from the cab and started toward her sleeping son, Bram said, "Let me get him, Thea. He's too big for you."

Tears filled her eyes then, but she was too tired to fight them. She let Bram carry Alex into the house, where she pulled off his smoke-damaged clothes and tucked him, still dirty, into Dwaine's sofa bed. She would give Dwaine's linens a good wash—tomorrow. Then Thea stumbled toward the back bedroom. Halfway through stripping off her grimy clothes, she turned with one arm out of her tee shirt and realized Bram leaned against the doorframe, watching her progress. Tired as he had to be, appreciative lights brightened his eyes. Slipping her arm back into her shirt, she stalked him, then slipped her arms around his torso.

"Don't quit undressing on my account," he murmured.

"I'm filthy," she moaned, then nipped the tensile muscle on one shoulder.

"You're not too tired?" He skimmed a hand up her side while the other wrapped around her waist and pulled her closer.

"We're both dead on our feet. But let's not let that stop us," she said.

After a searing kiss, he pulled her shirt off and back-walked her into the master bath. Once there, his touches and kisses ignited an entirely different kind of fire. Naked, slippery with soap and revived by the hot water from the showerhead, Thea came undone for the third time that day. She wrapped her legs around Bram's hips and let him take her to a new place, one free of insanity and destruction. As she rode a fire whirl toward another summit, Bram stopped his delicious movements and said, "Open your eyes, Thea."

She looked into his, hot and hungry.

"Now. Say the words."

"Don't stop." She slid against him, tightened her legs and he groaned, but he refused to give into her.

"Say the words, Thea."

"That's blackmail."

He nibbled her neck, giving just enough of himself to make her gasp. "The words."

"I love you, Bram."

He eased into her and she ignited. "Now was that so hard?"

"Just hard enough." Then he swept her into a firestorm.

Afterward she leaned against the shower stall and Bram dried her, then himself. They fell into bed still damp. Bram propped himself on an elbow and stared down at her where she sprawled, relaxed to her marrow.

"Aren't you tired?" Her words slurred.

"Uh-huh."

She could barely keep her eyes open, when something clicked into place. "You didn't have your weird response to fire."

"It's not *my* weird response."

"But it didn't happen."

"I know."

She smiled and rolled toward him, draping an arm and leg over his torso. "I must be good for you after all." The vortex pulled her under.

Midway through the night, she awoke to a warm body beside her. Happiness out of kilter to her losses filled her and she opened her eyes. Moonlight glowed through the window overhead and she saw Bram, still watching over her.

"You're still here. Why aren't you sleeping?"

"I almost lost you today."

She tangled her fingers in his thick hair, slightly damp from their shower, and pulled him toward her. Tracing the smoothness of his sleek chest to his muscular hip, she murmured, "I'm here now. And we've never tried a real bed before."

Chapter Eighteen

They gathered the next evening in Peabody's restaurant section. The banner over the extended banquet table proclaimed Thea's birthday celebration. However, as Potshot residents learned snippets of what happened the day before, the revelry gained momentum from those events.

Sissy Peabody displayed Thea's check from the art gallery under a sheet of Plexiglas at the center of the main table. The long awaited insurance check nestled beside it. Thea wavered over which she valued more.

"Guess this means I'll have to find someone else to do the wall painting at my place, eh, Thea?" asked Bud Senior, his cane cradled over his lap.

"Not at all. A bargain's a bargain, Bud. Besides I've blocked out the scene: Hercules and the Cretan bull." Already Thea visualized Bram as the hero wrestling the colossal red bull.

"The tourists and local ranchers will like that just fine." Bud hefted to his feet, then toddled away to spread his mural-to-be enthusiasm as he went.

Clusters of firefighters thronged to discuss how Ma Moran had set the fires. Her babbling, much of it nonsense, had allowed the two law officers to piece together most of her story. Now they explained and refined their theories with the help of Bram's grant team.

Dwaine said, "Evidently, Ma Moran read Zech's *Smokechaser's Gazette* even more faithfully than he did. She had a regular recipe book full of her favorite fire-starting methods. Kept it on the kitchen counter at Zech's place, where Sy found it."

"She must be a cousin to Coyote, eh, Bram?" Challie elbowed him, but Bram only smiled at the reference to a Native American mischief-maker, then winked at Thea.

Ian added, "The lab verified a combination of organic brake fluid with chlorine tablets as an oxidizer. This made for the slow, smoldering fire at Salinger's office."

"And that first fire Ma Moran laid under Thea's porch," Sy said, but Thea had reached her quota for fires and analysis, so she drifted toward a chattering group of women.

There she sat, sipping iced ginger ale and listening to the conversations swirling around her. Truly, she felt bone-weary, but the company of friends staved off the inevitable talk she had promised Bram. Hence, she stayed. Thea kept glancing over to where Alex sat amid a group of clamoring children, all hanging on his every word about his narrow deliverance. Every time she looked at her son, his face washed free of muddy tear tracks and glowing under the near adulation of his peers, her heart compressed. She had come so close to losing him. Twice. Then her gaze moved, seemingly of its own volition, to take in the man instrumental for getting her and her son through this.

Admiring cohorts also surrounded Bram. Instead of basking in the attention as Alex did, he merely looked thoughtful. As often as not, he caught her gaze with his own private look, punctuated by a sexy smile. Each time, Thea unraveled a little more. *Soon I'll be nothing but loose threads.*

She remained peripherally aware of her mother as Amarantha made her way from one group to another. She did notice, however, that Mother took great care not to come within hailing distance of either Meg or Jake. Some cures took time. Or maybe even time would be insufficient, but that

318

was not Thea's problem.

Thank goodness for the Serenity Prayer, which she had repeated to herself times without number over the last few months:

God,

*grant me the serenity to accept the things I cannot change, the courage to change the things I can,
and the wisdom to know the difference.*

This brought her around to another potential obstacle. Thea fiddled with the certified letter that the postmistress had hand-delivered before the party started. The unknown contents made her hands sweaty. She yearned to bask in the relief of being alive before grappling with another foe. At the kitchen entry hall, Hulon Peabody rang his triangle bell, salvaged from the chow hall of his long defunct cattle ranch.

"Ladies and gentlemen, our sheriff has asked for your attention."

Sy stood on the stage where local musicians played country and bluegrass on Friday and Saturday nights. He accepted the mike from the club owner and announced, "First, I want to wish Thea a happy birthday. A day late, but happy nonetheless."

A smattering of applause along with whistles and yells met his words. He held up a hand and said, "It looks like she's about to embark on quite a journey. Taking San Francisco and the rest of the art world by storm."

Ear-splitting whistles flayed her shotgun-blasted ears. She managed an embarrassed smile.

"Let's face it, folks. None of us are at all surprised, unless it's because the rest of the world has shown more sense than we gave it credit for. I'm real glad we got her signature on all her murals and such *before* this happened, though. Potshot will be on the map for two things now: our natural hot springs *and* our local prodigy."

Laughter met that pronouncement. Thea figured the heat from her face warmed everyone within ten feet.

"Mostly though, I'd like to give some credit to a local youngster. Alex MacTavish? You want to stand up, son?" Alex, more hindered than helped by shoves from friends, lurched to his feet. His face, too, turned crimson beneath the weight of stares.

"This here's the fella who was instrumental in catching our arsonist." The crowd met Sy's pronouncement with huge applause and stamping feet.

"Well, and it's time to put some local rumors to rest and restore Alex's good name. Because, folks, Alex is also the one who identified Potshot's abominable snowman, the ghost of Penny Ante Mine, and that wolf family who settled in our hills."

Some mutters met his proclamation, but little else. The sheriff said, "Jacob Seeger, you want to stand?"

Jake did, Meg beside him. "Folks, I want you to meet our local Sasquatch and miner's ghost." Alex's grandfather bowed his head, then nodded to Alex.

Sy continued. "If you set your minds to it, many of you'll remember Jacob, 'though you'll have to get past what time and war does to a body. He's a local boy made good, then lost to us for a spell. Earned all kinds of medals for valor and such in Vietnam. Kept those skills fresh over the last years by living off the riches of our land hereabouts. Scared Alex near to death a few times when he showed up all unexpected, but he's back with us now, and we're lucky to have him. With those other vets here in Potshot, looks like he'll be starting a construction firm."

Jake sat down hard on that, his gaunt face paling under Sy's praise. A hubbub of sound rolled over Thea before Sy continued. "Got some other unfinished business, too.

320

Turns out that our local highway patrol received calls on an abandoned truck a few months back. Looked like whoever left it had been transporting something live and probably illegal in the back. The Fish and Wildlife folks think there's a good chance that that's where our wolves came from.

"So before you all start pecking at the scratch I've given you, let me take this opportunity to publicly apologize to our young hero here." Heads turned to look at Alex as he fidgeted under their scrutiny.

"Believe me, son, it takes a lot of courage to speak the truth, especially when faced with skepticism. You just keep doing that, though. World would be a lot less bright without your brand of clear vision."

Thea joined in the applause. She blinked hard to keep tears from spoiling her son's belated tribute. Sy's appeal to cut the cake barely registered. The next thing she knew, Hulon wheeled a sheet cake out to her. Some wit handed her a pair of sunglasses as protection from the candle's glare. As she looked around for support, both Alex and Bram popped up, one at each elbow. The guys let her blow out the candles herself, which meant her wish really would come true. *Wouldn't it?*

She made the first slice, giving her son a corner piece laden with butter-cream frosting. Then she turned the cake cutting over to Sissy, who accepted with alacrity. Thea withstood the onslaught of well-wishers for a time before edging away from the center of activity and out the side door of the restaurant.

Night had long since fallen over Potshot. Moths and other night flyers gyrated around the streetlights. A sliver of moon peaked between White-Tail Rock and Skunk Ridge. Sissy's committee for beautification of Potshot had been hard at work. Along with banners, flower baskets hung from all available poles in preparation for the spa's Grand Opening next week. The stars looked close enough to tickle with her fingers.

321

To Thea, mid-June meant pink corydalis, yellow columbine, and white ivesia. It meant longer days of natural light in her studio, followed by evening soaks at the hot springs while the constellations slowly revolved above her. Thea inhaled the pungent smell of pine mixed with spicy floral scents from the baskets. The door behind her swung open. Bram's cedar smell made her stomach flip-flop.

Without looking at Bram, she said, "Missus and Mister bake peach turnovers and berry pies in June. On early mornings, the whole town smells of their baking. The scent alone is nearly enough to fill you up. Then, we always have a big community picnic on the Fourth of July. Bud Senior has family on one of the local reservations so we end with an evening of fireworks."

Bram drew up behind her and held her. She entwined her arms with his before going on, "In August, we plan all month for our Labor Day celebration. It's evolved into this extravagant contest with everyone making his or her best recipes. Missus and Mister are disqualified as contenders so they can judge the entries. I'm an honorary judge. That way no one has to eat my cooking. Dwaine almost always wins prizes for his pies. His strawberry rhubarb's to die for. We auction off picnic baskets with the proceeds going into the city coffers. That's one of the ways we were able to underwrite Bud's renovations on the hotel and build the spa complex." She leaned her head against his chest.

"Then in mid-September, you leave."

Street lamps buzzed with striking insects. Bram cleared his throat. "I've been thinking about that." He moved alongside her, handing her an envelope; the one she had avoided. "I found it on the floor."

She gave a huge sigh and ripped it open. By maneuvering it under the light, the message could be read. With disbelief, she saw that it came directly from Derek's father rather than

322

through his lawyers. She scanned the single sheet quickly before passing it to Bram.

He read it. When he consigned it to her, she stuffed it in the back pocket of her jeans. "What do you think?" he asked.

"I don't trust him. You'll notice it's not from his lawyers, which makes it less than binding."

"He states a willingness to make it legal, though. The man's probably gun-shy, Thea. You haven't exactly made things easy for him," Bram countered.

That brought her blood to full simmer. She swung toward him, "While he's been so trustworthy? So involved in his grandson's life?"

Bram hesitated. "I think he's trying to do something good here, Thea. He's acknowledging, as much as he ever will, that he hasn't done the right thing for his grandson or you."

"I don't need or want his money," she contended. "Remember Derek's revenge threat. How can I know that this isn't tied into that?"

"I'm sure a good lawyer could clarify those aspects for you."

She pivoted away from him. "I can't believe the old man feels guilt. He's never shown any remorse before. It's a payoff. Nothing more, nothing less. That's how his son's always dodged responsibility."

Bram put his hands on her shoulders, rubbing gently. "I'm not so sure. The man pretty much admits that he has no hopes of other grandchildren. Maybe he's being honest both with himself and with you. He knows Derek wouldn't be any kind of father to Alex and he seems interested in giving his grandson financial support. Since his own son's reneged on every other obligation to his grandchild, this could be where he draws the line."

"Is this a guy thing? You stick together, no matter how big a scum the other man is?" But she leaned into his hands at her shoulders and neck.

"Hardly. But old Salinger's finally realized what he's lost and is trying to make reparation." He turned her to face him. "Let him do that, Thea. Don't let Alex suffer because your vengeance isn't complete."

"It isn't revenge. Not strictly anyway. It's that I don't want either Salinger involved in my life or Alex's. I don't want the Salinger name connected to us. Besides, this doesn't involve you." She closed her eyes against the compassion and love she saw in his. "You don't play fair, Bram."

He kissed her forehead. "Sure I do, darlin'. Walk with me?"

Rather than give her a chance to say no, he caught her arm in his and started down the street. They passed the church, where a new saying graced the lighted board.

DON'T LET WORRY KILL YOU;
LET THE CHURCH HELP.

Bram laughed and Thea elbowed him. "What's wrong with that?" she kidded.

He only kissed her neck and pulled her along. A few blocks later, he aimed her toward the pine rungs that led to the hot springs. She went with him because it felt right. Arms interlaced, Thea nestled so close to him that both his scent and body heat enfolded her.

In silence they hiked the steps past the tent city. They sauntered by the Olympic-sized pool at the lowest level of the spa complex and on to the changing area, which housed showers and special therapy rooms. Thea reached above the lintel and retrieved the key to the compound, which she opened before switching on the lights.

Rich smells of sanded pine along with the dense oils that Jake used for preservation filled her nose. The mellow glow

324

of inset lighting against pale woods pleased her eye. The two wandered through the indoor complex and out another door that led to the hot springs. They meandered along the steps, well lit by solar torches. Thea guided them up one level, then to the next until they passed three hazy pools. She continued to the semi-enclosed area around the mud baths. From here, steam from the springs dissipated enough to allow them to view both the heavens above and luminous Potshot below.

Thea settled onto a smoothly hewn bench and patted the space beside her. Bram joined her. They relaxed into a warm peace treasured by Thea.

Bram finally said, "I have some friends who might be interested in restoring your place. It'd be easy to contact them for you."

Thea gripped her hands over a crossed knee and forced herself to maintain the casual swing of her lower leg. "Oh?"

"I know how important your home is to you."

"Yes. It is."

"When you told me about your fears yesterday—we both fear the same darkness, Thea. We've both been to hell and back. You must have figured out that having you in my life keeps me in the present and chases the ghosts away."

He grasped her hands, leaving her no room for attempted nonchalance. She held onto him for dear life. Ever since waking beside him this morning, she knew she would do whatever was necessary to make that her reality.

"I know I've been trying to eradicate every risk of fire here. I also know that's impossible. So J.D. and I came up with an alternate approach that will minimize danger, but maintain the soul of your town."

Thea forced herself to take a breath. "Such as?"

"Well, we can trim limbs on green trees within fifteen feet of chimneys. All dead limbs that hang over houses will have to be removed."

"Instead of cutting down trees, you mean?"

"Yes. Dead trees will have to be eliminated though."

"Even the ones with bird nests?"

"Only if they're within, say, thirty feet of homes," he countered. "Or we can try moving the nests."

Something resembling hope unfurled inside her. *Can my birthday wish come true?* "What about all the terracing?"

"Thea, even minor grades accelerate a wildfire's spread. However, there are composite materials available; some look like native rock. If residents would dedicate both time and effort, you could relocate plants from defensible home sites to the terraces."

"To soften the lines," she said.

"Yes."

Her imagination caught up with him. "I've seen some beautiful stone walls."

"An order of chimney and barbeque screens came in today. . ."

They stopped talking and considered each other. He spoke. "We can moderate the changes, but only if Potshot kicks in with work parties. J.D. had to leave today, although he could be back in late August. Still, we're one team member short. Thea, we're dealing with real financial and time constraints here."

A huge grin forced its way onto her face. "I think work parties can be arranged. Don't forget, Potshot has other resources now, with Jake forming his new construction firm."

"Good. That's good."

During their talk, Thea pulled Bram's hand to her chest, where she nested it between her breasts. His gaze flickered as he uncurled his hand from hers and lay his palm flat against the spot where her heart beat strongest.

"Yesterday, when that crazy old woman had you in her sights, I realized that my nightmares paled in comparison to losing you and Alex."

He recaptured her hands, lifted them to his mouth and kissed her knuckles. With subtle passion, he caressed each and every one of them. A spasm of anticipation uncurled in Thea.

"I have to leave in September, Thea. I'm an associate professor at the University with lectures to prepare and research grants to write. My team can stay if we get more grant monies and an extension. Come with me, Thea."

"To Oklahoma?"

"It's my home and I want to share it with you."

"But Oklahoma…"

"Oh, darlin', I love you and Alex so much it hurts. I want every morning to be like this one was and wakeup in bed with you. I want to be your husband and Alex's daddy. Any failings I have in those areas, well, we can work those out as we go."

"You want me to marry you?" *Birthday wishes can come true.* Her buoyant feeling rose, then burst as a chill swept over Thea that had little to do with the night air. "You want us to leave Potshot."

Bram's stillness queued her to his distress before he filled his pain with words. "I know you love this place, but I have a great condominium in Norman. Granted, it doesn't have the charm of your place. Or what your place had. Hell, truth is I'm only there when I have to be. But with your presence, it'll feel like home in no time. I have plenty of space—three bedrooms so Alex can have his own room."

"Norman, Oklahoma?"

An almost feverish gleam lit his eyes in the dusky light. "We could start looking for another house, too. One with a studio for you. And we won't have to leave Potshot permanently. We'll come back here for regular visits. Give Oklahoma a chance, darlin'. Give me a chance."

Thea raised her hands to frame Bram's face. "I love you, Bram. I do. But I have a life here that goes beyond a house needing rebuilding. Alex has lifelong friendships and grandparents. My roots are here and my friends, too. Will I have that in Oklahoma?"

He stood and began pacing. "I don't know. I've cut myself off from most of my childhood friends. Too many crazy-makers. I never wanted to live on the Rez, even though I have family there. But my work satisfies me and I've gained acceptance, even respect, at the university. Talk is that I'm being considered for a full professorship this year."

Thea fumbled for the thread that would weave the closeness back into their encounter. "There's my show this fall in San Francisco. Perhaps afterward, Alex could stay with Meg for a time while I visit. You can show me around Norman. Is it anything like Potshot?" Desperation made her voice crack.

He stopped in front of her and hunkered down onto his heels. She hated to see his hands tremble as he clasped hers. "I've made one hell of a mess of this, haven't I?"

She shook her head. His harsh laugh trapped words of reassurance in her throat. He said, "Yes, I have. I know how you love these mountains. I suspect you probably don't even bleed real blood when you're hurt. Anything out of your veins would have to be a combination of Jack Rabbit Creek and Boondoggle Pond with snowmelt off Ricochet Mountain thrown in for good measure." His head tilted as he took in the heavens. "I just can't bear the thought of living my life without you and Alex."

Thea leaned forward. "This isn't something we need to decide right now, Bram. Let's put our minds to it. I'm sure we can come up with a creative solution that'll work for all of us."

"Oh, Thea, darlin'. I don't want to be some problem you need a solution for. I want to be your lover, your husband. I want to be the Daddy that Alex always wanted." Silvery light etched the rim of his eyes. "I love you, Thea. You're so deep inside of me, I don't want a life that doesn't include you."

She slipped off the bench and clasped him to her. "And I love you, Bram. Please don't think I won't consider Oklahoma. I will. It just won't be simple—for me or Alex."

All the while she said the words, her mind screamed. *Leave Potshot, even for this man I love?* Yes, she could do it, even though the tearing sensation in her chest foretold a mortal wound. She closed her eyes against the vision of her hemorrhaging her lifeblood away on some barren plain in Oklahoma, all unbeknownst to this man she loved above all others. Yet she had found her art in the Bay Area while at school. She could find it in Norman, Oklahoma. Her love strengthened her.

"I'll love you forever, Bram. Like you said yesterday, all the other stuff is just window dressing." *If only her saying the words made them reality.*

"We can be so happy together, darlin'."

She took a deep breath of fragrant mountain air and said, "I guess you'd better marry me, then."

Bram's *whoop!* of joy echoed down the mountain and through the valley.

Chapter Nineteen

Late October nights in San Francisco made for clear skies and chilly winds off the bay. Galleries dotted the Mission district. At one particular gallery, sleek vehicles like powerful city cats prowled the curb, pausing to occasionally disgorge exotically clad people, then slink away. Chandeliers hovered from vaulted ceilings, shedding radiance in a wall of light around the outside of the crowded space. Fluted champagne glasses floated along on trays circulated by starched waiters while the uniformed doorperson opened and shut the French doors.

Bram inhaled sea scents mixed with exotic perfumes where he stood outside the nimbus of light from the gallery. A delayed flight from Oklahoma meant he missed Thea's opening earlier this evening. Now, he lingered at the edges of illumination, filled with both longing and fear. The glass front of the gallery filled him with full appreciation of how exclusive Thea's show was. Bram dug his hands deeper into the pockets of his tuxedo slacks. His fingers brushed against the jewelry box there.

He retrieved the case and snapped it open. Within laid the ring he and Thea had chosen for their wedding vows. Like his wife, the ring had everything to do with unique beauty and nothing to do with convention. Rubies and emeralds frolicked around an asymmetrical setting of white and yellow gold. Sizing the squarish band turned out to be impossible, so the jeweler had made an entirely new one. For the first time since the ceremony, she would wear it tonight, a month after their wedding. This gala event reminded Bram of their wedding rites.

Amarantha had demanded the whole hog for her daughter's nuptials. Thea's consent in her mother's traditional approach surprised Bram almost as much as her decision to wed. One never knew when his wife's inner sense of rightness would assert itself against societal rules. Of course, Amarantha bowed to Thea's choice of emerald green for her gown. Bram smiled at that. The color brought out the jewel tones of his wife. And, oh, what fun undressing her had been. How he loved her.

"Sir? May I be of assistance?" The doorwoman slid an appreciative glance over Bram.

Bram emerged from his side trip into recent memories. "Yes. I'm ready to chuck myself into the fray. If I'm not out by closing, send in the *Keetoowahs*." He placed Thea's ring in his lapel pocket.

"Hey, aren't you Ms. MacTavish's model?" she asked.

Bram laughed, "Not that I know of. Must have me confused with—"

"Oh, of course. Well, please, allow me." He grinned and accepted. *An Oklahoma Cherokee in the middle of highfalutin' San Francisco, who'd believe it?* Still, Bram got the definite feeling that the woman deferred to him out of a sense of fun rather than because she believed him innocent.

It took some time for Bram to discover his wife in the crowd. He rounded one of the many partitions and nearly barreled into a cluster of elegant people surrounding a painting under scrutiny. A women thin to the point of emaciation cooed, "He's breathtaking, my dear. Who is he?"

"How wonderfully this ties into the mythology of primitive man, arising from the quagmire of societal restraints," said her

331

male counterpart.

Over well-groomed heads, Bram ignored the painting as he spotted a bared back whose skin he explored in great detail every opportunity he got. Clad in a silk sheath the same ruby color as the stones in her wedding ring, Thea faced away from him, obviously deep into listening mode. Her newly cropped hair left an expanse of olive skin with warm overtones open to his perusal. As usual, her presence thrummed along his nerve endings, bringing him to a state of hyper-awareness that left him lightheaded. As though sensing his presence, she turned.

Unerringly, her gaze seized his. Shadows in the depths of her eyes cleared. "Here he is. My husband. . .and my inspiration." She held a hand out to him. The company parted as though before a ship's prow. Amid the outlandish fragrances that surrounded him, only Thea's unique scent tantalized.

He dipped his head for a lingering kiss before nestling her against his side. When she sighed, Bram appreciated a heady moment of joy. Thea needed him. Wanted him. A stocky woman fitted a lorgnette to one eye and gave Bram the once-over. Pre-Thea, Bram's hackles would have raised and he might have bared his teeth in a snarl. Now he just relaxed into his wife's loose hold.

"Yes, indeed. I do see where your inspiration comes from, my dear." She laughed the way a goose honks.

"Leave it to you, Thea, to find the one remaining beautiful heterosexual man on God's green earth,"quipped another.

"How do you feel, Mr. MacTavish, being your wife's muse?"

"Hayes," Thea corrected. "My married name is MacTavish-Hayes. And for your information, Bram's fondly known around the University of Oklahoma campus as *Dr. Youngwolf Hayes, sir*. Surprising as it may be, my husband has yet to see any of my paintings with him as subject."

Bram knew how the pole-axed steer felt. The group around them became a pocket of quiet in the maelstrom. "Indeed," said the lorgnette. "Well, no time like the present for Dr. Youngwolf Hayes to confront his celebrity."

Thea's gaze urged him to turn. Under her breath, she murmured, "I'm so sorry, Bram. I thought you'd be here for the pre-show tour. I wanted it to be a surprise, but not this much of a bombshell."

That's how Bram came face-to-face with himself. Well, not himself actually. A larger-than-life version. Coming out of the mists of hot springs, no less. Naked. Well, not truly naked. He'd had on his cut-offs after all, but the painting implied liberties with those facts. Misty unicorns, chimera, Pegasus and other mythical beasts surrounded this admittedly heroic looking guy in the painting. But was it him? With a *SOLD* tag across a bottom corner? Not in this lifetime.

"I guess you could mistake this guy for me. Obviously my wife has taken artistic license with her subject." There, that ought to cool their jets.

A sleek vamp gave a throaty chuckle too basso for a woman's. "Not that many privileges, I'll warrant. Unfortunately, it doesn't look as though Althea will give me the chance to find out."

The group joined in her laughter. Thea urged Bram through the crowd, making excuses as she went. When they won their way to a relatively quiet corner, she snatched a glass off a nearby tray and chugged it. Bram watched with growing concern. At his look, she giggled. "It's only white grape juice, man-of-mine. I have Stacy, here, shadowing my every move so I'm not without refreshment."

His gaze ranged the room. "I don't see Meg or Jake, although I did see my esteemed mother-in-law." The shadow that past over his wife's vivid face made him regret his observation.

"Meg and Jake came earlier, but left shortly after Mother arrived."

"Amarantha's pigheadedness isn't your problem, darlin'."

"I know." Her gaze searched his for a long moment. "I guess you'd better see the other paintings before you're cornered again. By the way, you look positively edible tonight," she whispered and slipped an arm through his.

"That's my line, darlin'."

Color suffused her already bright face. "When did you find time to change into your tux?"

"I stopped by our room at the Fairmont. Alex and Sherman were watching an action flick and feeding on a dessert tray like shoats at a trough."

Thea grimaced. "Oh, dear. I *did* give them permission to order from room service, but only once tonight. I thought they'd want dinner."

Bram gave into his yearning, and dipped to kiss the place where her neck met her shoulders. He trailed his lips to an ear. "You're so beautiful, darlin'. I'm not sure I'm going to get through tonight's little jubilee without making a spectacle of myself."

Her gaze swept over him and she gave a sultry laugh. "The cut of your tux doesn't offer much camouflage, does it?"

He groaned in answer. "I'm just going to have to display some of that discipline that's gone astray since marrying you."

Her fingers smoothed the lapels of his cutaway jacket. "I suppose I'll have to be good, too." As she flattened the material over his breast, a slight frown puckered her brow. "What's this?"

Bram glanced around to find themselves under covert scrutiny from any number of strangers, who continued to leave them their bubble of privacy. "Why, darlin', I'm finally going to make you an honest woman." He slipped the case from his inner pocket and snapped it open.

"My ring!"

As she reached for it, he snapped the lid closed. "All in good time. About those other paintings?"

She balanced on tip-toes and kissed his neck above the standing collar of his formal shirt, then nibbled an earlobe. "You'll regret making me wait, Bramden Hayes." The promise in her eyes sent shivers of delight down his spine.

"You're not thinking of tying me to the headboard again?" His voice sounded more thrilled than fearful.

"You wish. You'll just have to wait and see." She pulled him toward a different section, where a passel of onlookers surrounded yet another painting marked as 'SOLD'.

This one displayed a heroic man crouched in a meadow before a bubbling artesian well from which beautiful sirens rose. Spectral elements of other myths shimmered around the women. With a crown of ethereal vines around his brow, the portrayed man gazed at them with great intensity. His face held a rapt mixture of yearning and unbearable joy. Radiating out from his knees, where they touched the ground, a profusion of spring flowers bloomed and wended their way into the more distant wasteland. The title proclaimed it as 'The Healing'.

"My wounded king," breathed Thea.

"But that's not me, darlin'."

"Oh?" Her cat-eyed look sparkled. "You'll notice that he's learning secrets from the women at the well. He no longer needs the grail to heal him."

Their moment of solitude ended as Jarvis and his entourage gathered around them. Not long afterward, Amarantha joined them in full diva mode. Her arrival proved to be his and Thea's last moment alone together for the rest of the evening and Bram never did see the third painting. Even the ride back to the Fairmont gave them no surcease, as Jarvis, Thea's benefactor, and his longtime lover accompanied them in the gallery owner's luxurious vehicle.

Bram and Thea entered their suite to find the boys asleep, draped over each other like hunt-tired hounds in front of the blank television. The remains of their dessert-fest cluttered all available surfaces. Thea tenderly stroked the hair off her son's face. In a soft voice she said, "I'm so glad Sherman could join us here. Alex misses him and Keith."

"We'll be in Potshot for a few days after your showing. That'll give the boys plenty of time to create havoc and discontent." The wistful look on Thea's face pressed him to rush in with, "How about I lug these scamps into their bedroom?"

Bram carried first one, then the other to the second room off the sitting area. After removing the boys' socks and jeans, Thea tucked them in with a kiss. Only then did Bram and his wife retire into their room, a blessed respite from the chaos of the sitting room.

Thea, who stepped out of her shoes at the entranceway, glided to the windows overlooking the city. Bram sat on the bed to pull off his shoes before joining her. He slipped his arms around her waist, relishing the cool silk that covered her abdomen, loving the woman in the ruby cocoon.

"It's so hard to believe," she said.

"Your success?"

"Everything. The wonderful reception, my joy in our marriage, the special relationship you and Alex have formed. That we're standing here at all. . ."

"But Norman, Oklahoma, doesn't make you feel that way, does it, darlin'?"

Silence.

He said, "I went into the room you've been using as your studio. You painted over all the canvases you've been working on for the last two months."

She turned in his arms. "You shouldn't have gone in there."

336

"I know, but did you think you could hide your hurt from me? You'd never say anything about it without me bringing it up first. Truth is, Norman, hell, *Oklahoma*, isn't working out for you." Her limpid gaze clouded.

"I'm so sorry, Bram. I've been trying, really I have. I *do* love your grandfather and cousins. They're such a joy to be around. And their children—maybe I just need more time."

"Time. There's a funny thing about time. We're only allowed a certain amount of the stuff. So when you find a place and a person who makes your time rare and fine, you need to hold on for the ride."

"Bram—"

"Thea, darlin', truth is, Norman's not working for me either. Looks like I put down some pretty deep roots in Potshot, too."

Thea slipped her hands between jacket and shirt. She lay her head against his heart. "I don't think I'm blocked, Bram. I'm still finding the pulse in Norman."

He kissed the top of her head. "Maybe you don't need to get the pulse of anywhere in Oklahoma. Maybe we just need to hightail it back home."

His wife raised her head to meet his look. "But your work—the university—"

"Small potatoes when it comes to our happiness, Thea. *You're* my joy. I went stir crazy with you and Alex gone and decided to pursue some ideas. Then I got in touch with Jake last week and we discussed a few things."

She waited with that quiet intelligence Bram treasured.

"I contacted an old professor up in Seattle, Washington. Up there they call people who run businesses out of their homes *Lone Eagles*. I guess it's pretty big here in San Francisco, too."

Confusion obscured her eyes. "But, how could you. . ."

"Basically, it means that a person, a fire-safety consultant say, could operate his own business out of his house via fax, modem, and some Frequent Flyer miles."

"Oh?"

"There'll be a start-up phase, when we won't have much revenue, but I've been offered a guest lecturer position at the University of Nevada in Reno to get us past that. There're plenty of possibilities for contract work with firefighters, too. Seminars and such. I'm still crunching numbers and contacting my associates and people I've worked with over the years, but so far the response has been favorable."

Thea searched his eyes. "You know after tonight, money's not a problem. Not for a while, anyway."

"Aw, hell, darlin', I grew up on a Rez. Money's never been the pig's snout. It's just that you're rare, my own spring-loving centaury. Like those flowers you saved, you survived fire. But I want you to thrive. You do that best in Potshot."

"I want you happy, too, Bram."

"We'll be together, darlin', and nothing makes me happier than that. Since my work in Potshot, I'd been thinking about my own consulting firm. I've even found someone who'll take over my lectures this winter. By spring, Carlyle will have found a full-time replacement. The condominium market's peaking in Norman. I suspect we could find a buyer in no time. By then, Jake will have the plans drawn up for our new house, so I can have an office, too. With him as general contractor, Reno won't have a street person worth his or her salt. Hell, darlin', Jake may have to recruit from other cities."

Understanding rose in her face like sun over the desert. "You're serious about your own business? Moving back to Potshot?"

He laughed, his joy growing rampant as kudzu. "You bet your sweet cheeks I'm serious. We're a team, darlin' wife. Can't have one half of a team broody as an old hen."

"I haven't been moping."

338

"I have been, though. And I know you wouldn't complain, but I am. I want you back again in full regalia; the woman who saw the hero in me."

"That hasn't changed, Bram," she said. Her fingers started doing interesting things to his cummerbunds. Then she attacked his pleated shirt, studs, and bowtie before slipping her hands inside the stiff fabric and next to his skin. The double layers of shirt and cutaway dropped to the floor.

As usual, he flashed to full intensity with the slightest spark. Bram looped the spaghetti straps off of Thea's shoulders, enjoying the show as the silk whispered over her peaks and valleys to puddle on the floor. Beneath it she wore a body-hugging teddy, strapless and the same color as her gown.

Meanwhile, Thea managed to free the closure of his trousers. "Glad to see you haven't lost your agile way with my clothes, darlin'."

As she lick-kissed her way from his gaping waistband to his chest, she murmured, "I'm what you'd call *motivated*."

The sight of her pink little tongue at his nipple broke his restraint. With a groan, Bram lifted her and carried her toward their bed, nearly tripping as his slacks worked their way down his hips in transit. They tumbled onto the bed in a heap of tangled limbs and hot flesh. After an eternity of wet kisses and vocal harmonics, he laced her fingers with his. Only then did he realize that her ring finger remained bare.

"Hold that pose, darlin'," he muttered as he scrambled from the twist of sheets and blankets.

"Not now, Bram. Come back here and finish what you started."

Her delicious voice combined with his view of their rumpled bed with Thea *a la mode*. He damn near changed his mind. Instead, Bram scrambled for the pile of formal wear by the window and sorted through until he found what he was looking for. He launched himself toward the bed, prize in hand, and landed beside his giggling wife. She coiled her arms around his neck.

"This a new form of foreplay, Bram? Where you drive your wife wild with yearning. . ."

He stroked a hand up her left arm, gently tugging her hand away from his neck. "Not at all, darlin'. I'm trying to fulfill my end of an important contract."

With a snap, the jewelry case opened and he slipped the ring from the holder. After a glimpse of her moss-soft eyes, Bram slipped the band over her ring finger. It snagged on her knuckle, so he licked and kissed the joint before sliding the ring home.

"There," he said.

She laced her fingers with his. "There," she agreed.

After that, they sealed their vows with heated joy as wildfire claimed them.

About The Author

Jessie Jayne Smith is a pseudonym for Janine Donoho, who thrives in the Okanogan Highlands of Washington State. A former member of both *Pacific Northwest Writers' Association (PNWA)* and *Romance Writers of America*, she plants herself in the writing chair nearly every day. Her novel *WILDFIRE* tied for first in Stella Cameron's PNWA contest, while *CALLING DOWN THE WIND* proved a leading contender in the non-genre contest. *Writers' Weekend* judges chose another novel *SOUNDINGS* as a top competitor.

Fantasy, Folklore, and Fairytales, Indigenous Press, and *Legions of Light* have featured her short stories and for four years, she wrote as biologist-columnist for *EARTH, SEA AND SKY* in the *Bremerton Sun*.

343